Praise for
ROUGH JUSTICE

"Castille takes the MC genre and lights it on fire! I want my very own Sinner's Tribe Motorcycle Club bad boy!"
—Julie Ann Walker, *New York Times* bestselling author

"A sexy and dangerous ride! If you like your bad boys bad and your heroines kicking butt, *Rough Justice* will rev your engine. A great start to a new series!"
—Roni Loren, *New York Times* bestselling author of *Nothing Between Us*

"Raw, rugged and romantic, *Rough Justice* is so gorgeously written you'll feel the vibration of the motorcycle engines in the pit of your stomach, smell the leather and fall in love with this story!"
—Eden Bradley, *New York Times* bestselling author of *Dangerously Bound*

Praise for
***USA Today* and *New York Times* bestselling author**
SARAH CASTILLE
and her sizzling-hot romances . . .

"Castille's debut is steamy." —*Publishers Weekly*

"Hot, hot, hot." —*Nocturne Romance Reads*

"Smart, sharp, sizzling and deliciously sexy . . . a knockout."
—Alison Kent, bestselling author of *Unbreakable*

"I highly recommend this spicy book!"
—*Paranormal Cravings*

"It's a book that's gobbled up in giant bites"
—*Dear Author*

"This book would be for anyone who likes a tough alpha male and a heroine who is just discovering the joys of a kinkier lifestyle!" —*Harlequin Junkie*

"Hilarious, hot, and occasionally heartbreaking. I loved it!"
—*Maryse's Book Blog*

"I really REALLY enjoyed this book :)"
—*LoveLivLife Reviews*

"Sexy . . . I love a good alpha-male!" —*About That Story*

ALSO BY SARAH CASTILLE

Rough Justice

Beyond the Cut

Sinner's Steel

★ BEYOND THE CUT ★

Sinner's Tribe Motorcycle Club #2

SARAH CASTILLE

St. Martin's Paperbacks

BEYOND THE CUT

For information address St. Martin's Press, 175 Fifth Avenue, New York, NY 10010.

ISBN: 978-1-250-05661-0

Printed in the United States of America

St. Martin's Paperbacks edition / June 2015

St. Martin's Paperbacks are published by St. Martin's Press, 175 Fifth Avenue, New York, NY 10010.

10 9 8 7 6 5 4 3 2

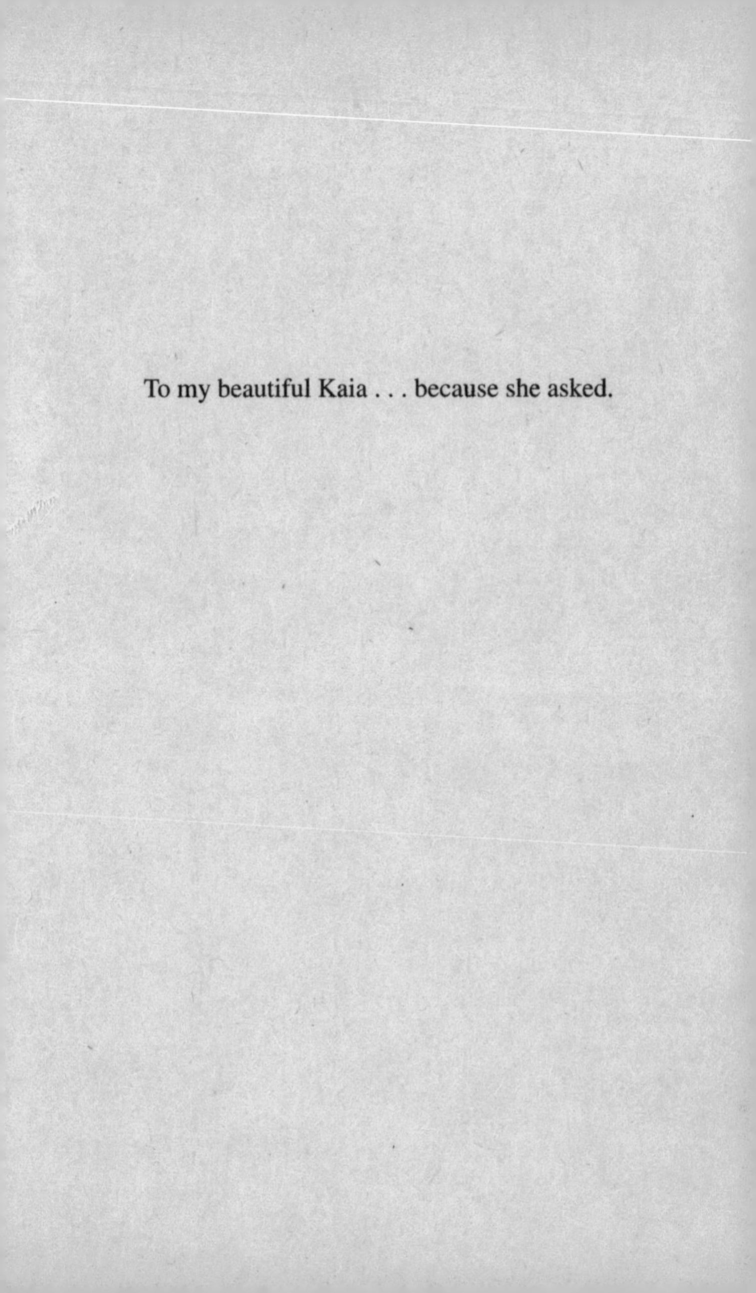

To my beautiful Kaia . . . because she asked.

★ ACKNOWLEDGMENTS ★

Thanks to my St. Martin's Press team—my awesome editor, Monique Patterson, who finds the heart in every story, her fabulous and patient assistant, Alexandra Sehulster, and the art team for the beautiful cover that made me drool. Thanks also to my agent, Laura Bradford, who gave me permission to believe in myself and who believed in me from the start. Thank you to my sisters, Sharon, Rana and Adele, for being there when I needed you, and to my brother, Tarick for his IT genius. To the bikers we met on the long dusty roads for all the ideas and for showing me just how worn a cut can be. And finally, to John and my girls, for all the little things you do to help my stories come to life.

★ ONE ★

Fear is the enemy. I will master my fear before it masters me.

SINNER'S TRIBE CREED

Dawn Delgado had to hand it to Kitty's Wig Emporium. They made damn good wigs. Well, except for the ill-fitting tribute to 1980s hair bands perched on her head.

She shoved yet another errant blond curl under the elastic. What the hell was going on? After twelve months of trial and error, Kitty's wigs were usually a perfect fit.

Her phone alarm went off and she yanked the wig down; it would have to do. If Shelly-Ann recognized her, she'd demand more money, but if Dawn didn't make it out the door in the next two minutes she'd miss the three thirty P.M. bell.

Tucking the last stubborn curl behind her ear, she grabbed a pair of sunglasses from the hall closet and raced out the door of her tiny rental bungalow. Spring had come early to Conundrum this year, which in Montana didn't mean soft April showers and lovely May flowers, but freezing rain, the occasional snowstorm, and gusting winds. More than enough incentive to cover the one-mile distance that much faster.

By the time she reached the throng of mums, prams, dogs, and nannies heading toward St. Francis Xavier's Elementary School, she'd given up all hope of the wig staying put. With one hand on her head, she slowed to a walk and then took up her usual position under a huge chestnut tree across the road from the school entrance. Although she was late, the girls would be later, dragging their feet down the school steps, the only unsmiling faces in a sea of cherubic grins.

They hadn't always been unhappy. One year ago, they'd had warm clothes, plenty of food, and a mother's love—things their aunt, Shelly-Ann, couldn't be bothered to give them, no matter how much blackmail money Dawn paid to spend a few extra hours with her girls every week.

Shelly-Ann's blue Volvo stopped in the school pickup zone just as Maia and Tia exited the school, dressed in identical faded pink jackets, worn jeans, and white sneakers. Matching pink headbands decorated with sparkly purple heart stickers adorned their long blond hair.

Although her seven-year-old twins always dressed the same, anyone who knew them could easily tell them apart. Maia, the older by two minutes, was always in the lead, protecting her little sister while at the same time dragging her along as she indulged her insatiable curiosity about the world. By contrast, Tia preferred to stay in the background—watching and assessing before diving in. But then Tia had a good reason for her reluctance to embrace the world: She had borne the brunt of her daddy's rage just before they left him for good. Jimmy hated his daughters, even more than he hated his wife. Dawn had celebrated the day their divorce went through, not realizing what Jimmy had planned for retribution.

The door of the Volvo swung open and Shelly-Ann barked from the front seat, her voice so loud, Dawn could hear her harsh words over the rumble of a motorcycle as the bike filtered through the SUV blockade. A kind, gentle auntie Shelly-Ann was not. But then she was from Jimmy's side of the family, and she had supported him when he took Dawn's daughters away.

The girls flinched as one, and Dawn took an involuntary step forward and away from the shelter of the tree. The wind gusted around her and with a delighted *whoosh* swept the wig off her head and carried it in a tumble down the street.

In that moment three things happened.

First, a biker pulled his motorcycle over to the curb and shouted her name.

She recognized the rich, deep baritone of Cade "Raider" Tyson's voice before she saw him dismount his Harley, his three-piece Sinner's Tribe Motorcycle Club patch clearly visible on the back of his cut—the sleeveless leather vest worn by all serious bikers. She heard that voice on street corners, in restaurants, and in bars. She heard it in her dreams and when she waited tables in Banks Bar. That voice had coaxed her deepest, darkest fantasies from her lips and made her believe, after two wild nights, maybe dreams really could come true.

Second, Cade's damn loud voice carried over the after-school chatter and the whistle of the betraying wind; it carried across the street and into the ears of two little girls who only saw their mommy once a week for three hours in the playground while Shelly-Ann had her nails done, and on the rare occasions Dawn had the cash to buy a few extra hours with her daughters.

Third, Maia and Tia spotted Dawn at the same time as Shelly-Ann, who cussed loudly three ways to the Sundays she was forced to bring the girls across the city for their access visit. With a glare for Dawn, she reached across the seat and tried to pull the girls into the car.

But although Shelly-Ann was fast, she wasn't fast

enough. By the time her fingers had breached the doorway, Maia and Tia were already halfway across the busy road, their arms outstretched, their twin voices screaming, "Mommy!"

Dawn's blood chilled for many reasons, not the least of which was the fact that she didn't have any extra money to give Shelly-Ann to keep her unauthorized appearance a secret from Jimmy. Also, her daughters were running through school rush-hour traffic heedless of the danger. And to make matters worse, it was Thursday. Payday for Shelly-Ann.

Usually, she would stuff the wig in her bag and meet Shelly-Ann in the parking lot behind the school to pay her for the extra visits Jimmy didn't know about—school plays and concerts, trips to the mall, and hikes in the mountains. This time, however, she didn't have any cash to spare. She'd taken a third job and dropped her college courses to pay a lawyer to help her overturn the court's decision to award custody of the girls to Jimmy—the result of a setup involving a shady private investigator, a Baggie full of crack, a corrupt judge, and a fabricated video of Dawn allegedly buying drugs—and after last month's outrageous legal bill, she had nothing left.

"Stop!" Her scream froze passersby but did nothing to deter her girls, now running hand in hand toward her and into the path of a blue pickup truck racing down the street at twice the school zone speed limit. Dawn's feet kicked into gear, but even as she threw herself forward, in her heart she knew she wouldn't make it in time.

A black blur shot in front of the truck. Cade swept her daughters into his strong arms, and out of harm's way. Moments later her outlaw biker savior deposited the girls on the sidewalk. Seemingly oblivious to their brush with death, Maia and Tia wrapped their skinny arms around her waist and squeezed her so tight she could barely breathe.

"I didn't know you had kids."

Dawn looked up at the man who had at once caused the chaos and saved the day, knowing as she did that she would fall headlong into the intoxicating sea of blue she had been trying to forget for the better part of a year.

"Cade."

"Give it to me, baby. I wanna hear my name on your lips when you come. Scream for me."

"Oh God. Cade!"

He smiled. She melted. As all women melted at the sight of his chiseled jaw and wide cheekbones, his firm chin and dangerously sexy crooked nose—the only imperfection in a face that could have been sculpted from the finest tawny marble. He wore his cut over a long-sleeved black tee, obscenely stretched to highlight the hard planes and angles of his broad chest. Her hands had traced every ridge of those bulging pecs, fingers clawing at his shoulders countless times during the two nights they'd spent together.

"Been a long time." His eyes dropped to Maia and Tia. "You never told me about your girls."

"'Cause they're not her girls anymore." The harsh rasp of Shelly-Ann's voice shattered the moment. "They're Jimmy's girls, and he won't take kindly to a Sinner laying his dirty paws on them or messing with his old lady."

"I haven't been his old lady for three years." Dawn glared at Shelly-Ann, dressed in her uniform of yoga pants and neon-colored sports tank, her red hair swept into a messy haystack on her head to show off her multiple ear piercings. Although Shelly-Ann wasn't part of Jimmy's MC, she knew full well that Dawn had ceased to be an old lady—the biker equivalent of a wife in the civilian world—when she ran away from Jimmy. And he'd lost the title of her old man. At least, that's how it was supposed to work. But of course, outlaw bikers didn't follow the rules, and because she'd made the mistake of also marrying him in a civil ceremony, she had to file for divorce to try to break his hold. And that's when Jimmy got really angry.

"Just wait until Jimmy hears about this." Shelly-Ann smirked. "You've shot yourself in the foot big time. We both know what'll happen if he finds out you saw the girls without asking me first. And if I tell Jimmy you're with a Sinner . . ."

"I'm not with him. He's just someone I know." But the Sinners were the reason she'd moved to Conundrum with the girls. After a brutal territorial war, Jimmy's MC, the Devil's Brethren, had been kicked out of town on penalty of death, which made it a safe haven for anyone wanting to stay out of the Brethren's reach. At least it was safe until Jimmy found a way around the ban by paying his sister to move to town.

Dawn stepped off the sidewalk, pulling the girls with her, to avoid two women with baby strollers. Her cheeks flushed when their gazes flicked from Cade to her to Shelly-Ann and back to her. After years of trying to put her past behind her, hints of an association with a biker made her feel sick inside. Bikers were bad news. Her little fling with Cade had been an indulgence, a nod to the wild child she kept buried deep inside. Sex and nothing more.

Shelly-Ann waited until the sidewalk was clear again. "Another five hundred a month might keep my mouth shut."

"I don't have another five hundred dollars." Dawn gritted her teeth and handed Shelly-Ann the money she owed her for the week. "I'm already working three jobs. I just sold my car to cover the extras you said you needed last month. You're getting money from Jimmy, too. How much do you need? You're not spending it on the girls."

"Your choice. But you've got a history of making bad choices, so you might want to rethink that attitude. You chose to piss Jimmy off, and look where it got you. No kids. I got my own problems to deal with, and looking after your brats is draining me dry. You know where I'll be on Sunday. And I know where Jimmy will be if you don't show up with the extra cash."

Heart aching, Dawn bent down to hug her girls. She assured them Sunday wasn't too far away, and that one day they would be a family again—a promise she'd been making every week, because she was damn well going to make it happen no matter what it took. No one was going to keep her away from her girls, and especially not Jimmy and his deadbeat sister.

After Shelly-Ann led her sobbing daughters back to the car, Dawn slumped against a streetlamp. Shelly-Ann had been right about one thing. She definitely had made some bad choices in her life, and the worst one was accepting Jimmy's offer to save her from the streets. In her sixteen-year-old naïveté, she had mistaken his interest for kindness and his possessiveness for love.

"You okay?" Cade gently brushed her hair back from her face, and her skin tingled at his touch. Focused on dealing with Shelly-Ann, she'd totally forgotten about him. And Cade wasn't an easy man to forget. Not with those faded jeans, tight in all the right places, those washboard abs, a body that moved with easy grace both in and out of bed . . .

Take me, baby. Deep inside. I want you to feel what I feel. Like there's nothing in the world but us.

What was supposed to be a one-night stand with Cade just over a year ago had turned into two nights, and in those two nights he had ruined her for other men forever.

Too bad he was a biker, the kind of man she'd promised herself she'd never fall for again.

"I'm fine. Sorry you had to hear that."

"My fault. Shoulda been more discreet. Not really one of my strongest traits."

Dawn gave him a dry smile. "As I recall, your strongest traits involve a bed."

She bit her lip as soon as the words left her mouth. What was she thinking? Flirting with him was a one-way street to disaster. And yet her subconscious was in the driver's seat and heading straight for "Route 69."

"Apparently not strong enough, since you dumped me." His blue eyes glittered, and she hit the mental brakes. No need to worry; it seemed she was traveling alone. Served her right. After all, *she* had walked away. Not him.

A flush stole across her cheeks. "We only slept together twice, so technically I didn't dump you. It was more like a permanent good-bye."

"Never had a woman refuse to see me again." Sardonic amusement laced Cade's tone. "Interesting experience. Not one I'm keen to repeat."

She wrapped her arms around herself to beat back the chill of the wind. "Well, as long as you're wearing that cut, you have nothing to worry about from me. As you can see, my life has already been totally messed up by a biker. I'm not interested in getting involved with another one."

"That why you walked away?" He stroked his thumb over the apple of her cheek, and warmth pooled in the pit of her stomach. "'Cause I'm a biker? We're not all the same."

"You're an *outlaw* biker, not just a biker. Isn't that what the one-percenter patch on your cut means? Mayhem and violence are how you live 'The Life' and it's a life I never want to be part of again. In simple terms, outlaws are bad and civilians are good."

His face softened. "What about Arianne?"

Damn. Caught out. Her bestie was the daughter of Viper, president of the Sinners' biggest rival MC, the Black Jacks. And although Arianne had spent a lifetime trying to get out of Conundrum and away from her father, she'd fallen in love with the Sinner president, Jagger, and returned to her outlaw biker roots. "I guess there a few exceptions."

The rumble of a motorcycle pulled her attention away from Cade and his gentle touch. Turning, she caught a glimpse of a Harley Classic motorcycle pulling to a stop beside Shelly-Ann's car.

No.

No way.

Dawn sucked in a sharp breath. What was Jimmy doing here? And by *here*, she didn't just mean in Conundrum or in front of a Sinner who, by all rights, could shoot him dead on sight for daring to enter the town, but *here* near her girls.

Jimmy hated his children. He blamed them for everything that had gone wrong in their relationship—in other words, Dawn had finally mustered the courage to leave after he took out his anger on Tia. Malicious and bitter, he had waged the custody battle not because he wanted their girls, but simply because he didn't want Dawn to have them.

"Jimmy! Get away from them." Heedless of the danger, she pushed past Cade and stepped into the street. Jimmy's presence here was nothing short of brazen, and tantamount to suicide. But then he'd always been an adrenaline junkie, a quality she'd admired until she discovered he got his kicks by listening to her scream.

Jimmy scowled when he spotted her, and she felt the familiar surge of adrenaline that accompanied the fear of knowing she'd displeased him. Once that scowl would have sent her running in the other direction. But she wasn't going to let him near her children ever again.

And besides, for the first time ever, she had backup. Not that she expected Cade to intervene in what was essentially a marital dispute, but Jimmy was a member of the Devil's Brethren, and he was on Sinner's Tribe territory. There was no way Cade would let that pass.

"What the fuck?" Clearly audible over the dwindling traffic, Cade's angry shout chilled Dawn's blood. She held her breath in anticipation of the moment Jimmy heeded the outraged biker only a few steps behind her and ran for cover.

Unfortunately, Jimmy didn't oblige. Instead he crooked his finger and motioned her forward, sending a shiver down her spine with a simple gesture that carried with it the memory of years of pain.

Dark where Cade was fair, slender where Cade was broad, Jimmy had a lean, wolfish face with razor-sharp cheekbones and a cruel slash of a mouth framed in a prickly goatee. When she first met him she'd thought him darkly handsome, but now, knowing just how vicious and brutal he could be, his cruel features were the stuff of nightmares, not dreams.

"That's your Jimmy?" Cade's voice dropped to a low, threatening growl. "Mad Dog, VP of the Devil's Brethren MC? What the hell is he doing in Conundrum?"

"Yep. That's Jimmy." Dawn's pulse kicked up a notch as she took full advantage of the opportunity that had presented itself in the form of a Brethren's mortal enemy, with absolutely no qualms about what she was about to unleash. If Cade were even half as passionate about the club as he was about sex, Jimmy would soon sport as many bruises as she had on the many occasions he'd raised his fists to her. "He's never dared come into

Conundrum before. Looks like he's decided to stick to the Sinners."

"Jesus. Fucking. Christ."

Dawn's mouth watered in anticipation. *Oh yeah.* Jimmy was about to pay for his crimes. His presence was a challenge to Sinner dominance in Conundrum, and no one challenged the Sinners without paying a price.

"You were an old lady in the Devil's Brethren?"

"Biggest mistake of my life." She hadn't realized just how big until she'd become pregnant with the twins at the age of nineteen. Only then did the blinders come off. Although the Brethren were hard, ruthless, violent men, they had bylaws and a constitution, rules and a creed. Jimmy followed the rules only to the extent he was forced to do so, and he lacked the fierce protectiveness most bikers had toward their property: bikes, weapons, clubhouse, women, and children—born or unborn.

Jimmy's dark eyes finally flicked from Dawn to Cade and back to Dawn. She trembled under his silent censure, wondering if he'd seen Cade's hand on her cheek and just how bad her punishment would be if he had. Jimmy's justice was swift and brutal, and she'd quickly learned that the price for breaking his rules was not worth even the smallest amount of defiance.

Cade took a small step forward, interposing his body between her and Jimmy. He seemed unaware of his subtly protective gesture, but Jimmy had seen it, and from the ferocity of his scowl he wasn't pleased. Of course, his displeasure was only the tip of the iceberg. She'd been caught breaking the deal. Now she would have to pay.

Cade didn't think of himself as a violent man. However, the string of blood patches lining the bottom of his cut said otherwise: One patch for every life taken.

A skull and crossbones for his tenth kill. And a Master of Mayhem patch telling the world he'd made violations for his club.

Violations he'd willingly make again.

The Sinners had given him the brotherhood and camaraderie he missed after leaving the army, and a way of life that made him look forward to every day when, for the longest time, he thought of nothing but ending it all.

And right now, his club's dominance was being threatened by a member of the Devil's Brethren who dared step foot in Sinner's Tribe territory; a biker who had stared at Dawn as if he owned her and Cade was the one in the wrong.

He wants to stick it to the Sinners.

Well, fuck that. No damn member of the Brethren would intrude on his territory, whether it was his town, nestled at the foot of Montana's Bridger Mountains, or a beautiful green-eyed blonde with a dry wit, a sharp tongue, and the sexiest body he'd ever had the pleasure to fuck.

Time had not diminished his desire in the least. When he'd seen Dawn standing under the tree, dark blond waves blowing gently around her heartbreakingly, beautiful face, lush curves filling out a slender frame, he almost crashed his bike. No one had ever affected him the way Dawn did, and over the last year he'd made the effort to find out.

"He's their father." A statement. Not a question. Although he had questions for Dawn. Like, what the fuck was she doing with such a loser? When did they split? And was it before she and Cade got together? Not that he had any issues with martial infidelity—he'd fucked plenty of married women, most of them better lays than the inexperienced hang-arounds at the club who were desperate to get into his bed—but he hadn't pegged Dawn as an old lady. And Arianne would have told him if she was still involved with the Brethren.

"Yeah, but we're not together anymore."

"I can't stand by and let one of the Brethren ride around my town like he's got the fucking right to be here. It's like a slap in the face."

Too bad Mad Dog was already rolling his throttle, preparing to flee. Except for the monthly fight matches at the clubhouse, Cade rarely got a chance to fight—properly fight—and he'd always been a brawler, taking out the stress of living in an abusive household on anyone who rubbed him the wrong way. Even after he'd joined the army he'd been disciplined countless times for scrapping.

"You have to do what you have to do." Dawn seemed surprisingly unconcerned that Cade was about to hunt down the father of her children. Her ex. Whatever had happened between them must have been bad.

Real bad.

Mad Dog accelerated into the traffic and Cade threw himself on his bike.

"I'm gonna take care of him." And not just for the club. He was more than happy to serve up a little justice. Sinner style.

Moments later he was off, mindful of the mothers and children crossing the street, not as mindful of the red lights or stop signs. He was an outlaw, after all, and the sheriff's department in Conundrum knew better than to interfere with Sinner business. Until last year, the Sinners had Sheriff Morton on their payroll, but after the sheriff had been picked up by the Bureau of Alcohol, Tobacco, Firearms, and Explosives (ATF) for selling confiscated weapons, a new sheriff arrived with a new deputy in tow and they weren't amenable to engaging in business with outlaws. In other words, they couldn't be bought.

Unlike Mad Dog's fucking sister. What the hell was going on there? Why did Dawn have to pay to see her kids? And how the heck did they wind up with their aunt? How was it he knew so little about her and yet she was the one woman he hadn't been able to get out of his mind?

He thought he'd had Dawn all figured out their first night together. Smart, savvy, and sexy, she knew what she wanted and she took no prisoners. He'd imagined nights of sweaty fucking, his cock buried inside her pussy, her generous breasts filling his palms, the sweet sound of surrender as he gave her the kind of pleasure only a man with his experience could give. And then, when he tired of her, or when she became clingy and demanding of his time, the inevitable good-bye. His first clue things weren't going to go as planned was when he woke up in bed alone after their first night together, the second, when it happened again.

But not this time. After he dealt with Mad Dog, he'd pull out all the stops and get her back in his bed. Then he'd fuck her until they were so exhausted neither of them could run away. She wanted him. He knew it from the way she licked her lips when she looked at him, and how her cheeks flushed when he touched her, the way her mouth parted, inviting him in . . .

Fuck me, Cade.

Sweeter words he'd never heard.

Shaking off the memory of Dawn moaning beneath him, Cade pursued Mad Dog through residential areas and then north on the interstate toward the airport. What the fuck? The Devil's Brethren had moved south of Conundrum after the turf war. If Mad Dog had any sense, he'd head to the Brethren clubhouse where Cade couldn't touch him.

But that was the problem with the Brethren. Whether it was stupidity or arrogance, they just couldn't accept Sinner dominance of the state. Even after the hellish battle in which the Brethren president, JC, was killed and his brothers were stomped, beaten, and chain-whipped to a pulp, their patches and bikes confiscated, legs and arms broken to prevent them from riding, they'd simply regrouped under a new leader, JC's brother, Wolf. No matter what the Sinners did to them, the Brethren just kept coming back. Like the roaches they were.

Leaning low on his bike, Cade closed the distance between him and Mad Dog, the icy wind sending a shiver down his back. Living in Montana had its challenges, not the least of which was winter riding. But with the advent of spring, he'd dumped the tire chains and Gore-Tex gloves. The bandanna, however, was still a must.

Mad Dog's bike screeched to a stop outside a warehouse nestled at the foot of the Bridger Mountains, just outside the town boundaries. Something about the warehouse niggled at the back of Cade's mind. He knew for certain he'd ridden past it last year in pursuit of a gang of Black Jacks intent on taking out Jagger and Arianne, but there was something else about the building . . . something he couldn't quite remember. An offhand comment made a long time ago.

Cade parked his bike, then did a quick reconnaissance of the building: Two windows, blacked out. A side door, locked. Tire treads near the front door. White panel van parked out back. He searched the trees nearby but found no other vehicles, bikes, or Brethren.

Maybe Mad Dog had run out of fuel . . . or courage. Or maybe he thought he'd be able to take Cade out from a secure position inside. He had to know Cade followed him here. So was it a trap or a challenge? Not that it mattered. Cade had a duty to address the wrong done to his MC: the blatant disrespect of daring to ride in Sinner territory wearing the colors of a rival club.

Steeling himself for the confrontation, Cade drew his weapon and stalked toward the door, a thrill of adrenaline shooting through his veins. Nothing Cade had accomplished as a child—school, sports, summer jobs—had been good enough for his father, but Cade excelled at using violence to solve his problems. Just like his old man.

He sent a quick text giving Jagger his location and the barest details of what had happened. He had no hesitation going in alone after Jimmy, preferring solo missions to group efforts where he invariably would be put in charge of inexperienced prospects or junior patch who had never fired a gun. Not that he had any issues with being in charge. He'd led his squad through countless missions while on tour in Afghanistan, until the night they were caught in an ambush. His discharge hadn't come about because he'd been the only man to survive, but because afterward he'd sought comfort the only way he knew how. And damned if anyone had told him that the lush blonde with the big blue eyes who tried to convince him life was still worth living by inviting him into her bed was the Lieutenant General's daughter.

But that was a long time ago. He no longer needed the soft sweetness of a woman to soothe his pain. He had the club, his bike, his brothers, and he had a fucking kick-ass weapon, a military-issue SIG Sauer P228 begging to be unloaded in a dirty piece of Brethren ass.

Cade slowly turned the handle on the front door, his weapon raised and ready. The hunt was on.

★ TWO ★

I do not fear death. Death will fear me.

SINNER'S TRIBE CREED

"Doors open in five minutes. Quit your yapping and get out front."

Joe Banks, proprietor of Banks Bar, lifted a warning eyebrow and glared at Dawn and her best friend, Arianne, engaged in a deep discussion in the middle of the stockroom.

"The bar isn't open yet." Dawn returned his scowl. "There are no customers I need to serve, and I haven't seen my bestie in a week. We have a lot of catching up to do."

"That's what phones are for."

Arianne laughed as she twisted her long, dark hair into a ponytail. Tall and slim, with startling green eyes and a perfectly oval face, she and Dawn had bonded her first day on the job over Banks's gruff manner, his pawing customers, and a shared fondness for flavored vodka.

"That's what stockrooms are for," Arianne said. "So wipe that frown off your face and let us have our little catch-up, or this bartender is going to walk and take your best waitress with her."

"Ever since you became Jagger's old lady, you got a serious attitude problem," Banks grumbled as he hoisted a box on his shoulder. "Before you hooked up with him, you were sweet, nice, easy to get along with. Now you're telling me how it is, wearing your damn cut while you're working the bar, throwing me out of my stockroom . . . I liked you better when you were just Viper's runaway daughter. Before, you had more respect."

Dawn laughed and kissed his cheek. Ex-law-enforcement, with one hell of a ripped body and the chiseled good looks to match, Banks was a close friend, and more often than not she found herself eating pizza and watching westerns at his apartment when she had a rare evening off. Arianne thought they were a good match, but Banks was too straitlaced for Dawn. She'd always had a wild side. And if not for the streak of rebel in her, she'd never have been able to run away from home the night she turned fourteen.

"It's not just Arianne; I don't respect you, either," Dawn teased. "Like you. But no respect."

"Fired." He pushed open the swinging door leading to the bar. "Both of you. Fired."

"Is that the first time we're fired tonight?" Arianne leaned against the wall, arms folded over the Sinner's Tribe cut Jagger insisted she wear when she worked the bar. The Sinner patch alone would have been enough to save her from roaming hands, but the PROPERTY OF JAGGER rocker above it kept all but the most ignorant away.

Dawn tied her apron around her waist. "Yep. But it won't be the last."

Banks wasn't given to overt affection. His threats to fire them were the closest he got to expressing friendship. That and saving Arianne from her psychotic brother, and then taking a beating from Jagger for his trouble.

Still, he was a good manager and the bar had always

done well. Dawn made twice as much money at Banks Bar as she did waitressing at Table Tops restaurant in the mornings, and arranging flowers at Cindy's Florals in the afternoons. One day, though, when she got her girls back and returned to college, she'd get that Accounting Technology Certificate she'd always dreamed about, a good, stable, high-paying job, and maybe even study for her CPA. Just like her dad.

At least that had been the dream a year ago.

Shortly after meeting Cade, she'd taken the bold step of filing for a divorce, and then she'd lost the girls. After that, determined to regain custody, she had no time for men, not the engaging new Conundrum deputy sheriff, Doug Benson, and especially not bikers, and most particularly not bikers who thought they were God's gift to women.

"So . . . finish telling me about Cade." Arianne gave Dawn a nudge after the door closed behind Banks. Arianne knew about Dawn's past, although not the reason Dawn had run away from home, or what happened to her on the streets before Jimmy found her—some doors were better left closed. "You gonna see him again?"

"No." Dawn checked the small mirror near the coat hooks and fluffed her curls. *The bigger the hair the better the tips.* "I broke it off last year after those two hot nights for a reason. And that reason was right in my face this afternoon. Present company excluded, of course, outlaw bikers are bad news."

"You can't judge all outlaw bikers solely on what you experienced with Jimmy and the Brethren. The Sinners care about their women, protect them." She gave Dawn a wry smile. "Some women even get respect."

"They have bylaws and rules, but they don't follow the law. And they're misogynistic to the core."

"True." Arianne gave her a wink. "But you just have to learn how to work the system."

"I'm not you," Dawn said. "I'm not badass to the bone and make all men except Jagger quake in their biker boots when I walk past. I've been betrayed in one way or another by every man I trusted, but I survived Jimmy and fought my way free. Now I'm fighting for my girls. I don't have time for men, and I'm not about to open myself up again, especially to a man like Cade."

"What kind of man do you think he is?"

"The dangerous kind," Dawn said. "The kind of man a woman dreams about, but never wants to meet because the reality of him overwhelms any fantasy. Powerful. Dominant. A biker. The kind of man I promised myself I would never fall for again."

And a womanizer, or so she'd heard after their two nights together. Charming, handsome, and seductive, but totally unfaithful, unable to commit, and unrepentant for his "crimes." The last time she'd been to a Sinner party, she'd heard rumors that Cade never slept with the same woman twice. She'd been tempted to share the fact that she had, in fact, slept with Cade twice, but she decided instead to slip out of the party and out of his life.

"I thought you liked him." Arianne rounded the bar and took up her position behind the polished wood counter.

Dawn grabbed a serving tray from the shelf behind Arianne. "I don't really know him. We didn't talk much. We were too busy ripping off each other's clothes and having sizzling-hot sex in his room at the clubhouse. And both mornings, coward that I am, I sneaked away at day-break so I didn't have to tell him to his face I couldn't see him again."

"And yet after that first night, you did." Arianne waved to the first customer in the door. Dawn grabbed her note-pad from the counter and stuffed it in her apron.

"But not after the second time." She turned away so

Arianne wouldn't see the regret on her face. She'd felt something the second time—a longing that tugged at her heart and kept her awake long after Cade had fallen asleep, an inexplicable certainty that nothing and no one would harm her while she lay in his arms.

She'd never felt so safe since her parents died, and the memories of their unconditional love and the good times they shared together—picnics and hikes in the mountains, playing number games with her dad and gardening with her mom—still made her heart ache. With Jimmy, she'd walked a fine line between affection and anger. One wrong step, one misspoken word and he would turn on her, his punishment swift, brutal, and invariably cruel.

She couldn't afford to have those longings. Dreams, hopes, and desires that did nothing to help get her kids back were a waste of time and energy. A heartbreak waiting to happen. Maybe one day, when she and her girls were together again and living far, far away from Jimmy and the Devil's Brethren . . .

"Hey, gorgeous."

She looked up as T-Rex, the newest full-patch member of the Sinners, joined them at the bar. Tall, blond, and built like a linebacker, with a broad face and a warm smile, T-Rex was a favorite in the club, and one of the few bikers who didn't set Dawn's teeth on edge. And that was saying something.

"Corona. Cold. No lime. No glass." Dawn rattled off his drink as T-Rex sat on one of the bar stools and chuckled.

"Damn. Don't know how you do that, but you impress the brothers every time they stop by for a drink. Even if Cade hadn't laid down the law, they wouldn't be cracking blonde jokes about you."

Dawn froze, her hand outstretched for the bottle Arianne was opening. "What do you mean, he laid down the law?" After she'd made it clear to Cade she wasn't interested in seeing him again, he'd respected her wishes and stayed away. She'd assumed he had found someone new, likely one of the club's sweet butts. Lower than old ladies and house mamas in the biker hierarchy, the young women who hung around the clubhouse, helping out and offering their services in return for food, shelter, and protection, were desperate to find a biker who would make them an old lady. And Cade, handsome, charming, unattached, and always willing, was quite the catch.

T-Rex's eyes widened, his usually affable expression turning to wariness. "You know."

"I don't know, or I wouldn't have asked."

"Well . . ." He coughed and looked around, but there were no other Sinners in the bar to save him. "He kinda . . . you know . . . warned the brothers away. Said you were his, 'cept you were wanting to take things slow. So no one was to touch you, hit on you, or disrespect you if they saw you at the bar or if you came with Arianne to our parties."

Dawn shot T-Rex an incredulous look. "Seriously? Except for this afternoon, it's been over a year since I've seen him. How slow do the brothers think I want to take it?"

"You saw Cade this afternoon?"

"Yeah."

"You tell Jagger?"

Puzzled, she frowned. "Why would I tell Jagger?"

But T-Rex already had his cell in his hand. "We're supposed to call in if we see Cade or hear anything about him. He sent a text to Jagger saying he was up at a warehouse in the North West checking out a Brethren sighting. He didn't report back. I figured he probably just hooked up with some chick and . . ." He cut himself off with a grimace. "Sorry."

"No problem. It's not like we're together. I'm sure he

was with some 'chick.'" But she wasn't so sure. Could Jimmy have hurt Cade? Although Jimmy hadn't made any effort to drag her back to the clubhouse after she ran away—he had someone new to warm his bed the next day—he'd told her through Shelly-Ann he would kill anyone who touched her. And Jimmy wasn't one to make idle threats.

"Actually . . ." She hesitated, not wanting to share her business, but sufficiently concerned to give him the most relevant information. "He saw Jimmy 'Mad Dog' Sanchez, VP of the Devil's Brethren, outside St. Francis Xavier's School about three-thirty this afternoon and went chasing after him. They headed north on Twenty-Seventh Avenue."

T-Rex texted her information and then looked up. "How do you know Mad Dog, or the Devil's Brethren? I thought you were just a civilian."

Damn. She'd managed to keep her past a secret from all but her closest friends. The last thing she wanted was Jagger breathing down her neck, hounding her for details of an enemy MC. Arianne described Jagger as a sensual, loving, caring man, but all Dawn saw was a powerful, violent, ruthless biker who would let nothing stand in the way of his goals. And Arianne had been one of them.

"I am just a civilian, and one who had better get back to work." She forced a smile and then quickly wove her way through the tables to the far end of the bar, away from T-Rex and his questioning looks, and out of range of a possible phone call from Jagger.

Although . . . Her hand dropped as she considered an option she had quickly dismissed in the past. Now that the wheels had been set in motion—Jimmy crossing the uncrossable line, Cade finding out about their relationship—maybe now was the time to ask for Jagger's help. No one in Montana except possibly Arianne's father, Viper, president of the Black Jacks MC, wielded as much power or had as much influence in Montana's criminal underworld as Jagger.

But why would he help her? Arianne's friendship wouldn't be enough for him to put any of the Sinners at risk. She needed more—leverage, a connection—something that would make it worth his while or call upon his sense of duty. And she'd have to give something back. Favors—or marks, as bikers called them—weren't free. They came at a steep price, and that price took her right back into the biker world she was determined to leave behind. Not only that, she had nothing to offer.

Fuck.

Cade tried to stretch the cramp out of his legs, but the Brethren had done a good job of hog-tying him before throwing him in the back of the van. At least they hadn't broken any bones when they'd jumped him in the warehouse. Six against one was hardly fair, especially in the dark. Three he could have handled. Maybe four.

But that's what he got for his arrogance. If he'd had any sense, he would have waited for backup before he entered the building. Now he could only hope the Sinners would find him before the Brethren decided he was worth more dead than alive. Killing him and dumping his body would send a powerful message, although he still couldn't understand how they thought they could take on his club.

Unless they weren't working alone.

He gritted his teeth as the van rattled over the bumpy road. Damn uncomfortable lying on the metal surface. But then he'd never thought about the comfort of the men he'd kidnapped, either.

The vehicle slowed to a stop and his heart pounded in his chest. He'd heard them arguing about what to do with him for most of the trip. Protocol, such as it was in the biker world, demanded they hand him over to their president, Wolf, to make the call. Cade didn't know any MC that would condone the kind of vigilante action these losers were contemplating. Executions were almost always at the discretion of the MC president, especially if the purpose was political.

The van doors slammed open and Cade blinked as his eyes adjusted to the light from the setting sun. Someone cut the ropes around his feet and he was hauled out of the van and pushed to his knees on the deserted gravel road. Mad Dog stood in front of him and pointed his Desert Eagle .50 at his head.

Pussy. With a fucking useless pussy weapon.

"Say your prayers, Sinner."

"Fuck, Mad Dog. This ain't right." A tall, gangly redhead with a scraggly beard and a name patch that read RUSTY put a hand on Mad Dog's arm. "This is Wolf's call. You off him and we're in a full-out war with the Sinners. We gotta wait until the patch-over, then the Jacks will have our backs."

Cade sucked in a sharp breath, as a memory twigged at the back of his mind. The warehouse belonged to the Black Jacks. Arianne had been kidnapped and held inside it last year. Jagger had saved her and almost lost his life. If the Jacks were letting the Brethren use the warehouse as a base, then the patch-over was a serious possibility.

Christ. A union between the Sinner's Tribe's most powerful rival, the Jacks, and a solid midsized club like the Brethren could spell the end for his MC. The Sinners wouldn't just lose territory or their dominance of the state; the Jacks would have the muscle to hunt them down and slaughter them one by one.

He needed to get the information to Jagger ASAP.

Problem was, he was tied and on his knees with a fucking gun to his head.

"It's my call." Mad Dog spat on the ground beside Cade's knee. "This is personal, not political. He was with my old lady. He had his fucking paws on her. Probably been fucking her, too. I gotta right to protect my property."

"Thought she wasn't your old lady no more." A burly biker with a massive beer gut toyed with his barbecue gun, a nickel-plated fixed-sight .38 super 1911, low on functionality but nice for cowboy shooter types to show off at barbecues or social functions. "And it becomes political once you off him, whatever the reason."

"Dammit, Trey. She's a bitch who needs to be kept in line. A man's got a right to punish his old lady. And that bitch has so much damn attitude, she needs it a lot. She thinks she's untouchable living in Conundrum, just like she thought she was untouchable when she filed for divorce. But those kids are her weakness. She wants them; she comes home to Daddy. This time tomorrow I'll be beating her into submission with a bullwhip until she learns not to defy me again, and then I'm gonna fuck her so hard she won't remember her own name."

Son of a bitch. Cade itched to get his hands around Mad Dog's throat. But first he needed to get his hands free.

Mad Dog's phone buzzed in his cut. He signaled to his Brethren brothers to watch Cade, and then he walked down the road as he engaged in a heated conversation with the caller. Cade continued working the ropes he'd loosened during the trip. Just another inch and he'd be able to show Mad Dog what a real beating was like.

Mad Dog returned a few minutes later, his face red and spittle bubbling at the corners of his lips.

"Wolf knows we got the Sinner. Wants us to let him

go. One of you musta texted him during the drive. Who's the fucking rat?"

Silence.

Although Mad Dog wore a vice president patch, Cade hadn't been around the group long enough to ascertain just how much power he held in the club. But if one of his supporters had reported the kidnapping to Wolf behind Mad Dog's back, then he didn't have the type of loyalty that inspired leadership. Which meant he'd be trying to prove himself, making him twice as dangerous as any of the other Devil's Brethren gathered around him.

"Fuck." Mad Dog kicked Cade in the side and Cade clenched his teeth against the pain.

"Wolf says we can rough him up a bit, but until the patch-over is a sure thing, he doesn't want to start a war with the Sinners." His lip curled and he spat again. "Wolf is a fucking old man. He's weak. Yeah, we need the Jacks, but why would we patch over and let them swallow us up instead of becoming a support club and keeping our power? It's time for a change. Once I'm president, I'll make this club great again like it was under my old man. I'm not afraid of the damn Sinners. We got lots of new blood. I say we start a war. Bring it on."

"You got ambition and good ideas but you gotta be patient." Rusty held up a warning hand. "You're not gonna help your case in the election if you outright defy Wolf. You gotta show you can toe the party line until it's your fucking party. We should do as Wolf says. Beat him good and let him go."

"But now he knows about the patch-over." Trey cuffed Cade on the head.

Dammit to hell. If they intended to rough him up, why not a few proper kicks and punches? Get it over with instead of pussyfooting around.

"What's he gonna do? Go to Viper and tell him it's a bad idea? Sinners can't stop a fucking patch-over. It's got nothing to do with them. And it's better this way." Mad Dog fisted Cade's hair and yanked his head back. "Now they'll be running scared."

"Sinners aren't scared of anything, especially not roaches like you." Cade felt the ropes around his wrists slacken and steeled himself to wait for the perfect moment. These bastards were so going down.

"You should be scared." Mad Dog lifted Cade's chin with the butt of his gun, forcing Cade to meet his cold, dark gaze. "Six to one on a deserted road in the mountains and your hands are tied. We might not be allowed to kill you, but we can hurt you pretty damn bad."

★ THREE ★

I will strive to better my skill of self-control.
SINNER'S TRIBE CREED

Dawn jolted into consciousness when someone banged on her front door.

Heart pounding, she reached under her bed for the .22 Arianne had given her as a birthday present. Trust Arianne to give her a gun, and an unregistered one at that. Although she had often talked about living in the civilian world, Arianne was a biker through and through. And no biker would ever leave his or her house unarmed.

Well, Dawn wasn't a biker. Not anymore. And the two days of lessons at the shooting range with Arianne hadn't changed her mind. Still, it was a comfort to know that she'd be able to defend herself from the crazy person trying to break down her door at three in the morning. Or at least threaten him. She never loaded the gun because she simply wasn't prepared to kill anyone.

Weapon in hand, she raced through the living room and stood on tiptoe to peer through the peephole. At first she didn't recognize the man standing in front of her door, his face swollen and bloody, his shirt in tatters, but it was his hair, golden strands matted with blood, glinting in the semidarkness, that made her look again.

Her breath caught in her throat and she undid the dead bolt, then threw the door open. "Oh God. Cade. What happened?"

"Jesus, Dawn. Put the gun away." He brushed past her and stalked into her tiny hallway, his clothes rank with blood and covered in dirt. "What the fuck were you doing with a piece of shit like him?"

Stunned, Dawn could only stare. "You almost break down my door at three in the morning, looking like you need to get to a hospital, to ask me that?"

"Yeah."

"If we knew each other better," she said, her voice tight. "If we were friends, or actually seeing each other, maybe I wouldn't be so annoyed at being pulled out of bed and ordered to explain my life choices. But we're not. We've slept together twice. We've never had a conversation that lasted more than two minutes, one minute of which consisted of deciding how we were going to have sex next. So you don't have the right to ask me that question, and unless you're in dire need of medical attention, I suggest you leave."

By way of answer, Cade took a step forward into the living room, staggered to the side, and grabbed the back of her sofa for support. "Damn. Gimme a minute."

With a sigh, Dawn closed and locked the door, then put the gun into her purse. "I see you've chosen door number three, 'dire need of medical assistance.' You want me to call the Sinner doctor or take you to the local hospital?"

"No hospital."

"Right. I forgot. Too manly for the hospital. You got a number for the club doctor?"

Cade shook his head. "No doctor. Just . . . water . . . bandages . . . maybe some whiskey. I'll be fine."

Hmmm. Fine *is obviously a relative word.* To her non-medical eye, he certainly didn't look fine. In fact, he looked like he was about to collapse, and from the way he was holding himself, he was clearly injured far beyond the cuts and bruises she could see on his face. But that was always the way with biker beatings. Why go for the small target when you could go for the big one?

"Kitchen. Now." Dawn gestured to the small kitchen area, visible through the open breakfast bar behind the couch. Living on her own, Dawn had more than enough space in her cheap, two-bedroom bungalow rental, although the pastel decor and white rattan furniture were not really to her taste. But she wasn't meant to be living on her own. The second bedroom held twin beds and the toys Maia and Tia had left behind the day they'd been ripped from her arms by an overzealous court sheriff after the devastating court case in which she was declared an unfit mother.

Cade followed her to the kitchen, decorated in country-chic pink and mint green, and pulled out a white wicker chair from the breakfast nook. As he lowered himself to sit, Dawn grabbed a tea towel and threw it over the seat.

"Lotta blood on you. Not sure how much is fresh, and the furniture isn't mine to stain."

"None of it since I was fighting a buncha deadbeats." Cade grimaced. "Six of them to one of me. I used the advantage of surprise to take Mad Dog down, and then went after the better fighters. When they were all moaning on the ground, I grabbed a weapon and took off in their van."

"I hope you parked the stolen vehicle nearby."

"Right out front."

"Excellent." Sarcasm laced her tone. "Now the Brethren and the police will know where to find you."

Dawn pulled out her first-aid kit and washed her

hands in the sink. Even though he was battered and bruised, his eyes full of questions she would never answer, Cade's presence soothed the nervous flutter that was always in her stomach. There was just something about him, beyond his obvious physical strength . . . Maybe it was the way he filled a room with his sheer, palpable presence. Or maybe it was the way he looked at her: Like there was no one else in the room. Like she was his and woe betide any man who dared hurt her.

Or maybe it was all in her imagination.

She eyed his bloody clothing and grabbed a garbage bag from the cupboard. "You'd better strip. I'll throw your clothes in the wash. Looks like you get to spend the night in your undies on my couch."

A smile tugged the corner of Cade's battered mouth as he undid his belt. "Will I be alone?"

"Condition you're in, you'll most definitely be alone." She eased herself between his parted legs to help him take off his T-shirt, freezing when he winced at her touch. "Well, that just settles it." She carefully pulled the shirt up his body. "I'm not about to take advantage of an injured man."

"I'm not injured everywhere." The deep rumble of his voice made her skin tingle.

"Seriously?" Dawn swallowed hard as her hands followed the shirt up his torso, her fingers brushing over heated skin and hard muscle. God, he was magnificent, all taut pecs and rippling abs. Even the bruises couldn't mar the perfection of his body. "How can you be thinking of sex at a time like this?"

His voice dropped, husky and low. "'Cause you're standin' between my legs wearing a tiny pair of shorts that only cover the top of your ass cheeks, and a damn tight top that doesn't hide what you're thinking." He leaned forward in the chair, so close she could feel his breath on her skin. "And nothing underneath."

Dawn's breath hitched and her blood heated, thundered through her veins. Until this moment, focused on Cade's injuries, her attire had been totally irrelevant. "How do you know I have nothing underneath?"

Cade traced lazy circles up the sensitive skin of her inner thigh, pausing at edge of her cotton PJ shorts. Dawn stilled as her brain clouded with desire. It was always this way with Cade: A chemistry so potent she was surprised they didn't combust.

"Let's see." He slid his finger inside her shorts and stroked along the sensitive crease at the top of her thigh, sending a zing of electricity straight to her core.

"Hmmm. Can't tell. Spread for me, baby. Let me in."

Her face flushed. God, the things he said did all the wrong things to the right parts of her body. "Cade . . . this isn't the time. You're hurt. Let me look after you."

He grabbed her hips, pulling her so close she could feel his heat through her clothes. Dawn breathed in his scent of blood and grass, mixed with heady aroma of leather and manly musk, and a delicious shiver ran up her spine.

"You are taking care of me," he said. "Man gets in a fight. Hurts all over. He wants to feel good. He wants something to make him forget the pain. And you—all soft and sexy and smellin' like flowers—will do the trick."

"I thought you came here for help." Dawn made a token effort at resistance and raised an eyebrow. "I didn't realize it was a booty call."

"You got the nicest booty I ever seen." Cade slid a hand down her hip, and gave her ass a squeeze. Before she could move away, his finger was inside her shorts, stroking over the bare skin of her folds. She gasped as moisture flooded her sex, and her nipples tightened beneath her thin cotton tank. Had she really thought things would be different from every other time they'd been together?

"Naughty girl," he whispered. "You go to bed without your panties and someone might take advantage."

"Cade." She pulled back just enough to dislodge his questing finger, at once disconcerted and aroused. "Why did you come here?"

His shoulders slumped and he leaned back in the chair, his easy capitulation more disturbing than his injuries. "The minute I got outta there, I called Jagger. Told him what had happened. The Brethren are planning to patch over to the Jacks. You know what that means."

"The Black Jacks could destroy the Sinners." She pulled the shirt over his head, biting her lip when she saw the extent of his injuries. Not an inch of his torso had been spared. His skin was a mass of swelling and bruises, with a few surface knife slashes across his abdomen below the fabulous tat of blue wings and twin pistons across his chest. And were those boot prints on his side?

Cade stiffened when she reached for his belt. "He called an executive board meeting for eight o'clock tomorrow morning."

"I'm not surprised." The executive board—consisting of a president, vice president, secretary, sergeant-at-arms, treasurer, road captain and two members-at-large—governed all outlaw clubs. The board made all the key decisions about the club and reported back to the members in weekly mandatory "church" meetings attended only by full-patch members of the MC.

Cade pushed himself to standing and unzipped his fly, wincing when he tried pushing off his jeans. Dawn gently moved his hands away from her body, taking a moment to collect herself, before she said, "Let me."

Licking her dry lips, she eased his jeans over his narrow hips, dropping to her knees in front of him to slide them over his powerful thighs and muscular calves.

Without taking his gaze off her, Cade stepped out of his clothes, seemingly unembarrassed to be standing in her kitchen, wearing only black boxers and sporting a sizable erection.

"Dawn . . ." Cade's voice cracked even as his gaze burned into her. Focused. Intent.

She should get up. Kneeling in front of him like this was sending all the wrong messages . . . for both of them. He was hurt. Badly. His injuries needed tending, and she didn't want this. Didn't want to open this door again. And yet she couldn't pull herself away.

"You still haven't told me why you came here," she said.

Cade sifted his hand through her hair, his touch more soothing than erotic. "I needed to tell you something . . . Fucking bastard's coming after you. He's gonna make you choose between going back to him or losing your kids."

Dawn stood, removing herself from temptation. "I knew the risks, but I couldn't help myself. I miss my girls so much I ache inside every minute of every day." Her throat tightened and she looked away. "I've been fighting to get them back for a year now, but the court process is slow and Jimmy has the money to pay a lawyer to drag out the case with frivolous motions that are draining me dry."

"How the fuck did the courts get involved?" He toyed with her curls, twirling them around his fingers as he cupped her jaw in his hand. "One-percenters don't do civil weddings. We find a woman we want to be with; we make her an old lady. Fuck the courts. Fuck the law. And when a biker says it's over, it's over. Simple."

"Simple if he says it's over. Hell if he doesn't. Double hell if he was the one who initiated the civilian wedding. Triple hell if he was clever enough to use the system against me." She sighed and tipped her head against his hand, his palm warm and soothing on her skin. "He was so angry when I filed for divorce, but he'd planned for it, and he used the system against me. He hired a shady private investigator to set me up. The guy wore a school sweatshirt and said he was selling tickets for the school picnic. I handed him the money. He handed me a Baggie filled with crack. I was thrown off for a moment, trying to figure out what it was. Even though I'd seen quarters like that before, because we were behind the school, and I wasn't expecting it, I thought for a moment it was a sugary treat for the kids, or some kind of fairy dust. By the time I figured it out, it was too late. Someone was secretly filming our encounter. Jimmy produced the tape at the custody hearing. He paid off the judge so no questions were asked. My lawyer did everything he could, but on its face, and given my history, it looked bad."

"Bastard."

"I was so scared for the girls," she said softly. "I didn't know he planned to give them to Shelly-Ann just to spite me. He'd hit Tia once before . . ."

"He hit your kids?"

Instantly she realized her mistake. Cade was nothing if not protective. The first time they'd met, she and Arianne had been fleeing the Black Jacks and Cade offered to take her to the safety of the clubhouse and spend the night watching over her. One motorcycle ride pressed up against Cade's broad back later, and she'd let him watch her in more ways than one.

"Yes, he did. That's when I finally left him." She didn't mention the years of abuse she'd endured as Jimmy's old lady. The day she'd left Jimmy was the day she put the past behind her; the day she realized she was a fighter and a survivor. The day she'd started her life as Dawn, and not Dee.

Cade thudded his fist against the cabinet. "Fucking cowardly piece of shit beating on children. Gimme my clothes and I'll go out there—"

"Cade."

"I'll find him and show him just how it feels to be beaten up by someone bigger and stronger. Then I'll flay him alive—"

"Cade."

"And when he's on the ground whimpering and pissing in his pants, I'll pull out my gun—"

"Cade, honey." She pressed her hands against the only unmarked skin on his chest, stilling him in a heartbeat. "Can we save the beating and flaying talk until tomorrow? I have a feeling you won't be able to get off the couch in the morning, much less pulverize Jimmy, and I'll have nightmares if you keep it up. Not that I'm turning the offer down. I'm quite happy to endorse the beat-him-till-he-pisses-his-pants plan. But not right now."

"You want revenge?"

"When someone messes with my children, I'm not going to shed any tears if someone lands a few good blows on the bastard's face, except for the fact I couldn't do it myself."

Cade gave a satisfied growl. "At your service."

She licked her lips and Cade slid his hand over her hip, pulling her against him. His erection pressed against her belly and Dawn bit back a groan. Even battered and bruised, Cade turned her on like no man ever had. "I'm sure you are. But why?"

* * *

Why?

Because when he'd been on his knees on the gravel road with a pistol pointed at his head, he was sure he was going to die. But instead of thinking back over his life, trying to relive thirty years in the space of a heartbeat, he'd thought about her: The softness of her skin. The warmth of her smile. The way the sunlight glinted on her hair, making it look like spun gold. He'd thought about running his hands over her beautiful body, in and out of her sweet curves, cupping her breasts in his palms and licking her dusky-rose nipples until she writhed on the bed. He remembered how easily she rode pillion on his bike, the feeling of her arms around his waist, the way men looked at her in the bar and how everyone wanted what he'd had for only two nights.

Cade had been with more women than he could count. But the only face he could remember was hers.

When Mad Dog had pressed the barrel of the pistol against his forehead, he thought about every detail of those two nights with her. And in that moment he decided two things. First, it wasn't a good day to die. And second, if he did manage to escape, he would find a way to make those two nights into something more.

But Jesus fucking Christ if he didn't get her away from him right now his more-than-two-nights dream would be over in two minutes. Already the throbbing in his cock far exceeded the pain in every other part of his body.

"Cade?" She looked up at him, big green eyes wide and glistening, her lips pink and plump, wet from the little flicks of her tongue.

Cade let out a tortured groan and tightened his hand in her hair. The urge to settle her back on her knees, shove down his boxer briefs, and slide his cock into that soft, sweet mouth was overwhelming. And from the way she was looking at him, he was damn sure she wouldn't say no. He'd never met a woman whose needs so matched his own, who knew what he wanted before he did, and was totally and absolutely uninhibited in bed. There was nothing she wouldn't try and in the two nights they'd spent together, they'd tried a lot.

"You got some whiskey?"

She turned away, breaking the spell. Cade sat heavily in the chair thanking God for the small mercy of whiskey and its miraculous powers of healing, numbing, and taking a man's mind off soft plump lips and little pink tongues.

By the time she finished tending his wounds and settling him on the couch, he was rock-hard again, but fairly certain he wouldn't be able to do much about it with his veins now running at least 75 percent alcohol.

"I think you'll live." Dawn handed him a blanket. "I'll see you in the morning."

"Where are you going?"

"Bed. I have a job waitressing at Table Tops and I have to be there at seven A.M."

He stretched out his arm, motioning her back, and gritted his teeth against the pain. "You're gonna leave an injured man alone all night? What if I lose consciousness?"

She lifted an admonishing eyebrow and Cade grinned. He liked that about her. She didn't easily take offense, nor did she take any crap. And she totally got his sense of humor, although right now he wasn't being funny.

"It's called sleep, and you know what it's like when we're together. We can't . . ."

"I'll be good. You have my word." Part of him couldn't believe he'd been reduced to begging. He'd never begged to sleep with a woman. In fact, he'd never had to pursue a woman. Nor had he ever been rejected.

But then he'd never been interested in anything other

than a casual hookup. Relationships required intimacy, and he had no template for a healthy, intimate relationship. He enjoyed the company of women, their gentle temperament, and the softness of their bodies. After he had what he wanted, whether it was to be teased, tempted, or sexually relieved, or to ease the ache in his soul, he was just as happy to walk away. But he was always up front. He was there for a good time, not a long time. And when he left, he did so with no regrets and no trail of broken hearts.

Her head fell back and she groaned. "You can sleep in my bed only because you're badly injured, but if your hands or any other part of your body moves off your side, I won't be responsible for my actions. Arianne gave me a gun and taught me how to use it."

"You'd shoot me for a little cuddle? It's a scientific fact that sex releases healing hormones. Don't you want me to get better?" He couldn't help but turn on the charm he used to lure women to his bed, and yet, for the first time, the teasing banter left a bitter taste in his mouth.

Her lips quivered with a repressed smile. "I highly doubt you'd be able to perform in your current condition."

"Performance is never an issue." He whipped off the blanket to reveal the erection tenting his briefs. Apparently his cock could withstand the effects of excessive alcohol consumption and bone-numbing pain in the presence of a beautiful woman in ass-revealing shorts and a skimpy tank top.

Dawn's gaze lingered below his waist and her cheeks flushed as she crossed the room toward him. "I'm not someone who functions well without sleep." She helped him off the couch and he leaned against her shoulder, trying to decide which was worse: the ache in his balls, or the damn cuts and bruises.

Her body was soft and warm against him, trembling as she tried to bear his weight. So delicate and yet so strong. Beautiful. Compassionate. And damn tempting in that little outfit. How had he ever let her get away? And how could he resist her now?

"I'm not someone who functions well without a good-night kiss." In one swift move he turned her to face him, then bent down and covered her mouth with his, one arm sliding around her waist to pull her against his body before she could protest.

She softened against him with a sigh, as if she'd been waiting for him to make a move, her lips parting for the sweep of his tongue, her nipples hard against his chest. She smelled of flowers and sunshine and antiseptic. She tasted of mint and honey, and oh God, she tasted of sex.

His groin tightened and his cock throbbed, pressed tight against her belly. When she moaned and slid her hands around his neck, deepening the kiss, he truly thought he would lose control. But Dawn wasn't like the other women he'd had in his bed. One night wouldn't be enough. Plus, he'd given his word, and a biker's word was his bond.

Drawing in a ragged breath, he released her. Dawn staggered back a step, her face flushed, lips swollen from his kiss, confusion wrinkling the smoothness of her brow.

"Cade." Her voice caught as she whispered his name. A plea. A warning.

"On second thought . . ." He gritted his teeth against the tightening in his groin. If he climbed into bed with her, he wouldn't be able to hold back. Not with adrenaline still streaming through his veins, stirred up by her gentle touch, her barely concealed curves, and the memories of the two nights they had spent together. "I think I'll sleep on the couch."

She stared at him, nibbling her lip, then swallowed hard. "Probably a good idea. I mean . . . nothing has changed."

What did she mean "nothing has changed"? Everything

had changed. He knew about her kids and about Mad Dog and what he intended to do. He understood now why she had pushed him away. Just like his mom, she needed protection, but couldn't ask. Maybe this was another chance to do it right. And this time, when he walked away, the person he wanted to protect wouldn't die.

"Right?" She stared at him, her beautiful eyes liquid with desire.

"Right," he lied.

Who was he kidding? He wanted her more than any woman he had wanted in his life. He was hurting and he wanted her. Her every touch would be agony, and still he wanted her. His want was a living thing inside him, hungry, clawing at his insides, desperate to be free.

He couldn't give in to the want.

He wouldn't succumb to temptation.

Even if it killed him.

And given the current state of his cock, it just might.

★ FOUR ★

I will stand ready to help any biker who truly needs my help.

SINNER'S TRIBE CREED

Silence.

Cade shrugged on his cut and turned to face his brothers, seated around the table where they'd convened for an emergency executive board meeting this morning. Revealing the defiled tattoo on his back hadn't been easy, but Dawn had treated the slashes that went through the symbol of his brotherhood last night with a quiet understanding that made this moment slightly more bearable.

"Jesus fucking Christ." Zane, the Sinner VP, pounded his fist on the large oak table, carved with the same Sinner's Tribe patch that the Brethren had butchered on Cade's back. "Mad Dog is a dead man."

Dax, official secretary and unofficial torturer, nodded in agreement, as did T-Rex, the junior patch member-at-large. Sparky, the road captain, joined in with a "hear hear."

Cade didn't bother looking over at Shaggy or Gunner. The senior patch member-at-large and the club's sergeant-at-arms, like Zane, lived and breathed for the club, and this kind of dishonor screamed for Sinner justice. No questions. No mercy. No regrets.

"I say we adjourn the meeting and go now." A war vet and Sinner since before Jagger's time, Shaggy had earned his road name because of his full beard and unkempt long hair, now almost fully gray, that he claimed had never been trimmed in twenty years.

T-Rex snorted a laugh and gestured to the patch covering Shaggy's left eye. "That's 'cause you only got one eye and you can't see in the dark when normal bikers do their killing."

"I'll kill you with both eyes closed and my dick buried in a sweet butt's pussy, young pup." Shaggy drew his weapon and placed it on the table.

"Enough." Jagger folded his arms across his chest. An inch taller than Cade, and broader, dark where Cade was fair, he'd served with Cade in Afghanistan until a rocket propel left shrapnel near his heart. After being honorably discharged, he'd found a home with the Sinners, and when Cade had returned home, burdened by the crushing guilt of losing his squad in a desert ambush, Jagger sobered him up, straightened him out, and invited him in.

"I hear you, brothers. I feel Cade's pain. This disrespect screams for justice, but Wolf called me this morning to apologize for Mad Dog, and he made me an offer that we need to seriously consider." Jagger spoke with his usual implacable calm, and yet his sheer presence and power left no doubt he could enforce his will if anyone dared step out of line.

"We don't want any fucking apologies. And we don't want anything the damn Brethren have to offer except Mad Dog's head on a plate and the bodies of his men lying on the street." Gunner slammed his coffee cup on the worn, wooden table. With his head shaved military short, and his body thick with muscle, he was perfectly suited for the position of sergeant-at-arms, responsible for keeping order in the club.

"Hear him out." Dax put a cautioning hand on Gunner's shoulder. "It's not a done deal. Whatever Wolf proposed will be subject to a vote."

"I vote no." Gunner held out his hand, thumb pointed down. "Done. Let's get going."

"Viper approached Wolf about a Brethren patch-over." Jagger held Gunner in place with the fierceness of his scowl. "Wolf says the club is undecided, and he personally doesn't think it is a good fit. The Brethren have an election coming up. Wolf made it clear he would be interested in patching over to the Sinners if he wins."

Cade stood so abruptly his chair toppled over, banging against the worn wooden floor. "You can't seriously be considering patching in those motherfucking pieces of slime. We kicked them out of Conundrum for a reason."

"I'm with Cade," Shaggy said. "We lost good men in the war with the Brethren all those years ago. Good friends of mine. There'll be bad blood if we let them into the club."

"There won't be a club if we don't expand our numbers." Irritation laced Jagger's tone. "The Jacks are actively recruiting supporters, and if we want to maintain our status as the dominant MC in Montana, and put the fucking Jacks in their place, we need to expand our membership. A solid midsized club like the Brethren could tip the balance either way."

"The Jacks and Brethren together would be hard to beat," T-Rex said. "The Brethren have their own network of support clubs. Not big ones, but enough that we would be spread thin if we had to defend against them and the Jacks."

Jagger rubbed his brow, a sure sign he was conflicted

about his proposal. "We need the bodies, but we don't need them all. We can pick and choose. Right now these discussions are just between Wolf and me, and the executive boards. The way I see it, as long as Wolf is tied up in negotiations with me, he won't be negotiating with Viper. And since the election is still a few weeks away, we have a chance to investigate his MC and make a decision about whether any of his brothers are worthy of the Sinner name. None of the men who beat on Cade will wear our patch, guaranteed. And Mad Dog—"

"Dead," Shaggy said.

"Not yet." Jagger rubbed his brow again. "Wolf had a condition. He knows the value of his club, and he knows the advantage the Brethren numbers will give us over the Jacks. Mad Dog is his nephew. He wants our word he won't be touched."

"Mad Dog is JC's boy?" Zane let out a strangled groan. "He'll have a vendetta against us for killing his dad."

"Mad Dog doesn't wear our patch." Jagger firmed his voice. "Ever. Wolf knows that. But he wants us to spare his life. In exchange for our mercy, he's offered us a shipment of AK-47s, just in from Korea, that he has stored in a warehouse up in Whitefish."

There were a few angry murmurs around the table but Jagger's gaze fixed on Cade. "This is your call, brother. Your justice. Your vengeance. If you don't agree, we turn Wolf down and we go after Mad Dog and his men as soon as this meeting ends."

Cade took a deep, calming breath as he stared at the picture above Zane's head, a half-naked woman leaning over a Harley Fat Boy, not unlike almost every other picture nailed to the walls. The meeting room had once been a dining room, but the fancy fixtures and fittings had been removed, and after it was painted, it was decorated in true biker form.

And a true biker lived by the code "Club First."

Although he burned to jump on his bike and hunt down Mad Dog and his men, Wolf's proposal could secure the club's future, and end the war against the Jacks that had already claimed too many Sinner lives. He had to protect his club at any cost.

"I'll waive my claim against Mad Dog for the club. He's still bound by the restriction on any Brethren coming into our town so it's not like he can rub it in our faces. But we have to take some action to address the Brethren's disrespect or everyone will think we're weak. Since Mad Dog's men will never wear our patch, I say we hunt them down and give them a taste of Sinner justice."

"All vote." Jagger raised his hand, and rest of the board members followed suit.

"No one will forget the sacrifice you've made for the club," Jagger said quietly. "And you have my word, as soon as the Brethren are patched into our club, and subject to Sinner law, Mad Dog will die."

Cade swallowed past the lump in his throat. This is why he had joined the Sinners. Honor. Brotherhood. Loyalty. Men who would stand up for him. Men who always had his back.

His club.

His tribe.

"If the Jacks approached the Brethren, then they must be feeling vulnerable," Cade said. "We should take advantage of the opportunity. If we weaken them enough while you're negotiating terms with Wolf, we won't even need the Brethren support."

Jagger nodded his agreement. "We should hit them hard, and hit them now."

"We'll need more weapons to launch an offensive." Gunner shoved a piece of paper across the table. "I got a lead on an arms shipment coming across the border heading for that Mafia boss in Helena, Franco Rizzoli. He hired the Jacks to run protection. If we ambush them, we'll get fifty thousand dollars worth of weapons and take out some Jacks as a bonus."

Jagger leaned back in his chair and folded his arms behind his head. A man content. He hadn't always been that way, but Arianne had smoothed out his edges. Cade had edges, too, but he was pretty damn sure no woman could smooth them out. Some wounds just couldn't be healed.

"Gunner can organize the Rizzoli ambush." Jagger pointed to each man as he assigned tasks. "Cade and Zane, you go up to Whitefish with the prospect and get Wolf's AKs. Demon Spawn is our support club in the region. They can help out."

"Sounds like we're in for some good times." Tall and dark, his skin lightly tanned, and his hair just brushing his shoulders, Zane stroked the goatee he had grown during his mysterious disappearance at the end of last summer. Although Cade wasn't a fan of facial hair, Zane's goatee had caused such a stir among the club's women, Cade had almost considered growing one himself.

Cade snorted a laugh. "I didn't know 'good time' was in your vocabulary."

Reserved and fiercely private, Zane was the least fun guy Cade had ever known. He rarely drank or socialized at club functions, and Cade could count on one hand the number of times he'd seen Zane with a woman.

"That's 'cause my idea of a good time doesn't involve hot tubs, booze, and multiple women in my bed," Zane shot back.

Cade couldn't refute that statement, but right now

there was only one woman he wanted in his bed, and he'd put her in danger. "What about Dawn? Mad Dog threatened to drag her back to his clubhouse. He's using their kids as leverage."

Zane gave a derisory snort. "She's a civilian. If she needs help, she can call the police."

"Zane's right," Jagger said. "We can't get involved in a marital dispute between a Brethren member and his old lady, especially if we're negotiating terms of a patch-over. If you want to get involved in their affairs, you'll have to do it without your cut."

Without my cut? Cade barely processed the rest of Jagger's words. He hadn't gone anywhere without his colors since the day he first put them on. Hell, sometimes he slept in them. Jagger might as well ask him to cut off his right arm. His colors were everything—a symbol of a new life where he wasn't burdened by the past, where the only person he had to look out for was himself, and where his brothers had his back. His cut was his creed: freedom, loyalty, and brotherhood.

Life.

"One thousand dollars?" Dawn stared at Shelly-Ann aghast. "I don't have one thousand dollars just sitting around the house. I've given you the money for this week. I have the girls for six hours."

Maia and Tia clung to her, their fingers digging through her clothes. Tia's soft whimpers sliced through a heart. Her girls weren't stupid. They knew exactly what was going on and it twisted her heart that they understood blackmail at the tender age of seven.

"You got three hours with them unless you come up with the cash," Shelly-Ann rasped from the window of her vehicle. She looked worse than she sounded today, her face pale and sallow, dark circles under her eyes, and her nose rimmed red. "You found a way to give me what I wanted before; you'll do it again."

Dawn pushed the girls behind her and out of sight of Shelly-Ann. "I have nothing left and you know it. I'm working three jobs. I sold my car. I'm renting my house. I buy nothing. I go nowhere. What do you need more money for?"

Shelly-Ann pressed her lips together. "Kids are expensive."

"Not that expensive." Taking a chance, Dawn leaned in and lowered her voice. "You're in some kind of trouble, aren't you? Don't involve my girls, Shelly-Ann. They're just children. It isn't fair."

"Life isn't fucking fair," Shelly-Ann spat out. "Thought you'd already figured that one out."

"I'll give you what I've got." Dawn pulled out her purse and gave Shelly-Ann her tip money and pay from Banks Bar. "There's six hundred there. I can ask my landlord for a month grace on my rent. But I can't do it again next week."

"Then you won't see your kids next week." Shelly-Ann snatched the money and stuffed it in her purse. "You're lucky I got a massage and hair appointment booked for this afternoon. You got your six hours but you owe me. Next week I won't let them outta the car till you make it good."

Dawn sagged against a tree as soon as Shelly-Ann's vehicle peeled out of the parking lot. For the longest time, Shelly-Ann had been content with the money Dawn and Jimmy paid her, but in the last few weeks her demands had increased, and Dawn had nothing left to give. What was going on? Between her and Jimmy, they had to be giving Shelly-Ann at least five thousand dollars a month.

"Mom. There's a biker staring at us?" Maia tugged on Dawn's arm and pointed across the playground to a lone biker in the parking lot. From this distance, Dawn couldn't see the patch on his cut, but he didn't look like any of the members of the Devil's Brethren she knew. Still, given what Cade had said about Jimmy coming for her, she couldn't take any chances.

"Let's go to the concession stand." Feigning calm, she slowed the swing and helped Tia down. She tried to make the most of every minute of her Sunday access visits with the girls. Now that the weather was warmer, they could venture outside again, and the park was their favorite place to play.

"He's getting off his bike." Tia's voice dropped to a whisper and she plastered herself against Dawn's side.

"What if it's Jimmy?" Maia's small face paled. "What if he wants to hurt us or take us away?"

"I won't let that happen." She gave Tia a squeeze and reached for Maia's hand, wondering if they believed her. After all, she had effectively let Jimmy take them away last year, albeit through the courts, and she hadn't been able to stop him from hitting Tia . . .

Stop. She slammed a mental wall down, blocking out all the feelings of despair, frustration, and self-doubt that had plagued her since she lost custody of the girls. That road led right back to Jimmy and a loss of the self-worth that she had rebuilt, brick by brick, over the three years since she left him. No one could have foreseen how he would use the courts against her, or that he had the wherewithal to fabricate evidence and pay off a judge. If she couldn't stay strong and believe in herself, she would never get them back.

The biker drew closer, eating up the distance between them with easy strides of his long, lean legs. Tia whimpered. Shy and withdrawn as a result of Jimmy's abuse, Tia was afraid of strangers and reluctant to talk outside her close circle of friends and family. The school counselor had assured Dawn that over time, in a stable and loving environment, Tia would eventually recover. And in the two happy years they'd had together after leaving Jimmy, Tia had come out of her shell.

And then it all came crashing down.

Her heart kicked up a notch as the biker drew closer, passing through the shade of the massive chestnut trees that separated the playground from the playing fields, but damned if she would run and show the children her fear. There were at least thirty other caregivers in the playground, along with their children. Even Jimmy wouldn't try anything in front of so many witnesses.

"Mom. He's waving." Always the brave one, Maia took a step forward. She hadn't emerged from their time with Jimmy unscathed—she still suffered from nightmares—but she had been the most successful at putting the bad times behind her. Dawn admired her resilience and optimism. No matter how bad things got, Maia could always make her smile.

"I know him." Maia's voice rose in pitch. "That's the biker who saved us on the street. The one who scared Jimmy away."

Dawn studied the biker as he pulled the bandanna from his hair, revealing a head of slightly damp, golden curls. Her gaze traveled down over his broad shoulders to his toned pecs and the ripples of his abs beneath his tight black T-shirt. He bent slightly to the side, one hand against his ribs, almost as if he was . . . injured.

Cade.

Her heart rate slowed and she released the breath she hadn't realized she was holding. Then her heart kicked up again, for an entirely different reason. "Yes, you're right. He's a . . . friend. He won't hurt us." The latter she said for Tia's benefit, but her daughter was already behind her, face pressed against Dawn's back as if she could make the biker disappear just by erasing the sight of him.

He stopped a few feet away, and Dawn tensed. "Cade. What are you doing here?"

"Checking up on you. I gotta go out of town, and I just wanted to make sure you were okay before I left."

He glanced down at Maia, and then at Tia, still pressed against her side. "Hello, lovely ladies. I hope you haven't run in front of any more trucks."

"Did you catch Jimmy? Did he do that to your face?" Maia tilted her head to the side and studied Cade's bruises. He looked even worse than he had when he'd stopped by Dawn's apartment on Thursday night, the bruises now a greenish yellow and covering most of his face. He'd removed the bandages from his forehead and cheeks, and the cuts were dark and crusted. No doubt, they would leave scars. And yet they only added to his rugged charm.

"Unfortunately, he caught me first." Cade bent down, grimacing in pain and dropped to one knee in front of her. "But I'm pretty damn sure he looks worse than me today. Which twin are you?"

"Maia. I do the talking. Sometimes I get in trouble for talking too much. Mrs. Walker made me stay in for recess because she gave me three warnings and I forgot. Tia's the quiet one, but she's smarter than me and does more thinking. She likes purple. I like pink."

He gently lifted her hand and gave it a shake. "Nice to see you again, Maia-who-likes-pink. Musta been important stuff you were saying to forget to follow the rules."

She nodded, her face grave. "It was."

Cade leaned to the side, trying to catch Tia's gaze. "And this must be Tia."

Tia tightened her grip and turned her face away. Dawn patted the tiny hand on her stomach.

"It's okay. Cade's a good biker."

"He's still a biker," Maia said, withdrawing her hand from Cade's grasp. "And bikers are bad."

"Maia . . ."

"It's okay." Cade pushed himself to his feet. "I'm guessing living with Jimmy wasn't all flowers and sunshine."

"There were flowers." Maia's gaze dropped and she toed the grass underfoot. "He bought flowers sometimes after he hit—"

"Maia." Dawn's cheeks heated and she bent down and lowered her voice. "We don't talk about that. Especially not to people we don't know. That time is gone. We live in the now."

Maia's bottom lip trembled. "I thought he'd feel better if he knew that Jimmy hurts everyone."

"Not for fucking long," Cade muttered.

"Cade!"

"He swore." Maia gave him an assessing look. "Just like Jimmy. And he wears the same clothes as Jimmy. But he has a nice face. Jimmy has a mean face."

Unabashed, Cade twisted his lips to the side. "I'm nothing like Jimmy. First, I'm much better looking. Second, I save the swearing for special occasions. And third, I'll bet he never bought you ice cream." He looked to Dawn for confirmation. "If that's okay with your mom."

"Bribery. Very nice." Dawn laughed and sent the girls to the concession stand to choose their flavors, pushing all thoughts about Shelly-Ann to the back of her mind. "I thought you'd scare the girls away in your leathers and chains."

He gave her a cocky grin and placed a hand on her lower back, guiding her along the path. "What can I say? I have a way with the ladies no matter how old they are."

"You have a way of finding ladies, too. How did you

know where we were?" His hand was warm against her back, and she tried to ignore the curious glances of the other parents in the park. As far as her neighbors knew, she was a conservative, hardworking single mom with shared custody of her kids and no connection to unsavory biker types who looked sinfully good in worn, low-rise jeans.

"Drove by the park on my way to your house and saw Jimmy's sister dropping the girls off. Decided to make sure she wasn't giving you a hard time."

Warmth pooled in her belly, and for a moment she considered sharing her concerns about Shelly-Ann. But her business wasn't his business, and it wasn't like he could help. "We're doing fine. Thanks for checking up on us. I'm glad to see you're up and about."

His fingers tightened around her waist, sending a delicious tingle up her spine. "That's 'cause I had a good doctor. Although after seeing you in those little shorts, I had an ache that just wouldn't go away."

"Cade. Behave." She jabbed him lightly with her elbow, and he laughed, his deep rumble reverberating through her body. Before Cade, her sexual experience had been limited to a few fumbles with inexperienced teenagers, and then Jimmy, for whom sex was a purely selfish event. But in the two nights she and Cade had been together, they'd done things she'd only fantasized about, and then some things she could never have imagined. Even now, her cheeks heated at the memories.

"I can't behave around you." His voice dropped, husky and low. "Last time we were together—"

"Was the last time we will be together." Disconcerted by the intensity of her feelings, she pulled away. "I had a good time with you, but I'm not interested in getting involved. I have my hands full with work, the girls, and the custody fight." She was good at building walls to protect herself. Even with him, she'd given her body but kept a lock on her heart.

At least, she thought she had, but when he leaned down and brushed his lips over hers, her betraying heart stuttered in her chest.

"You're interested in getting involved with me," he whispered. "Otherwise you wouldn't have invited me to sleep in your bed. You think I'm hot."

Dawn lifted an eyebrow. "Is this part of the seduction technique you use to lure sweet, sexy young things into your bed?"

He nuzzled her neck, feathering kisses along her jaw as one hand curved over her ass. She should push him away. Run. Hide. Pretend she didn't enjoy having a badass biker whisper naughty words in her ear in the middle of the playground as he set her blood on fire. But she couldn't move. Couldn't speak. Instead, she closed her eyes and went along for the ride, tilting her head to the side to give him better access.

"That's my girl," he murmured against her ear. "She's sweet. She's sexy. And she wants me in her bed, my hands on her body, my mouth between her—"

"Mom."

Somewhere in the distance, someone was calling her name. This wasn't a dream; it was real. And she'd almost made the same mistake with him again. She jerked back, her cheeks flushing at her uncharacteristic loss of control.

"I can't believe you." She shook off her lust-induced haze and pulled away. "We're in the playground."

A sly smile tugged at his lips. "Swings. Chains. Gives me so many ideas."

"You're filthy." And she loved it. But she would never let him know.

"So are you, if I recall correctly." He licked his lips

and Dawn's throat tightened. God, he looked like he wanted to do her right here. And if not for her girls, and the playground full of people, and the fact it was illegal, and it was the middle of the day, she might have agreed.

But she knew better than that. She'd walked away from him for a reason—and it had as much to do with the fact that he was an outlaw biker with a reputation for sleeping around, as with how easily she succumbed to his touch and how much it scared her. Yes, he was hot. And, apparently, good with kids. But she had a history of trusting the wrong people for the wrong reasons, and his world was not a place she wanted to be ever again.

They stopped beside the concession stand where Maia and Tia had made it to the front of the line. Maia turned to wave Dawn over, and a tall, bearded, giant of a man pushed past her, knocking her down on his way to the counter. Dawn ran over and picked a sobbing Maia off the ground.

"It wasn't his turn." Maia looked down and saw blood on her knees and her sob turned into a wail. Tia's eyes widened and she clung to Maia's hand.

"You're right." Her face flushed with indignation, Dawn leaned over the counter and caught the attention of the server. "These girls were next."

"Not fucking waiting for kids who can't make up their minds," the man growled. "I just want a soda."

"The back of the line is over there," Dawn gestured behind her. "You can wait like everyone else. And on your way, you can apologize to my daughter. You knocked her down and she scraped her knees."

"Fuckin' bitch. Don't tell me what to do."

Dawn sucked in a breath and her vision sheeted red. A tiny niggle at the back of her mind warned her this was a fight she couldn't win. But she'd done enough running away in her life. And this time, she had backup.

"You got this, Dawn?" Cade appeared at her elbow, his calm, steady presence spreading over her like a warm blanket.

She scowled at the man in front of her. "Yes, thanks. This gentleman was just heading to the back of the line."

The giant looked back over his shoulder at the angry crowd, then he locked gazes with Cade. Electricity crackled between them. Cade growled, ever so softly, cold and menacing, dark and threatening. Dawn sensed rather than saw the shift in the balance of power.

"Didn't want a damn soda, anyway." The bully lowered his gaze and stepped out of line.

"Wait." Dawn's voice cracked through the shocked silence. "You owe my daughter an apology."

"Fuck you."

Wham. Cade shoved him up against the wall, with a strength and ferocity that made Dawn's heart pound. He closed his hand around the bully's throat and Dawn leaned right up in his face.

"Apology. Now."

Eyes glittering with repressed anger, Cade loosened his hand enough for the man to speak.

"Sorry, kid."

"Thank you." Dawn took a step back and nodded at Cade, indicating he should release his grip. Cade lowered his hand and the man stumbled away to the murmured appreciation of the crowd.

"Thanks for having my back. Whenever anyone threatens my children, I just see red."

"Pretty damn hot seeing you go all mama bear on his ass." Cade chuckled and put his arm around her shoulders while the girls leaned over the counter to choose their ice cream. Although outwardly he appeared calm and relaxed, she could feel the blood pounding through his veins and the quiver of his muscles from unspent adrenaline. "Good thing we're in public."

"Pretty damn hot seeing you go all alpha wolf and slam his sorry ass against the wall," she whispered. "Definitely a good thing we're in public."

Cade leaned down, and his voice rumbled in her ear. "We don't have to be in public. We could go back to your place, and I'll show you how to make an alpha wolf howl."

"It will be a howl of frustration," she said. "There is no being alone when you have two little girls who only see their mommy on Sunday." And thank God for that because after Cade's show of dominance, and with the adrenaline still streaming through her veins, she was ready to tear off his clothes at the first available opportunity.

For the next half an hour, Dawn and Cade took turns pushing Maia and Tia on the swings. Cade took Tia's refusal to speak to him in stride, including her in their conversations even though she didn't respond. Dawn hadn't seen the girls as relaxed around a man as they were with Cade, and when he finally told them he had to leave, Maia didn't hold back her disappointment.

"Do you have to go? You pushed Tia three times and you only pushed me twice."

"Got work to do, Maia-who-wears-pink, but I'm glad I passed the swing test."

Her mouth turned down and she squeezed Tia's hand. "Will you come back? You make Mom smile."

Cade didn't miss a beat. "Your mom has a beautiful smile. Just like her girls."

Dawn fought back a sigh. So charming. And yet why would he be interested in a woman with a fucked-up life, two kids, three jobs, fifteen extra pounds, and baggage in the form of a psychopathic outlaw biker ex who had already tried to kill him? Maybe it was just his way of getting back at Jimmy, or maybe he wanted another notch in his belt.

Cade leaned down and brushed his lips over her cheek before mounting his bike. "See you later, beautiful."

Or maybe not.

★ FIVE ★

I shall savor the ignorance of those who do not know me.

SINNER'S TRIBE CREED

"He's on his way."

Cade startled when Zane stepped out of the shadows. He'd brought Zane and four brothers with him after receiving a tip that Rusty, the redheaded bastard from Mad Dog's van, was at Peelers Strip Club, but Zane had the unnerving ability to move without making a sound and damned if he'd known his brother was right behind him.

"Christ." He lowered his weapon and drew in a calming breath of night air, cool but damp with an oncoming storm. "Don't sneak up on a man with a gun. I almost shot you."

"Your gun was pointed in the other direction," Zane said. "Mine was aimed at your back. Wasn't feeling the threat."

Shaggy joined them from the far side of the parking lot, located at the side of the small brick building. "He's got a woman with him. There's a buncha Brethren inside, but doesn't look like they're planning to go anywhere. We should be good if we keep it quiet. If any of his buddies decide to join him . . ." He raised his weapon. "I figure the only good Brethren is a dead Brethren."

"In a normal situation, I'd agree with you." Cade checked his magazine and holstered his gun. "But we're here for Rusty only, and the rest of those Brethren will soon be our brothers."

Shaggy's face curdled beneath his beard. "I voted to protect the club, same as you, but I still don't like it. The Brethren can't be trusted. We learned that lesson the hard way and had to run them outta town. Why the hell are we bringing them back?"

"To win the war against the Jacks. I don't want to bury any more brothers over at Sandy Hill Cemetery."

The front door opened and Rusty emerged with a woman beside him, her red hair twisted into a messy bun on top of her head. She wore workout clothes, and not stripper gear, and Cade didn't recognize her until he heard her raspy voice.

"C'mon, Rusty. I'm in big trouble here. I need the cash you owe me and I need it fast or Jimmy's gonna slit my throat."

Shelly-Ann. What the fuck was she doing at Peelers when she was supposed to be looking after Dawn's kids?

Rusty shoved her away. "I don't owe you nothin', bitch. I paid for that coke by giving you the pleasure of my dick."

"That's Mad Dog's sister," Cade murmured to Shaggy. "The one who's blackmailing Dawn."

"You want her taken out?" Shaggy jerked his chin in Shelly-Ann's direction. Vicious, loyal, and trigger-happy, he'd once claimed he would shoot his own mother if it would benefit the club.

"Just keep her quiet." Motioning to his brothers to follow, Cade unholstered his gun and crossed the parking lot, blinking to clear his vision when the first few raindrops fell.

"Hey, Rusty. Remember me?" He smashed the butt of his gun into Rusty's head, and the smaller man staggered back against the wall.

"Stop! No!" Shelly-Ann's hand flew to her mouth as Cade threw punch after punch, easily dodging Rusty's retaliatory strikes. He hit Rusty's nose and blood sprayed over Shelly-Ann's jacket and splattered on the wall.

"Oh God."

Shaggy grabbed Shelly-Ann and pulled her away when Zane and Gunner joined the fray, the three men pummeling Rusty until he fell to his knees.

"You like that Rusty?" Cade kicked him in the ribs. "You want my boot prints on you to match the ones you left on me?"

"Damn Sinner. We shoulda fucking killed you when we had the chance." Rusty heaved in a breath, and pushed himself to his feet. Then he ran at Cade, knocking him back.

"Your mistake." Cade grabbed Rusty and twisted his arm behind his back, then pushed him to the ground. Raindrops splattered on the pavement around them, streaming off Cade's jacket. "Six against one and my hands tied? You must have known I'd come for you."

"Didn't think you were that stupid," Rusty grunted, his cheek flat against the wet pavement. "We're patching over to the Jacks, and then we're all coming for you. There won't be a Sinner left alive when we're done."

His free hand slid out from beneath him and Cade caught the glint of steel. "Look out!" He dived to the side just as Rusty fired. The bullet hit Shaggy in the leg and his brother went down.

"Die, fucker." Rusty jumped to a crouch and aimed his

gun at Shaggy's head. Cade threw himself forward, knocking Rusty off balance. Rusty fell to the side and his head cracked against the cement parking bumper. Then he went limp.

"Fuck." Shaggy fell back, clutching his leg. "One more second and I woulda been a dead man. Gratitude, brother."

"Oh. My. God," Shelly-Ann shrieked. "You killed him. You killed Rusty. He owed me money. Now what am I going to do?"

His body still pumped with adrenaline, rage seeping through his veins, Cade grabbed Shelly-Ann by the shoulder and shoved her hard against the wall. "You are one damn coldhearted bitch. Man's dead and all you care about is money. And what the hell are you doing at Peelers when you got two kids at home to look after?"

Shelly-Ann's face twisted in anger. "Not that it's any of your business, but I got a babysitter. And I need money. Since you killed Rusty, his debts are your debts. You owe me."

"Son of a bitch," Gunner said. "She's either incredibly stupid or she'd got the biggest fucking balls this side of the Bridger Mountains."

"You owe me," Cade growled. "I saved your fucking life. Shaggy here wanted to off you the minute you stepped outside."

"I know you." Shelly-Ann leaned up and stared into Cade's face. "You're the Sinner who was with Dawn outside the school. Just wait till Jimmy hears you offed Rusty."

Cade snorted a laugh. "You tell him, princess. Let him know I'm coming for him, although I think he'll guess." He tipped his chin in Rusty's direction, drawing her attention to Gunner, who was spray-painting the Sinner's Tribe symbol on Rusty's cut.

Shelly-Ann's eyes narrowed. "Kinda hard to go after

him if you're in jail. Gimme the money Rusty owes me and maybe I won't say anything to the police about what I saw."

"How about you go home to those girls and I won't tell Shaggy to slit your fucking throat?"

"How about I get someone to slit yours?" Shelly-Ann gave him a sly look and then she screamed. "Help! Shifter! Trey! The Sinners got Rusty!"

Cade clamped a hand over her mouth a moment too late. The door to the club burst open and Brethren bikers flooded the parking lot.

"Let the fun begin." Zane drew his weapon, and the brothers followed suit.

"Stand down," Cade ordered, gesturing the brothers back to their bikes. "Zane and I will cover. Everyone out of here now. We've done what we came here to do. They know what Rusty did. Even with the possible patch-over, they'll have been expecting some form of retaliation, although it wasn't meant to go that far."

Cade's heart pounded in his chest, adrenaline crashing through his body in waves. Yeah, he wanted to off that Brethren scum. But tonight wasn't a good night to die.

"You staying for a drink?"

Banks handed Dawn her share of the evening's tips as she untied her apron. *Not a bad night.* If she could find more ways to cut costs, she might be able to scrape up another couple hundred dollars for Shelly-Ann. Enough to keep her quiet, at least in the short term.

"I have to get going. I have an early shift tomorrow." And she wanted to get home and lock her doors tight. Before Jimmy crossed the Conundrum border, she wouldn't have been concerned, but something spurred him to take the life-or-death risk of coming into town, and she desperately wanted to know what it was. Jimmy only took chances when he knew he would win. She could only hope he wasn't after the girls.

"Just one drink." Banks held up a glass. "Then I can finish up and walk you out."

"Thanks, but I have to run or I'll miss the last bus." Usually she caught a ride on the back of Arianne's motorcycle. Her bestie bartended at Banks Bar four nights a week, and they tried to arrange their shifts so they could work together, but Arianne's work at the Sinner garage was taking up more and more of her time and she'd cut her shifts this week down to two.

Dawn grabbed her jacket and picked up the trash bags near the stockroom door leading to the parking lot. Although she missed her car, she wouldn't trade the extra time it had bought her with the girls for anything.

"Don't like you taking the bus at night," Banks said.

Dawn put her hand in her purse and pulled out her .22. "I have this to keep me safe. A present from Arianne."

"Jesus Christ. Put that away before you hurt someone, namely me." Banks jerked to the side. "Don't know why Arianne would give you a gun. You aren't in that life."

"She gave it to me because that life won't let me go. And until I get my girls back . . ."

"You won't be shooting anyone." He placed a gentle hand on her wrist, and she lowered the gun. "And I know this first, 'cause I know you got a soft heart; second, 'cause I can see that gun isn't loaded; and third, 'cause I got faith you'll find a way to cut Jimmy deep and get back those girls without spilling any blood and landing your pretty ass in jail. You're a fighter, but not a killer."

"I'll take that as a compliment." She tucked the gun into her purse and zipped up her jacket.

"Meant as one." Banks twisted his lips to the side, considering. "How about I call you a cab?"

"You don't give up, do you?" Dawn unlocked the dead bolt on the door leading to the parking lot. "It'll take at least an hour to get a cab out here at this time of night. The bus is coming in five minutes. I'll be fine. It's not like I have far to go."

"I'll wait at the bus stop with you," Banks called out. "Just gimme a minute and I'll meet you there."

The door closed behind her and she crossed the deserted parking lot toward the Dumpster. She tossed the bags, and pulled her leather jacket tight around her neck. Where had the warm spring weather gone? This winter had been the longest ever, and she so wasn't a winter kind of girl. Now, Florida. That was more her style. Her parents had owned a condo on Miami Beach and she'd spent the summers with them building sand castles, learning how to in-line skate, and never appreciating her safe, secure loving world until it disappeared when a drunk driver crossed the median and hit her parents' car.

She wanted that kind of happy life for her children—a life without stress or fear, a life where they were surrounded by love and laughter, a life where parents kissed you in the morning and didn't disappear in the afternoon.

Keeping to the lit side of the street, she walked toward the bus stop. The streetlights had been changed out for energy-saving orange a few months ago, giving the area an eerie glow. She reached the crossroad and looked up and down the street. Time to jaywalk. She just couldn't help breaking the law. Maybe it was genetic. After all, her uncle had broken at least ten different laws the first time he trapped her in the bedroom.

Footsteps rang out behind her, and she turned, half smiling, expecting to see Banks. But her smile faded and her pulse went into overdrive when Jimmy stepped out of the shadows.

"Time to come home, love."

Dawn's gaze flicked back to the bar and then down the street. Where was Banks? The drunks were still inside. The streets were deserted. It was just her and Jimmy, and a lifetime of regret.

"I'm not going anywhere with you." She took a step toward the bus stop, and Jimmy grabbed her arm and yanked her back.

"You'll come with me or you lose those girls forever. I'll take them someplace you'll never find them."

She stared up at him, his face at once foreign and familiar. They'd shared a bed every night for seven years. At first, she'd thought of him as her knight in shining armor, rescuing her from a pimp who had discovered her unprotected and living on the street. It was only after Jimmy turned vicious that she saw him for who he truly was: a monster. In biker's clothing. There was no way she would allow herself to get caught up in a relationship where she could fall into that trap again. Especially not in a world where women were property and everyone turned a blind eye to abuse.

Still, it had taken years to push aside the childish teenage fantasy, break the emotional bond, and gather up the courage and enough money to leave him. And in the end, she'd done it for her girls. Not for herself. Caught in an endless cycle of abuse, she'd lost her sense of self-worth. Her mama bear instincts had saved her as much as she'd saved her children and taught her an important lesson: She was a fighter and a survivor, and she would never let anyone take that away.

"I'll find a way to get them back." Her heart thundered so hard she thought she might break a rib. She was intimately familiar with Jimmy's moods. Her safety had depended on reading him correctly and responding accordingly. And right now, she read danger with a capital

D. He wasn't just angry; he was enraged, and his control would slip the longer they dragged out the conversation.

Jimmy gave a bitter laugh, tightening his grip on her forearm. "You've tried for a year and what do you have to show for it? Nothing. Shelly-Ann has you over a barrel and now I'm gonna have you back in my bed. I lost the last election 'cause the brothers thought I was too weak to control my woman. But there's a new election coming up and I've let this stupid little game go on long enough. You're mine until I let you go. Until death do us part. Nobody leaves Jimmy, especially not you, and never for a Sinner."

"Wrong." She tugged the unloaded .22 from the pocket of her jacket and Jimmy released her with a jerk, his hands flying up in a defensive gesture.

"You don't want to that, love. Think about the kids. You'd go to jail for life. They would have no one but Shelly-Ann."

Love. The term of endearment made her feel sick inside. He'd called her "love" from the day he took her back to the clubhouse. New name for a new life, he'd said. Now she associated that name with only one thing: Pain.

"Drop the gun and stop playing games." His grin turned feral. "I know you. And I know it's not loaded."

For a split second, Dawn wondered what she would have done if there had been a bullet in the gun. But he'd called her bluff, just as Banks had. Now she had only one option.

Run.

Turning quickly, she raced across the street. In the distance, the headlights of the bus glowed warm in the night. It would all come down to timing.

"Fuck." Jimmy's voice echoed in the darkness, and the thud of his shoes on the pavement sent her heart into overdrive.

But although she was fast, Jimmy was faster. Just as she reached the bus shelter, he grabbed her hair and yanked her head back. Using her momentum, he slammed her face into the glass. Pain shot through her skull and she shuddered beneath his grip.

"Wrong. Fucking. Decision." Jimmy pressed his lips to her ear and growled, "Looks like someone needs to be reminded of her lessons."

Well conditioned to what usually followed those particular words, Dawn froze. Jimmy had rules, and every lesson she'd learned after breaking one of his rules resulted in a trip to the hospital.

The growl of an engine shattered the silence. Light flooded the shelter and the bus slowed to a stop. In the distance the bar door slammed and she heard Banks curse.

"Let me go or I'll scream." She mumbled the words against the glass, unable to move an inch with his body pressed hard against her. "They have armed security on the night bus, and my manager is coming."

Her gamble that Jimmy knew nothing about buses or the limited resources they had to run at night—resources that most certainly didn't include salaries for security guards—paid off. With a last smash of her forehead against the glass, he released her and backed into the shadows.

"We're not done, love." His words sliced through the darkness, piercing her heart. "Not even close."

"Son of a bitch." Cade slammed his fist on the chipped Formica table, and the six customers seated at the counter of Table Tops diner on the corner of Fourth and Pine stilled.

"Would you like coffee with that?" Dawn tried to keep her voice steady and willed everyone to go back to their respective conversations. Anything but watch the drama unfolding in the corner booth of the cheap restaurant where she worked six mornings a week, remarkable only for the fact there was absolutely nothing notable about it. Brown vinyl booths lined the walls across from the curved counter; a plastic palm tree, its leaves heavy with dust, took up an empty corner; and a newspaper stand filled with day-olds perched in the corner. The kitchen was partially open, filling the restaurant with scents of grease and coffee, and the walls were decorated with pictures of cats. Lots of cats.

"What the fuck happened to your face?" Cade stared at her aghast.

"Cream and sugar, sir?"

Conversation resumed around them, slowly rising to a gentle murmur, and Dawn's tension eased. Hopefully her boss, Stan, had missed Cade's outburst.

"I had a run-in with a bus shelter." She kept her voice low and her eyes on her notepad. There seemed little point lying to him. Although she'd done her best to cover up the bruises with makeup, she couldn't hide the swelling around her eye.

Cade's lips pressed into a rigid line, a far cry from his warm, affable expression of only moments ago. "It was Mad Dog, wasn't it? I'm going to fucking kill him."

She caught a flash of red out of the corner of her eye and saw Stan standing by the door to the kitchen in his Table Tops uniform: black pants, red polo shirt, and white apron. Dawn wore a skirt instead of pants and instead of the word MANAGER stitched across the top left corner of her uniform, her shirt read WAITRESS. As if people wouldn't know when she took their orders.

"Quiet," she whispered. "I can't afford to lose this job." And then she raised her voice loud enough for Stan to hear. "How would you like your eggs, sir?"

Cade ripped the napkins from the holder and crumpled them in his fist. "Scrambled."

"Any toast?"

"Yeah," Cade muttered. "He'll be fucking toast when I'm done with him."

Dawn leaned in and tugged the napkins out of his fist. "Bad pun. And get it together. My boss isn't the most understanding of people."

"How the fuck am I supposed to get it together when I walk in here and see your face all banged up? I don't see you for one day and look what happens."

"Life is what happens. My life. And yeah, it's fucked up. But I have a plan to get back at him."

Resolved not to let Jimmy scare her, she'd come up with her plan last night while tending to her cuts and bruises. This was her town. Her safe place. Jimmy had never assaulted her in public before, and she'd never had a friend in the sheriff's department. Maybe this time, the police could help.

"I'm going to see the sheriff's deputy after work tomorrow to report the assault." She tucked her order pad in her apron and gave Cade a cheeky smile, hoping to calm him down. "Want to come?"

"Why the fuck would you go to the police?" Cade attacked the napkins again, grabbing the bundle she had just tucked away and tearing it apart with one fierce yank. "They can't help you."

Dawn glanced quickly behind her and saw Stan frown. When he took a step in her direction, she turned back to Cade and cupped his jaw in her hand then bent down to touch her cheek to his, whispering in his ear. "Cade, honey, please calm down. Stan is on his way over and I really, really need this job."

Cade gave a contented rumble and stroked his thumb over the bruised apple of her cheek. "I shoulda been there. He said he was going to give you an ultimatum. I shoulda realized he wouldn't do it over the phone."

"It's nothing to do with you." Dawn drew his hand away from her cheek and backed away. "It's my messed-up life and I have to deal with it."

"Everything all right here, Dawn?" Stan came up behind her, so close she could smell the bacon on his breath and feel the faintest brush of his belly against her back. Stan never went farther than surreptitious touching, but even that made her skin crawl.

"Yes, just taking this order."

He rested a clammy hand on her shoulder. "You're taking a long time and we've got other customers waiting to be served."

Dawn gritted her teeth and shook Stan's hand away. "I said it's fine, Stan. I'll finish here and then I'll go and check on the other tables."

Cade tossed a wad of twenties on the table. "Buy 'em some coffee on me. I'm not done deciding what I want."

Stan frowned. "I'm afraid I can't allow—"

"Now." Cade shoved the money to the edge of the table. "Or I call up a bunch of my brothers and invite them all for a free meal."

"Cade!"

Stan reached for the money, and Cade slammed his hand over the man's thick wrist. "Before you take that cash, one thing you need to understand. You. Touching her. Not on." He squeezed Stan's wrist and Stan paled. "Looking at her. Thinking what we both know you're thinking. Also not on."

"Stop it." Dawn tugged on Cade's arm but he was in full-on alpha mode and didn't flinch.

Sweat beaded on Stan's brow. "I get it."

"Make sure you do."

"I cannot believe you did that." Dawn's voice shook so

hard she could barely get out her words after Stan scurried away. "How am I supposed to work now? Stan's going to hate me."

"He didn't get that boner in his pants 'cause he hates you." Cade pulled out his phone and stabbed at the screen. "But I agree, you might want to find a different job. I know his type. He'll keep pushing unless you push back in a way he understands."

"*You* don't understand." She glanced back over her shoulder to make sure Stan couldn't hear. "This is the only restaurant near the school, and Stan lets me go during our busy time so I can see the girls. I don't just *need* the job; I need *this* job. And I have my own way of handling Stan." Although Cade was right that Stan kept pushing despite her firm rebukes. But she couldn't go much farther without risking her job, and for all that he was annoying, Stan was harmless.

"Your way of handling Stan means Stan gets to touch something that doesn't belong to him." Cade leaned back in the booth, arms folded, legs spread. "Something I want. That causes a problem."

Dawn's eyes crinkled in amusement. "For him or for you?"

"For him, since I always get what I want."

"Cocky."

Cade licked his lips. "Maybe you should drop a napkin and bend over and pick it up so I can show you just how cocky I can be."

"Always about sex."

He reached for her hand and stroked a thumb across her knuckles, sending a wave of heat through the body. "Always about you. What happened last night won't happen again. I'm gonna protect you and keep you safe."

Without thinking, she stroked a hand over his hair. So fierce. So passionate. What would it be like to have someone like Cade in her life? An idea stirred at the back of her mind, but she quickly dismissed it. Yes, she liked Cade, but not enough to embrace the biker life that had caused her so much pain.

Reality kicked in and her hand dropped. It would never happen. Wrong life. Wrong world. Entirely the wrong guy.

★ SIX ★

I will avenge all wrongs done to me and my club.
SINNER'S TRIBE CREED

Christ. Cade pulled open the door to the Conundrum Sheriff's Department and steeled himself for a takedown. Damn cops would just love to toss a one-percenter in jail. If the Sinners still had Sheriff Morton on the payroll, he wouldn't have been concerned, but the idiot had been caught stealing weapons from the evidence room, and that was the end of what had been a damn fine arrangement with the local police.

"Can I help you?" The receptionist glared through a Plexiglas window, her hand hovering over the conspicuous emergency call button at the side of her desk.

Yeah, he needed help. He needed someone to shake him up, slap him around, and tell him to get his sorry ass back to the clubhouse instead of panting after the only woman on the planet who didn't want him.

What the fuck was he doing here? She'd been joking around when she invited him to go with her to the sheriff's office, and if she had any sense she'd boot his ass out the minute he showed up, if the cops didn't throw him in jail first. But dammit, she had no one looking out for her, and the cops wouldn't be able to help. Conundrum was a biker town. The kind of protection she needed was the kind of protection only a biker could provide. Still, showing up here took things to a whole new level. Maybe she'd think he wanted more than another night with her in bed.

Maybe he did.

"Sir? If there's nothing you need, perhaps you could step out of line."

And leave Dawn to the inept fumbling of the local police?

"I'm meeting a friend who's seeing the deputy sheriff. Dawn . . ." *Christ.* He didn't even know her last name. Par for the course. He usually didn't care about a woman's last name when he was buried deep inside her. Or her first name, for that matter. But Dawn wasn't like the others and he silently berated himself for not making the effort.

"Dawn. No last name." The receptionist lifted a manicured eyebrow in censure, and Cade scowled.

"Just make the call."

Five minutes later, accompanied by two suspicious police officers, he walked into the intake area of the sheriff's office. An assortment of drunks, vagrants, and a few high school girls in cuffs were seated in the waiting area. All the desks were in use, and the air was thick with the stench of unwashed bodies, old cigarettes, and pastrami.

The lead member of his entourage gestured to a desk in the corner where Dawn sat across from a cop with brown hair and the chiseled good looks of those losers on the front of men's magazines. Cade snorted at the frickin' gigantic shiny badge on the dude's blue shirt, but his derision faded when the deputy met Cade's gaze and then reached over the desk to clasp Dawn's hand.

A growl escaped Cade's lips. So that was the game.

Bastard thought he could put his hands all over Cade's girl.

Okay. Technically, she wasn't his girl. But he'd slept with her, wanted to sleep with her again, and he'd had a good time with her and her kids on Sunday afternoon. Hell, he'd even missed joining Gunner and Sparky at a little pool party with Delilah and the girls from Peelers Strip Club. Now, that was something he would never live down.

His gaze still on Cade, the deputy stroked Dawn's hand.

How fucking pathetic. Was that his idea of a challenge? Seated at his fucking desk in a collared shirt, patting Dawn's hand? He'd give anything right now to get the deputy outside in the alley. Pansy ass would go down with one punch. Guaranteed. And the guy was an idiot if he thought he'd rile Cade up enough to risk assaulting a police officer. Not that Cade was afraid of doing time, but he had business to take care of first, and item number one was to get the deputy's paws off his woman.

"Thought you were done with bikers," the deputy said, loud enough for Cade to hear. Cade snorted and put more effort into thudding his boots across the tiles and rattling the chain hanging from his belt.

Let the fucking games begin.

Dawn looked over her shoulder, her brow wrinkled in confusion. "I am. He's just a friend."

Friend? Ha. He didn't fuck his female friends. He didn't give free rein to all the kinky, twisted shit in his brain and have them demanding more. And he certainly didn't come so many damn times in one night that the sight of blond hair the next day made him instantly hard.

"A biker friend. Same poison. Different color." The deputy's face soured when Cade bent down and brushed his lips over Dawn's unbruised cheek, a direct response to the challenge in the deputy's eyes.

"Babe." He stroked her hair for good measure and then sprawled on the empty chair beside her, ignoring the salivating police officers behind him. They knew who he was. And they also knew they had nothing on him. The Sinners kept their illegal activities under the radar, and if someone did get caught, they had a big-shot criminal attorney on retainer.

"Um . . . this is Cade." She gave the deputy a weak smile, and then her cheeks flushed and she pulled her hand away. "Cade, this is Deputy Sheriff Doug Benson."

"Cade."

"Benson." He deliberately used the deputy's last name, not his first name or his title, letting him know with that one small gesture where Benson stood in the hierarchy of things. But just to make sure, Cade lifted his arm and placed it over the back of Dawn's chair, his hand dangling with deliberate casualness over her shoulder, fingers brushing her bare skin.

Benson's jaw clenched, and they locked gazes, trying to stare each other down.

"Enough," Dawn snapped. "Both of you."

Didn't see that one coming. His girl had backbone. No doubt about that.

Benson's eyes glittered, and then his gaze dropped. Cade puffed out his chest and gave a satisfied grunt. *Challenge met. Dominance established. Woman claimed.*

"What are you doing here, Cade?" Dawn looked up at him and his fingers took advantage of her exposed neck, tickling their way to her ear.

"You invited me the other morning. In the restaurant."

Dawn's eyes widened. "It was a joke. I would never, in a million years, have expected you to show up."

"Shows how little you know me." He rubbed his knuckles over her cheek, the gesture at once intimate and possessive. "You want me to go, just say the word. But I don't trust the cops, and Benson here is gonna be able to do dick-all about Mad Dog. I can."

Benson bristled. "Actually . . ."

"Am I wrong?" Cade leaned forward and tilted his head to the side. "You suddenly got the balls to take on the Devil's Brethren?"

"Yes, you are wrong," Benson said, his expression smug. "The town recently installed CCTV cameras in high-traffic areas. Dawn says she was assaulted in a public place. We may be able to pull some footage and get enough evidence to charge Jimmy . . . Mad Dog with assault."

Cade chuckled and leaned back in his seat. "That kind of evidence will disappear so fast you'll wonder if you even had it in the first place. Evidence rooms aren't as secure as you think. And even if the evidence doesn't disappear, strings will be pulled and he'll be walking out the other door as soon as you hand in the paperwork."

"Doesn't mean we stop trying. Justice needs to be served. And I promised Dawn I'd do my best to get her justice."

Cade toyed with Dawn's curls, his fingers brushing over the back of her neck. Damn she was soft—soft skin, soft hair, and a soft heart. But he was learning she had a core of steel inside.

"There's the big difference between us," Cade said. "I serve justice hot. You serve it cold."

Benson tipped his chin, a tacit acknowledgment of the truth of Cade's words. There was no due process in biker culture. No rules or laws or procedures that had to be followed. Biker justice was swift, and often brutal, but it was always effective. Just as it had been the other night.

One down. Five to go.

"Dawn, you want to give that statement now, or after your friend leaves?" Benson picked up his legal pad, but

Cade didn't heed his dismissive tone. He wanted to hear the details of the assault as much as Benson did, but unlike Benson he would do something about it.

Dawn studied Cade intently, her eyes boring into him as if she could see into his soul. Well, there wasn't much to see except a black hole that he'd spent a lifetime trying to fill with countless women in countless beds, and enough whiskey to ensure his remains would be well preserved when he finally passed.

"You can stay."

Score! He caught Benson's gaze and made no effort to hide his triumphant grin. *Take that, bastard. She wants me.*

Benson's hand tightened around his pen, but to his credit he remained professional. "That's fine. You can give me the details, and after you're done, you can talk to someone in our Victim Services—"

"I'm not a victim," she said abruptly. "I'm a fighter. That's why I'm here."

"Damn right," Cade said. "Of course, coming here is the equivalent of trying to fight Mad Dog with a feather, but as a civilian you're doing the best with what you've got."

Benson put down his pad. "I take offense at that statement."

"Good. It was meant to be offensive." Cade stared at the scowling deputy. "Admit it, Benson. This is a biker town, and in a biker town the police have no power. You get Dawn's girls back yet? You got Mad Dog jail? And Victim Services? How's that gonna stop him?"

"I didn't choose the name and the unit is there to help people who have suffered as the result of a crime." Benson shifted in his seat. "Looking at Dawn's face, I would say she suffered. And as for being a feather . . ."

"You're not going to win that one, Benson." Cade gave

him a grin. "Don't even try. Plus, I got a plan to keep Dawn safe."

"What plan?" Dawn turned to him and frowned.

"Later. Benson already looks pale. Don't want to give him a heart attack by revealing too much about our evil biker ways."

Dawn tipped her head down, hiding a smile. "I kinda like your evil biker ways," she murmured.

His groin tightened and he leaned over to whisper, "Next time I get you in bed, I'm gonna show you just how evil my biker ways can be."

"Cade!"

He threw back his head and laughed. Really laughed. He loved the way she shrieked his name.

Dawn gave her statement and answered Doug's questions with Cade's arm around her shoulders the entire time. Although she considered shifting his arm away, especially since his overt possessiveness clearly made Doug uncomfortable, she liked his warmth and quiet support. Even Doug had never made her feel as safe.

"If you change your mind about Victim Services, the number is here." Doug slid a piece of paper across the desk. "And if you think of anything else . . ."

"I'll call." Dawn moved to stand, and Cade helped her from her seat.

Chivalry. From a biker. Fancy that.

"Anytime," Doug said. "You have my number."

Dawn made her way to the door after a farewell wave. Yes, she had Doug's number, but she suspected the reminder wasn't entirely directed at her.

Friends since meeting at Doug's self-defense class at the community college, she and Doug had met up for coffee every few weeks for the past year and often bumped into each other at the monthly get-togethers with their self-defense class. Doug made it clear early on he was interested in more than friendship, but Dawn turned him down again and again. He was too nice, too straight, too rigid, too . . . good for a girl with a wild side and a résumé that included aiding and abetting a criminal organization, and stripping in some of Montana's seediest clubs.

"Is he still watching?" Cade slid an arm around Dawn's waist and pulled her into his side.

"There was no need for a pissing contest," Dawn said. "Doug understands that I just want to be friends. I've made it clear to him on several occasions."

"Ha." Cade barked a laugh, and they descended the concrete stairs to the main level under the watchful gaze of Cade's police escort. "No man understands when a woman wants to be friends. All a man hears when a woman says that is, 'I'm not gonna fuck you right now, but maybe later.' That's why he hangs around. For a guy who isn't getting some on a regular basis, 'maybe later' is a chance not to be missed. Not that I've ever had that problem."

"Of course not." And she would be wise not to forget it. Cade wasn't a one-woman man. But what if he was? What would it be like to be with Cade? She amused herself as they walked down the sidewalk, imagining how many jobs she would have to go through before she found a boss he deemed acceptable, and how many sheriff's deputies he would cow into submission with the fierceness of his scowl. And then she imagined how it would feel to be under the Sinners' protection. Jimmy would never have dared take her children if he had to face Sinner justice. Nor would he be able to threaten her ever again.

"I thought we were friends," she teased.

Cade stopped and pulled her to the side after they exited the station. "Aside from Benson, any of your friends want to fuck you?"

"Um . . . no. Not that I'm aware."

"Well, I do," he said. "Means we're not friends."

She tugged him forward. "So what does that make us?"

"Still trying to figure that one out."

The light turned green and Cade led her across the street, his eyes darting from side to side as if he expected a vehicle to blast through the intersection at any minute. *Always keeping me safe.* He probably had no idea how much those small gestures meant to her.

"The police can't help you," he said as if reading her thoughts. "You got a biker problem; you got to deal with it the biker way. Look what happened when you got the courts involved in your custody dispute."

"Easy to deal with things the biker way when you are a biker. Not so easy when you're a civilian."

Cade slowed his steps and stared at her, his face thoughtful. For a moment she wondered if he was thinking of asking her to join the MC, but when she saw his bike parked in an alley near the bus stop, she figured he'd been leading her this way. Always in control, but in a subtle way. She liked it. Maybe too much. She didn't have to sweat the small stuff when she was with Cade. But what if he took that control too far, the way Jimmy had? She had learned the hard way that in the biker world no one would be there to help her.

"You don't have to take the bus to work." He gestured to his bike. "I could give you a ride."

Dawn's lips tipped at the corners. "Last time you gave me a ride, we wound up in your bed."

"That was a good night."

"A very good night." She turned to face him. "But it's almost dark and I have to work tonight, so I think the bus is my safest bet."

He stroked a warm finger along her jaw. "You're probably right. Made me hot when you told me 'n' Benson off in there. Don't think I'd be able to take you to work without a detour."

"Are you joking?" She gave him a quizzical look. "I thought alpha male bikers who show up in police stations and do everything except pee on the floor to mark their territory wouldn't like being told to stand down." Her cheeks flushed, but she wanted to know. Was he really so different from Jimmy?

Cade pulled her into the alley beside his bike and wrapped one arm tight around her waist, rolling his hips against her. His erection pressed into her stomach, and she bit back a moan.

"Does that feel like joking?" He licked his lips and stared down at her. "I don't joke about serious things. Painful things."

Dawn leaned her forehead against his chest and laughed. "Well then, I'll try not to call you out in public again. I wouldn't want to cause you any more pain."

He cupped her jaw in his warm palm and tilted her face up until she met his gaze. "That kind of pain I can take." His voice dropped, softened. "When it's 'cause of my sexy girl."

She was ready for his kiss. Knew it was coming before he lowered his head. And as his lips touched hers, she threw caution aside and pressed up against him, twining her hands around his neck to pull him close so she could feel every inch of his hard body against hers.

"Christ, you're so fucking hot," he murmured against her lips. "You're like a fucking drug. All I was thinking about at the police station was how sweet you'd look naked, and bent over Benson's desk with my cock in your pussy." He deepened the kiss, his tongue stroking firmly inside, devouring her. Dawn's body flamed, sweat trickling between her breasts, and she pulled him down for more.

"I love it when you talk dirty." She ground her hips against him, pushing him deeper into the shadows, seeking even the smallest bit of friction where she needed it the most. "Talk dirty some more."

"Fuck."

"That's a start." She nuzzled his neck, frowning when he pulled away. "What's wrong?"

Cade drew in a ragged breath, his gaze focused on something behind her. "We got trouble. Brethren. Two of 'em. They're watching us from the other end of the alley. Goddammit. They aren't supposed to be in town. Jagger and Wolf are negotiating a patch-over but the rules haven't changed."

The Brethren patching over to the Sinners? She couldn't imagine the two clubs had anything in common, and from what she'd seen they didn't share the same ethos. The Brethren bought, sold, and traded women; they prostituted their sweet butts and turned a blind eye to abuse. The Sinners might be misogynistic, but that kind of behavior didn't go on in their MC. Jagger and Arianne would never have allowed it.

Dawn followed Cade's gaze and her heart skipped a beat. "It's Jimmy. He's with Trey. They're always together."

"Trey is one of the guys who grabbed me," Cade growled. "Jesus Christ. This is too fucking much. Wanna shoot them dead right here, right now. Trey is fair game, but Mad Dog . . . I had to agree to let him go. Looks like he's decided to rub his 'untouchable' status in my damn face." He grabbed her hand and yanked her toward his bike. "Hop on, sweetheart. We're gonna run them out of town."

She hesitated, her gaze flicking from Jimmy to Cade and back to Jimmy. If she got on the bike, she would be as good as telling Jimmy he was right about her and Cade: She'd hooked up with a biker, and she was totally and irrevocably finished with Jimmy and the Brethren. But more than that, she would be doing the one thing she'd promised herself she would never do. Was she really ready to get involved in the biker life again?

The bus pulled up at the stop outside the alley, wheels squeaking as it ground to a halt. The door slammed open and Dawn watched the people mounting the stairs into the warm interior. Ten steps and she could be on that bus, warm and safe, and on her way home.

"Come." Cade straddled his bike and held out his hand. "I can't protect you if you're not with me."

How could she resist an opportunity to finally stick it to Jimmy and run him out of town? She'd never been on the offensive before. Even when she left him, she was running away. And how could she refuse the protection of the man who made her heart pound and her knees weak?

With one last look at the bus stop, she threw a leg over the bike and wrapped her hands around his waist. "Let's ride."

Cade cranked the throttle and the engine of his modded Harley Fat Boy roared to life, the sound echoing down the alley. Jimmy and Trey turned their bikes and sped away. Cade raced after them, veering out into the traffic and accelerating after the fleeing bikers as if there were no other vehicles on the road.

Dawn had ridden pillion on Jimmy's bike, but she'd never experienced anything as breathtakingly exciting as riding with Cade. They flew through stop signs and traffic lights, wove in and out of traffic, and sent pedestrians scurrying off the sidewalk. Dawn clung to Cade as if she were a first-time rider, barely able to keep her balance when the bike tipped on hairpin turns that sent her stomach plummeting. The wind whipped through her hair, the motorcycle vibrated between her thighs, and the world became a blur once they hit the open road. She had never been as exhilarated in her life.

"Babe. Grab my gun from the holster," Cade shouted over his shoulder.

Tightening her free arm, Dawn reached beneath his cut and removed the weapon, sliding it across his chest. She held it in front of him, but Cade shook his head.

"Going too fast to ride and shoot. You gotta do it. Shoot 'em."

Dawn sucked in a sharp breath and pressed herself tighter against Cade's back. Her legs clamped around his thighs when he suddenly changed lanes to accelerate past a truck. "I can't shoot," she yelled. "What if I hit someone?"

"That's the idea. If you don't, he'll just keep coming back like a fucking roach."

"I hate Jimmy, but I can't kill him." She slammed the gun into his stomach, her arm tightening around him to keep her balance when he hit a bump.

Cade grunted. "Well, then shoot out their fucking tires."

Tires. I can do tires. How much harder could it be than trying to hit the tiny targets at the shooting range where Arianne had taken her for her birthday? She hugged Cade with one arm and peered around his side, aiming her weapon at Trey's tires. Then she pulled the trigger.

Crack. The recoil almost threw her off the bike. The bullet pinged off the rocks and ricocheted overhead. Cade's weapon was nothing like her .22. And clearly, she'd missed her target because Trey and Jimmy were still speeding ahead.

"Again," Cade shouted.

Dawn's hand shook as she tried to aim the gun, but with the wind whipping around her, and Cade leaning so far forward she could barely hold on, she worried her aim was off. And if the bullet hit one of the men instead of the bike . . . "You need to get closer."

"What the fuck do you think I'm doing? They're almost at the border." He kicked up the acceleration and Dawn gave up any further thoughts of shooting out Trey's tires in favor of making it through the ride alive.

But although Cade was fast, he wasn't fast enough. Jimmy and Trey shot across the Conundrum border and Cade slowed his bike, pulling up in the empty parking lot behind Big Bill's Custom Cycles and Paint. CLOSED ON SUNDAYS.

For a long moment, neither of them moved. Dawn's heart thudded against her rib cage, the beat matched by the throb of the pulse at the juncture of her thighs and the heated rush of blood through her veins.

When she was able to loosen her fingers from Cade's cut, she slid off the bike. Cade followed suit, and then he turned to face her.

"What the fuck kinda shooting was that?" His voice rose in frustration. "When I give you an order, I expect it to be carried out right away."

Shocked by his anger, a curious mix of adrenaline and desire boiling through her veins, she answered him back with the same vehement tone. "Don't shout at me. I spent two days at a shooting range with Arianne. That's all the experience I have. I couldn't get a clear shot, and I didn't want to take the risk I'd hit one of them. And I don't take orders from you."

His eyes glittered in the setting sun, his body quivering with unspent adrenaline. "If you're gonna ride with a biker, you're gonna have to suck it up. The man is the boss. And you're gonna have to learn how to shoot in a straight fucking line."

"I did the biker thing," she spat out. "You saw how that turned out. I don't know why I got on the back of your bike, but I'm sorry I did. I should have just taken the bus." Her voice rose in pitch as she struggled against the conflicting needs to slap some sense into his thick, chauvinistic skull, and to tear off his clothes and soothe the ache between her thighs.

"Jesus Christ." Cade whirled around and thudded his boot into the brick wall of the store. "Don't be so damn difficult. I'm just trying to keep you safe."

"Difficult? I don't spend my time taking shooting lessons because I don't want to shoot anyone. And this ride was a onetime thing. I've never been in position to act against Jimmy before, much less run him out of town. But it wasn't an invitation to be bossed around."

Damn it felt good to shout and stand up for herself without being afraid of the repercussions. Jimmy would have beaten her for much, much less. But Cade stared at her, feral hunger in his gaze, burning her with its intensity.

Then he turned and walked away.

"Where are you going?"

"Wound up too tight," he muttered. "And you . . . that fire . . . those green eyes . . . your hair wild around your shoulders . . . fucking beautiful when you're angry . . . too damn hot. Need to cool off."

Caught in a maelstrom of emotion, adrenaline, and lust, Dawn heaved in a breath. "Cade Raider Tyson," she shouted. "You get back here and fuck me right now."

He stopped.

He turned.

And in less than five seconds he had his hand twined through her hair, his body pressed against her, his thick thigh between her legs, and his tongue down her throat.

She loved that about him. No questions. No second-guessing. No uncertainty. She wanted him and he was with her all the way.

"You don't know what you've unleashed, sweetheart." He sank his teeth into the sensitive spot between her neck and her shoulder and Dawn shuddered at the exquisite sensation.

"Yes, I do."

He yanked open her jeans and shoved her up against the cold, brick wall, his face almost fully obscured by the lengthening shadows of the forest behind him. "Not gonna be gentle. Not gonna take my time. Need you so bad, I'm gonna fuck you hard and fast, so you'd better be ready for me."

"If I wasn't ready for you, Cade, I wouldn't have asked." She eased her jeans down over her hips, toeing off her boot to slide one leg free. God, if anyone came out here . . . But why would they? The shop was isolated and, thankfully, closed.

Cade pulled a condom from his back pocket and shoved down his jeans. "Didn't hear much asking. Heard a sexy girl telling me she wanted my cock."

"I didn't . . ."

He grabbed her hair, tugged her head back, and cut her off with a kiss. Fierce. Demanding. Possessive. His tongue delved into her mouth and she tangled it with her own, savoring his taste.

With a low growl, he pulled away and sheathed himself, then slid his hands over her ass, cupping her cheeks as he lifted her against him.

"Open for me, sexy girl."

Dawn couldn't contain the moan that escaped her lips, deep, hungry, and full of need. She'd been with other men since Cade, but none was as rough, driving her past all restraint to touch the wild side she had buried long ago.

"Seems you can't help being bossy." She nuzzled his jaw, prickly with a five o'clock shadow, and then braced herself against his shoulders to wrap her legs around his hips.

"Only 'cause I know you secretly like it." Cade slicked

a finger through her folds and groaned. "So wet and ready for me."

"It's the whole vibrating motorcycle, chasing bad guys, pressing up against you, dangerous speed, shooting at people, shouting at me, being sweet, and fucking me in a parking lot thing. It turns me on."

Cade growled his appreciation. "You were fucking made for me, sweetheart."

"It's just chemistry." She buried her face in his neck, breathing in his masculine scent, laced with leather and crisp mountain air.

"Fuck, yeah." He yanked her down, his cock thrusting deep inside her slick, wet heat. Dawn groaned as he filled her. So hard. So thick. So . . . perfect.

His fingers tightened on her ass and Dawn trembled. Cade had no limits in the pursuit of sexual pleasure, and after two nights with him neither did she.

"You promised me hard and fast."

"Christ. You're killing me." Cade gripped her hips and hammered into her with a primal intensity that took her breath away. Passion burned between them. Her head smacked against the brick wall, and the rough mortar dug into her back, but she wouldn't have traded this moment for anything. Only Cade could drive her wild.

"Come for me. I wanna hear you." He slid a thick finger between them to stroke over her clit, and her arousal peaked. She screamed as her orgasm ripped through her body, a pleasure so intense she could only hang on for the ride.

Cade pounded into her, fingers digging into her skin. Sweat beaded on his forehead as he rode out her orgasm, prolonging her pleasure, before his body finally tensed and he came with a groan. His muscles bunching beneath her hands, cock pulsing inside her. Then he fell forward, cradling her against him with one arm, bracing himself against the wall with the other.

He held her as they came down, chests heaving together, hearts pounding in unison. Then he released her, and they straightened their clothes in comfortable silence.

"Maybe sometimes it's okay if you're bossy," Dawn murmured as he fastened his belt. "Especially if it means chasing after Jimmy and having hot sex in a parking lot."

"Good to know." His mouth quirked at the corners, and then he stilled.

"What's wrong?"

"Someone's behind us."

He leaned down and kissed her slowly, reverently, lingering, as if they were alone, while he reached between them and drew his gun from its holster.

"Close your eyes, sweetheart," he whispered. And then in one smooth move Cade spun around, pushed her behind his back, and fired.

★ SEVEN ★

What's mine is mine and I shall strive to protect it
to the best of my ability.

SINNER'S TRIBE CREED

"I can't fucking believe you got into a high-speed chase only three blocks from the police station. Or that you fucking shot at the Brethren on the highway." Jagger glared at Cade as they stretched out on the rocky outcropping just above the valley where Rizzoli's truck full of weapons was due to cross at any moment. "Or that I had to hear about it on the fucking news."

"I was just trying to run them outta town. Dawn grabbed my gun and started shooting. Nothing I could do about it. I was going so fast it woulda been dangerous to let go." He looked over at Jagger and grinned. "Safety first. And there was nothing stopping her from taking Mad Dog out except for the fact she can't shoot for shit."

"Jesus Christ. Someone put a bullet in his head." Jagger turned to face him. "You think I'm stupid?"

"Calm the fuck down," Zane muttered from behind them. "Sound echoes in this valley. We don't want to tip them off. The point of an ambush is to stay hidden until the last moment."

"You would know, since you live in the fucking shadows." Cade snorted when Zane scowled. Nothing he liked better than riling Zane up. The guy was wound up too damn tight. Just once he wanted to make the VP laugh.

Cade's dad hadn't had much of a sense of humor, either. But on the good days, when he was kind to Cade's mom, Cade would try to make him laugh with practical jokes he bought from the corner store with the money he saved from his paper route. He'd felt an incredible sense of achievement when he made his dad smile or, even better, ruffle his hair and toss him a compliment the way he tossed their dog, Selma, a bone.

"At least I do something useful in the darkness," Zane shot back. "I'm not holed up in bed banging Arianne's friend. You do to her what you do to your other women, and Arianne's gonna give you a belly full of lead."

"How about a little respect?" Cade snapped. "She's my girl."

"Your girl?" Jagger's voice cracked through the stillness.

"Yeah." Cade checked his weapon, an M107 .50—caliber long-range sniper rifle, in the stunned silence, unwilling to share his rationale for his split—second decision to involve Dawn in the chase and his even more uncharacteristic decision to claim her in the parking lot. He barely understood it himself. But after listening to her story in the police station, and then looking down at her beautiful, bruised face in the alley while her attacker hovered nearby, he'd been seized with an utterly overwhelming need to protect and avenge her. And that meant keeping her close, taking her with him, and then claiming her in the most primitive way.

Mine.

"You have a girl? What does that mean in Cade-speak?"

Zane's incredulous voice grated on him even more than Jagger's curious stare. "Just one?"

"Lotsa brothers got just one girl. Why not me?"

" 'Cause you're you," Gunner said. "Voted 'Least Likely Ever to Settle Down' five years in a row. Winner of the 'Most Sweet Butts in the Bed at One Time' prize. 'Biker Manwhore of the Year.' Author of 'How to Get Laid in Less than Thirty Seconds and Leave Your Friend Drinking Alone at the Bar.' The man who researched beds big enough for six. The list goes on."

"And I'll be taking those prizes home again this year." Cade bristled. "It's not like I'm making her an old lady. Not interested in that level of commitment, or becoming an old man. Hell, I almost got her killed when we stopped at Big Bill's bike shop and Big Bill came around the corner with a shotgun."

"I can fucking imagine what you were doing at Big Bill's at that time of night." Gunner snorted a laugh. "How much did you have to pay him off?"

"Five hundred."

And it had been worth every penny.

Laughter echoed around him, dying quickly when Shaggy whistled to let them know the convoy had entered the valley.

"You're fucking obsessed with this chick." Zane called it straight as he always did. "She dumped you a year ago, and still you still warned the brothers away. You meet her again and suddenly she's your girl? Just get over her, and be glad she didn't rip out your fucking heart, rub it in salt, and stomp it into the ground while she fucked every other damn guy on the planet."

"Christ. He's at it again." Gunner sighed. "Sometimes I want to hunt down the bitch who hurt Zane so bad just to put him out of his misery."

Cade rolled to his side and drew his pistol, aiming it

at Zane's chest, fighting back an unexpected burst of anger. "I'll put him out of his misery now."

Zane drew his own weapon, and adrenaline surged through Cade's veins. This wasn't about sex. He didn't just want Dawn in his bed; he wanted more. He wanted to know everything about her. He wanted to hold her and keep her safe. His want was a craving, an addiction that had only grown worse since he'd met her again.

"Stand down, brothers." Jagger barked. "Save it for the Jacks."

Cade lowered his weapon and Zane did the same.

"Fucking bastard," Zane muttered.

"Come here and say that." Cade gestured Zane forward, but as he did, he caught the flash of headlights on the road below. "They're here."

All their differences vanished in a heartbeat, and they took up their positions. Cade, Zane, and Jagger were on point. Shaggy, T-Rex, Tank, and Gunner had their backs. They'd ambushed protection runs before and everyone knew what to do.

The first Jack went down under Zane's gun, but before Cade could get a clear shot at the Jack in the lead, a bullet pinged off the rock near Jagger's head.

"Fuck. They've seen us."

"Scouts," T-Rex shouted. "They're off to the side. Two Jacks and a civilian."

Another bullet thudded into the dirt only two feet from where Jagger was now crouched and ready to run for cover.

"They're after Jagger." Cade jumped to his feet and moved between Jagger and the shooter. "Zane. You and Gunner get him out of here. Tank, T-Rex, and I will cover."

"Jesus Christ," Jagger growled. "I'm not running away from the fucking Jacks. Bring them on."

"The Sinners need their president." Cade kept low and

followed Jagger behind the cover of a large rock at the edge of the outcropping. "Especially now. Without you . . ."

"They'll have you," Jagger said, checking his clip. "You can lead them. I trust you."

Cade swallowed past the lump in his throat. Jagger's faith had pulled him out of a nightmare and into a world of friendship, honor, loyalty, and brotherhood. He'd helped Cade bury the past and look to a new future where he had something to live for beyond the bottom of a bottle and a mountain of guilt. But he had no desire to replace a great leader and a true friend.

"You're making it damn hard to protect you. Go, or I'll shoot you myself."

"When your men were falling around you in that desert, did you run away?" Jagger fired a shot around the side of the rock and someone screamed. "Were you the last man standing because you were right where you wanted to be—with your men—or because you were hiding and watching them die?"

Cade gritted his teeth against a memory that had almost destroyed him. He'd lived through the ambush only because the slaughter had been so sudden and so violent that his men had fallen dead on top of him, ironically saving his life. Even now the guilt lingered. "Fuck you."

"Fuck you back. Don't expect me to be any less of a man than you were. And don't even consider fighting the Jacks without me by your side." He lifted his hand and Cade did the same, their knuckles bumping as fists collided.

"To the end," Jagger said.

"To the end and back."

Jagger ducked a bullet and then returned fire. "You planning to come back from the dead?"

"I'm not planning to die until I'm an old man."

* * *

It was a little after seven when Dawn arrived at Banks Bar. She'd stayed late at the florist shop, helping her boss get the bouquets ready for a weekend wedding, and then missed her bus when she stopped to grab a snack from a nearby deli. She stuffed the sandwich in her mouth and grabbed her apron from the hook in the stockroom, hoping Banks wouldn't be around. She had never been late before and she didn't want to blemish her perfect record.

"That supposed to be your dinner?" Banks emerged from the parking lot with a crate of bottles in his hands.

Damn. Dawn nodded, her mouth too full of chicken salad to speak.

"Not very healthy, always eatin' on the go. You need to sit down, relax, and enjoy your meals. Better for digestion."

"No time," she muttered through a mouthful of bread. "Not really a sit-down-and-relax kinda girl. I think they call me an A-plus personality."

Banks pulled a bottle from the crate and placed it on the stock shelf. "You're killing yourself to feed Shelly-Ann's shopping habit. Those girls of yours should be livin' in style with the amount of money you're giving their aunt."

"One day," she said. "I haven't lost hope yet. I reported the assault to the police this time and Deputy Benson thinks there's a good chance they'll be able to put Jimmy behind bars. My lawyer says that kind of offense will likely be enough to convince an appeals judge to overturn the custody order."

"You want him outta the picture, you just say the word." Banks shelved another bottle. "I got friends who can make him disappear."

So did she, but she wasn't about to share. "Then you'll have the Devil's Brethren hunting you for the rest of your life." Dawn handed him another bottle. "My fight, Banks, and I'll deal with it my way. But I appreciate the offer. Always nice to know I have friends who are prepared to kill for me."

He gave her a rare Banks grin. "Anytime."

The bar was hopping by the time she hit the floor. She counted at least a dozen Sinners scattered throughout the room, most of whom she didn't know. Arianne waved to her from behind the counter and Rob, the bouncer, nodded a greeting. Dawn picked up her tray and headed to a table of rowdy biker wannabes in the corner, looking utterly ridiculous in their TV biker show cuts.

After one minute of putting up with their fake biker talk, she signaled to Rob to keep an eye on them. Invariably, they would get drunk and approach one of the real bikers in the bar. If they were lucky, they would get turfed out. If they picked the wrong bikers or really pissed someone off, they would be hauled outside and beaten half to death; their vehicles would be trashed, their money stolen, and she would be mopping up blood and calling for a bevy of ambulances to take them to the hospital.

By the time she filled their drink orders, the place was full, every seat taken, and it was standing room only at the bar. Dawn worked as quickly as she could, hoping to pick up enough tips to keep Shelly-Ann quiet, at least for the rest of the week. The Pretty Reckless's "Messed Up World" blasted through the speakers and she returned to the bar from an umpteenth trip across the floor only to find Deputy Benson sitting at the counter.

"Hey, Doug. What are you doing in the wrong end of town?"

His crisp dark-blue jeans, hand-tooled leather belt, cowboy boots, and button-down denim shirt made him look more like a country singer than a law enforcement officer, but he greeted her with his usual firm handshake.

"I pulled the CCTV tapes from the night Jimmy attacked you and stopped by to check the positioning of the cameras at the bus stop. Thirsty work staring at hidden cameras, so I thought I'd come in for a quick drink before I went home."

Arianne pulled his beer and Dawn chatted with him every time she hit the bar with a new order. He seemed in no hurry to get home and was content to talk in abruptly interrupted snippets, with Arianne pulling up the slack when Dawn was serving tables.

"He seems quite decent for a cop," Arianne whispered as she loaded Dawn's tray. "A bit straitlaced for me, but nice."

"He is nice." Dawn shuffled the glasses around to balance them out. "Too nice. I'd probably taint him forever if I told him my whole life story. But he can also be very intense. Sometimes he gets fixated on a case and he can't let go. He told me all about it over coffee one afternoon. He hinted that it had something to do with one of his sisters."

Arianne loaded Dawn's empties in the dishwasher. "Where's he from? He doesn't sound local."

"Chicago. He wouldn't tell me why he moved out here, but he doesn't have any family or ties to the town." Dawn gave her a grin. "Maybe he's running from something. I think he has dark secrets. The quiet ones always do." She lifted the tray, freezing when Arianne hissed in a warning breath.

But she didn't need a warning. She knew Cade was here, felt his eyes burning into her skin, had sensed him the moment he walked through the door.

"Where is he?"

"How did you . . . ?" Arianne cut herself off with a grin. "Sort of like I did the first time Jagger came to see me." She looked over Dawn's shoulder. "He's heading to the back. Section four. Not sure why because all the tables are taken." She snorted a laugh. "And suddenly there's a table free. Your customers from table sixteen have been relocated to section five with only minor injuries. I guess he enjoyed your sordid activities at Big Bill's bike shop."

"I shouldn't have told you. And it's not serious. It was just . . . sex." Turning slowly, Dawn spotted Cade at the back of the bar, sitting in the corner in an I'm-so-dominant-I-need-the-space-of-three-men pose, his legs spread wide and his elbows resting on the arms of the chair. God, he was gorgeous.

"I'm surprised to see him." Arianne pulled a bottle of bourbon from the shelf. "Last I heard, he and Gunner were at Peelers Strip Club with some of the brothers for a hot night watching Dancing Delilah and the other strippers. They were celebrating some secret thing that happened a few days ago that I'm not supposed to know involves fifty thousand dollars' worth of stolen guns, five injured Jacks, and one angry Mafia boss."

"Seriously? And now he's here?" Dawn turned and Cade beckoned her to him with a waggle of his finger. "Oh. My. God. Does he think I'm going over there after he's spent the evening with a woman in his lap? The strippers were the warm-up and I'm the booty call?"

"From the way he's looking at you," Arianne said, "that would be a yes. And I have a feeling that if you don't go over, he's going to pounce. But, like you said, it's not serious, so why do you care?"

"I don't."

Arianne gave her sly grin. "Maybe you should kiss your cop friend. See how not-serious Cade thinks things are between you. Because I'll tell you one thing I've learned during my time at the club: The Sinners are a possessive bunch. Once they claim you, there is no going back."

After enduring all the posturing at the police station, Dawn could just imagine what would happen if she kissed Doug. But she didn't want Doug to get the wrong idea, or for Cade to wind up in jail. "Maybe I'll just ignore him instead. I'm not going over there to be someone's sloppy seconds."

Arianne poured a shot of bourbon and placed it on Dawn's tray. "He's watching you like a predator about to pounce. If you don't go over there, he's gonna hunt you down, and I don't think he'll care who gets in his way. Maybe you should spare Banks the bloodshed."

Dawn unbuttoned the top two buttons on her shirt and pulled the ponytail holder from her hair. "How about this? He wants a hot night; I'll give him a hot night. But it will be look and don't touch."

"I can hardly wait." Arianne laughed. "Cade's never been with a woman who pushed back. He's always the one running the show."

Dawn lifted the tray and wove her way through the tables, flirting and joking with her other customers as she steeled herself for a professional but distant conversation with the man who made her blood hot and her heart cold. By the time she reached Cade's table his lazy smile had disappeared beneath a mask of disapproval.

"You look like you need a drink." She handed him the last glass on her tray.

His fingers brushed over hers as he took the glass. A zing of electricity shot through her body and she stifled a gasp.

"What the fuck was that?"

"What?"

"That." He gestured toward the sea of tables between

them and the bar. "Taking down your hair. Unbuttoning your shirt. All that laughing and smiling and touching guys. That dude on the right in the red shirt is still staring at your ass. And those two suits haven't stopped looking at your legs."

"That is called being friendly with the customers. Happy customers give better tips."

"This customer isn't happy." He sipped the bourbon, his eyes boring into her with an intensity that took her breath away. "You're my girl. You don't be friendly with anyone but me."

Dawn lifted an admonishing eyebrow. "First, I don't recall us discussing an exclusive arrangement in which I would be your girl. And second, you get to be friendly with the dancers at Peelers? Hardly seems fair." She tried to keep her tone light, but her words came out slightly sharp and she cringed inwardly. She didn't do jealous. And really, she didn't care what Cade did in his free time. So they'd shared a few kisses. And blazingly hot sex in parking lot behind a bike shop. No big deal.

Cade finished his drink and placed the glass on the table. "I had a shit week, so yeah, I went to Peelers to relax. Watched my friend Delilah on the pole, but afterward, when she wanted to dance in my lap, I turned her down. All I could think about was you."

"Really?" Dawn raised an eyebrow. "I've always wanted a guy to tell me he was thinking about me while a stripper was offering to writhe naked on his lap."

"She wasn't completely naked."

"Oh well then. That's so much better." She grabbed the empty glass and held it to her nose, inhaling the strong scent of liquor. She'd never been tempted to drink while at work, but being this close to Cade gave her a burning need to cool off.

Cade leaned back in his seat, wincing when his shoulders hit the wooden frame. "You're making me think you care."

"I don't. Go see all the strippers you want, but not if you think I'm your girl. Some women might not have a problem with it, but I do." She stared at him for a moment, torn between turning and walking away and asking him if he was okay. She'd seen the deep knife cuts over his Sinner's Tribe tattoo when she'd fixed him up the other night, the ultimate disrespect from one biker to another, and wondered if her household antiseptic was enough to clean wounds that deep. Now she suspected it hadn't been, but knowing Cade, he'd be falling off his bike before he'd see a doctor.

"Something wrong with your back?" She licked the edge of the glass, and the burn on her tongue made her eyes water.

" 'S good." A smile played at the corners of his lips. "You thirsty?"

"Um. No. Just tasting." She put down the glass. "Something is wrong with your back. I saw you wince and I saw what they did to you the other night. Why don't you come to the stockroom and let me check it out?"

Cade's brow creased. "Nothing's wrong, so there's nothing to check out."

"Fine. I'll just leave you to think about the stripper in your lap and the cuts on your tat and I'll get back to work." She turned to leave, at least she thought she did, but her feet were still planted firmly on the floor.

"You're damn sexy when you're riled." His hand slid up her thigh, curling around her hip, and he pulled her gently between his spread legs. "And even more sexy when your compassion gets the better of you."

Game over. She should never have let him touch her. Dark hunger gripped her belly, and she struggled against the heat coursing through her veins.

"My face is still bruised. Bruises aren't sexy."

"Yours are. Everything about you is sexy." He shoved up her skirt, just an inch, his thumb stroking along her inner thigh. Dawn trembled, wanting more and hating herself for it. He'd just come from a goddamn strip club. She knew exactly what would have happened in the back room. And the kind of guys who used them . . .

"I'm in my work clothes."

"Sexy little skirt." He caressed her with both hands, smoothing his fingers over the curve of her hips to her waist. His fingers tightened and he stood and spun her around, guiding her the few steps to the hallway leading to the washrooms. Then he pushed her against the wall, his massive body hiding her from view.

"Cade. I'm working." She studied the slightly off-kilter set of his shoulders, the weariness of his face, breathed in his scent of beer and bourbon. "And you've been drinking. A lot."

"Stuff came up during an ambush. Stuff I'd buried a long time ago."

Dawn frowned when his voice cracked. She didn't really know that much about Cade—his family, his past, what he'd done before joining the Sinners, and what led him to the club. "You okay?"

Ignoring her question, he drew her closer, trailing his fingers over her ass, then cupping it in his broad palms, grinding her hips against his. "More compassion. And a sexy white apron with strings that hang over your lush ass.".

"No . . ." Her voice caught. "You were just with . . . Delilah."

He clasped her hand and placed it over the bulge in his jeans. Her fingers tightened involuntarily over his erection, hard as steel beneath his fly.

"You think I'd be this hard if I did anything at Peelers

other than hanging at the bar, having a few drinks, and shooting the shit with some of the brothers? I put in my time so no one felt let down when, really, I wanted to be here. With you. I can't fucking stay away."

A soft groan escaped her lips and she glanced around, concerned someone might see. But his hands were already on the move, sliding up her abdomen, circling her rib cage, and stopping just below her breasts.

"Sexy tight top that makes a man hard just looking at it," he whispered in her ear. "If we were anywhere else, I'd tear it off and spend an entire evening worshipping your tits."

She tried to pull away, but Cade wasn't done. He tangled one hand through her hair, pulling her head back, exposing her neck to his heated slide of his lips. He'd never been so aggressive with her before. So demanding. Dominant.

"Sexy beautiful throat." He kissed the hollow at the base of her neck and her knees went weak.

"If you're lying to me about Delilah—"

"Sexy soft jealous lips tell me you care." He covered her mouth with his own and kissed her hard and fast.

"I'll . . ." What? She'd never threatened anyone in her life. Even when she'd lived on the streets, she managed to find a safe haven with other street kids. What would Arianne say?

"Shoot off your balls."

Seemingly unconcerned, Cade feathered kisses along her jaw. "Good thing I'm not lying 'cause I'm gonna need them right now. One taste of you and I gotta have more." And then he thrust his thick thigh between her legs and rocked her gently. "Sexy wet pussy."

"Cade. Stop." Gritting her teeth against the delicious sensation, she wrenched herself away. "I don't know what's gotten into you tonight. And even if we're just having a good time, even if this isn't real, I can't handle your . . . other . . . Dancing Delilah."

Oh God. Did she just say "Dancing Delilah"?

"I don't want her. I want you."

"If you wanted me, why did you go to Peelers?"

"Because I didn't want to want you."

She stroked his cheek, rough with stubble. He hadn't shaved in a couple of days, and now that she was closer she could see lines of weariness marking his brow. Haggard.

"Then why did you come here?"

"Because everything is better when I'm with you." He clasped her hand and pulled her down the hallway. With a quick look back over his shoulder, he pushed open the door to the ladies' restroom and dragged her inside.

"What are you doing?" But she knew exactly what he was doing, and she was more than fully on board with the program.

He closed and locked the door, then flicked on the light. Both stalls were empty. He pushed her against the burnt-orange wall and settled his hands possessively on her hips.

"I need you, sweetheart, and I need you now." He angled his head and claimed her mouth in a fierce kiss that ripped a moan from her throat.

"What happened when you were on the road? Talk to me, Cade. Let me help."

Cade smoothed his broad hands over her hips and raised her tight skirt, his fingers curling around the hem as he tugged it up to her waist. "Nothing for you to worry about." He kicked her legs apart, cupped her mound. Dawn gasped, her brain trying to catch up with her body's instant response to the focused intensity of his sensual assault.

"I am worried. I've never seen you like this."

His hand rocked, rubbing her through her panties until she was grinding against him; so wet she ached to feel him inside her.

He clasped her hand and pressed it against his shaft, rock-hard beneath his fly. "I want to be inside you. I want to forget. Something about you. So sweet. Soft. Sexy. You light up the darkness." He brushed his lips over her ear, whispering dark secrets, things he wanted to do to her, all the ways he wanted to make her come. Then he slipped his hand into the front of her panties and slid his fingers through her folds, teasing her clit. "Only thing you need to know is I won't let anything happen to you."

She tried to pull back, but he thrust his finger deep inside her wetness and she panted her breaths, head spinning as the rush of sensation threatened to carry her away.

"You need me." He added a second finger, stretching her, thrusting harder this time. Dawn's heart thundered, blood pounding through her ears.

"You need me like I need you. Say it."

The door shook with a heavy blow and Banks shouted outside. "Dawn? You okay? What's going on?"

"Just a minute," she called out.

Cade's eyes narrowed. "He wants you."

"You think everyone wants me." She reluctantly pulled back and tugged down her skirt.

"They do. You're sexy as fuck." His chest heaved, his eyes hot, the bulge in his jeans betraying his need. "Benson I can handle. Mad Dog, too. Banks might be a problem. He took down six men in less than three minutes when Jagger decided to bring him to the clubhouse for questioning. Might just have to shoot him."

Her lips turned up in a bemused smile. "I'd appreciate it if you didn't. You've already put one of my jobs at risk."

Cade made a quick self-adjustment and then nodded

for her to open the door. "Won't shoot him unless he touches you."

"Much obliged."

He brushed his knuckles lightly over her cheek. "Still wanna fuck you."

"I get off at midnight."

★ EIGHT ★

I will never dishonor my colors.
SINNER'S TRIBE CREED

Jesus. Fucking. Christ. Cade shot back his bourbon and closed his eyes as the thick, sweet liquid burned its way down his throat. What the hell was wrong with him?

If Banks hadn't knocked on the door, he would have taken her in the restroom. Over the sink. Her hair twisted around his hand, back arched, legs wide as he plunged his cock deep into her hot, wet pussy.

Only Dawn could push the demons away. He'd never felt a connection with anyone in his life, but during the two nights he'd spent with her, he'd felt no pain, suffered no flashbacks. He had wanted those nights to go on forever, and when she left him, he hadn't been able to shake the memories. He'd imprinted. Like a goddamn newborn chick.

He watched her work her way through the bar, the grace of her movements, the ring of her laughter, the brightness of her smile marred by the fading bruises on her face. He imagined his hands on her ass, his fingers in her hair, his mouth on her soft lips, his cock inside her slick, wet heat. He liked her compassion, her sass and directness. When she was annoyed, she let him know it, and damn she'd been pissed about Delilah.

Christ, he'd liked that little flare of jealousy. Her indignant sniff and the flush in her cheeks were the only things that told him he wasn't wasting his time. Everything about Dawn screamed sex, but there was something more that kept bringing him back. He'd never been so inexplicably drawn to a woman in his life.

Apparently the bunch of losers in the corner felt the same. They'd been harassing her all evening, but the bouncer kept them in line. Now, however, the bouncer was occupied with a belligerent drunk and one of the biker wannabes was trying to pull Dawn onto his lap.

Cade shoved back his chair and stalked across the bar, knocking tables and the odd person out of his way. Dawn struggled in her captor's grasp, then jabbed him hard in the ribs with her elbow. The dude bent over and she spun around and clipped him a good one in the chin. Damn fine woman could look after herself, but the dude's friends didn't look so happy. Time to make sure they got the message the party was over.

But before he reached the table, a black blur shot in front of him and Deputy fucking Benson stole the show.

"I suggest you keep your hands to yourself." Benson put one protective arm around Dawn and pulled his fucking shiny sheriff badge from his pocket. The dude Cade had intended to pound into the floor paled.

"Didn't mean anything by it, Officer. Just joking around."

"Good to hear." Benson tucked away his badge., "But I suggest you move on. There are real bikers in this bar who might not take kindly to you playing dress-up." He nodded to Cade, but Cade wasn't interested in playing the game. Not while Benson had his hands on Dawn.

"Let her go, Benson. Dawn had this fight."

"She was in danger. Someone needed to step in and save her."

"I deal with this all the time." Dawn struggled to free herself from Benson's tight grip. "There's no need for them to leave. I can handle guys like this." But Benson wasn't listening. His hand tightened around her shoulders and he glared at the miscreants.

"Go."

The wannabe bikers threw some money on the table and raced out of the bar.

A sliver of annoyance slid through Cade's chest. Earlier this week, he'd thought Benson wasn't a threat, but now he saw him in a totally different light. He wanted what Cade wanted. He'd come to the bar to make his move while Cade had been getting drunk and squeezing tail at Peelers.

"She's fine, Benson. Get your paws off her. Last thing she needs is more of the same."

"You okay, Dawn?" The soft murmur of Benson's voice grated on Cade's already taut nerves, but not as much as his fingers stroking her neck.

Cade's body reacted before his mind had processed what he was about to do. One minute he was standing beside Dawn, the next he had Benson up against the wall, his hand pressed against Benson's chest. The depth of his fury shocked even him. "Thought I told you to let her go."

"Cade. Stop." Dawn's voice barely registered through the pounding of blood in his ears. "You're doing exactly what you just told him not to do." Dawn stepped between Cade and Benson, her head barely reaching Cade's outstretched arm.

Benson met his gaze, his direct stare raising Cade's hackles and loosening the last threads of his self-restraint.

"You don't want to do this, honey."

"Outta the way, babe, or you're gonna get hurt." Cade tried to maintain his resolve, but it was damn hard with the scent of her perfume surrounding him, the soft brush of her hair against his skin, and when she wrapped her arms around his waist and pushed him back, he couldn't hold on.

"Fuck. Dawn. Stop."

But she didn't stop. And even though he could have easily pushed her aside, he let her back him up until five feet separated him and Benson.

She looked up and glared, her beautiful face doing strange things to his stomach. For a moment he lost himself in her gaze, perversely pleased that she was here and not five feet away. She'd put her arms around him. Not Benson. She'd determined *he* was the bigger threat. Not Benson. And now she was looking up at him with those big liquid eyes and all he could think about was kissing her soft lips.

"You don't have to solve every problem with violence," she said softly. "I can't go down that road again."

"You don't have to." He bent down to kiss her.

She turned her head so his lips brushed over her cheek. "I like that you let me handle this myself. I liked knowing you were there as backup. Don't ruin it by playing into Doug's hands. He wants to arrest you. Don't give him an excuse. I'm safe. Isn't that all that matters?"

Cade looked up and stared at Benson. The deputy was leaning against the wall, arms folded, the faintest smirk playing out on his lips. Cade needed to hit something. Benson's face being the most desirable target. Sensing Dawn might not be pleased, he smashed his fist into a table instead, his anger dissipating as the legs cracked and the table tipped sideways toward the floor.

"Tsk. Tsk. Destruction of property." Benson's voice was

laced with amusement. "Maybe you should cool your heels down at the station."

"Doug." Dawn looked over at Benson and scowled. "Don't make it worse.

"And you . . ." She poked Cade in the chest and lowered her voice so only he could hear. "I told you to let it go."

"Dawn."

She looked up when his voice cracked, and her face softened. Pressing herself against him, she wrapped her arms around his chest and gave him a hug.

"Must have been a really bad week."

And it just had gotten worse. What the hell was he doing? Leaving his brothers at Peelers? Walking away from Delilah? Fighting over a woman? Women fought over him. And assaulting a police officer? No doubt Arianne had seen what he'd done and would report back to Jagger. Not that he was afraid of Jagger, but he structured his life so he was rarely in a situation where he could lose control.

He needed to get away from here. Clear his head. These confusing feelings he had weren't rational. This wasn't him. After growing up in a household where he could only sit by and watch his mom suffer, control was of the utmost importance to him, and right now it was slipping away. "I gotta go." He pulled away and caught Benson studying them with interest. Their gazes met, locked, and then Benson dropped his eyes.

Primal satisfaction flared in Cade's chest.

Mine.

And then he turned and walked away.

Not Benson.

"I hate her." Dawn screamed and threw her phone across her living room. In an incredible show of agility, Arianne leaped over the coffee table and caught the phone before it hit the wall.

"What did she say?" Arianne stumbled to a stop and then fell heavily on the couch, her chest heaving.

"She won't bring the girls because I don't have the extra money. She says it's not worth her time. The court order gives me three hours with them every Sunday. I can call social services, but she'll just make something up about how she brought them here and I was high and she was afraid to leave the girls. She did it once before, and because of that damn court decision the people at social services believed her over me."

"I can vouch for you." Arianne thumped her boots on Dawn's coffee table. "I'll tell them she didn't even bother to show. I'll even put on civilian clothes so I look civilized."

Dawn scrubbed her hands over her face. "Thanks, but by the time we jump through all the bureaucratic hoops, it'll be too late. I tried calling my lawyer last time and we didn't get an emergency court hearing until Monday morning. It was a waste of time and the legal fees almost broke me."

"That's one of the things I like about the outlaw life," Arianne said. "No hoops to jump through. You want something, you take it, and fuck everyone else."

"The girls will be so upset." Dawn sat on the couch beside Arianne. "I'm so worried about them. Especially Tia. She's withdrawn so much since they moved in with Shelly-Ann. She just watches and lets the world pass her by. Maia's more resilient. She gets hurt, and then she moves on. And they're both still wary of men, especially bikers. Well, except Cade. He made quite an impression. Tia called me every night last week to ask if he was going to be at the park again today. It breaks my heart that the one man she wants to see is the kind of man we don't need in our lives, and someone who doesn't want to get involved."

Arianne frowned. "You went on a high-speed chase with him down the highway and had sex in the parking lot. He hunted you down at Banks Bar and dragged you into the restroom for some more kinky loving. Sounds pretty involved to me."

"Then he left. Walked out of the bar. No good-bye. No explanation. Nothing until morning when he sent a text saying he was in Whitefish on a job, and he'd sent the prospect to watch out for me while he was away." She took her phone from Arianne and flicked to Cade's text. Brief. Abrupt. To the point. No hint of warmth or intimacy. "I don't know where I stand. Is this just sex or something more? If it is, I'm good with that, but then why send the prospect and why all the posturing around Doug?"

"What are you saying? You'd rather be with someone like Doug?"

Dawn's lips twisted to the side. Doug was honest, stable, and kind, although a little intense about his work. So why hadn't her knees gone weak or her heart pounded when he came into the bar? Why had her gaze locked on Cade when the biker wannabes started causing trouble?

"And there's our answer," Arianne said into the silence. "The good girls always want the bad boys."

"I'm not that good." After running away from her abusive uncle only a year after her parents died, Dawn had done what it took to survive on the streets. She had never shared the details of those years with anyone. And she never would.

"You're better than me," Arianne said. "Although I heard about your MMA TV marathons with Banks, and how you're the one shouting for blood. You don't like violence but you're attracted to violent men. No wonder you and Cade got together."

Not that it mattered. Whatever had happened at the bar had put a stop to the runaway roller coaster she and Cade had been riding since they'd met again.

Which was a good thing.

So why did she feel so bad?

"So, what about a plan for seeing your girls?" Arianne stood and walked over to the window. Dawn could see the glint of the prospect's bike out front, an ancient Harley Classic that was far too big for him but screamed old-school biker.

"What can I do? Nothing. That's what." She grabbed the bag of cheesy puffs she'd bought for the girls and ripped it open. No better balm for her sorrow than a kilo of cheese-covered corn snacks. And she had a tub of Crunchy Caramel Cookie ice cream in the freezer . . .

"Thought you were a fighter."

"I am a fighter." She offered Arianne the bag, but as always Arianne passed on the unhealthy treats. So irritating. Her bestie didn't drown her sorrows in junk food, preferring instead to go running, or cycling, or sprint up a mountain in her bare feet with one hand tied behind her back, which was why she wasn't packing any extra pounds. Maybe Dawn should do the same. Or maybe she should stick her hand in the garbage disposal, because the pain would be same.

"But this is one fight I don't think I can win. I'm doing everything I can to get the girls back, but every week she asks for more money. I talked to my lawyer and the social worker, even Doug, but without proof there is nothing they can do."

"Dammit, Dawn. She's holding your girls for ransom."

Ransom. The word echoed in her mind. Shelly-Ann was

holding her girls for ransom. She couldn't just sit here and do nothing. Dawn tossed the cheesy puff bag on the table. "I'm going to call Doug."

"Look around you." Arianne unsheathed her weapon and placed it on the table. "You might be confused about what's going on between you and Cade, but he's not. The prospect wouldn't be out there if you didn't mean something to him. And although I'm your bestie, and I was coming over here anyway to see the girls and get a sparkly princess pink manicure so Jagger could laugh at me at the shooting range, Cade asked me to swing by, too. Take advantage. Pretend you're a Sinner. Dig deep and find the strength I know you have to take what you want. Then let's go get your girls."

"Open this door, Shelly-Ann." Dawn thudded her fist on the door to Shelly-Ann's brand-new, sprawling ranch home, tucked away at the back of Conundrum's Bow Creek Estates. She doubted Shelly-Ann's ritzy neighbors had ever seen an outlaw biker, but once she'd made the decision to confront Shelly-Ann, it was a matter of go big or go home, and why show up with one outlaw biker when she could show up with two?

"I know you're in there. I saw you through the window."

"Get lost," Shelly-Ann's voice crackled over the intercom. "The girls aren't here and I got company unless you're standing on my doorstep with two thousand dollars. Then I might come out and say hello."

Dawn looked over her shoulder at the prospect, standing guard behind her while Arianne plucked petals off a begonia in Shelly-Ann's flower box. Damned if he wasn't the most gorgeous man she'd ever laid eyes on, aside from Cade. With that thick dark hair, lean frame, and chiseled jaw, he could have graced any runway. Instead he'd chosen the outlaw life, and from the uneasy way he wore his cut, he was still growing into it.

"You got a name, prospect?" She'd waved to him from the back of Arianne's bike before they headed out to Cindy's Florals where her boss had kindly given her an advance on her salary, but she hadn't had a chance to talk to him until now.

"Nick. But I haven't earned a road name yet, and Jagger doesn't trust me so everyone calls me Prospect."

"Nice to meet you, Nick. Could you please open the door?" She glanced over at Arianne, still unsure about how far she could push the prospect around. After all, she was still a civilian.

"Old ladies don't say please," Arianne whispered.

"I'm not an old lady," Dawn whispered back.

"Prospect," Arianne barked. "Open the damn door."

Nick ran forward, bent at the waist, and hit the door with his shoulder. He staggered back from the impact, and tried kicking at it instead, a totally ineffectual move that brought a smile to Dawn's lips. Prospects. They were all the same.

Arianne pulled the last petal off the begonia, then pulled out her weapon and screwed a silencer onto the barrel. "Men." She sighed and motioned Nick back, then fired at the lock until the wood cracked. "They always have to do things the hard way."

"She scares me," Nick said quietly as he followed Dawn into Shelly-Ann's house. "Never met a woman like her. Not even sure she is a woman."

"I hope you're saying nice things about me," Arianne called out. "I'm in a good mood right now, but I promise you wouldn't want to see me riled."

Dawn walked down the polished, dark wood hallway; past gilt mirrors and painted alcoves containing vases of silk flowers; and into the expansive living room, decorated in dark brown and cream, with floor-to-ceiling windows overlooking the Trecher Valley. Two men in suits were loading Baggies containing white powder into a suitcase from a box on the coffee table, while Shelly-Ann lounged on the couch watching them. Sunlight glinted off the sparkly purple heart stickers decorating each bag—a common indicator of low to mid-end product—and Dawn blinked as her eyes adjusted to the light.

"My next clients are here, boys. Hurry it up please."

"You're selling drugs with my children in your house?" Dawn's voice rose in pitch, and one of the men frowned.

"Thought you said they were clients."

"Thought you said you didn't want anyone to know which senator you work for," Shelly-Ann shot back. "Take your quarters and go."

The two men shared a glance, and the one who had spoken snapped the suitcase closed. Dawn waited until they left the room before she spoke again.

"Where are Maia and Tia?"

"Not here. I hired a babysitter to look after them for the day. Didn't want them to get the wrong idea when they saw the stickers." Shelly-Ann leaned back on the white leather couch and rolled her eyes. "So what is this? You got some new friends? We gonna have a party? Or did you come for your weekly fix?" She gestured to the box on the table and bile rose in Dawn's throat.

"You know I don't do drugs."

Shelly-Ann fixed her gaze on Arianne and Nick. "Did she tell you she's a little crack whore? She was a crack whore when she was with Jimmy, and she just couldn't shake the habit after she left. She got caught buying drugs behind the school and made up a story about Jimmy setting her up. Of course no one bought it. That's how she lost her kids."

Dawn's body trembled and she fisted her hands by her sides. Jimmy had tried to get her addicted to crack when she first moved in with him, but she'd resisted, terrified that if she didn't keep her wits about her, he'd beat her to death. "That's a lie and you know it."

"Is it? Tall, dark, and handsome isn't too sure."

Dawn looked back at Nick, her heart sinking when he averted his gaze. "It's not true."

"We know that," Arianne said. "She's just trying to wind you up. Don't play her game."

"So you got my money?" Shelly-Ann stood and held out her hand. "No money means no kids. No money means I call the cops and report a break-in and a breach of the custody order. No money means Jimmy hears about your visit."

"No money beyond what we originally agreed." Dawn's voice wavered with emotion. "I'm tired of playing this game. I'm tired of having you use my children to blackmail me. I don't know why you need so much money, and frankly, I don't care. Now tell me where they are."

"Or what?" Shelly-Ann's face twisted in anger. "You think I'm afraid of you? You think I'm gonna break 'cause you showed up with a damn prospect and a Sinner old lady? I don't think so. You don't have what it takes, or you woulda done something long ago."

"I did do something." Dawn dug her nails into her palms, wishing for the first time in her life that she was the kind of person who could solve problems with her fists. "I started a lawsuit, and I've just filed an assault complaint. I'll drag Jimmy through the courts until I get my girls back."

" 'Cause using the legal system worked out so well for you last time." Shelly-Ann sneered. "Get the fuck outta here and stop wasting my time."

"Here." Dawn pulled a handful of cash from her purse. "I've got twelve hundred."

Shelly-Ann crossed the room and snatched the money. "It's not enough."

"Don't give her any more." Arianne put a cautioning hand on Dawn's arm. "I know her type. It will never be enough. The blackmail will never end."

Which was exactly what had happened last week, but what choice did she have? Sure it was nice to have Arianne and Nick here, but she wasn't about to ask them to beat up Shelly-Ann, or even threaten her, and she'd never hit anyone in her life. Shelly-Ann had effectively called her bluff, leaving her with no choice but to pay her off.

"How much?" Cade's growl reverberated through the room, so rough and harsh, even Dawn trembled. For the first time since Dawn arrived, fear flickered across Shelly-Ann's face.

"Where did you come from?" Dawn gave him a puzzled frown. "I thought you were on the road."

"The prospect texted me just as we were leaving. He thought I might want to know you and Arianne were planning to bust your girls outta Shelly-Ann's jail. I figured you might need some help, and the door was open. Looks like Arianne's handiwork. No one can shoot up a lock like her."

"Thank you." Arianne gave a mock bow.

"Thor to the rescue." Shelly-Ann snorted. "Where's your hammer? Oh. I forgot. You don't need one. You prefer to kill men with your bare hands."

"What's she talking about?"

"How much?" Cade said to Shelly-Ann, pointedly ignoring Dawn's question.

"She owes me another eight hundred."

Cade pulled out his wallet and counted eight hundred

dollars into Dawn's hand. "Your choice, sweetheart. You can pay her, or you can walk out of here and leave her to me."

"Hey." Arianne gave an indignant sniff. "I was here first. If anyone gets to throw a few punches at Shelly-Ann it's me, and only if Dawn doesn't want to do it first."

Dawn stared at Shelly-Ann, considering. But how could she inflict violence on someone after what she'd suffered at Jimmy's hands? She hated Shelly-Ann, but she couldn't physically hurt her, and she couldn't ask anyone else to do it. "I'll pay her."

"Good call," Shelly-Ann let out a breath. "Didn't think you were the type who could live with blood on her hands. Thor, on the other hand, probably went drinking with his brothers after killing Rusty the other night." She scrawled the babysitter's address on a piece of paper and handed it to Dawn.

"You killed Rusty?" Dawn whirled around and stared at Cade aghast. She remembered Rusty from her time in the Brethren—a tall, thin, redhead with a scraggly goatee, and one of Jimmy's closest friends.

"Club business."

"Club business is the same in every club," Shelly-Ann said bitterly. "It's all about blood and pain. And bikers are the same wherever you go. Does your man beat you like Jimmy did? 'Cause from what I saw there's not much difference between them."

Dawn's mouth opened and then closed again. Why was she so surprised? The Sinners were outlaw bikers. They would do anything for their club—even if it meant taking a life. Cade was the Sinner treasurer and one of Jagger's right-hand men, positions that had to be earned by proving yourself in the MC. Plus, Rusty had been part of the gang that had kidnapped and beaten Cade. He would have known justice was coming . . .

Still, she couldn't shake the niggle of doubt Shelly-Ann had planted in her mind. Cade was a violent man. Just like Jimmy. And what if that violence spilled over to her?

★ NINE ★

I will follow the creed before I follow my heart.

SINNER'S TRIBE CREED

The Whitefish trip wasn't going as planned.

Although Cade had initially been glad to take off with Zane and the prospect right after the altercation with Shelly-Ann, he couldn't get Dawn's shocked expression out of his mind. Not during the spectacular three-hour drive through the mountains. Not when their new prospect had to keep pulling the cage off the road because every damn cop seemed to be on the lookout for black SUVs. And especially not when they arrived at the house of the Brethren's weapons broker and found him dead.

"Well, damn."

From the state of the poor bastard's body, and the pungent smell of rotting flesh, the broker had been dead for a while, and from the fact his body was untouched, no one really cared.

"His guards are out here," the prospect called. "They're dead, too. Looks like there was a gunfight."

"Weapons are missing from the shed," Zane called out. "I'll text Jagger and let him know. My guess is they were taken weeks ago."

Could this day get any worse? Dawn had acted almost as if she were afraid of him outside Shelly-Ann's house, and yet he'd exercised almost unbelievable restraint when he'd let Shelly-Ann off with only a warning. And what did she expect? That he'd slap Rusty on the wrist and tell him not to do it again? Dawn had been part of this world. She knew how it operated. She knew he might have had to take a life. Or eight. But only to protect his brothers. And now they were short the weapons they needed to launch an offensive against the Jacks.

Cade did a walk around the small, isolated, villa-style house that had served as the broker's base. But other than the four dead guards, and two whining pups, he saw nothing that would give a clue as to who might have stolen the weapons.

He fed the dogs and filled their water bowls, then went in search of the prospect. Damn, he couldn't remember the dude's name. Of all the prospects they'd had over the years, the quiet, geeky, pretty boy with blazing green eyes and sharp features had to be the least likely prospect ever to want to be patched into the club. But he was a tech genius, and could fill a gap in the club's knowledge base that was getting larger by the day.

He found the prospect throwing up in the bathroom with Zane looking on in disgust.

"Why the hell did you bring him?"

"Prospects need to learn," Cade said. "Plus there was no way I was driving the damn cage and I knew you wouldn't volunteer." Brothers rarely drove in vehicles when they could ride their bikes, leaving the cage driving to old ladies, prospects, and junior patch.

"That prospect can't learn dick." Zane turned and Cade followed him from the bathroom to the small patio out back.

"What did Jagger say?"

"He wants us to go see Demon Spawn. Hard to believe five men were shot on their turf and they didn't know anything about it."

While Zane checked the rest of the house, Cade went to get the prospect, now pale and pasty after losing his lunch. "Ready to go?"

"We should take his tech." The prospect pointed to a computer as they walked through the house. "Might be a clue in his computer or phone about who took him and his men out."

"Take what you need," Cade said. "And then put the dogs in the truck. We'll drop them at the shelter."

"Christ. They're just dogs." Zane gave an exasperated sigh. "They got the sense to run away."

"They're pups and they didn't have the sense to run away from a house full of dead bodies." Cade whistled for the dogs. "And why not help them find a home instead of letting them run loose on the streets?"

He had a soft spot for strays. Selma, the golden Lab, who had been his comfort and constant companion since he was four years old, had wandered into his yard one evening and never left. He had been shocked his dad allowed the dog to stay, but Selma was smart enough to understand his father's insecurities. Loyalty was the way to win his affection. Whenever Cade's father was home, Selma never left his side, but Cade always knew he had her heart.

After dropping off the pups, they arranged to meet up with Matchstick, president of Demon Spawn, and some of the club members at a bar in town. Demon Spawn had been forced into their role as a Sinner support club, which meant all meetings had to be public in case resentment got out of hand.

By the time they reached the bar, Cade was ready for

some serious distraction. Smelling of JD and tobacco and made up to look like an old western saloon with some scratchy Bob Seger on the jukebox, the bar was the perfect place to relax. Matchstick, a Zane look-alike with dark skin, dark hair, and brooding looks, brought two sweet butts and a pitcher of beer to their booth, and Cade settled down for what promised to be a much better evening than he'd expected.

A blonde with short, curly hair immediately slid onto his lap. The other girl, a petite brunette, took the seat next to Zane. Usually Zane sent the girls away, but they were gifts from the host MC and asking them to leave was the ultimate in disrespect.

"Don't know much about that broker," Matchstick said after they'd dispensed with the pleasantries and turned to business. "He usually kept to himself."

"Hard to believe a major arms dealer was shot in your territory along with four of his men and you didn't know anything about it." Zane toyed with his glass, his free hand under the table, no doubt within easy reach of his weapon.

"We're a support club, not a fucking babysitting service."

Zane withdrew his weapon and placed it on the table. "Maybe you don't understand the role of a support club."

"I'm sure he does." Cade put a warning hand on Zane's arm. "I think it was just a poor choice of words. He knows what would happen if Jagger had to send up some of our brothers to remind him that we tolerate Demon Spawn's presence only as long as they remain loyal."

"Yeah, that's right. Poor choice of words." Matchstick ordered a bottle of whiskey on the house and then waved over his old lady, a statuesque blonde with fake tits and an orange tan.

"You want her for the night, Cade? I heard you appreciate a fine piece of pussy."

Christ. His reputation preceded him, even up north. Usually, he would have laughed and made a joke, then accepted the offer, but tonight the reminder grated on his nerves. "Appreciated, but I got this little sweet butt in my lap to keep me busy . . . and a girl at home." He squeezed the girl's ass and made her squeal, cutting off Zane's snort of disbelief.

Matchstick apologized again and excused himself to take a call. His VP, Skid Mark, a short, stocky man with a military buzz cut, took his seat and they segued into a conversation about the arms trade up north. But Cade felt a growing sense of unease. Whether it was the way some Demon Spawn brothers kept looking at them or the VP's slightly off manner, Cade's instincts were blasting a warning at full volume.

The blonde nuzzled his neck and Cade tensed. He'd almost forgotten about the sweet butt in his lap. Her hair wasn't soft or curly like Dawn's hair, and he was damn sure that color wasn't real. He picked up his phone and sent a quick text to Jagger expressing his concerns about Demon Spawn, then flicked to Dawn's number. He liked seeing her name in his address book. What she was doing right now?

Zane and Skid Mark were deep in conversation, and the girls were talking to each other. A quick glance around the bar assured him nothing was obviously wrong. Why not send a quick text and find out what the hell was going on?

Hey

He couldn't think of any better way to start so he pressed SEND and drank his beer as he waited.

Hey yourself

Hmmm. No humor in her tone, but at least she'd texted back.

U working tonight?
Took the night off to spend with the girls. Just dropped them off. U back from Whitefish?
Still here
Nice place 2 be working
Not nice work 2 be doing. What r u doing on ur night off? ?
Fixing the sink
My kind of woman
Not so sure about that. You alone?
At a bar with a local MC
Another strip bar?

Fuck. Why hadn't he lied when she asked him about Peelers? He wanted her to forget he'd gone there. Ever. He wanted her to forget the rumors about him. He wanted her to trust him, but how could he expect trust from her when he couldn't even trust himself?

Just a bar
They give you a sweet butt?

Ah. Of course she would know what went on when bikers visited another club. He should lie this time. Zane wouldn't tell her what was going on, and the truth would just reinforce in her mind that he was exactly the kind of man she thought he was.

And she would be right.

"Hey brother." Zane leaned across the table and tapped

a spoon on Cade's glass. "Skid Mark asked you a question about passenger pegs. Wake the fuck up."

The blonde looked down at the phone and laughed. "He's busy texting Dawn."

"Jesus Christ." Cade pushed her off his lap. "You don't look at a man's phone."

"But you can text one woman while you've got another on your lap?" Zane refilled Skid Mark's glass from the pitcher on the table. "Cade's got a way with the ladies. A good way. No relationships. No complications. No women making promises they can't keep. No shattered dreams or promises. No betrayals or jumping into bed with the first bastard who knocks on the door. He's got it right. Women can't be trusted. Not to keep the faith. Not to hold true. Not to respect a man's soul." He thudded his fist on the table and the woman beside him beat a hasty retreat, pulling the blonde with her.

"Whoa, brother." Cade held up a hand. "Maybe you've had one too many. You wanna step outside for some fresh air?"

Zane nodded and they excused themselves from the table and walked out into the night.

"What the hell did that bitch do to you?" Cade asked as soon as the door closed behind them.

"Nothing I want to talk about." Zane kicked at a stone and then leaned against a pillar, his arms folded. "It was a very long time ago, like when Jagger and I were kids long."

"Well, you scared those girls pretty good, so it looks like neither of us is gonna have a good night. You wanna go back to the motel? Something felt off in that bar."

"Thought it was just me," Zane said. "Didn't like the way they were watching us. I'm thinking we should head back home tonight. Not keen on having my throat slit while I'm sleeping."

After texting the prospect to meet them outside the hotel, they walked down the main street, and then turned up an alley. The air had cooled rapidly since the sun set, and Cade's skin prickled despite the hoodie he wore over his T-shirt.

Or maybe it wasn't the cold.

Too late he heeded the warning. Gravel crunched behind them, and two men stepped into the alley from the road ahead.

"Two behind us," Zane murmured, half turning.

"Son of a bitch." Cade drew his weapon as the two men in front walked toward them. "It's Mad Dog. What the fuck is he doing here? And with Matchstick?"

"Maybe he came to help us load the missing weapons." Zane drew his weapon and positioned himself to cover Cade's back.

"Maybe he's tired of living and came here to find me 'cause I'll be happy to take care of that problem for him tonight."

"Jagger gave his word. He's untouchable."

Cade's lips pressed into a thin line, his body tense and thrumming with energy as the enemy approached. "I'm beginning to regret that decision. You shoulda seen what he did to Dawn's face."

"I saw what he did to your tat." He glanced over his shoulder at Cade. "Noted that you weren't enjoying Demon Spawn's hospitality."

"Nope."

"So . . . you and Dawn . . . there's more than just the usual one-night stand?"

Christ. Of all people to call him out, it had to be Zane. The dark horse. The man who'd been burned by a woman so bad, he kept all women at bay. But what the hell. Even if they made it out of this ambush alive, it wasn't like Zane was going to tell anyone. The dude had no close friends except Jagger and, except for tonight's outburst, he rarely talked to the brothers.

"Yeah. Maybe. I dunno. Never met a woman who's gone through so much shit and come out of it so soft and sweet. But she's a fighter. No matter what Mad Dog throws at her, she meets it head-on."

A smile played about Zane's lips. A fucking smile. Cade had never seen Zane smile. He looked almost . . . normal.

"I might just be looking the other way if something happens to Mad Dog. Man's gotta protect what's his."

He almost couldn't believe the words he'd just heard. Zane? On his side? And because he thought Cade and Dawn were tight?

"You looking the other way now?"

"I am indeed."

Dawn felt like a human sacrifice. Summoned to the Sinner clubhouse to meet Cade when he returned from Whitefish, she had dressed in her favorite red, stretch knit dress, added a pair of killer heels and prepped like she was going out for a night on the town. Sexy and sophisticated, her dress had a fitted bodice with a deep V neckline, an open back with double straps, and a fitted midi-length skirt that hugged her curves. He wanted to see her; then he would see her. And after she told him just what she thought of his evenings full of blood, strippers, sex and sweet butts, she'd take the damn welcome out the door. He'd had one free pass. He didn't get another.

Yesterday had been a brutal reminder of the violence and misogyny inherent in the one-percenter lifestyle. And yet she couldn't reconcile the man who had allegedly killed Rusty and spent the night with a Demon Spawn sweet butt with the man who had pushed her children on the swings and done so much to protect her. So she'd come to the clubhouse to assure herself she wasn't making a mistake, to end it before she became emotionally entangled with the wrong kind of guy. But damned if she wouldn't give him something to remember her by.

"Smile. You look like you're at a funeral." Arianne jabbed her in the side and Dawn shifted along the worn, brown couch.

"I am. My funeral." She lowered her voice so only Arianne could hear. "How awkward is this going to be? I don't even know why he asked me to be here. Maybe he just wants to tell me it's over, which would save me from having to do it. Or maybe he just wants someone to warm his bed now that he's finished with his Demon Spawn sweet butt. He wasn't ashamed or even apologetic. He didn't even bother to answer my text last night until an hour later, and only then to ask what I was wearing. Like he'd done her and was ready for more. I believed him last time about Peelers, but this is too much."

"What happens on the road . . ." Arianne turned up the volume of the crime show they'd been watching, sufficiently violent to keep T-Rex and Tank entertained, but not violent enough for Dax or Bandit who were throwing darts at the far side of the living room . . . at each other.

"Stays on the road," Tank said with a grin. The heavily built junior patch could have been T-Rex's dark-haired twin. He had the same build and easygoing nature, although he didn't seem too bright.

Tanya, the house mama, looked over from her seat beside Dawn and scowled. "Stupid rule. If you ask me, it's just a license for men to sleep around." She brushed back her sleek chestnut bob, and Dawn felt a stab of jealousy. Even her stylist, Kitty, couldn't fight Dawn's curls, and had suggested wigs as a preferable disguise for her secret before- and after-school visits.

"We all know you're hot for the new prospect, and

you're wondering if he enjoyed some Demon Spawn hospitality up in Whitefish," Tank said.

"If I was his old lady and he did, it would be . . ." Tanya drew her finger across her throat and Dawn laughed.

"I'm with you there, except I told Cade I would use a gun on certain delicate parts of his anatomy."

"You can hurt a man worse by breaking his heart," T-Rex said. "We're not made of stone. Take Zane, for example. He was hurt so bad, he can't even look at a woman."

"He doesn't have a heart." Tank snorted a laugh. "It was ripped out, rubbed in salt, stomped on . . ."

Laughter rang out around them as the brothers shared their impressions of Zane muttering about the inconstancy of women.

"We need to get him out to a strip bar," Tank said. "He doesn't even go to Peelers and Cade's got a table—"

T-Rex cut him off with a sharp, indiscreet jab to the ribs, but Dawn forced a laugh.

"I know about Peelers. And was thinking I might get some of the ladies to join me over at Lucky Larry's on Thursday nights. They have free booze and male strippers, and for an extra twenty dollars we get a private dance."

"I'm in." Arianne licked her lips and grinned. "I wonder what Jagger will do."

But her smile faded when Cade staggered into the room, his face bruised and bloody, and his shirt torn.

"What happened to you?" she said.

"Ambush. But we managed to take a prisoner. Zane's locking him up downstairs." His gaze flicked to Dawn and his mouth tightened. Aside from the fact he'd been badly beaten, Dawn could tell right away he'd overheard the conversation, and he wasn't pleased. The cords in his neck were standing in sharp relief, and he looked like he wanted to punch someone.

She hoped it wasn't her.

"You're here." His voice cracked and in that moment she knew this wasn't meant to be a good-bye. But knowing where he'd spent the night, she wasn't about to jump into his arms.

"You summoned me so nicely, I couldn't say no."

Seemingly oblivious to her sarcasm, he gave an almost imperceptible nod and then his face tightened. "No strippers."

Dawn swallowed hard. Well versed in biker politics, she knew she couldn't challenge him in front of his brothers. Not even a lady could do that. But despite her lack of status, this was their first public interaction and everyone was watching. She couldn't disrespect him, but she didn't have to toe the line either, especially if this was their last time together. Arianne would never have tolerated Jagger sleeping with anyone else.

"I don't go to watch. I'm just there to drink and talk with the girls." She threw his words back at him, then stood and closed the distance between them, working her dress like she just couldn't wait to get him into bed. "Watching all those sweaty, ripped guys, dancing and showing off their tackle, makes a girl all kinds of hot." She breathed out the last word and ran her hands along her curves, then looked up at him through the thicket of her lashes. "We wouldn't want that, now, would we?"

Cade's heated gaze drifted down her body, then up again. He licked his lips and beckoned her toward him, his voice dropping to a husky growl. "How hot?"

She slid one hand over her hip, her fingertips dangling suggestively over her mound, and trailed her free hand down the vee of her dress to the crescents of her breasts. "Ditch the panties and take care of business in the restroom hot."

Tank and T-Rex whooped in delight. Arianne snorted

a laugh. Cade choked back a grunt, and then his lips thinned. "You wanna go see strippers, I go with you."

"What are you going to do in a bar full of male strippers?" she teased, stopping close enough for him to appreciate the low-cut neckline, but not close enough for him to touch.

"I'm gonna be there to fucking take care of business." He reached for her and she turned out of his grasp, giving him a naughty glimpse of her bare back before facing him again.

"So does that mean when you go to Peelers, I can come, too?" She met his smoldering gaze and licked her lips. "Just in case there's business that needs to be taken care of?"

Cade growled low in his throat and then he pounced, yanking her against his chest. "You got business to take care of right fucking now."

Dawn pressed her hips against the bulge in his jeans. "If you're wanting something," she said softly, "and I feel you are, maybe you should have turned down the hospitality last night."

She heard murmurs of appreciation from behind her, male and female, and her lips quivered with a repressed smile. Damn this was fun, but she had a point to make, too. She might not be an old lady, but she wasn't a sweet butt, either, willing to sleep with any of the bikers in exchange for their protection and a place to stay. And if they were to have any sort of future together, which it sounded like he wanted, but which she still hadn't decided was a good idea, she wanted the kind of respect she hadn't had with Jimmy. And that respect wouldn't come if he thought it was okay to spend the night in another woman's bed.

Cade's arm tightened around her, almost cutting off her air. "What happens on the road, sweetheart . . ."

"Isn't anywhere near as good as what could have happened upstairs in your room, honey." She arched her back and hooked one arm around his neck, her breasts lifting for his viewing pleasure, and then she lowered her voice to a soft whisper only he could hear. "But maybe you weren't interested in seeing what's under this dress. I love lingerie, but some men just don't get off on red lace garter belts—"

"I didn't fucking touch her."

Yes!

"I'm happy to hear that." Dawn leaned up to kiss him, but as soon as her lips brushed over his, he lifted her and threw her over his shoulder.

"Time to take care of business."

★ TEN ★

I will give respect only if I get respect.

SINNER'S TRIBE CREED

"You don't go out without me. You do not go to see male strippers. You don't see other men. No clubs. No dates. No drinking. No Benson." Cade barked out each rule as he mounted the stairs leading up to his room. The chandelier overhead rattled with each step he took, but upside down, over his shoulder, the only thing Dawn was in a position to appreciate was the worn wooden floor, and Cade's very fine, tight ass.

He pushed open the door to his room, and then slammed it closed and dropped her lightly to the ground. "You answer the phone when I call or text. You don't hang with the brothers dressed in the kind of dress a man wants to tear off you."

Dawn gripped the door handle to regain her balance as Cade stalked across the floor to the window. The room pulsated with the intensity of his emotion, or maybe something was alive beneath the piles of clothes, pizza boxes, bike gear, and magazines. At least it didn't smell as bad as it looked, just a tad . . . fetid, but laced with the fragrance of his cologne.

"Don't you think you're taking this too far? I mean, Jimmy's not about to grab me from a bar or a club. At heart he's a coward. That's why he's always approached me in the dark or from a distance."

"This isn't about him." His puzzled frown almost made her laugh. "You're mine."

"I'm not yours." Dawn folded her arms. "But since we're laying it on the line, and if you're wanting me to stick around, I have terms, too. You don't go to strip clubs, even for a drink. Nor do you let sweet butts wriggle in your lap. You don't flirt with women or bring them back to the clubhouse. You're a one-woman man unless you want a woman who isn't me, and then I walk out this door."

Tension coiled in the room between them. He stared at her for so long she was afraid she'd crossed some hidden line and nothing would ever be the same again.

"I guess now that we have that straight, I'll take care of those cuts and bruises," she said to fill the silence. "You got a first-aid kit in here?" Her gaze swept over the room, bare of any decoration save for the detritus, a gritty contrast with the huge four-poster king-sized bed and heavy dark wood furniture, remnants from the days before the country house had become the Sinner clubhouse.

Cade scowled. "I'm not finished saying my piece."

Dawn wasn't sure she wanted to hear the rest of his "piece" if it involved any more one-sided rules and restrictions. She studied the room again for any sign of first-aid equipment, trying not to look at all the empty condom boxes or the shiny wrappers strewn across the floor or think about what they meant.

"I got something else to say." Cade's voice held an uncharacteristically sharp edge. "What are you looking at?"

Her cheeks heated and she scrambled for words. "Lots of . . . pizza boxes. What kind of pizza do you like?"

"Pizza?"

"I don't know that much about you. What kind of pizza do you like?"

"Meat."

She let out an exasperated sigh. "Can you be more specific? Pepperoni, sausage, ham, bacon—?"

"Just meat. Lots of it." His brow creased. "You?"

"I'm kinda into veggies. Not that I don't occasionally indulge in a Slim Fred's Meat Feast when I'm hanging with Banks at his place watching the fights, but usually I like to keep it healthy."

He lifted an eyebrow. "What else you want to know?"

Hmmm. A rare insight into Cade and what made him tick. She wanted to know everything, but from the way he was looking at her—focused, intent, like a predator sizing up its prey—she would have to be judicious with her questions. "Music."

"Mostly 'seventies legends like Bob Seger, Lynyrd Skynyrd, and the Allman Brothers and hard-rock bands like W.A.S.P. and Great White."

"Typical of a biker and not very revealing." Dawn sighed. "I don't suppose you harbor a secret love for Justin Bieber or Taylor Swift?"

Cade's nose wrinkled. "Girl crap. Don't listen to it."

"I like 'girl crap,' as you call it. I also like jazz."

"That's 'cause you're a girl."

"I'm a woman." She lifted an eyebrow in censure and he gave her a smoldering, sensual look that made her instantly wet.

"That I fucking know. And 'cause of that, there's no hanging out with Banks, 'cause he knows that, too." He crossed the floor toward her, eating up the distance between them with easy strides of his long legs. "You want to listen to girl crap and hang out and eat pizza, you do it with me. And forget the veg. How are you gonna keep those curves if you're just eating green shit?"

He was so close now she could feel the heat radiating off his body, breathe in his scent of leather, crisp spring air, and the sharp odor of blood. "You like my curves?"

"Love your curves, babe. Couldn't have made it through that fucking ambush if I didn't have these curves to think about."

Dawn took a step back, and then another. She hit the door and he slammed into her, momentum melding their bodies together, sparking a firestorm in her blood so hot she thought she might combust.

"Did you . . ." She shouldn't ask, but she couldn't help herself. "Kill anyone?"

Cade's face softened. "Club business, sweetheart. But I know this is something that bothers you so I'll let you know it's never easy taking a life. We do what we gotta do to protect the club. Rusty had a gun on Shaggy, so Shaggy lived and Rusty died. It wasn't meant to be that way, but that's the life we've chosen to live."

"It's a violent life."

"It's a life where I protect the people closest to me the best way I know how. Being part of the MC means I don't worry about rules or laws or orders when my brothers are at risk. It means I can do what needs to be done to protect what's mine. It means I can live a life without guilt or regret."

Cade wrapped his arms around her and pulled her into his chest. For a long time they stood in silence, hearts beating together, and then he brushed his lips over her forehead and pulled away.

"You okay with that?"

"I don't think I can handle it," she said. "I saw too many things when I was with the Brethren that still give me nightmares. I don't want to be part of that life, even if we're just hanging out and having a good time."

"What I do with the club doesn't come back on you, sweetheart." His voice tightened. "It doesn't touch you. And what Mad Dog did to you is not something I would ever do. Yeah, I may be violent, but it stops outside that door. I don't need to hit a woman to feel like a man. I don't get off on dominating a woman until there's nothing left but an empty shell. I am always in control."

Dawn released the breath she'd been holding. She hadn't realized just how much she needed his assurance. But more than that, he seemed to understand abuse at a fundamental level. Almost as if . . .

The door vibrated under the pounding of someone's fist. "Jagger wants to see you."

"Fuck off."

"He said now." She recognized Tank's voice and T-Rex's low chuckle. God, this was like being in high school all over again.

"I *said* fuck off."

"You busy in there, Cade?" Tank knocked again. "You need any help taking care of business?"

Hmmm. Not as busy as they should be. And since everyone already assumed they'd be at it by now, and she could see her way forward through the forest of the biker world, maybe they should get on with the program.

"You wanna lose a fucking hand?" Cade barked.

Dawn slid her hands under Cade's shirt and pushed it up and over his head, grimacing at the four white bandages on his pecs. She leaned forward and pressed her lips to his chest. His skin was warm and dry, tasting slightly salty, deliciously male.

She felt the low rumble of his pleasure at the juncture of her thighs and yanked open his jeans. Oh God. He'd gone commando. She wrapped her palm around his shaft and he let out a groan that made her mouth water. The floor outside the door creaked and footsteps faded down the hallway.

"Christ. I fucking ache for you." He hugged her face with his hands and took her mouth in a deep, hard kiss, almost violent in its intensity. Tongues tangled, teeth clashed. He devoured her mouth as if he'd been starving for her, giving her barely enough time to take a breath. He tasted of bourbon, and the thick, sweet taste sent her pulse skyrocketing, ripping a moan from her throat.

"Here I am." She dropped to her knees and wrapped her mouth around his shaft, just as she'd wanted to do when he'd been standing in her kitchen. Except this time his injuries weren't bad enough to keep her desire at bay.

Ah God. He wasn't going to be able to hold out for long. After letting her dance that little dance downstairs in her fucking sexy dress, and seeing the lines of worry disappear from her forehead after he gave her the assurance he wouldn't be taking his fists to her pretty face—his father's son he was not—he wanted nothing more than to bury his cock in her pussy and drown himself in her sweetness.

But damn her hot, wet little mouth was impossible to resist.

Cade slid a hand through Dawn's hair, pulling her forward until she took all of him in. "So fucking hot seeing you on your knees, those beautiful lips wrapped around my cock."

She pulled away and smiled. "So fucking hot doing what I wanted to do the last time I had you injured and at my mercy."

Cade bit his lip as she teased, licking and sucking his cock until he had to fight back the urge to pump into her mouth. In the distance he could hear the low murmur of voices, the rev of a motorbike, the rustle of leaves outside his window. In his ears he could hear the thud of his frantically pounding heart. He tasted his own blood on his tongue, and his fingers tightened in her hair.

"You keep teasing and it will be you begging for mercy."

"Naughty." She withdrew and gave him an admonishing look. "You should be nice when your girl has your cock in her mouth." She cupped his balls in one hand, squeezing gently while she flicked her tongue over the swollen head of his shaft. His hips jerked forward and his cock prodded at her lips.

"My girl." He liked the way it sounded. He'd never had a woman exclusively his. Never wanted one. Not since he'd left the military. But damn he wanted her, and not for just one night.

Dawn laughed and slid her hand between her legs, grinding her palm over her clit. "Maybe your girl will just take care of herself."

Cade's eyes locked on her hand, positioned exactly where he wanted his cock to go. "You want to touch yourself, you do it with no clothes on, and when I got a good view."

She leaned forward and took him deep while she tightened her hand around his cock, squeezing him so hard his eyes watered. "Is that a request?"

Cade's breaths came out faint and shallow. "It's me telling you how it is."

Flexing her fingers, she gripped the base of his shaft and worked her hand in counterpoint to her mouth. *God, so good.* But just when he felt the warning tingle in his spine, he gently pushed her away. After reassuring her that he was always in control, he couldn't let go now. Not only that, he wanted her pleasure. He wanted to hear her scream.

"Not like this." Cade pulled her up, and leaned down to kiss her as he straightened his clothing. "I wanna give it back to you."

He slid her dress over her lush hips then ran his finger along the lacy edge of her underwear. Red. Like she'd promised and she wore a matching garter belt, but no stockings. There was nothing Cade liked more on a woman than lacy lingerie. Maybe this time he'd exercise a little restraint.

"Cade . . ."

"Shhhh." He eased her panties down. But the second he caught sight of her golden curls, restraint went out the window. With a growl, he ripped the panties away.

"Beast. I'll need another job to pay for all the panties you destroy."

Cade knelt in front of her and nuzzled the soft down over her sex. "I'll buy you a truckload of panties if it means I can tear them away."

Her voice caught when he parted her legs. "You're not . . ."

"I am. Same as you did to me." He lifted her right leg, hooking it over his shoulder, then shifted until she was spread wide, bared for him.

Beautiful.

"Cade . . . I've never . . ." Her voice trailed off when he licked, his tongue parting her folds to dance over her clit. She gasped, and her hand tightened in his hair.

So sweet. He loved her taste. Could never get enough.

"Something about you . . ." he murmured. "Sexy and sweet, vulnerable but tough inside. Whenever I see you I want you. I have to have you, like I need air to breathe. And when I can't have you, I think about the next time I'll see you and how beautiful you look when you come."

His tongue slid up and around her clit, and then down through her folds, over and over again, until her body trembled and her nails dug into his scalp, sending jolts of painful pleasure down his spine. Even when she dug her heel into his back where the defiled tat still burned, he maintained the steady gentle rhythm, staying close, but not close enough to where she clearly wanted him to go.

"Give it to me, babe. I want to feel you come in my mouth." His blood streamed like lava through his veins and sweat trickled down his back. Every sensation heightened, the softness of her skin beneath his fingers, the cool air, the scent of her sex, her sweet slickness beneath his tongue . . .

"Cade." She breathed his name, cupped his head to hold him still. He knew exactly how far he could take her, just when to suck her clit, and when to hold back, keeping her on the edge. Moisture trickled down the inside of her thigh, and she finally let go, grinding her sex without abandon into his mouth.

So damn hot.

"Tell me what you need." He wanted to hear her need, feel her surrender.

"Make me come, Cade." She pulled him forward. "Make me come hard."

With a grunt of pleasure he cupped her ass in both hands then slid his tongue into her entrance.

"Oh God."

He plunged deeper, alternating thrusts with light flicks over her clit. She bucked against him, and then he nipped the swollen bud, ever so lightly. With a low, sensual groan, she came undone, rocking against his mouth, her knees trembling as he lapped up her sweetness. Then she released his hair and fell back against the door.

Worthy.

Cade stood and shoved down his clothing, freeing his erection. He didn't care if Jagger was waiting. Hell, Viper could show up and he wouldn't be able to stop himself. Grabbing a condom from his pocket, he sheathed himself and then cupped her ass in his palms. "Too fucking sexy, babe. Can't wait."

He lifted her to the bed, and then shoved down the top of her dress, exposing a red lace bra to match the panties he'd torn away. *Fucking divine.* Some night, when he wasn't so desperate to come, he'd get her to wear her lingerie and then strip for him so he could spend more time appreciating her beautiful curves. But not now.

Cade yanked down her bra and claimed one nipple, tugging into it his mouth, while he teased her other breast. He rolled her nipple between his teeth and gave a gentle nip, delighted when she gasped.

"Fuck me." Her plea turned into a growl of pleasure when he nipped again. God, he could play with her tits all night.

"Now."

"I got a bossy girl." Cade flipped her over to her hands and knees, and then tugged up her ass, pressing her legs apart with his knee. He smoothed his hands over her lush cheeks, and almost lost it right then. No more time to play. Without any warning, he shoved into her hard and fast, sliding deep through her wetness until she whimpered.

His brow creased. "You okay?"

"Hard, Cade. Fuck me, hard." She braced herself on the bed, spreading her legs to accommodate him. Then she gave him a wiggle.

Too much. Too hot. Too sexy.

With a grunt of pleasure, he hammered into her, his firm hands gripping her hips, holding her still. Her pussy tightened around him, and a moan ripped from his throat, and in that moment he was hers to command.

"More."

Cade shifted behind her, changing his angle so his cock hit her sensitive inner walls, driving her to come a second time. Again and again he hit that sweet spot, and then he reached around to stroke her clit. Dawn stiffened and climaxed again, her pussy clamping around him, pulling him over the edge.

"I'm coming, babe. Fuck. So good." Cade thrust deep and hard. His balls lifted, tightened. Then sensation exploded from his spine. His cock thickened and jerked inside her as he came in heated waves of pleasure.

He collapsed over her, brushing kisses over the soft skin on her neck, covering her with his body.

"You have no end of talents." Dawn looked back over her shoulder. "But I kinda liked being in charge."

"You weren't in charge. I was in charge."

Her lips quivered with a smile. "I let you be in charge."

He gave her that because she wanted it. But seriously, who did she think was running the show?

"Cade!"

Dawn startled awake when someone banged on the door. Cade jerked up beside her in the bed and stumbled to his feet.

"What the fuck?" he shouted.

"The Black Jacks are outside," Tank yelled. "They've taken out the guards. They're trying to burn down the clubhouse."

They dressed quickly and Cade yanked open door.

"Where's Jagger?"

"On his way." Tank wiped a hand over his face, black

with soot. T-Rex stood behind him, bare-chested save for his cut, his belt undone, hair a messy rumple. Gunshots rang out below and fire lit up the night sky, the acrid stench of smoke only now filtering through the windows.

"What do you want us to do?" Tank panted. "There are only twenty men brothers here and the prospect."

Cade morphed from gentle lover to fighter in a heartbeat, his words coming fast and clipped as he strapped on his weapon. "Tell the prospect to start calling up the brothers. Get as many men out here as we can. Barricade the road where it meets the highway so they're trapped here unless they want to chance riding through the bush. We gotta guard the Rizzoli weapons. I want five men out at the weapons shed. Everyone else should arm up and get out front." He grabbed Dawn and shoved her forward. "T-Rex, take her home through the trail out back."

"He's not a fucking babysitter," Tank spat out. "We need him here."

Cade's hand shot out and he shoved Tank up against the wall. "I'm giving the fucking orders and your job is to obey. If I say we can spare him, then we can spare him. End of discussion."

"I can help. I know how to use a gun." Dawn tugged on his arm and he brushed her away.

"What you did out near Big Bill's wasn't shooting. You coulda got us killed. And I can't lead the brothers if I'm worrying about you. I want you out of here, and I want you safe. We took out five Jacks the other night and they're here for revenge. Go with T-Rex. Now." He tagged his cut, shrugging it on as he stalked down the hallway with Tank following close behind.

Dismissed.

Dawn gritted her teeth at his abrupt departure. He hadn't even considered her offer. As with Jimmy, he thought she was a liability. But dammit, she wasn't helpless and in need of protection, and she didn't want him to be a man down because he thought she couldn't look after herself.

An explosion shook the clubhouse, and the chandelier in the hallway rattled. T-Rex ran over to the window and swore. "The weapons shed is on fire. They musta thrown something at the roof. If it blows, we'll have the cops, the fire department, and the fucking ATF out here. We'll all go to jail."

"Then we'd better put it out right away. I was part of a fire line during a vacation with my parents in North Carolina. We need buckets, hoses, and as many brothers as can be spared. We can run water from the kitchen and any outside taps." She didn't wait for his agreement, but ran barefoot down the hallway, wishing she'd brought something to wear other than her slinky red dress.

Within minutes T-Rex had rounded up some buckets and Dawn organized the brothers. She filled bucket after bucket from the tap in the sink, passing them to T-Rex who sent them down the line. Gunfire peppered the front of the clubhouse and thick, black smoke billowed through the windows, choking her and making her eyes water, but she didn't slow her pace.

Please let Cade be okay.

She didn't know how long she filled the buckets, but when Tank came to tell them the fire was out, she collapsed against the counter beside T-Rex, soaked, sooty, and exhausted beyond belief. But she had only a moment of respite before Cade stalked into the kitchen.

"I thought I told you to take her home." Cade rounded on poor T-Rex. "I give an order. I expect it to be obeyed. The Jacks are still outside. They got reinforcements through the northeast trail. I got enough to deal with and now I gotta worry about Dawn being here."

"We needed all hands to put out the fire." T-Rex swallowed but he didn't back down. "We woulda lost the shed and all the weapons if it wasn't for her idea to set up a fire line. We'd used up all the fire extinguishers and the hoses didn't go out that far."

"We're fighting a damn war." Cade cuffed T-Rex so hard, he staggered to the side. "You do what I fucking tell you to do or people die."

"It was my decision." Dawn pushed her way in front of Cade. "T-Rex wanted to take me home. I didn't let him."

"You're half his fucking size," Cade spat out. "If he wanted to take you home, there's nothing you could do to stop him. I want you out of here. Now." He gestured to Nick, who had just come in with the last of the buckets. "Take her home. Do what you gotta do to get the job done. If I see her here, or I find out she's anywhere else, you'll be picking your fucking teeth off the floor."

"Oh my God. What are the police doing here?" Dawn slid off Nick's bike and raced over to her house, glowing alternately red and blue from the lights of the two police cars parked out front. She ran up the sidewalk and hit Doug square in the chest as he stepped out her front door.

"Dawn! Thank goodness you're okay. I heard a report of a break-in over the police radio and when I saw the address on the scanner I came right away. Where have you been?" His gaze drifted down her body, taking in her soaked hair, ruined dress, sooty skin, and bare feet. Too terrified to let her back in the house for her jacket and shoes, Nick had raced her out to his bike and ridden like hell was on his tail. It had been the coldest ride of her life.

"Party." Her teeth chattered and consternation laced Doug's brow. He slid off his jacket and wrapped it around her. "You look terrible. And cold. Who goes to a party without any shoes?" His gaze lifted and he spotted Nick on his bike across the street. "Oh, Dawn. You weren't with the Sinners, were you?"

Shivering from the cold, and irritated by his patronizing tone, she pushed past him toward her house. "What happened here?"

"We got a call that your front door was ajar and one of your neighbors saw someone suspicious inside. I've been through the house and I have to say, I don't think it was just an ordinary break-in. The intruder was looking for something."

Dawn tapped the initials MD spray-painted in angry red on her front door. "Jimmy. And I'm guessing he was looking for me."

Doug put an arm around her shoulders as she took a step forward. "Actually, I think he might have been looking for something else. Brace yourself. It's not going to be easy to see."

Now, that was understatement. Dawn stared at the destruction in her living room and kitchen, her breath catching in her throat. Every drawer had been opened and overturned; curtains were torn and cupboards emptied. Her bedroom had fared even worse: Clothes strewn across the floor. Ornaments cracked. Mattress slashed, and box spring broken. But it was the words scrawled across her dresser mirror in red lipstick, the handwriting sickeningly familiar, that sent her into the comfort of Doug's arms.

WHERE IS THE FUCKING MONEY?

"Hey. It's okay." Doug ran his hand down her back. "We'll catch him. On the bright side, someone must have scared him away because the rest of the rooms are untouched."

"It's definitely Jimmy." She lifted her head, taking a breath to banish the almost cloying scent of his cologne. "I know his handwriting. But I don't know what this is all about. I don't know anything about any money." She grabbed some clothes from the floor and excused herself to change, tugging on a pair of yoga pants and a hoodie before joining Doug in the hall and handing him back his jacket. "I need some fresh air."

"Of course." Doug placed a hand on her lower back and guided her out the door. He stopped to speak to the two police officers examining a set of footprints in the garden beneath her broken living room window, and then joined her on the front step. "Is there anything that might help us? Do you think this might have to do with your new biker friend?"

Cade. She toyed with the idea of calling him, but he had enough to deal with right now, and after what had happened, he was the last person she wanted to see. She pushed away the nagging thought that Cade might not make it through the fight with the Jacks. He was a survivor. Just like her.

"I don't think so. Jimmy's insanely jealous, and he's seen me with Cade. But I don't know if that would be enough to make him take the risk of being caught in Conundrum. And the money thing doesn't make sense." She shivered and Doug tucked an arm around her waist, pulling her into his warmth. Dawn leaned her head on his shoulder. God, she just wanted a hot bath, a warm bed, and two days' worth of sleep.

"Do you have somewhere you can go for the night?" Doug said. "We'll be putting police tape around the property until forensics has finished collecting evidence, and you'll need a new window and all your locks changed before you can move back in."

Not the clubhouse, if it was even still standing. And Arianne was probably there with Jagger. Most of her other girlfriends had kids and she didn't want to disturb them.

"I can call Banks. He'll come to get me."

Doug leaned down and tucked a rogue curl behind her ear. "Or you can stay with me."

★ ELEVEN ★

I shall show no mercy to those who have cause
to fear me.

SINNER'S TRIBE CREED

Cade parked his bike outside Dawn's house and took his first deep breath of the night. They had only just chased away the Jacks and tended their wounded when the prospect called to tell him about the break-in at Dawn's place.

So here he was, his body thrumming with adrenaline, his brain still wired for action, and his trigger finger itching for another workout.

All of which were going to be a problem if Benson didn't get his fucking paws off his girl.

Cade gritted his teeth as he slid off his bike. He needed to calm down. Still primed and in full-on fight mode, he was inclined to stalk down the sidewalk, rip Dawn away, shove his fist in Benson's face, and then take Dawn someplace safe where he could strip off her clothes and make sure she hadn't been injured. Then he would mobilize the brothers and hunt down Mad Dog. At least he'd done Cade the favor of letting him know just who had trashed Dawn's house.

MD. Mad Dog. Bastard clearly wasn't afraid of the police, or the Sinners.

Or did he know the Sinners would be busy fighting off the Jacks? The timing of the break-in couldn't be a coincidence. But if that was the case, how did he know? And what the fuck did he want?

"There are two cops out back." The prospect stepped out of the darkness. "Looks like he got in through the window. The house is totally destroyed. I heard them saying he was looking for something. Dawn and that cop have been sitting there for about ten minutes. She seems pretty rattled."

"You did good, prospect. Go back to the clubhouse. Tell Jagger I'll be at the meeting tomorrow."

He scrubbed his hands over his face after the prospect walked away. Okay. He could do this. Walk in. Get the girl. Find out what the fuck was going on. Walk out. Solve the problem. Keep his hands to himself.

He crossed the street and headed down the walk.

And that's when it all went wrong.

Dawn looked up and the despair on her face sent his heart crashing into his gut. Not only that, she was shivering, and wrapped in an overly intimate cop who had timed his comfort for the exact moment Cade arrived.

"It's okay . . . Cade." Benson held up a warning hand. "I've got this. Dawn's coming home with me tonight where she'll be safe, and we've got a forensics team on their way. We'll find the perpetrator and put him behind bars. Guaranteed."

Jesus Christ. Is the cop purposely winding me up? He'd managed to restrain himself at Banks Bar, but he was way past restraint now. A night in jail would be worth the pleasure of wiping that smug smile off Benson's face.

Cade pulled up short, the chain on his belt swinging

violently against his thigh. "We both know Mad Dog did this. We also both know you won't be able to touch him, just like you can't keep Dawn safe. But I can." He held out his hand to Dawn. "Come."

Of course, she didn't come. Damn woman had a problem following orders. That had become abundantly clear when she'd stayed to help fight the fire, risking her life in the process. He had to respect a woman who knew her own mind, but not if she put herself in danger. Right now, he needed to assure himself she was safe and protected. And if she didn't get off the step, and let him hold her, he didn't know what he would do.

As if she sensed his inner struggle, Dawn slid out of Benson's grip. "Could you give us a minute, Doug?"

Benson gave her a curt nod, then headed around the back of the house. Dawn made her way over to Cade. Her bare feet slapped softly on the pavement, bright in the darkness, white from the cold.

"Thank you for coming. I'm glad you're okay."

Beyond speech, overwhelmed with the need to hold her, Cade grunted and reached out, but Dawn stepped away. "I didn't appreciate how you spoke to me at the clubhouse," she said softly. "I didn't like feeling like a liability. I was with the Brethren for seven years, and they treated me like I was worthless, but I survived and I learned a lot. And in the three years since I left, I learned even more. And one of those things is that I have value. I get that you want to protect me, but you need to get that I can look after myself, and sometimes I can even help."

He knew what she wanted to hear, but he couldn't say it. And if they faced the same situation again, he would make the same decision. "I can't give you what you want, sweetheart. I can't put you in danger. My dad beat on my mom for as long as I could remember, and until I turned fourteen there was nothing I could do to protect her. Even when I was strong enough to stop him, she wouldn't leave. When she finally did leave, she went back. I could never understand why. And in the end she died by his hand. So now I got a need to protect you that is part of my soul. Whether you want it or not, I'm gonna keep you safe."

He tagged her around the waist, drew her close, bent down and rested his forehead against hers, grounding himself in the moment, savoring the feel of her soft body in his arms.

"I'm sorry about your mom." She slid her arms around his waist and hugged him tight. "I understand why she didn't leave. It's a cycle, Cade, and you can't see your way out. For the longest time, I believed the horrible things Jimmy said about me. I believed I was worthless and every day I stayed made me feel even more humiliated about the fact I hadn't run away the day before. It was only when he turned on the girls that I broke free. I survived and found my worth and made a life for myself. That's why it was important to me that you didn't think I was a liability. I will never be that woman again."

"Never thought you were a liability." He pulled her against his chest. "Just wanted you to be safe." And then, because he wanted to see her smile, he said. "But you can't shoot for shit."

"I'll learn."

"How 'bout I take you somewhere we can warm you up first. Then you can tell me what happened in there, 'cause I've got a feeling Benson's not gonna be too keen to let me inside. After that, we can do some shooting."

She looked up at him and licked her lips. "Is there some hot sex in a bed involved?"

Cade rumbled his satisfaction. "Sweetheart, I don't need a bed."

"Dawn?" Benson came around the corner, his shiny deputy badge glinting under the streetlight. "Are you ready to go?"

Dawn turned to face him and Cade clamped an arm around her waist and pulled her tight against his chest, pleased when Benson's smile faded.

Mine.

"Actually, um . . . I'm going with Cade. But thank you for the offer, and for coming out here tonight. You've been such a good friend to me."

Benson's lips thinned. "Friendship doesn't seem to matter when there are bikers around who make a mockery of our laws and lure women into a violent world with promises they'll never keep. Think about what you're doing, Dawn." His voice took on a sharp edge, and the hair on the back of Cade's neck stood on end. "I'm certain Jimmy came here tonight because of your involvement with the Sinners. You tried so hard to get away from that world and make a good, stable life for you and your girls. Don't throw it all away."

"I appreciate your concern," she said sharply. "But I can make my own choices."

Cade drew in a deep breath and his hands clenched into fists. Only Dawn's quiet "hush" stopped him from shoving his fist down Benson's throat. Yes, the dude wanted her. But he was also trying to do his job and protect her. He just needed to understand that protecting Dawn was Cade's job.

"A biker's word is his bond." Jagger folded his arms and leaned back in his chair in the boardroom. "I'm not about to go back on my word because Mad Dog broke into Dawn's house."

"He's taking advantage of the fact he's untouchable."

Cade could barely contain his ire. The early-morning meeting wasn't going the way he'd hoped. In other words, Jagger wouldn't back down.

"If we can't keep him out of town, she's in danger. He attacked her outside the bar, showed up at the police station . . . He thinks she belongs to him and he just won't quit. By making him untouchable, we've taken away the only safety she had."

Jagger held up a warning hand. "I know how many times he's been here. And every time I have the same need as you to hunt him down, but we made a deal with Wolf and I'm not about to break my word. You agreed to this, Cade. We all did."

Gunner, silent until now, along with the rest of the brothers at the table, exhaled a breath. "Wolf broke the deal when he sent us up north for weapons that weren't there."

"He says he doesn't know what happened to the weapons. He's looking into it."

"And you fucking believe him?" Cade stood abruptly, no longer able to contain his anger.

"Of course not. Dax is going to interrogate Matchstick today about what he knows, and you and Zane can do some investigating when you take a team up to Whitefish to deal with the Demon Spawn betrayal. But the Jacks are clearly stronger than we thought if they could launch the kind of attack they did last night. We have to retaliate but we have to be smart."

"I'll start asking questions about where the Jacks are drumming up their new supporters," Zane said. "I didn't recognize some of the patches on the guys who were in the raid last night."

"How about we just tell the Brethren where to fucking go?"

Jagger regarded Cade with a damn irritating calm, implacable expression. "Do you really want to risk sending the Brethren running into their arms? Wolf has another weapons shipment coming in and he's arranged for it to be delivered straight to us. We can use those weapons in a new offensive. The election is coming up in three weeks. After Wolf's presidency is secure, we patch the Brethren in and the deal no longer stands. That's when we tell them where to fucking go. Mad Dog dies that day, and no other."

"I can't sit by and let him harass her." Cade shoved his chair against the table. "I can't be with her every minute of the day, and he always shows up when I'm not there. And does anyone wonder how he knew to break into her house when we were all busy with the Jacks? I think he knew about the raid."

"He's the one pushing to join the Jacks," Zane said. "Maybe he has a connection. Maybe he's made the same kind of deal with Viper that Wolf has made with us: If he wins the election, he'll patch the club over to the Jacks."

Jagger shook his head. "Wolf says he doesn't have that kind of support, and from what I've heard from other clubs, that's true. He'd have to win over the senior patch or buy up a lot of votes to beat a ten-year president who rebuilt the club. And as Cade said, Mad Dog doesn't want a patch-over. He's young. He wants to lead. At best, he'll have made a deal to be a support club. We'll deal with that problem when the time comes, but for now, we don't touch him."

"Fuck." Cade wanted nothing more than to yank open the door and leave the goddamn board behind, but Jagger hadn't adjourned the meeting and he didn't want to put his good friend Gunner in the position of having to deal with his breach of the rules. "How can I protect her if my hands are tied? I shoulda voted to off him that very first day."

"Then we would be having a very different conversation right now," Jagger said. "The Brethren would have been part of the attack last night. We barely fought off the Jacks as it was."

"Why are you so damn riled?" Gunner's forehead creased with a frown. "It's not like she's your old lady. You never cared this much about the other women you took to bed . . ."

"What if she was?" He felt the rightness of the idea the moment he spoke the words. "She would be entitled to Sinner protection as my old lady."

Jagger quirked an appreciative eyebrow. "Mad Dog would no longer suffer under the illusion that Dawn belonged to him. And if he did harass her, you could act to defend your old lady, regardless of the agreement we made with the Brethren."

"No fucking way." Gunner shot out of his seat. "You can't take an old lady. You're you. You got a rep to protect. And who am I gonna go drinking with? We got parties lined up every weekend for the next couple of months. And the twins with the biggest—"

"It wouldn't be permanent," Cade said quickly. "Just until Mad Dog is no longer a threat."

"I'm good with that," Jagger settled back in his chair. "Dawn's got herself in a bad situation and Arianne has been harassing me about our decision not to touch Mad Dog for the last few weeks."

"What does Dawn think of this idea?" Zane voiced the question on everyone's lips.

"I haven't asked her." Cade inhaled and released a long breath. "Might take a lot of convincing because she's made it pretty damn clear she isn't interested in being anyone's old lady."

"I got faith in you, brother." Jagger gave him a wicked smile. "If anyone can convince a woman to do anything, it's you."

* * *

"Dawn. Wake up."

Half asleep in Cade's bed, his warm, naked body tucked around her, Dawn wasn't inclined to climb out of her cave of oblivion. "Sleeping," she mumbled.

"Babe. I need to talk to you." He turned her gently, resting her head on his shoulder so he could harass her face-to-face. "I couldn't sleep."

"I wasn't having any problems." She squeezed her eyes closed and buried her face in his neck, breathing in his warm masculine scent. She'd dragged herself to work in the morning, stumbled through her job in the afternoon, spent a few hours sorting her house while the workmen changed the locks and window, and barely made it through her shift at the bar before Cade picked her up and took her back to the clubhouse.

Too tired to eat, she'd allowed him to put her to bed, expecting to sleep until the sun came up.

Apparently, Cade had other ideas, and now that she was awake, she had some ideas, too.

"I know a cure for insomnia." She eased herself on top of him, perversely pleased she'd gone to bed without any clothes. Cradling his hips with her thighs, she slid down until he was perfectly placed, his semi-erect shaft nestled against the curve of her sex.

Cade groaned. "You're making this hard."

"Yes, I am." She wiggled on top of him, delighted at his instant response. One thing about Cade, he could perform at a moment's notice.

"What happened last night at your house, can't happen again." Cade stroked his hand down her back. "I can't touch him, but I can't sit back and let him threaten you, either. It's gone too far."

"What are you going to do?"

He spread his legs, parting her wide, and his cock slid through her wet folds. "I've thought of another way."

"What way? And don't think I don't realize you're trying to distract me."

Cade leaned up and caught her nipple between his teeth, licking and sucking until she moaned. "You're gonna be my old lady."

"I don't want to be your old lady." She reared back, her breath catching in her throat. "I don't want to be anyone's old lady. Been there. Done that. Got the bruises and the emotional trauma to show it."

"Shhhh, babe." Cade's strong arms wrapped around her and he pulled her down to his chest. "It won't be permanent. Right now, Mad Dog still thinks you're his, and he's using the pass Wolf bought him to ride freely through town. That puts you in danger. So we make him understand you're taken and he's got no claim on you. And if he does come near you again, I can deal with him without going against the club 'cause I'm defending my old lady. No one fucks with a biker's old lady."

"I haven't even gotten used to the fact that we occasionally have hot sex. Being an old lady is too big a step. I can't deal with the violence, Cade. I can't be part of this world again."

He rocked his hips against her, his erection sliding against her clit. "You're gonna say yes, because you can't fight Jimmy alone. He's part of the Brethren and to stand a chance you need a club on your side. And it's not forever. There's an election coming up and once it's done and the Brethren patch over to us, Mad Dog is dead. You'll be safe and . . . "He hesitated. "The Sinners can help you get your girls back."

Now that caught her interest. "How?"

"'Cause if you're a Sinner, then they are Sinners. Shelly-Ann can't hold them for fucking ransom, and no one's gonna do shit if I pick them up and bring them home.

This is a Sinner town and the cops and social services will have to toe the fucking line."

"I'm going to say no." She pushed up, trying to get his cock where she wanted it to go. Although tempting, his solution didn't address the fact there was a court decision out there that said she was an unfit mother. If this ended when Jimmy died—and she didn't want to think about being in any way complicit in his death—then she'd be on her own again and the authorities could still take her girls away.

But oh, for a chance . . .

Cade gave her an evil grin, then rolled until he was on top of her, his shaft hard and heavy between her legs. "If you want a taste of me, you're gonna have to be mine."

Desire curled through Dawn's belly, and she squeezed her eyes shut. "Maybe I don't want a taste of you. Maybe I just want to go to sleep and pretend this conversation never happened."

He eased to the side then thrust a thick finger into her wetness. "You're gonna say yes, sweetheart, because by the time I'm done, you won't be able to say anything else."

"If you're planning to sex me into agreeing to be your old lady, then there's something I want," she said as a plan formulated in her mind.

Cade kicked her legs apart and pressed the head of his shaft against her entrance. "And you'll get it when you say yes."

"That's not what I mean. I know someone who might know how to find Jimmy's private investigator, or the identity of the person who filmed the fake drug deal behind the school. If I could find at least one person who could testify it was all a setup, I would feel better about your promise to get my girls back because then I wouldn't have to worry about the police or courts taking them away. Ever."

"The people who were involved in that scam aren't the kind of people who are going to stand up in court and confess."

Dawn heaved a sigh, her arousal fading. "I have to try. I can't live under the shadow of that decision. And I'm not about to do anything stupid. I'm just going to have a conversation, but it isn't with someone I can see alone."

Cade's eyes darkened and his arms came up around her. "Who do you want to see?"

"Bunny." A shady underworld kingpin and sometime human trafficker, with connections everywhere, Bunny was a man who traded in information. He knew everyone and everything. If you wanted something, he could get it. If you needed information, he knew it. But his services came with a price.

A price Dawn had already paid. Bunny had her mark, and it was time to call it in.

"Son of a bitch." Cade's muscles bunched under her hands. "No. Absolutely not. No fucking way are you gonna see that slime-sucking dirt bag. Look what happened to Arianne."

"He's not the one who chained her in his basement and tried to sell her into slavery. That was her brother. And that other guy, the ex-Sinner who tried to slit her throat . . ."

"Axle."

"Jeff and Axle were the ones who hurt her. Bunny saved her."

Cade gave an irritated snort. "Only because Jagger beat the shit out of him after you brought Arianne to him to negotiate a deal."

"He owes me, Cade. Jimmy made me dance. At strip clubs." Her words came out so fast they ran over one another. This was a part of her life she didn't want to share, but Cade had opened up about his past and she wanted to do the same. "Bunny had a table at the club where I danced. We had an arrangement Jimmy didn't know about. So now I can call in a favor. If you don't come with me, then Arianne will."

"He saw you naked."

She knew from his tone of voice exactly where this conversation was going to go. "Yes."

"No."

"I was asking for your help. Not your permission." Dawn glared, although it wasn't easy to be angry when he was naked, on top of her, and their heated conversation had clearly not diminished his arousal in the least.

"You get neither."

"Then you don't get an old lady." She tilted her hips until he was poised at her entrance. "And you don't get your sexy times."

"That was supposed to be my line."

Dawn eased down the tiniest bit. "Say yes, Cade, or we're both going to suffer."

He thrust deep and hard, filling her so completely she almost came right then.

"Yes," he said.

Dawn leaned up and kissed him. "Yes."

★ TWELVE ★

I will ride until the ride is done, and then
I'll ride again.
SINNER'S TRIBE CREED

Saturday night. Party night.

At least for the brothers without old ladies. For the brother whose impulsive nature had landed him with an old lady who didn't want to be an old lady at all, the party Jagger had staged for the big announcement of Cade's new "old man" status was a sedate affair. Sure the sweet butts, lays, house mamas, and hang-arounds had been invited, and as usual they were dressed to undress in skimpy minis and tiny tanks, but it was hands off for Cade and hands on for the unattached brothers in Riders Bar.

Cade had spent last night at the clubhouse, catching up with his executive board work. His aptitude for numbers had made him a natural for the position as treasurer, but he wasn't looking forward to sharing the news that their finances had taken a massive hit as a result of the war with the Jacks. Unfortunately, the time alone had made him second-guess his plan to make Dawn his pretend old lady.

What the hell had he been thinking, baring his soul to

her the other night? No one knew about his parents. Not even Jagger. And he didn't want her sympathy. He'd dealt with that situation and moved on. After he'd received the letter about his mother's death, he never returned to his hometown, never contacted his father in jail; hell, he'd never even visited his mother's grave. Even when his aunt emailed a few years later to tell him his father died of a heart attack in prison he hadn't gone home for the funeral.

Although Dawn had opened his eyes to the possibility some situations just couldn't be controlled, he couldn't accept that there were times he wouldn't be able to protect the people he cared about. He wouldn't let her suffer the same fate as his mother. Not when he had the strength and resources to ensure it would never happen. Not even if it meant turning his back on the club. And in the boardroom the other day, he'd almost been there.

Jagger thudded his beer bottle on a wooden table to quiet the room, and the DJ turned down Pink Floyd's "Comfortably Numb." The DJ was crap but he owed the Sinners money and what better way for him to work off his debt than to DJ at Riders, one of several bars the Sinners owned, operated, and laundered money through in Conundrum. At least Riders looked like a biker bar: worn wooden tables, posters of girls, bikes, and girls on bikes pinned to the walls, beer bottle sculptures in the alcoves, dim lighting, and a central dance floor that gave the brothers a good view of the girls. And of course, it smelled like stale beer and leather.

Cade grimaced when Jagger cleared his throat. He wasn't up for this at all. Pretending to have a relationship had been a lot easier when they were just having a good time. But now he felt open, raw, totally and utterly exposed. Not a comfortable feeling.

He shot back his whiskey, swallowing the smooth,

bitter liquid in one gulp. Time to back off, regain perspective. This relationship wasn't real and he had to stop thinking of it that way.

Arianne put two fingers in her mouth and whistled, quieting the room. She winked at Jagger and his face softened. Secret joke that wasn't much of a secret. Arianne had saved Jagger's life with that whistle not so long ago.

"As you all know," Jagger shouted. "Cade has an announcement for us." Jagger looked over at Cade and winked. Club tradition said that when a brother took an old lady, he had to make a formal declaration to the club. Usually the brothers brought it up in church, but Jagger wanted the word to get out. The Brethren had to believe it was true, and what better way than to invite a bunch of support clubs and support wannabes, splash the cash, and send them out to spread the word that the "Sinner of Sinners" had finally been tamed.

Now he had to make a damn speech when all he really wanted was to get on his bike and ride until he ran out of gas.

After refilling his glass from a bottle on the bar, he searched the crowd and spotted Dawn deep in conversation with Tanya. She looked up and met his gaze, her expression wary. Mustering all the charm he'd relied on to woo women into his bed, he smiled and held out a hand, indicating for her to join him.

"Finally found a woman who lit my fire," he said, raising his bottle. "Sweet, sassy, and sexy and a bit of a sinner like all of us. She may look soft, but she's got a core of steel. Sweet butts, dry your eyes. She's got my heart, my wings, my protection, and my patch. I'm taking Dawn as my old lady and if anyone has a problem with that, I'll shoot them between the fucking eyes."

Everyone cheered. Dawn gave a cool smile and, after

a nudge from Tanya, joined him in the center of the room, her fuck-me stilettos tapping lightly on the wooden floor. Her gold dress shimmered in the light, hugging every curve of her beautiful body, and her hair fell in soft golden curls past her shoulders. Damn. Why did she have to dress like that? He was hard just looking at her. Every damn brother in the room would be panting after her . . .

But they couldn't touch. Dawn belonged to him now and no one touched a biker's old lady.

Mine. He felt no small amount of satisfaction when he took the new cut from Jagger and slid it over her shoulders. Dawn spun around to show off the PROPERTY OF CADE patch on the back: the skull and stars in the center and his personal rocker on top, and Cade thought he might burst from pride. His cut. His woman. A more beautiful sight he had never seen.

Too bad it wasn't real.

After the cheers died down, he clasped Dawn's hand and wove his way through the crowded bar, forcing a smile as he endured the congratulations, handshakes, and pats on the back, counting the minutes until they could be free.

"Hey Cade." One of the few non-board-members who knew about the ruse, Arianne greeted him warmly when he reached the bar. "Nice speech. All I got from Jagger was a cut wrapped up in brown paper with PROPERTY OF JAGGER written on the back and suddenly I was his old lady."

"That's 'cause you were his old lady the second he laid eyes on you. Just took you both a while to realize it." That and Jagger almost dying in a ditch after rescuing Arianne from her Black Jack family.

"Never seen anyone scowl so much about getting hitched." Jagger leaned against the bar beside him after Arianne took Dawn to meet her new family. "People are starting to talk. Totally defeats the purpose of what you were trying to do here. Go dance with her, kiss her, make out—something to make it seem legit. Or are you having second thoughts?"

"She's not fully on board with the plan. Took a lot of convincing." He finished his beer in one swallow. "I get that she had a bad experience with the Brethren. And Mad Dog . . . every time I think about him, my blood fucking boils, but we're not them, and I'm not him. Why can't she see the difference?"

A shadow crossed Jagger's face and he glanced over at Arianne and Dawn. "She's fought hard to get away from the Brethren and make a life for herself, so it's gonna be hard for her to trust us or give up her independence. You can't run around swinging your club. I know about strong women, brother. You need a subtle touch."

Subtle. Sure. He could do subtle.

Cade pushed his way through the sea of brothers, parting the group of women now crowded around Dawn with a scowl.

"Thought it was time I had a dance with the old lady." He held out his hand, his heart pounding as if he were sixteen and back in high school wondering if the girl with the biggest tits in middle school would shoot him down. He'd always had a thing for big tits, and Dawn . . . damn she looked fine.

Dawn paled and for a moment he thought she'd refuse him, but she rallied and took his hand. "Of course. Can't let the old man dance alone."

He led her to the dance floor where a few brothers and their girls were making out on the pretext of dancing, but that was because the DJ was playing some shit boy-band pop crap. Cade caught the loser's eye and shouted. "Put on some real music or I'll rip off your balls."

"Nice." Dawn put her hands around Cade's neck. "Our

first dance and you threaten to rip off the DJ's balls. If I had any illusions about being back in the biker world, they have now been well and truly dispelled."

"My woman doesn't dance to shit music," he muttered. God she smelled good, like the flowers his mothers had planted every spring, no matter how disparaging his father was about her choices.

"Sounds like your woman now has to dance to the Forest Rangers' 'House of the Rising Sun.' " Dawn snorted a laugh after the DJ changed the tune. "Why do civilians think every bike gang is like the ones on TV?"

" 'Cause if they knew what we were really like, we'd all be locked up for our own protection."

Her hips swayed gently to the music and he slid his hands around her waist, pulling her close, molding her soft, lush body to his own.

"You watch biker shows on TV?"

Dawn's face flushed a delightful pink. "Yeah, I like them, although they're so far removed from reality sometimes I laugh the whole way through. I also like watching boxing and MMA, and . . ." Her voice trailed off.

His interest piqued, Cade gave her a nudge. "She gives me a hard time, but she likes her violence. What else?"

"Survival shows. Whenever I'm feeling down or having regrets about the past, I watch survival shows and think about how I'm a survivor and how hard I fought to get where I am."

"Damn right you should." His heart warmed with pride. "And you're still fighting, but now you got me by your side."

She sighed and melted against him. And then everything changed. All his anger and tension, even the pain in his back, just faded away. She just felt so . . . right—perfect—like they were meant to be together and the world had gotten in the way.

"We never danced before," she said softly. Her breath was sweet, citrusy, and he was tempted to lick that sugar from her lips, but uncertainty held him back.

"We never did a whole lot of anything before except fuck." Exactly what he wanted to do now. And afterward, maybe they could talk, or do what couples did, although never having really been part of a couple, he didn't know what that would be. Watch TV? Go for a ride? Fuck some more?

"Maybe that's 'cause that's all we're good for together."

That gave him pause. Yes, he enjoyed sex with Dawn, but he genuinely liked her. She was smart, sweet, sensitive, and funny. She had more grit and determination than anyone he'd met, working three jobs, putting up with Shelly-Ann, never giving up hope she'd get her girls back. He wanted to spend more time with her, but she was always running away.

"Well, we gotta have something together, because now you're wearing my cut and there's no turning back." He brushed his fingers through her beautiful long, blond hair. They had that in common. But Dawn was soft, where he was hard. Curved where he was straight. Sweet where he was bitter.

"If you'd told me three weeks ago I'd be in a biker bar, dancing with a biker and wearing a cut, I'd never have believed you. This was the last thing I ever thought I wanted. Me. A biker's old lady again."

His old lady. He liked the sound of it. He liked watching the words on her lips, tumbling over the silky softness and into his heart. Three weeks ago, sitting in his booth at Peelers with Delilah in his lap, he never would have believed he'd have an old lady. "Say it again."

She licked her lips, and the sight of her little pink tongue made him hard.

"Old lady."

"My old lady. Say it."

Dawn studied him for a minute, considering. "Yours." She leaned up and kissed him and he lost the last threads of his control.

His fingers convulsed, digging into her flesh, pulling her hips against his until he could feel the softness of her belly against the hard length of his cock. He didn't know if she was teasing or torturing or where this was going to go, but right now, if he didn't get her out of here, Jagger was going to get more of a show than he had bargained for.

"Let's go." He pulled away just as the DJ spun Preacher Stone's "Not Today."

"I want to dance." Dawn slid her arms over his shoulders, dropping her hands to his back. Cade winced and bit back a hiss.

She stilled and dropped her arms. "Does it still hurt?"

"No. It's fine." He couldn't feel the pain except when she touched him, overshadowed as it was by the pain down below.

Dawn pressed her lips together. "Doc Hegel is here. If there's something wrong, he can fix it."

"The only fixing I need involves you, me, and a bed."

"Cade, honey." She slid her arms around his hips and then cupped his ass, just as he had done to her, little fingers digging into his flesh as she ground her hips against his painfully hard shaft. "Don't you want to have sex on the night you got hitched?"

Arousal pounded through his veins, a thunder so loud he couldn't think straight. Or was it Van Halen's "Everybody Wants Some" coming through the speakers? Seemed like everyone was getting some except him. Unable to get words past the lump in his throat, he grunted.

"I bought something special for my first night as your

old lady." She pressed a soft kiss to his throat. "Under my dress. You can have a little taste."

He smoothed his hand over the curve of her hip, skimming his fingers along the bottom of her dress, his mouth watering in delicious anticipation. But it wasn't the promise of what lay beneath her golden dress that tightened his throat; it was the fact that she'd bought something for him. For tonight. To celebrate being his old lady. As if it was real. "I thought you were pissed at me."

"I am." She licked her lips. "Using sex to get your way is not on. But I'm willing to forgive you and give you your present if . . ."

"If what?"

The music segued into Aerosmith's "Sweet Emotion" and she swayed to the beat.

"If you show me your back."

"The wounds are infected. You need to go to a hospital." Dawn grimaced as she patted an antiseptic cloth over the angry red streaks marring the Sinner's Tribe tattoo on Cade's back. Although she tried to stay calm, her voice wavered. His back was in worse shape than she'd thought, the cuts obscuring most of the tattoo and forming wheals on his back. Jimmy must have used a rusty knife or coated it with something before he went out. She'd seen him do it before and it had sickened her then as it sickened her now. There was no honor in poison or tainted blades, but then Jimmy was far from an honorable man.

"No hospital." He shifted in the chair, his elbow hitting the desk with a loud thunk. Riders' manager had let them use his office, a small, windowless room with faux-wood paneling, a cheap metal desk, and a credenza covered in papers and empty beer bottles; it smelled almost as bad as Cade's room before she tidied it up the night after the fire, worried she might suffocate in her sleep.

"Well, then let me go get Doc Hegel. He's on call tonight so he hasn't had anything to drink."

"Fine. I'll give you this one 'cause I want that present and I want it soon."

She found Doc Hegel by the bar. A solidly built redhead with a small goatee and a big stomach, he helped club members with injuries that would ordinarily draw police attention at a hospital, and in return he had been granted nomad status at the club. No voting rights, but he was allowed to ride and participate in most club functions, save for church meetings.

"What he did to your tat is unforgivable," Hegel said as he tended to Cade's back. "And because of the infection, you'll have scars. It will never be the same."

"I know." Cade looked up to where Dawn perched on the desk. She saw more than anger in the depths of his eyes. Pain. Confusion. Betrayal. She understood why the Sinners hadn't avenged Cade right away, but it had clearly affected him deeply.

Hegel gave Cade a shot of antibiotic, and instructions about caring for and dressing the wound, and then Dawn walked him to the door.

"Do you think he knows how bad it is?" he said quietly.

Dawn looked back over her shoulder. "They defiled it the second they touched it. Doesn't get worse than that."

"Are you going to be okay?" Dawn asked after Doc Hegel left to rejoin the party.

"Yeah. A few cuts aren't gonna slow me down."

"Even if they're here?" She placed her hand over his heart. Cade jerked back and her hand fell. What had she been thinking? After Doc Hegel's treatment he was probably hurting. "Sorry."

Cade clasped her hand and brought it back to his chest.

"I like your hands on me. It was just what you said . . . like you knew what I was feeling."

Heat sparked between them and she wondered if he knew what *she* was feeling. She liked her hands on Cade. Maybe too much. She liked everything about him, from his loyalty to his possessiveness, from his gentleness to his ferocity. And he was right about Jimmy. She couldn't take him on alone when he came part and parcel with the Devil's Brethren. Would it really be so bad to accept the Sinners' help?

And afterward? What would happen when they both had their justice? Already, she couldn't imagine not having him around, feeling his arms around her, watching him laugh with her girls, lying with him in bed at night knowing she was totally and utterly safe.

A dangerous place to be for a woman who had sworn off bikers for life.

Standing in his arms right now was also a dangerous place to be. Especially with the weapon straining against his fly. She had plans for that weapon and they involved the white lace corset, garters, and panties she'd bought for the occasion.

Time to focus on now, and worry about the future later.

Weapons shouldn't be wasted.

★ THIRTEEN ★

I will do without question what has to be done for honor, for loyalty, and for my brothers.

SINNER'S TRIBE CREED

He couldn't stop himself. Even though his back burned, it was nothing compared with the pain of keeping his desire at bay. He had to have her. And it had to be now.

"You made me a promise. Now I intend to collect." His arms snaked around her and he crushed her to his chest, trapping her hand between them. He could hold her forever. A balm for his soul.

"Here? Wouldn't you rather go somewhere . . . private?" Her head tipped back and he leaned down and kissed her. Soft lips. Sweet kiss. She tasted of the bourbon she'd sipped from his glass, smooth and rich, and he licked the stickiness from her lips. Dawn melted against him and his cock throbbed, pressed against his fly, blindingly painful, as if he'd been wanting her forever.

Maybe he had.

"Can't wait. I'll do you here, then I'll take you home and fuck you there, too."

"Does this mean you aren't angry at me anymore for twisting your arm to see Doc Hegel?" She reached up with her free hand, tangling her fingers through his hair, pulling him down. Her soft moan cranked him higher and he thrust his tongue in her mouth and devoured her, leaving no inch untouched.

"I could never be angry with you, although you seem to have picked up the old lady attitude pretty damn fast."

"Good to hear." She dragged his hand up her thigh, pulling up her dress until the tops of her stockings were visible, complete with their little elastics. "Because I bought this for you."

"White lace." Cade breathed out his appreciation. "I would have picked white for you if I bought it myself. So beautiful against your skin. Like an angel."

He yanked her dress up higher, revealing her garter belt and the thin strip of matching lace panties. "A naughty angel."

Cade traced his finger along the edge of her garter belt. God, he loved the lingerie women wore. Light and filmy, smooth and sexy, lace and leather, and ribbons that he wanted to pull, unwrapping the treasures just visible beneath. Did women have any idea what it did to a man to get a peek at something he shouldn't see?

But Dawn . . . in this . . . So fucking sexy he could barely breathe.

He lifted her and settled her on the desk, parting her legs with his hips to give him better access.

"You're hurt . . ."

He cut off her protest with two hands around her heart-shaped face, tilting her head back so he could ravage her mouth some more.

"Cade . . ."

Even as she kissed him, even as her hands smoothed over his shoulders and her fingernails dug into his skin, he heard the hesitation in her voice. Desperation seized him. He wanted her to want him as much as he wanted her. He wanted her to need him as he needed her. He wanted her to know him as he was now, consumed by her, and not the Cade that went from bed to bed looking for what now trembled in his arms.

So he threaded his hand through her hair and tugged her head back because he knew she loved it.

So he slid his lips down her neck, to that sensitive spot on her shoulder that made her moan.

So he yanked the dress over her head, baring her to him, knowing his dominance aroused her.

But he wasn't prepared for what lay beneath. Creamy, voluptuous breasts nestled in a froth of white lace. A pure, lush, decadent feast. A bride. And he was a bastard because he was going to take her here on a hard desk in a filthy office, instead of a nice soft bed in a fancy hotel room, and there was fuck-all he could do about it. He'd never felt want as he felt it now: pulsing, throbbing, pounding want.

"Dawn, babe. You are so beautiful you could make a priest sin."

"Good thing then I already have a Sinner."

When his palm cupped the smooth perfection of her breast, and his thumb brushed gently over her taut, rosy nipple, he couldn't hold back. With a groan, he eased her back on the desk, wrapping her legs around his hips.

"Touch me," she whispered.

"What my old lady wants, my old lady gets." He smoothed his hands along her inner thighs, his fingers brushing over the lace tops of her stockings and along the garter elastics, until he reached her lace panties. She liked lace. He remembered tearing lace panties off her before, the soft rend of material as erotic a sound as her whimper when he stroked her wet pussy.

"More, Cade. Don't tease."

His body shook like it was his first time, like he had at

the age of fourteen when he discovered he could lose himself in a woman's embrace and the shouting and crying and screaming he heard at home would fade away beneath moans and whimpers of desire. He couldn't stop the pain, but at least he could give pleasure.

He cupped her breast in his hand, tugging down her bra to take her nipple in his mouth.

"Oh God." Dawn arched off the desk, offering him more. Her hands slid over his chest, sending wave after wave of heat down to his cock. Unable to stop himself, he ground his erection against the curve of her sex until he was on the verge of spilling himself like a teenage boy.

Her hips rocked against him, her heels digging into his back. With her head thrown back, her hair spread around her in a golden wave, she was a goddess, devastatingly beautiful, irresistibly wanton . . . and his.

Mine. Overwhelmed with a need to claim her, he grasped the edge of her panties and eased them over her hips, sliding them over her lean legs and off. Too pretty to tear away.

He heard her gasp, and if he hadn't been so wound up, he would have savored her, licked the salty sweetness from her skin, and teased her nipples until she writhed beneath him. But that was for another time. Another place. A night when they weren't the guests of honor at their own party and everyone would be wondering where they were. Now was about sex. Rough and raw. Pure and primal. Now was about making her truly his.

"Are you wet for me, babe?" His hand dropped to his belt and he worked at the buckle.

"So wet."

"Are you hot?" The buckle gave way and he tore open his fly.

"So hot."

"Legs on my shoulders." He pulled a condom from his

pocket and ripped it open with his teeth, then sheathed himself as she positioned herself, calves on his shoulders, her glistening pussy wet and inviting.

"Now," she demanded.

He entered her with one hard thrust, his hands around her thighs, holding her in place. Dawn arched against him, rocked into his rhythm, her hands clenched tight on the lip of the desk.

"God, you feel so good."

The desk squeaked across the floor as he hammered into her. When he felt the little quivers in her sex that told him she was close, he traced his thumb over her clit, spreading her moisture up and around until her legs tightened around him and her heels dug into his freshly dressed wound. Pleasure-pain suffused his body and he felt a familiar pressure at the base of his spine.

The doorknob rattled and Cade froze. "Jesus. Fucking. Christ. Not again. Someone's gonna die."

"Hey you two," Tank yelled. "Come outta there and join the party, or else we're coming in."

Cade heard laughter and the sound of voices. His cock throbbed so painfully his eyes watered. "Fuck off."

"Maybe we should . . ."

He thrust deep and Dawn's back arched. "Oh God. So close. Make them go away."

"Pleasure." Cade reached across the desk for his gun. Sex with his old lady was serious business. Not to be disturbed. Especially when he was so damn close he had to grit his teeth against the pain.

"No. I didn't mean—"

He fired at the door, aiming his shots at the ceiling. A woman screamed. The brothers gathered outside the door roared with laughter.

"Catch you at a bad time, brother?" Sparky shouted. "We need to know if you're fighting at the next fight."

"This is worse than a civilian wedding," Dawn muttered. "Although we're supposed to be in a fancy hotel room when we're hazed."

Cade placed the gun on the table beside her. "My woman doesn't get interrupted when she's about to come."

"That's sweet, in a terrifying-ruthless-biker-I'll-be-totally-humiliated-when-we-walk-out of-here kinda way."

"Fucking me is not humiliating. Most of the girls out there would die to take your place."

Dawn glanced from side to side, taking in the dingy room, and then laughed. "First of all, I am reassured that you do not suffer from a lack of self-confidence. Second, how about you get on with the program? Since they all now know what we're up to, we might as well enjoy it so I can lord it over all those girls who are dying to take my place. And third, if you do any more shooting, someone probably will die."

He wasn't sure if she was joking, but he would be damn proud if she wanted to share just how hard he made her come. After all, he might have an old lady, but he still had a rep to protect.

"C'mon, old man. Keep up."

With a growl, he pulled out and slid deep inside her. He slicked her juices up and around her clit until her hips bucked against him and her cheeks flushed. His balls tightened, lifted, and he pressed hard on her clit. "That's it, babe. Come with me."

Dawn threw an arm over her mouth and climaxed, muffling her scream as her pussy clamped around him. Cade hammered into her until his body stiffened. He gripped her hard and climaxed in long hot heated jerks, listening to his old lady moan with pleasure.

"Not bad for an old man," she murmured.

He collapsed on top of her, taking his weight on his arms. "I aim to please."

Dawn tunneled her hand through his hair. "So you liked my present?"

"Best present I ever got." He nuzzled her neck. "But I like what's inside the present better."

"We should get back to the party or your brothers are going to break down the door. What fight were they talking about?"

"We hold fights on the last Saturday of every month at the clubhouse with our key support clubs. Mandatory attendance. Get a fire going, barbecue, coupla cold ones, old ladies and sweet butts . . ."

"I usually work on Saturdays."

He wanted her there. He wanted her to watch him fight. His woman should see his strength and rest assured he could defeat anyone who challenged him. Or threatened her. "Take if off."

She gave him a tight smile. "I need the money so I can see the girls."

He withdrew to dispose of the condom. When he turned back, she was already off the desk, her dress in her hand. Frustrated that their moment of intimacy had been so brief, he dressed in silence. But when they were both ready to go, he leaned against the door.

"I got money . . ."

"I don't want your money. I earn enough to pay Shelly-Ann and my expenses and save up for when the girls come home." She hesitated. "They are coming home, right? That was the deal."

Cade shifted his weight and rubbed his palms on his jeans, unaccustomed to asking for anything, and especially something he desperately wanted. "Yeah. I talked to Jagger after the meeting. He's gonna speak to Wolf as a courtesy to let him know what's going down. But the fight . . . you got an obligation as my old lady to be there."

"I have on obligation to my children, Cade. They come

first." She straightened her clothes and ran her fingers through her hair. "I'm sure you'll be amazing."

When his brow creased, she looked away and bit her bottom lip. "I thought you'd be happy. We both benefit from his arrangement and the sex is hot. But I'm not looking to tie you down, and I don't want to get too involved with the club."

His hand fisted by his side. He knew her well enough to know she wasn't being entirely truthful with him. This wasn't just about sex to her. She cared enough to bring Hegel to check his back, and to dress up tonight; she'd opened up to him outside her house. And those little glimpses into who she really was made him greedy for more. He figured her hesitation stemmed from a lingering fear of Jimmy. But if she came to the fight, he could show her he could protect her. He had ten straight wins under his belt. Maybe then she wouldn't run away.

"I want you there."

She gripped the purse in her hand so hard her knuckles tightened, and when she looked up the pain in her eyes shocked him. "I can't handle the violence, Cade. Okay? Is that what you want to hear? Trust doesn't come easily to me. And the way I feel about you scares me. The things you do scare me. If I have to see you actually fight in the ring, I don't think I'll be able to trust you not to hurt me. Every time I've trusted someone I've been hurt and betrayed, and I don't want to feel that way about you."

"Every time?"

She hesitated and dropped her gaze. "It wasn't just Jimmy."

His body went taut, blood heating through his veins. Jesus Christ. His girl just couldn't catch a break. "Who?"

"After my parents died in a car crash, I was sent to live with my uncle. I didn't have any other living relatives. He . . . touched me. At first, I thought he was just comforting me. Then he wanted more. He wanted me to show my gratitude for his care. I didn't know what to do or where to go. I was lonely and lost. I didn't have any friends or family in Seattle, and I was afraid if I told someone, I would have no one. So I endured it for a year until my fifteenth birthday when he made it clear touching wasn't enough."

Cade couldn't move for the pounding of his heart. If he'd ever thought his life had no purpose, he had a path now. First, Mad Dog. Then the uncle. Then every other person who had ever hurt his girl.

"That night when he came to my bedroom, I grabbed my bedside lamp and knocked him out. Then I ran away with my purse and the clothes on my back. I didn't even take a picture of my parents with me. I took a bus out of state and got off in Helena when my money ran out. For a while, I lived with in an abandoned building with a group of street kids, and when my luck ran out and a pimp decided to add me to his stable, I met Jimmy."

"Never again." His seething brain couldn't form the words he knew she needed to hear. The murmurs of sympathy and understanding. The words of consolation. He couldn't even touch her, because if he did he would never let her go. Her pain was his pain. Her past was his future.

"It's okay, Cade. It's over. It was one more lesson about how to survive and fight for what I want. I don't waste any time thinking about it."

Fucking hell. What a woman. All the fucking abuse she suffered, and she owned it.

"You're the only person I've ever told."

"Means everything to me," he said. "Tells me everything I need to know."

"What do you know?"

He crossed the distance between them and took her in his arms. "I know I never met a woman as strong and smart and beautiful as you are. Never met a better mom than you, doing so much for your kids with so much damn love it fucking shines around you. Never met anyone I wanted to share the worst part of my life with. And I never had a woman give me a present that made me want to ditch my own party so I could spend the night showing her how much it was appreciated."

"I bought two presents." She went up on her toes and kissed him, her voice a breathy whisper. "One naughty. One nice."

His tongue parted her lips and he thrust inside, consuming her. The world melted away until there was only Dawn, her soft body pressed up against him, her fingers threading through her hair, his hard length between them, and her hot, wet mouth on his.

"Please tell me this is the naughty one 'cause I'm fucking hard all over again."

Dawn feathered kisses up his neck and along his jaw, and then she pressed her lips to his ear. "Cade, honey, this is the nice one."

★ FOURTEEN ★

I will wear the symbols of brotherhood with pride.

SINNER'S TRIBE CREED

Dawn placed the steaming plate of bacon and eggs on her tray and lifted it from the counter. The diner was unusually quiet this morning so the cooks had been overly generous with the portions. Stan wouldn't be pleased. He was only just back from a vacation he'd decided to take the day after Cade visited the restaurant and things had slipped in his absence.

"Table three wants more coffee." He came up behind Dawn, his belly brushing against her back as he reached for the coffeepot. Dawn cringed. Despite Cade's warning, nothing had changed. Or maybe, it had. She felt different today. Although she needed the job, she wasn't prepared to sacrifice her self-worth to keep it, or to tolerate any disrespect.

Just like a Sinner.

She spun around and shoved Stan away. "Back off."

Stan's mouth dropped open and he took a step back. She'd never warned him off so forcefully before, but today the words slipped out before she could stop them.

"I like working here, Stan. This is the only restaurant

close to the school and you've been very accommodating by letting me take my morning break during our busy time so I can see my girls. And of course, I need the money. But all this touching has to stop. Whether it is accidental or intentional, I don't like it, and if you touch me again, I'm going to break your arm."

She didn't know if she could, in fact, break his arm, although Doug had taught arm bars in his self-defense class and she figured if she twisted hard enough, it just might break. But it sounded good and it felt even better. Resolved. Like she was holding a loaded gun. Maybe if she showed that kind of attitude to Shelly-Ann she wouldn't be hiding under trees wearing a wig to see her own kids. And she wouldn't be forking out all her extra cash so Shelly-Ann could drive a Cadillac while she had to take her girls around on the bus.

The front door slammed open and the little bell in the doorframe tinkled. She looked up and smiled when Doug walked into the restaurant, still riding the high from making Stan back down.

"I'll take table six." She gestured Doug to an empty booth in the corner and joined him a few moments later.

"Hey, Doug. You're looking good." He always looked better in civilian clothes than in uniform, and today he was clean-shaven and all decked out in a blue-and-white-striped shirt with crisp blue jeans—the kind of jeans Cade would never wear. Her mouth watered at the thought of Cade's worn, low-rise jeans, tight in all the right places, and she almost missed Doug's next words.

"You missed our monthly drinks last night. And you didn't return my calls. I was worried about you. After what happened at your house . . ."

Damn. She'd totally forgotten about the monthly meet-up with her self-defense class. After moving to Conundrum, she'd taken the course as part of a therapy program to get over Jimmy's abuse, and made some close, supportive friends, including Doug. After the course finished, Doug suggested a monthly drinks night to stay in touch, and Dawn had never missed a night.

"I'm so sorry. I totally forgot. I was at . . . a party." She couldn't bring herself to tell him she'd spent the night becoming Cade's old lady in more ways than one.

"Good to hear you're getting out." He fiddled with the napkin on the table. "I thought maybe you'd turned to the dark side and joined the Sinners. Your friend Cade can be pretty overbearing. Kinda like Jimmy."

Ouch. That stung. And so unlike Doug she almost couldn't believe he'd said it. Sharp barbs were so not Doug's style.

"He's nothing like Jimmy." Aside from the violence, beatings, and torture that seemed to be as much a part of Sinner life as it was with the Brethren. But the violence was directed outside the club, not in.

Doug clasped Dawn's hand and gave it a squeeze. "I came to see you this morning because I've got some exciting news. We've been through the tapes from the bus shelter and the sheriff agrees we have enough evidence to charge Jimmy for assault. When we bring him in, we'll question him about the break-in as well."

"That's great." She smiled through clenched teeth while her stomach twisted in a knot. What had she been thinking? There was no way the police would be able to hold Jimmy. Once he was out on bail, he'd come for her, and he would show no mercy. Where would the police be then? According him due process while she bled out on the floor? Although she hated to admit it, the biker system worked better. There was no presumption of innocence, no proof beyond a reasonable doubt. There were no long delays before trial, plea bargains, or paying off judges. Jimmy did something bad, Jimmy was punished. End of story.

"You don't sound happy." He released her hand and sank back in the booth.

"How long can you hold him?" This plan didn't just put her at risk; it put Cade at risk, too. She didn't want to see him dead on the street as a result of Jimmy's wrath.

"You're afraid of the repercussions." Disappointment laced his tone and Dawn instantly felt contrite.

"There's just other stuff going on right now . . ." She hesitated, weighing her words. Club business couldn't be discussed outside the club and now that she was ostensibly a Sinner, she had to be careful what she said. "Stuff that will make Jimmy more volatile than usual. If you can't hold him, he'll come after me the second he's out on bail."

Stan coughed discreetly and she pulled out her order pad and gave him a wave. He knew Doug was a cop and he wouldn't intervene the way he had with Cade. Still, she didn't want to push what little advantage she'd just bought herself.

"I have to work, Doug. But I've changed my mind. Can we just pretend I didn't give the statement?" If her plan to find out who had filmed the setup panned out, she might be able to get her girls back without provoking Jimmy, and then she could find another way to deal with him. Now that she was a Sinner she had access to an entirely new set of tools, and they didn't involve civilian law. She'd already crossed the legal line long ago; she just needed a little kick to cross it again, and Sinners had done that for her.

"I can't do that." Doug's face crumpled. "The sheriff is involved. He intends to wage war against all bikers, and he's going to use Jimmy as an example."

"You won't have a case without a witness. I won't testify against him."

"Dawn . . ." Doug laced his fingers through hers and

stroked his thumb along her hand, a decidedly intimate gesture that sent her pulse skittering. Except for that night outside her house, he'd never crossed the friendship line, and this small, earnest gesture was definitely more than friendship.

"We can protect you. I can protect you. That's what the police do. That's what the system is there for."

"I made the biggest mistake of my life when I thought I could rely on the system to get my girls back." Dawn gently removed her hand from his grasp. "Not only was the system not there for me, Jimmy was able to turn it against me. I should have known. When Jimmy beat me, the cops would never come out, no matter how many times I called, and eventually I just gave up."

"I would have been there for you." Doug's dark eyes glistened. "I would have come out. I would done everything I could to get him behind bars."

"But it wasn't you. And now I don't know why I reported the assault. I just felt like I wanted some control over my life, but I never really thought it through. For some reason I thought you'd lock Jimmy up and throw away the key. But there's a long period between arrest and trial, and it puts my girls and me at risk. There are other ways, Doug. Biker ways. I just never had the courage to try them."

"Don't be ridiculous," Doug snapped, shocking her with the vehemence in his tone. "Everything will be different this time. I can make sure you're protected. And . . . this is the second news I wanted to tell you . . ." He glanced around and lowered his voice. "I've secured a place for you in the witness protection program. After you testify against Jimmy and the Brethren, you'll get your girls back. A new life, Dawn. You'll be safe. Forever."

Safe. On the surface, it seemed to be a perfect solution—she would have her girls and her freedom away from the biker world she hated with a passion, and Jimmy would spend some time in jail. Except she'd be safe and alone. No Banks and Arianne. No Doug.

No Cade.

Curiously, the idea of running away with her tail between her legs didn't appeal. Sinners didn't run. Sinners didn't hide. Sinners were fighters. They met their enemies with both guns blazing. They stepped into the ring and stayed there until there was only one man standing. This was her town. Her life. Her friends. Why would she let Jimmy chase her away?

"I appreciate everything you've done," she said gently. "But this is all very sudden, and you should have discussed it with me first. Testifying against an outlaw MC is serious business, and I'm not sure if it's the right path for me. And I've made a life here for myself. I have a job and friends. There's only one way for me to have justice and it doesn't involve—"

"No." Doug thudded his hand on the table. "This isn't you. You're not a violent person. You're not vengeful. You're not a biker anymore. You're a good, honest, upstanding citizen who's been dealt a bad hand in life."

"You don't know me," she said. "I'm not the person you think I am."

He leaned in closer and his voice dropped to a quiet murmur. "I care about you, Dawn. Much more than as a friend. You know that. And I've waited all these years because I understand the trauma you went through. You could take your stand by testifying against Jimmy and the Brethren, and when you're done, if you want, I could come with you in witness protection. I've already looked into it. I would be there to look after you and your girls. As a friend, or something more."

Warning bells clanged in her mind, and yet his expression was so earnest she instantly felt guilty. Doug was a good man. He had started the self-defense class in his free time to help women feel more confident when they had to walk alone at night. Upstanding, conservative, and dedicated to his work—he was everything she should have wanted, and the total opposite of Cade. And yet he didn't push any of her buttons. There was no wild in Doug. No blasting through stoplights or having sex in parking lots. No cheeky smiles and devil-may-care grins. She couldn't imagine him tossing her on a table in a dingy office, shooting at his friends to keep them away, and giving her one of the best orgasms of her life.

"I'm sorry, Doug. I'm with Cade now." Well, not entirely true, since the cut was only temporary, but maybe that would get the message across. "And I have no intention of running away from my home."

"This is about you. Your safety. Your life. If you're happy, your children will be happy. And more important, they'll be with you. Please. Promise me you'll think about it." He stroked her cheek and she felt . . . nothing. No zing of excitement. No tingle between her thighs. No desire the throw him on the table and rip off his clothes. Cade could do that to her with just one look.

As if on cue, the door opened, and Cade stalked into the restaurant, the chain on his belt rattling as he walked. T-Rex and Gunner followed behind him.

Dawn's lips tipped at the corners, but when she saw his face, his eyes cold and hard, jaw taut, lips pressed into a thin line, her smile faded. She'd seen that look before—at Banks Bar, and when he'd seen Jimmy in front of the school. That look meant someone was about to get hurt, and a sickening wave of dread rose in her stomach.

"Restaurant is closed," Cade shouted. "You got one minute to clear out otherwise I'll have my boys pay your table a visit."

T-Rex pulled down the shades in the windows. Gunner

yanked people out of their seats and ushered them out the door. The cooks ran out the back. When only Stan was left, gaping at the empty restaurant, T-Rex locked the door.

"What's going on here?" Doug's tone switched from friendly to officious, and he rose from his seat. Although in civilian gear, he still carried a weapon in a holster on his belt, and his hand hovered near his hip.

"Benson." Cade turned his steely gaze in Doug's direction. "Always a pleasure to find you sniffing around my girl, but I'm afraid I don't have time to toss you around today. This is Sinner business, and it would be best if you step outside."

"I'm not going anywhere." Doug reached for his weapon, and Tank came up behind him and pressed a gun to his head. Dawn hadn't even noticed him coming in the back door.

"I'll take that weapon." Tank reached around and pulled the gun from Doug's holster. Then he patted Doug down and removed his phone.

"You just bought yourself a night in jail," Doug spat out.

"See. That's where you and I disagree." Cade folded his arms and leaned against the nearest booth. "This is a Sinner town. The police don't get involved in Sinner business and we don't get involved in police business. Sheriff Morton had that all figured out, but since you've only been here a short time, and your sheriff is new, I'm giving you a little leeway. So you got a choice. You can walk out of here and let us do what we have to do. Or you can stay and put yourself in the difficult position of witnessing a breach of the law that you're not gonna be able to do anything about."

"I'm not leaving Dawn." He put an arm around Dawn's shoulders and Cade's scowl deepened.

"You like your life, you're gonna take your hands off my old lady. Now."

"Old lady?" Doug gave her a puzzled glance. "Dawn? What's going on?"

"I was . . . going to tell you." She gently removed his arm and took a few steps away.

"What have you done?" He stared at her in horror. "You hate bikers. Look what happened to you in the Brethren. Look what happened with Jimmy." His jaw clenched and he glared at Cade. "What did you do to her? You've coerced her. Or is it blackmail? Did you promise to get her children back? Did you tell her you'd kill Jimmy? You're going to commit murder to protect her? Are you beating her, too?"

"Doug, please." Dawn put a hand on his arm. "It's a complicated situation. But this works out best for both of us."

"What about your girls?" His eyes blazed, startling Dawn. She'd never seen Doug so heated about anything, and he'd never imposed his views on her choices in life.

"Don't patronize me, Doug."

"With that videotape out there, you'll always be considered an unfit mother." He shook off her hand. "I'm offering you a way out of this mess. In exchange for your testimony, we can get that tape examined, the case reheard—"

"My old lady's not a rat." Cade slowly unfolded his arms and took a step forward. "And you need to calm the fuck down."

"Whoa, brother." Gunner put a warning hand on Cade's shoulder. "We got a job to do, and we need to get it done before someone calls the cops." He looked over at Doug and laughed. "No offense intended."

"Sit him down." Cade tipped his chin at Tank. "Keep him quiet. If he opens his mouth again, close it."

"What's going on?" Dawn edged closer to Stan. She had a fair idea what might be going on since T-Rex had stopped Stan from leaving with the rest of the staff, but really, if this was about Stan touching her, it was overkill. She had the situation in hand.

"Have a seat, babe," Cade pointed her to the nearest booth. "Stan and I are gonna have a little talk."

Dawn's blood turned to ice and she stood in front of Stan, blocking Cade's path. "My fight."

Cade stared at her, pinning her with blue eyes filled with fury. "He had his warning."

"I've talked to him. I've laid down the law. He's not going to touch me again." She looked over at Stan, and he vigorously shook his head.

Cade threw a USB stick on the table. "You gonna deal with all the footage he has of you naked in the restroom and change room? T-Rex found the cameras. The prospect checked them out. He's been recording you and the other staff, selling the images on porn sites, and jerking off to them at home at night."

Bile rose in her throat, but it wasn't fear that made her shake, but rage. "Stan? How could you?"

Stan bolted. But, of course, Cade had someone waiting for him at the back door.

"Look what I found." Shaggy shoved a quivering Stan back into the restaurant only a few moments later.

Cade tipped his head from side to side, cracking his neck. "T-Rex. Take Dawn and Benson out back. Gun, watch on the door."

"I'm not going anywhere." Dawn glared at Cade. "What he did, he did to me. And what happens to him is my choice."

"I can arrest him," Doug said. "What he did was illegal. Give him to me and he'll be subject to the full force of the law."

Cade barked a laugh. "Invasion of privacy? Taping someone without consent? What's that gonna get him? A fine? A slap on the wrist? A night in jail? You think that's gonna stop him from doing it again? Is that gonna make Dawn feel any better knowing dirt bags across the country saw pictures of her that no man should see? Is that justice?"

"It is justice," Doug said. "The right way. The legal way. You have to trust in the system."

"Don't trust in the system at all," Cade said. "Legal justice is no justice. My old lady has been disrespected. That means my club has been disrespected. That means justice, Sinner style."

"Cade . . ."

Cade grasped her arm and pulled her forward. Her cheek hit his chest and he brushed his lips over her ear and murmured. "You're a Sinner now, babe. You are my old lady. I like that you're a fighter but this is one of the times I'm stepping in and you're just gonna have to suck it up."

She trembled at the press of his body, hot and hard against hers, the feel of his heart, thudding in his chest, his anger, barely contained.

Wait. That was *her* heart pounding. *Her* anger. *Her* rage. Dawn took a deep breath and let the unfamiliar feelings wash over her. She had never been angry with Jimmy. In the fight for survival, emotion had taken a backseat. But now she felt indignant, powerful, and capable of exacting her own revenge. Yes, Stan deserved to be punished. But not without her.

"Don't kill him."

Cade looked down, amusement flickering in his eyes. "Is that a *request*?"

"Yes." She caught her breath at his gentle reminder that old ladies needed to ask permission if they wanted to get involved in Sinner business. Chauvinism at its finest.

"Since you asked so nice, sweetheart, I'll give you

that. I won't kill him. But I'm gonna take it pretty damn close to the line."

Dawn bit her lip, considering. Her decision to wear the cut meant acknowledging the way things worked in his world, including the use of violence. She didn't have to like it, but she couldn't judge Cade for wanting to handle this the biker way. And he was right. The justice Doug was offering was no justice at all. Would Stan really stop if he got a slap in the wrist? Would she feel the horrific violation of her privacy had been addressed if he had to pay a fine? Why not dive in a little deeper and embrace what Cade had given her? Do the one thing she secretly desired.

Vengeance. The Sinner way.

"I want the first punch."

"Dawn!" Doug's outraged shout drew chuckles from the Sinners. "What are you doing? What have you become? This isn't you. You're not violent. You don't break the law."

"Actually, I think this is me." She tipped her head to the side, musing over her decision. "This feels right. And I have broken the law, Doug. I did it to survive. And I'm about to do it again."

"Fucking Sinner old ladies," Sparky said, his voice laced with admiration. "They always gotta have a turn."

Cade's voice softened, his eyes dropping to her lips. "Is that another *request*?"

"My fight. The first punch is my business. Then you can address the disrespect done to the club. After that, and this is my final request, I would like you to give him to Doug, as well as all the evidence. He'll face justice twice. Our way and Doug's way."

Our way. It hadn't taken long for her to start thinking of herself as a Sinner. Maybe because she'd always been a Sinner at heart.

"Can't refuse my old lady." Cade turned her to face Stan. "He's all yours."

"Mommy. Cade's here."

Dawn almost didn't hear Tia's whispered words above the chatter of monkeys in the Conundrum Valley Zoo. They'd been visiting the animals all afternoon, and although she'd sent a text to Cade telling them where they were, she didn't expect him to show. But there he was, cut, chains, skull bandanna, Harley-Davidson buckle, and kickass biker boots, all ready for some clean family fun.

She registered the concerned looks of the parents around them, but the delight on Tia's face more than made up for her slight embarrassment at being outed as an outlaw biker groupie.

"Babe." Cade leaned down and kissed her cheek. Dawn could almost hear the gasps of disapproval.

He knelt down in front of Maia and Tia, all decked out in matching pink-and-purple T-shirts, purple sparkle skirts, and rainbow jelly shoes. "Ladies." He shook hands with them one at a time. "You are looking lovely as always."

Maia and Tia giggled, and Dawn smiled. So what if everyone disapproved. He might be a biker, but he had heart.

"What's on your hand?" Maia pointed to the brown streaks on Cade's knuckles, and he jerked his hand away.

"Just something I forgot to wash off."

"It's blood, isn't it?" Dawn whispered when he stood. "Are you hurt?"

"Not my blood." He headed for the washroom, and her stomach churned. Was it Stan's blood? Did she want to know what he'd done? How could he switch off the violence to be so gentle with the girls?

"So, where are the animals?" He joined Maia and Tia in front of the monkey exhibit a few minutes later.

"Here." Maia pointed to the cage. "We've got names for them all. Tia named the biggest, strongest one with the long hairy arms, Cade."

He looked down at Tia and grinned. "My arms aren't hairy."

"She thinks they are," Maia said. "But she doesn't mind."

His face softened and Dawn almost forgave him for coming to the zoo without washing up first, but the real-life reminder of what had happened at the restaurant sent a shiver down her spine. What had she done? What kind of role model was she for her girls if she had to resort to violence to solve her problems? She was no better than Jimmy.

"Monkeys are lame," Cade said. "How about we go see some real animals. Predators. Lions, tigers . . ."

"And bears?"

Cade cracked a grin. "Saw that movie when I was a kid. Mom loved it. Me not so much. Dorothy put the damn lion to shame. Made me appreciate a strong woman, though. Damn, you made me proud this morning."

"What happened to him?" she asked when the girls were out of earshot.

"We taught him a lesson, then handed him over. Benson called an ambulance and when the bastard is all fixed up, he'll spend some time in jail. Probably get out on bail. Trial a coupla years away . . . Due process. Just like you wanted." Cade stopped walking and pulled her into his arms, his hands smoothing down the back of her cut. "Having second thoughts?"

"Yes. I've never done anything like that in my life."

"Did it feel good?"

Dawn bit her lip. "It felt . . . great." So great she'd

wished she'd been able to do that to her uncle and Jimmy. Maybe even Shelly-Ann. Although Shelly-Ann had been almost decent when she dropped the girls off. Not only had she bought Maia and Tia new clothes and toys, she took the money Dawn gave her without asking for more. If Dawn hadn't been so shocked, she might have asked why. Shelly-Ann had acted almost as if she felt guilty, overcompensating the way Jimmy had the days after the nights he lost control.

Maia led them to the lion enclosure and they arrived just as the lion trainer began his presentation. Dawn's nose wrinkled at the sharp scent of blood coming from the lions' evening meal. She turned her focus to the talk as the girls settled on the bench between her and Cade.

When had she last seen them so relaxed and happy? She gave Tia's hand a squeeze and her daughter looked up and beamed. Dawn's eyes teared. Nothing warmed her heart more than her daughters' smiles.

Turning her attention back to the talk, she learned that male lions did little but eat, sleep, and copulate multiple times a day. By contrast, the female lions did all the hunting and raising the young.

"What does copulate mean?" Maia asked.

"It means have fun." Cade whispered. "And the lions have it right. Males need to conserve their energy to protect their females and cubs from predators, and for important nighttime activities."

"You can be the male lion," Maia said. "Tia and I will be your cubs. You can protect us from predators like you did at the park."

Cade tucked one girl under each arm. "Good idea. And how about your mom pretends to be a lioness and gets us some burgers while I keep people away from her seat?"

"Male lions don't get to partake of nighttime activities

if the lioness is tired from running around hunting for food." Dawn folded her arms. Seriously, sometimes she wondered if Cade belonged in the Stone Age.

Cade quickly detached himself from the girls. "So, what does everyone want on their burgers?"

"We all just want ketchup and Mom also wants candy floss," Maia said as he turned to leave. "Pink."

"Pink candy floss?" Cade's mouth turned up at the corners.

Dawn blushed. "My happiest childhood memories involve pink candy floss, roller coasters, and stuffed animals my mom won for me at carnival games. When she was young, she dated a carnie and he taught her all the tricks."

"Candy floss, three stuffed animals, and five burgers coming up." He winked at Dawn. "I was a carnie when I was a teenager. My mom thought a summer job would keep me out of trouble, but carnival folk aren't a conservative bunch."

Maia counted five fingers and frowned. "That's one burger too many."

"I'll need two." Cade grinned and lowered his voice. "Extra energy for nighttime activities."

Dawn snorted a laugh. "From what we've just heard about lions, I don't think you can compete. Didn't the trainer mention something about one hundred times a day?"

"Babe." He leaned forward and brushed his lips over her ear. "You've got to be fucking kidding. Lions have nothing on me. I haven't even begun to show you my best moves."

And didn't that just put all the wrong thoughts in her head for a day at the zoo.

They spent the rest of the afternoon watching the animals, and then Cade and Dawn pushed the girls on the swings in a nearby playground. They were having so much fun no one saw Shelly-Ann arrive.

"Well, look at this." Shelly-Ann's eyes lit up with a gotcha smile and she pulled out her phone. "Jimmy's not gonna be happy to see a picture of his old lady parading around in a Sinner cut. Didn't notice it when I dropped off the girls. Maybe I shoulda got out of the car."

Dawn clamped her hand around Shelly-Ann's wrist and pulled her close. "Then let's not make him unhappy. Put the phone away."

Shelly-Ann jerked her head away and her hair swung back behind her ear. Dawn stared at the massive bruise on ex sister-in-law's cheek, the size and shape eerily familiar.

"What happened to your face?"

"Nothing." Shelly-Ann's face shuttered, and she tugged her hair down.

"It was Jimmy, wasn't it? He always uses his right hand and his Brethren ring leaves a mark."

When Shelly-Ann didn't answer, Dawn pushed a little harder. "Did you ask him for more money because I don't have enough? Is that why he trashed my house? Does he not believe I'm giving you everything I've got?"

Guilt flickered across Shelly-Ann's face, but it disappeared so fast Dawn wasn't sure if she'd seen it. "Don't know anything about Jimmy. Or the money he's after." She turned to shout for the girls and Dawn saw finger-shaped bruises on her neck.

"He tried to strangle you." Her voice caught. "Shelly-Ann, you don't have to let him do that to you. I can help."

"Don't you fucking be nice to me." Shelly-Ann's face curdled. "You think you're something now that you're wearing that cut? You think being with the Sinners will solve all your problems? You're too damn good to be bad. You don't have what it takes to be a biker chick. When

Jimmy finally comes for you—and nothing will stop him now that he thinks you've got his money—I'll be fucking relieved 'cause I'm tired of watching you fight. Just give up. You'll never beat him. I don't understand why you never give the fuck up."

"What money? I don't understand."

Cade put a steady hand on Dawn's shoulder. "I almost forgot. I brought some ammo for your gun, babe." He reached into his pocket and handed her a magazine. "That enough?"

She stared him in disbelief. "Um . . . thanks for giving me that ammo, and so subtly threatening my ex-sister-in-law in the parking lot of the zoo."

Totally oblivious to her sarcasm, Cade smiled. "Pleasure, sweetheart."

Shelly-Ann rubbed her wrist, bouncing back to her nasty, officious self in seconds. "You're quite the pair. A regular Bonnie and Clyde. I'll be glad when Jimmy's done with you and I can go back to my nice quiet life."

Cade's eyes lit with humor. "Teamwork. You should try it sometime."

Five minutes later, after a flurry of tears and good-byes, Dawn followed Cade to his motorcycle in the parking lot. But when he put out a hand to help her mount, she took a step back.

"Did you really think I would shoot her? I felt good when I hit Stan because what he did was so utterly wrong, and so deeply personal, but it doesn't mean I've changed my views about violence. I'm not going to run around with a gun shooting anyone who pisses me off. Not Jimmy, and certainly not Shelly-Ann."

Cade cupped her face between her hands and stared at her intently. "You can't avoid violence in this life. Even when you left Mad Dog, you were still a part of his world. He's playing the game by different rules. Now you're on even footing. You have options. And one of them is me. Not just now. Always."

"What are you saying?" Her heart thudded in her chest. She knew what he was saying. She just didn't want to hear it.

He leaned down and brushed a soft kiss over her forehead. "I'm saying I'm here for you. Anything I am and anything I have is yours. However you want to deal with this situation, I'm on board. And when we both get what we want, when you've got your girls, and I've got justice, I'm not gonna let you go."

★ FIFTEEN ★

My ink is my heart. My cut is my bond. My bike is my soul.

SINNER'S TRIBE CREED

Cade joined Gunner, Zane, and a handful of Demon Spawn brothers crammed into the only strip bar in Whitefish. The dark, scuzzy dive in the center of town contained a small stage with a pole, no more than twenty worn, wooden tables, and enough smoke to conceal a wildfire. But it fitted Cade's mood to a T. He didn't want to be here. The Sinners didn't want to be here. And Demon Spawn definitely didn't want to be here since they suspected the Sinners hadn't come for a simple social visit.

And they were right. The Sinners hadn't just traveled to Whitefish to deal with the Demon Spawn members who attacked Zane and Cade in the alley. Dax had obtained some very disturbing information from Matchstick in the Sinner dungeon, and Cade and Zane intended to find out if it was true.

So now they were all pretending to celebrate, but the only person with a smile was the stripper on the pole.

Gunner slid over in the booth and Cade joined him,

falling back against the plush, black velvet cushions. The prospect hovered at his shoulder, and he sent the kid away to find him a drink.

"Nice of you to join us." Gunner grabbed a beer from the collection in the center of the table. "I wasn't sure you'd make it tonight."

"Neither was I," Cade said, keeping his voice low. "Who woulda thought I'd be spending my honeymoon offing a bunch of betraying Demon Spawn bastards?"

"Whaddya think of our girls?" The Demon Spawn VP, Skid Mark, soon to learn he was the new president, leaned over to shout above Warrant's "Cherry Pie," while the dancer spun around the pole. He was clearly drunk, his eyes at half-mast and his words slurred. "I hear you're the expert."

"Not anymore. Got an old lady now."

"That's right. I heard about that, too. You stole Mad Dog's old lady."

Gunner tensed, but Cade played it cool. "Can't steal something if it didn't belong to him."

"You steal his kids, too? They'll ruin your life, man. Suck your wallet dry."

Gunner was out of his seat now. And Zane, too. The prospect put down the beer he'd brought for Cade and moved to intercept the bouncer heading their way.

"You got a lot of personal information about Mad Dog's situation." Cade sipped his beer and fought for calm. "Kinda curious since Mad Dog lives way down south and you live way up north. But then, he likes to visit up here, doesn't he? Maybe he's a big skier, or does he come for the roads? Or maybe he likes disrespecting a brother's old lady, just like you."

Theory of a Deadman's "Bad Girlfriend" blasted through the tinny speakers and a new dancer took the stage, but the audience was now watching the conversation between Cade and Skid Mark. Tension thrummed through the bar, a powder keg ready to explode.

"Hey man, no offense. Just rumors. Congrats on getting hitched."

"He didn't mean to offend." Skid Mark's companion offered Cade a beer. "Sometimes he runs off at the mouth when he's had too much to drink."

Cade pushed the beer away. Disrespect was disrespect and it couldn't be smoothed over with words. Plus, he'd been itching for this fight since he left Conundrum. According to Matchstick, a handful of Demon Spawn members were Black Jack puppets, bikers who did the Jacks' dirty work in exchange for the promise of being allowed to form a new Black Jack chapter, or be patched over to the club, and it was time to put them in their place.

Justice for their treason would be swift and fierce, and Cade was leading the charge.

"Not interested in beer, but I am interested in teaching shit-for-brains a lesson in respect." He grabbed Skid Mark by the hair and smashed his head down on the table. "You can fucking apologize to me outside for disrespecting my old lady."

The music kept playing.

The dancer kept dancing.

The bikers drew their weapons.

Zane paid off the bouncers.

Cade's phone buzzed in his cut.

"Gotta take a call." He thudded Skid Mark's head on the table again. "You gonna walk outside or I gotta drag you?" He hadn't expected to have to make a show of the Sinners' dominance so soon, or in public, but what the hell.

Let's get the party started.

"Fuck you," Skid Mark said.

Cade pulled his gun from his cut and held it to Skid Mark's head. Skid Mark's Demon Spawn brothers pointed their weapons at Cade. He almost laughed at their lack of resolve.

"Tell your brothers to stand down or someone is gonna get hurt and I promise it will be you."

"Stand down," Skid Mark shouted, blood trickling from the side of his head.

The dancer on the pole did a Hands-Free Marley to Mötley Crüe's "Girls, Girls, Girls" and the dudes in perverts' row at the front clapped. Clearly there had trouble in the bar before. Cade had never seen a more brazen performance of "the show must go on."

Once upon a time, Dawn had been that girl on the pole. She'd danced, not because she wanted to dance, but because she had been given no choice. She would have finished her show and then gone down to perverts' row for the lap dances that were a dancer's bread and butter. Men would have touched her. Maybe more. And all the while Mad Dog would have watched and done nothing to protect her. Cade clenched his hand by his side, pushing the thoughts away as he tried to focus on the task at hand. As if he weren't wound up tight already.

His phone buzzed again. Zane, Gunner, and T-Rex disarmed the Demon Spawn brothers and tossed their weapons into the prospect's backpack. They wouldn't have been quite as bold if there hadn't been twenty more Sinners waiting on their bikes outside.

Cade threw a wad of money on the table and forced Skid Mark up at gunpoint. "Let's go for a walk. I'll leave your mouth alone so you can apologize and tell me which of your members are Black Jack puppets."

Skid Mark paled and Cade snorted a laugh. "Yeah, we know about the Jacks, and you're gonna give us a list of the puppet members. If your list doesn't match the one we got from Matchstick, you get to make up the difference." He yanked Matchstick's cut from his pack and threw it at Skid Mark. "Congrats, by the way. Looks like you got a promotion. Matchstick won't be needing that anymore. Wear it while you can, 'cause it won't be for long."

His phone buzzed again—probably Jagger wanting an update. Damn irritating. He nodded at Gunner and Zane to take his hostage, and then he turned off his phone. Punishment time. Jagger would damn well have to wait.

He headed outside where his Sinner brothers had herded the rest of the Demon Spawn members into a field behind the strip club. The local sheriff and his deputies were hog-tied in the police station, and the roads were blocked. No one was coming to help Demon Spawn now.

Cade handed Skid Mark a piece of paper and a pen. Skid Mark shuffled over to a patch of grass, silver in the moonlight, and wrote down a list of names that matched the one Dax had given to Cade. The traitors, including Skid Mark, were culled from the rest of the herd, and Gunner ushered the remaining Demon Spawn members away. Cade held a gun to Skid Mark's head.

"Bad fucking decision."

"Yeah. We should never have listened to Mad Dog, but Matchstick trusted him. They were friends going way back. He told us the Jacks were the stronger club. He said they'd been making up puppet members all over the state, hiding their numbers so they could take you down when you weren't expecting it. He said we should join the winning team before it was too late."

Cade didn't know what Mad Dog had to do with the Black Jack puppets in Demon Spawn, because Matchstick had kicked the bucket before he could share that information. Usually Zane kept Dax under control during torture sessions, but he'd been busy gathering intel on the

Jacks and Dax got carried away. He loved his work, but sometimes the sadist in him got a little too greedy.

He kicked the gravel underfoot, struggling between offing the bastard now and pumping him for more information. "Mad Dog didn't think his own club was the winning team? Demon Spawn and the Devil's Brethren would have been a good fit."

Skid Mark cast a worried glance at his brothers and Cade cuffed him on the head. "Don't look at them. Look at me. I'm the one who chooses whether you live or die. If you're cooperative, you might wind up in the hospital instead of the grave the brothers are digging just outside of town. I'm interested in Mad Dog and why he's sniffing around.

"Mad Dog is a Black Jack puppet in the Brethren, like some of his men. The Jacks are backing him to win the Brethren election on the condition he patches the entire club over to the Jacks. He's been paying off Wolf's supporters to vote for him 'cause the Jacks made him all sorts of promises if he can get the job done."

Good information. Cade shared a glance with Zane who nodded in silent agreement. If they'd picked up Skid Mark instead of Matchstick, Dax wouldn't have had any fun. They hadn't even had to break a finger. "You shoulda called us."

Sweat beaded on Skid Mark's forehead, and he wiped it away with the back of his hand. "Hell . . . we're a small club. Most of us have families and we support them mainly by running guns for the bigger clubs. I'm a single dad with two little girls. Mad Dog came here recruiting for the Jacks. He said the Jacks would let us form our own chapter, fully funded, and give us a cut of the arms trade up north. How could we pass that up? You Sinners just came in here, forced us to be a support club, and walked away. We helped Mad Dog empty a warehouse where the

Brethren were storing their weapons, and he paid us for our trouble."

Gunner kicked him in the side. "You pass it up because you're a Sinner support club. You pass it up out of loyalty, respect, and the fact that if you don't you fucking die."

Cade felt a curious stab of conscience. By rights the Sinners could beat the shit out of all the Demon Spawn traitors, trash their bikes, burn down their homes, take their women, and anything else they owned. And yet he couldn't shake the image of Skid Mark's little girls and how they would feel if their daddy didn't come home. What would Maia and Tia do without Dawn?

You don't have to solve every problem with violence. Dawn's words filtered through his mind, and yet, his dad had taught him the opposite. His dad used his fists to make a point, regardless of who was on the other side, or whether his little boy was watching.

Still, he couldn't let it slide. This was the life he'd chosen to lead and if the Sinners didn't make a show of force, word would spread, and the vultures would start circling. But death wasn't the only way.

"Destroy their bikes, burn their cuts, then beat the fucking crap out them."

Gunner frowned. "You don't want 'em dead?"

"No. I want them punished. Then I want them thrown into a van and driven to the Black Jack clubhouse. Paint 'em with the Sinner's Tribe logo and toss 'em by the back door like the trash they are. They wanna play at being Jacks, they can find out what it's really all about. And the Jacks will get the message. We're gonna find their puppets and root them out. And then we'll be coming for them."

"I can't believe you dragged us here. Jagger is going to go ballistic when he finds out we're meeting with Bunny."

Arianne followed Dawn through Sticky's Pool Hall, weaving through the crowds milling around the vast sea of pool tables. Banks followed behind Arianne, growling at anyone who crossed his path. He'd come along as muscle and he was doing a bang-up job at playing the part.

"I can't believe Cade agreed to this." He side-stepped a trip of college girls, and fell back in line.

"I didn't give him a choice," Dawn said over her shoulder. "And I have a feeling he wasn't really paying attention. But Bunny knows everyone. He'll know the private investigator in the video and through him, he may be able to find out who was on the other side of the camera. I can let the Sinners bring the girls home through force or politics, but I'll always be looking over my shoulder. This way, no one will question my ability to look after my children."

"Is Bunny gonna drag them to court and make them talk, too?" Banks asked. "Or you got another plan? No way is that PI gonna hold up his hand and say he handed you a bag of crack and then lied to the court for money."

"I'm working on that part. I might need some help to convince him." She skirted around a table and headed for the back where it wasn't as busy. Located in the basement of an ancient brick building on the far edge of Conundrum, Sticky's was famous for its pristine tables, local beer, and sticky floors. Dawn had never been in the bar when it was less than packed and she couldn't believe her luck when she'd spotted an empty table at the back when they walked in the door.

"You'll need a gun, maybe a knife, and a whole load of Sinners to make him show his face in court."

Dawn staked her claim on an empty pool table, tossing her jacket on the padded bumper. Yeah, she knew her plan had holes, but secretly, she was hoping Bunny might have some dirt on the PI, or his accomplice, that would make the second part of her task that much easier. If not, she would have to deal with her violence issues and ask for Cade's help because nothing was going to keep her away from her girls.

"Why didn't you meet with Bunny before?" Arianne ran an expert hand over the pool table. Viper had given her a pool cue for her third birthday, and she was now the best player in the MC. None of the Sinners would play against her because of the shame of possible defeat by a woman, so the lure of a good match at Sticky's had been enough to convince her to help Dawn out, despite the bad memories she had of Bunny's dungeon.

"I was just so desperate to be done with this world, I pushed everything away. Even when I brought you here last year, I didn't really think about how I knew Bunny or what he could do for me. I just thought about helping you."

"And now I get to return the favor."

"Don't like pool," Banks muttered as he stared at the table. "Don't like Sticky's. Don't like spending my night off playing pool at Sticky's just to keep you outta trouble."

"You love pool," Dawn countered. "I know for a fact you spend hours playing with the bouncers after the bar closes at night. They say you win back all the money you paid them for the night so they have to keep working."

"Gonna fire them when I get back to the bar." Banks stared down at the empty table and shook his head. "Crooked. Felt's not been looked after. Cues are bent. Balls are probably weighted."

Arianne laughed. "Well then, since you know everything that's wrong, I guess you won't mind playing against me. I promise to go easy on you." She grabbed a cue and a block of chalk. "We'll have a quick game until Dawn needs us. How much do you want to put down? I'm thinking of buying a new bike and I'm a couple grand short."

"Don't like playing against sharks," Banks said, but he took a cue and the faintest smile curved his lips.

"I'll go let him know I'm here." Dawn left them and headed over to the bar. Back when she'd been a dancer, Bunny paid Jimmy a small fortune for Dawn's exclusive attention at the Pink Cherry dance club, and although Jimmy didn't allow her to have sex with her clients—that privilege was his alone—he did allow almost anything else. Bunny took full advantage. However, he was always respectful and civil, often chatting with her after a dance despite the extra cost, and they forged an understanding. Sometimes Dawn would break the rules. In return, she earned a mark in Bunny's book.

Tonight she had come to collect.

She recognized the tall, broad-shouldered bartender from the last time she'd visited Bunny's pool hall with Arianne and shoved a fifty-dollar bill across the counter. That night she'd left with Cade and wound up in his bed for the second time. He made her come four times in as many hours and then she sneaked out before daybreak, ashamed of herself for breaking her own rules about one-night stands, but more afraid that if she stayed she'd break them again.

"I'm looking for Bunny. Tell him Dee wants to see him."

The bartender pocketed the bill without looking up. "He knows you're here."

Dawn gestured for Banks and Arianne to join her, but when they reached the counter, the bar phone buzzed and the bartender put out a warning hand.

"One second." He answered the phone, listened, and then hung up without saying a word. "Leave Jagger's bitch and the muscle outside."

Banks moved so fast all she caught was a blur at the corner of her eye, before he grabbed the bartender by the throat and yanked him down on the counter. "Don't much care for your disrespect, beer boy. Maybe you want to rephrase your request."

The bartender's face turned red, then purple, and he flailed and struggled in Banks's powerful grip.

"He can't talk." Dawn made no effort to hide her exasperation. "You're crushing his windpipe. I'm sure he'll be more polite if you allow him to breathe."

Banks huffed and released the bartender, shoving him backward from across the bar. "How 'bout you try it from the top?"

The bartender paled and his hand flew to his throat. "Not my rules. No leather. No muscle."

"Am I the muscle or are you the muscle?" Arianne grinned at Banks. "Since we're both wearing leather it's hard to tell."

"I'll go in alone," Dawn said with a bravado she didn't feel in the least. Cade was in Whitefish, and for once he wouldn't be around to swoop in and save the day. Tonight was her night, and although she felt apprehensive, she also felt a tingle of anticipation. This was the world she had run from. Now she was back, and this time no one would push her around.

"We're here if you need us." Banks folded his arms. "And I'm watching the door."

The bartender nodded and she followed him down a narrow hallway to a door guarded by two bald, thick-necked bouncers. They moved to let her pass and Dawn stepped into Bunny's office, a drab room containing only a metal desk, a small window, and three chairs.

Pasty-faced and balding, with rounded shoulders and a visible paunch, the man sitting behind the desk could have blended into any crowd save for his eyes, cold, hard, and obsidian black.

"You." Bunny leaned back in his chair and folded his arms behind his head. His two security guards, tall and heavily built, shifted on either side of his chair.

"Me."

"What do you want?"

Dawn twisted her hands together. "I'm calling in my mark. There's a video out there that shows me supposedly buying crack from a PI. Jimmy set it up to take my kids away. I want to find the PI, and I want to know who was behind the camera. I got a copy of the video from my lawyer." She put a hand into her purse. The security guards moved forward as one. Bunny shook his head.

"You don't have a mark with me. And if you did, you used it up when you brought Jagger's old lady here and his goons almost slit my throat."

"You and Arianne made a deal. That had nothing to do with me. I just made the introduction."

"I wouldn't have met with her if not for you. Don't like to get involved in biker business." He waved a dismissive hand and picked up his pen.

"But . . . I . . ." Her throat tightened and she couldn't say the words out loud. God, she'd been so naive when she was with Jimmy, so goddamn trusting in a world where everyone was ready to stab you in the back.

"You want a favor from me, Dee, you know the price." He looked up from his desk. "Been a long time since I saw you dance."

Bile rose in her throat. She couldn't do this again. She wouldn't pay for favors with her body even for the slim chance of getting back her girls. This was a line she wouldn't cross. There had to be another way, something Bunny might want from her . . . or from the Sinners.

"I'm not Dee anymore. I'm Dawn and I'm a Sinner old lady." She spun around to show him her cut. "I don't dance anymore, but I'm sure the value of having a mark with the Sinners would far outweigh any pleasure my dancing might give."

"A Sinner mark?" Bunny sat back and stared at her as if seeing her for the first time. "I heard you ran away from the Brethren. Didn't think you'd ever come back into the game."

"Neither did I, but I discovered a strength I never knew I had."

"Sinner strength?" He gestured at her cut.

"My strength."

Bunny smiled. "I got dealings with the Jacks. Don't want to get on their bad side."

"That's nothing compared with what will happen if you get on the Sinners' bad side. You got a taste of that last year." She tapped her throat in the same place Bunny sported a scar from Jagger's knife. "My old man has a protective streak, same as Jagger's, and he won't be happy if he finds out you asked me to dance."

He raised an appreciative eyebrow. "Maybe the Jacks won't hear about it."

"Maybe they won't."

"Maybe I'll look at the tape. Sinners can owe me a favor." He held out his hand, and Dawn gave him the USB stick she'd picked up from her lawyer's office on her way to the pool hall.

"Maybe we will, or maybe we'll come back and slit your throat and finish the job we started last time."

"Christ." Bunny chuckled. "You're almost as bad as Jagger's old lady."

"I'll take that as a compliment." She turned to leave and the door burst open. Chest heaving, Cade stepped over the bodies of the two guards in the hallway and pointed his gun at Bunny. Gunner, Arianne, and Banks tumbled in after him.

"End of the fucking line."

Dawn sighed and covered the gun with her hand, pressing it down. "Put that away, honey. We're done here."

"He's a dead man." Cade gripped Dawn's elbow to steer her clear of a drunk on the sidewalk. His body shook with unspent adrenaline and the remnants of the fear and anger that had been pulsing through him since Jagger called to tell him what was going on. Jagger had a sixth sense for when Arianne was doing something he wouldn't like, and when he'd texted to find out where she was, she told him the truth. The message got passed along. Already at the Conundrum border after dealing with the Demon Spawn scum, Cade had raced to Sticky's, arriving only minutes too late.

"He's doing me a favor," Dawn said. "Why do you want to shoot everyone who makes you angry?"

"I'm a Sinner. That's what Sinners do."

"Not always," she said softly. "That's not what Arianne does. Or T-Rex. That's not what the club agreed when Wolf offered an olive branch. And if you'd hurt Bunny, I would never have had a chance to find out who was responsible for that video."

He winced inwardly as her barb hit home. Every day he held back from going after Mad Dog was a day a piece of him died. That bastard was still on the streets, when by all rights he should be lying in a cold grave. If not for fucking Mad Dog, Dawn wouldn't have put herself in danger by going to see Bunny. If not for Mad Dog, she wouldn't be in danger at all.

And she wouldn't need Cade.

"I told you not to go there." He tightened his grip on

her arm, close to dragging her down the street. Damn. He couldn't calm down. It was too much . . . Bunny, the pool hall, all those bastards eyeing her up . . . the things that could have gone wrong . . .

"And then you said yes."

"I didn't think you were serious." He growled his frustration. "Or that you would even consider going there without me. And I was . . . distracted." Too agitated to continue the conversation in public, he led her into an alley off the street, and drew in a deep, calming breath, his nose wrinkling at the fetid smell of decay and the cloying scents of piss and stale beer.

"Nothing happened. He refused my mark and asked me to dance. I changed his mind. I didn't go there alone. I'm not stupid. He knew Arianne and Banks were outside. He wasn't going to hurt me." Dawn folded her arms and leaned against the brick wall. "In the end it worked out well. I don't always need you to rush to my rescue whenever there is a hint of danger."

"You're in danger every fucking minute of every fucking day, and I can't take it anymore." He thudded his fist against the brick wall. "I got a need to protect you that I don't even understand. I thought my heart was gonna explode when Jagger called to tell me where you were. Only reason everyone in that pool hall isn't dead is 'cause I brought Gun with me and he held me back." He leaned in, resting his forearm beside her head, caging her with his body.

Startled, she looked up, and he almost drowned in the emerald depths of her eyes.

"I know you can protect me," she said softly. "I don't doubt that. But I need to stand on my own feet. It felt good to see Bunny. It felt good to tell him I wouldn't dance. And it felt damn good to come up with a solution that didn't involve fists or firearms. I want to stand up to

Jimmy the way Arianne stood up to Viper, the way I stood up to that guy in the park. I know you're planning to go after Jimmy after the election, and I want to be part of that."

His body shook with emotion. "I get that you want to fight your own fight, but some fights you can't win. My mom never won her fight with my dad. After years of abuse, she finally moved out, but the week after I was sent overseas, she went back to him. In the end he hit her one too many times, and she died from a subdural hematoma. I never confronted him. Never saw him again. He died in jail. I could never understand why she went back."

Dawn stroked his jaw, her eyes warm with understanding. "Because that kind of abuse twists your mind. It saps your strength and confidence. You feel worthless and incompetent. You believe the demeaning comments. You don't think you deserve any better. You think no one cares. Every day is a fight to survive. Every night you hate yourself for not running away. You feel humiliated and alone, and sometimes the abuser can seem like a comfort in the storm, especially on the good days."

"What did he do to you?" he asked, although he knew. He'd lived through it. And it was all he could do not to jump on his bike and shoot Mad Dog dead, or die trying. Just the thought of Dawn suffering the way his mom had suffered stoked a fury inside him so fierce he thought he might explode.

"He beat me." Her voice was surprisingly calm and even, a startling contrast with the rage that suffused his veins. "He made me strip and dance for his friends. He treated me like a piece of property and shared me around. He kept me isolated and humiliated me. Sometimes after it was really bad, he would apologize and buy me flowers, and then it would be okay until it started again."

"I wasn't there to protect my mom in the end, but I'll

damn well be there for you." Cade clasped her chin between his thumb and forefinger and turned her head roughly, forcing her to look at him. "I'll do what has to be done to end this. You may want to face him, but we both know you'll never pull that trigger. And even if you could, I won't let you bear that burden."

"Cade . . . no."

Overwhelmed by a tumult of emotion, he stepped away. "You may not want my help and protection, but you will have it. Even if it means going against my club so you never have to face Mad Dog again."

★ SIXTEEN ★

I will show no mercy when mercy is not deserved.
SINNER'S TRIBE CREED

Dawn waved to the bus driver as the city bus lurched out from the bus stop and into the street, somehow working its way past a black cat that had bedded down for the night on the asphalt. Exhausted from a late shift and the emotional upheaval of the day, she wanted nothing more than to fall into bed, and she was profoundly grateful to Cade who had arranged to have her bed replaced, and the damage to her home repaired by a small army of junior patch. Maybe tomorrow she would be able to think clearly again and decide just how deeply she wanted to get involved in the Sinner's Tribe. As if she weren't drowning already.

She unlocked the front door and then stepped inside, closing and bolting it behind her. But as she reached for the light, her skin prickled in warning.

Too late. Maybe she shouldn't have made that wish the other night.

"Welcome home, love. Come give your old man a kiss."

Ice flooded her veins and she turned to see Jimmy

sprawled on a chair in her darkened living room. "How did you get in here?"

He gestured for her to approach him, scowling when she didn't move from the door. With his face half in and half out of shadow, his hoodie bunched around his neck, and his all-black attire, he looked every inch the monster she knew he was.

Run. She should run. But dammit, this was her house. Plus she knew he wouldn't let her get away that easy. There would be some trap lying outside: Brethren hiding in the bushes, a gun in his hand hidden by his side.

"You know me. I can get in anywhere." He leered and she recoiled at the double entendre, wishing she could erase every minute she had spent in his bed.

"Get out or I'll call the police." She pulled her phone from her pocket with one hand and reached into her purse with the other, feeling for her weapon. She'd loaded the gun after Cade dropped her off at work, never thinking she would have to use it so soon.

Jimmy pushed himself out of the chair and ambled toward her, seemingly unaffected by her threat. "I want my fucking money. Then you're gonna come home where you belong and I'll teach you again what it means to be mine." He struck her with his closed fist, sending her flying sideways across the room. The purse fell from her grasp and she landed on her back beside the coffee table.

Stunned, slivers of pain shooting up her back, her face throbbing, she could only watch as he tugged open his belt and closed the distance between them.

"Did you think I wouldn't find out you stole from me? Or that you've been parading around town in a Sinner cut? Did you think Shelly-Ann wouldn't tell me? I've put up with your shit far too long." He whipped off his belt with a crack and Dawn's breath caught in her throat. Jimmy had left her alone for the better part of three years. Why did he want her back now?

"Time for a reminder about how this relationship works. Then you'll get that money and come home with me so you can be reminded of it every day."

"I don't understand. I thought we were done. You have someone new." Grimacing at the pain, she pushed herself to sitting and searched for her purse.

Jimmy tugged open his fly and scowled. "I'm sure you'll understand just fine when it's my dick inside you instead of that fucking Sinner's dick. Shelly-Ann saw you playing happy families in the park." His face twisted and spittle bubbled at the corner of his mouth. "*I* saw you," he screamed. "I saw him kiss you. I saw his fucking paws all over you. You're my old lady. My wife. And you're a fucking whore and a thief."

Every alarm bell in her body triggered in warning. He was past the point of restraint, past the point of rational thought. The few times he'd been like this she'd barely managed to get out of their apartment alive.

Dawn rolled, her arm outstretched toward her purse, but Jimmy was on her before her fingers caught the handle. He straddled her hips, his weight pinning her to the floor.

"You got two choices, bitch." He caged her jaw, forcing her mouth open with his thumb as his fingers pressed against her windpipe, cutting off her air and making it impossible to scream. "You can lie nice and quiet and take what I'm gonna give you, or you can put up a little fight and I'll whip you and fuck you and beat you and fuck you again."

Dawn's heart pounded so hard she thought it would crack a rib. How had she ever looked into those cold, dark eyes and seen a savior? How had she ever thought Jimmy cared? She inched her fingers toward her fallen phone, fighting the darkness threatening her vision.

"Tsk. Tsk." Jimmy released her and snatched the phone from her grasp. "You thinking of calling for help? Do your new Sinner friends know how you earned your keep for the Brethren, little whore? Does your damn Sinner? I'll bet he'll lose interest pretty quick when he finds out just what a skanky bitch you really are, when it's my cum filling your pussy. Maybe we'll make some more damn brats. He's not gonna want you all knocked up. I sure didn't."

Dawn sucked in a breath of cool, clean air and tried to stop the trembles racking her body. She closed her hand into a fist and remembered the moment she hit Stan and how she'd imagined he was Jimmy.

"No one's coming to help you, love. Not the police. Not the Sinners. And definitely not that fucking prick who can't keep his dick out of other people's business." He threw her phone against the wall, grinning when it slid to the floor with a sharp crack. "Cheap. Like you."

"Jimmy. Please. Stop."

Without hesitation, he shoved up her top. Dawn shivered as the cool air slid over her heated skin. The urge to hit, slap, punch, and fight him away was almost overwhelming, but experience had taught her if she used her hands against him, he would either pin them above her head or bind her wrists, and right now she needed her hands free to get her gun.

"Fuck, I missed these tits." He gave her breast a vicious squeeze through her satin bra. "Did you know I picked you up off the streets just 'cause you had the nicest tits I'd ever seen? Whore tits."

Bile rose in her throat as he pawed at her breasts. Her purse lay discarded, open, and within reach. While Jimmy was distracted, she slid her fingers inside, barely daring to breathe until she felt cold steel. When he moved to shove up her bra, she yanked out the gun and held it with two hands, pointing the barrel at Jimmy's chest.

"Off."

Jimmy froze and then he smirked. "You playing that game again? You think I don't know it's not loaded? You don't have what it takes. You never did. That's why you never fit in with the Brethren. And deep down you'll never shoot me. I'm the man who saved you from the streets, gave you a home, a life, a job, discipline, two sniveling brats, and all the fucking you couldn't handle."

"Last time. Off." She felt different holding a loaded gun. Resolved. And Jimmy could clearly see the difference.

He sighed and pushed himself up, his belt still dangling from his grip. "Okay. I'm off. Now give me the gun before someone gets hurt."

Dawn scrambled to her feet. "Out."

Too late she saw the danger. His hand shot out and he cracked his belt, whipping it across her bare arm. The violent sting of leather on her exposed skin made her gasp and she lost her grip on the gun.

Crack. He struck again, this time whipping the belt over her wrist. Pain fuzzed her brain and her hand wavered.

"Stop, Jimmy. Stop. I dropped the gun."

But Jimmy never stopped. No matter how hard she begged, he never stopped until he was sated or she was unconscious, or both. He yanked a blade from beneath his cut and raised his arm to whip her again. "Gonna mark you, bitch. Gonna carve my initials into those pretty cheeks so no one will ever mess with my property again."

Heart pounding, she ran at him, using momentum to knock him off his feet. Jimmy stumbled over the coffee table, falling heavily to the ground. The belt fell from one hand and the blade fell from the other.

"Jesus Christ. You're gonna be sorry for that."

Dawn threw herself forward and grabbed the knife. Acting purely on instinct, she stabbed the blade into his thigh.

Jimmy screamed. The world slowed. She released the blade and backed away as Jimmy's face twisted into a mask of horror.

"Fucking bitch. You stabbed me." He grabbed his leg with one hand and pulled his phone out of his cut with the other.

"Drop it." Dawn grabbed her gun from the floor and pointed it at Jimmy. "It is loaded. If you look closely, you'll see the magazine."

He stared at her for a long second, and then he placed the phone on the floor. "Christ. The Sinners have turned you. Little Dee carrying a loaded gun. Have they made you into a killer, too? Are you ready to pull that trigger?"

"You want to take that risk? Look what I just did to your leg. You think I won't do that to your head after everything you did to me? Throw the phone to me."

"Crazy bitch. You want me to bleed out all over your floor?" With a snarl, he threw the phone and Dawn kicked it away.

Sweat beaded her forehead as she contemplated the wounded man in front of her. She hated Jimmy, had imagined having him at her mercy countless times, although in every scenario he died and she lived with her girls happily ever after. But now that the moment was here, she knew she would never be able to live with herself if he died because of her. He needed medical attention but no way could she call the Brethren and tell them she'd stabbed one of their brothers.

As if he sensed her confusion, Jimmy softened his

voice and tilted his head to the side. "I need your help or I'm gonna bleed to death. How many years were we together? You gonna let the father of your children die?"

She took a step forward and then caught herself. He wasn't bleeding that badly, which meant she hadn't hit any major veins or arteries, and he wasn't screaming the way he had years ago when he'd taken a shot in the leg that had hit a bone. Her stomach knotted at the idea of someone in pain—even him—but she knew better than to trust him. 911 wasn't an option unless she wanted to go to jail for stabbing him and carrying what she was damn sure was a stolen gun.

Jimmy groaned and clutched his leg. "I know you're pissed at me, but I promise things will be different this time. I'm gonna be president of the Brethren. I won't have to do things I don't wanna do and I won't be answering to no one. We'll get a big house with a yard for the girls. We'll be a family, just like you always wanted."

Cade's phone buzzed in his pocket, and for a moment he considered not answering it. Gunner was waiting for him outside the clubhouse, and he was just about to bail on him for the very first time. He'd promised Gunner weeks ago he would go with him to a party tonight. At the time, he'd been more than happy to accept the invitation, envisioning a night in a hot tub with a girl tucked under each arm, an endless supply of champagne, and a room with a bed big enough for three. But now there was only one woman he wanted, and she kept him plenty busy in bed.

Well, at least she had until he lost it outside Bunny's pool hall. She hadn't spoken to him since their encounter in the alley. But he couldn't let her put herself in danger, especially after she'd just made a narrow escape from Bunny. Sure, she said it all went fine. But who knew what went on behind closed doors?

With an irritated growl, he checked the screen. *Arianne?*

"Is Dawn with you?" She sounded breathless, anxious. He could hear people talking, glassware clinking, and the faint sound of the Kongos' "Come with Me Now" playing in the background.

"No." His skin prickled. "Haven't seen her since I dropped her off at work."

"She didn't call after her shift to let me know she was home and she's not answering her phone. I thought maybe she was with you."

"Maybe the bus broke down."

"I called the bus company," she snapped. "The busses are all running on time. I'm worried, Cade. It's not like her to forget to call."

That warning prickle returned, but worse, and his heart raced like he was running a damn marathon. Cade closed his eyes and tried to pull it together. But he couldn't shake the damn past: memories of his mother's face covered in bruises, her body limp on the floor, her arm in a cast, bandages on her head; the nights he spent sitting with her in the hospital. Abusive guys like Mad Dog—like his dad—never let go and they never gave up.

"Gunner and I were about to head over that way for a party. We can swing by her place."

"Hurry, Cade. Something's wrong."

★ SEVENTEEN ★

I may not always agree with my brother, but he is always my brother.

SINNER'S TRIBE CREED

A family.

Yes, she'd always wanted a family like she'd had before the car crash, but when she imagined a family it was much like what she'd had at the zoo: her children playing in the sunshine, and a partner who made her laugh, someone who respected her need for independence, but was there when she needed him.

"You don't know what a family is."

A shadow crossed his face so quickly she wondered if she'd imagined it, but when he spoke, his voice was gentle, the same voice he'd used when he coaxed her off the streets with promises of a better life, the voice he used on the good days just before everything turned bad.

"I've got a gun in my cut, love. If I wanted to kill you I would've done it already. But I want you back. I miss you . . . and the girls. A president needs a family so the old boys think he's stable and . . . settled. And . . . the money. It doesn't all belong to me."

As if she would ever believe him. The red wheal on

her hand from his belt and years of hospital visits had taught her that the soft words were usually followed by a hard beating, and she hadn't missed the hesitation before he mentioned the girls. He didn't want them. Never had. And he was crazy if he thought she had any money.

"Slide your weapon across the floor to me. And your belt. When I've got them, I'll call Wolf and he can send someone to pick you up."

Jimmy's smile didn't reach his ears. "That's my girl."

A loud thud on the door startled them both. Jimmy froze and drew his weapon. Resting against the wall directly across from her in the living room, he was in clear sight of the door.

"Who the fuck is that?"

"Dawn!"

She recognized Cade's voice and her lips quivered with a smile. "Maybe it's the mailman."

"It's Cade. Open the door."

"I knew it." Jimmy's harsh voice echoed in the tiny room. "You are fucking that Sinner. You betraying little bitch. That's why you wouldn't come back. You were spreading your legs like the whore you really are. Open the damn door. I'm gonna blow so many holes in him you won't be able to find his dick."

Dawn glanced around the room, assessing potential places to hide. The kitchen lay behind her, visible through the opening at the breakfast bar, but accessible only if she could make the ten feet to the door. The small hallway leading to the bathroom and the bedrooms was directly across from the front door and also in Jimmy's line of fire. If Jimmy started shooting, her best bet for cover was the couch beside her.

Jimmy put a finger to his lips. His black eyes gleamed and she knew right away if she'd gone to help him he would have found a way to hurt her. Drawing in a ragged breath, she threw herself behind the couch and screamed. "Jimmy's here. He's down but armed and at nine o'clock from the door."

Silence.

And then the door splintered and Jimmy fired.

"You can't kill him."

Plastered against the walls on either side of the front door, Gunner and Cade shared a glance.

"He just fired at us." Cade kept his voice to a low murmur. "We have to defend ourselves. My old lady is a hostage inside. Of course we can kill him."

"Jagger says no." Gunner lowered his phone. "He gave his word to Wolf that we wouldn't touch Mad Dog. He wants us to go in, rescue her, and get out before the cops show up."

"Do you hear sirens?" Cade checked his magazine. "The cops aren't coming. No one heard the shot. There's no one on the street and I didn't see any lights go on. Not even a dog barked."

Gunner twisted his lips to the side. "How 'bout we do as Jagger said and try and get her out without killing him?"

"He's a threat to my old lady. I have a right to defend her and Wolf's not gonna be able to say dick about it. No one fucks with a biker's old lady." Cade peered around the corner and a bullet zinged past his head, embedding itself in the wall behind him.

"Fuck." Gunner sighed. "Where is she?"

"She's behind the couch in the middle of the room, directly across from him and slightly to the right of the door, maybe twenty feet away. There's a small hallway between the living room and us. She's got her gun."

"I'll distract him and you get her out." Gunner took a step toward the entrance.

"You get her out and I'll kill him."

"Jesus, Cade." Gunner exhaled an exasperated sigh. "He's down and injured, and we've got a clear run to Dawn and out again. We won't be able to spin this in a way that justifies taking him out. The Brethren election is only a week away. We'll patch them over and then we'll go after him together. We've come this far. Why risk it all now? If Wolf calls Jagger out for breaking his word, we'll be done for."

Sirens wailed in the distance. Maybe the neighbors were more vigilant than he thought. And although he wanted Mad Dog dead so badly he could taste it, Gunner had a good point. Could he put the club at risk over a matter of seven days? But how could he let Mad Dog live after what he'd done? Never had he been so conflicted about his duty to the club. Never had he questioned the creed.

Sensing his hesitation, Gunner checked the magazine in his semi-automatic and raised his weapon. "She's your girl. I'll cover. You rescue. And by the way, you're gonna owe me big time if the twins ditch us tonight."

"Get over it. You love shooting things."

"This ain't the weapon I was planning on shooting tonight, brother."

Brother.

He couldn't let his brothers down. *I will follow the creed before I follow my heart.*

Cade tensed, adrenaline pounding through his veins as he mentally prepared himself to go in, grab Dawn, and get out with succumbing to the almost overwhelming desire to get rid of Mad Dog for once and for all. "If your aim is a little off and you hit Mad Dog by mistake . . ."

"I don't make mistakes." Gunner stepped into the doorway and fired, his bullets thudding into the wall above Mad Dog's head. Cade dived past him and landed behind the couch beside Dawn. Although pale, she appeared remarkably together given the circumstances.

"Rescue time. Stay low and head for the door." He jumped up and fired a few random shots to keep Mad Dog occupied while Dawn crouched and ran. Mad Dog grunted and the gun fell from his grip.

"Fuck. I shot him." Gunner slammed a hand on the doorframe.

"No, I shot him." Cade half rose from behind the couch, his weapon still trained on Mad Dog.

"Are you fucking kidding?" Gunner raced across the room to kick the bastard's gun away. "You didn't have a clear shot."

Cade knelt down beside Mad Dog and pressed two fingers to the pulse on his neck. "Damn. He's still alive."

"It's our lucky day." Gunner heaved a sigh. "We woulda started a war and been kicked out of the club."

"Um . . . boys." Dawn motioned them to the door, but Cade didn't move.

"I would have been kicked out," Cade said. "It was my bullet."

"You can't shoot for shit." Gunner tugged at Mad Dog's shirt to check the wound. "No way would I let you take the fall."

Dawn raised her voice to a shout. "The police are almost here. I can see flashing lights. You have to go."

"Fuck." Gunner slapped the bullet-ridden wall. "He was wearing a vest. He'll be bruised but not broken. Let's go."

"You can't leave him here." Dawn's voice rose in pitch.

Cade frowned. "Why not? Break and enter, assault with a deadly weapon? Taking a hostage? Even our lawyer wouldn't be able to get us off without some jail time."

"We'll do time together," Mad Dog mumbled. "You

bastards don't get me outta here before the cops show, I'll tell them I came to visit my wife to talk about our kids and Dawn stabbed me unprovoked. Then a buncha Sinners tried to off me. My bullets are near the door. Makes it look like I was defending myself. By the time the cops sort it out we'll have spent months cooling our heels in jail."

"I'm not your wife," Dawn bit out. "We're divorced."

"And look what happened when you pulled that shit." Mad Dog gave a bitter laugh. "Not that a civilian piece of paper means dick all. And that cut you're wearing is a joke. You're still my old lady until I'm dead or I let you go."

"Your call, brother," Gunner said.

Cade pointed his gun at Mad Dog's head. "I wanna shoot the fucker dead."

Dawn looked at Cade aghast. "We have to let him go. There's not enough time to clean up and hide his body. I can't go to jail, Cade. I can't leave the girls with Shelly-Ann and no one to watch out for them."

"Can you walk, fuck face?" Cade shoved Mad Dog's head back with the gun barrel, his finger itching to pull the trigger.

"Just get me to my damn bike," Mad Dog spat out. "I'll call someone to pick me up." He turned to Dawn. "Bitch. Gimme my phone. And go get the money."

Cade jabbed his knee into the wound on Mad Dog's leg and Mad Dog screamed.

"You disrespect her again and I'm gonna say fuck the MC, fuck the cops, and fuck you breathing another fucking breath."

"I need the money, dammit," Mad Dog leaned on Gunner to pull himself up. "I know she has it."

"Shut the fuck up." Cade smashed the butt of his gun into Mad Dog's head. Maybe if he hit the bastard enough times, he would do Cade the favor of dying.

"Take him out the back door in case someone sees him." Dawn handed Mad Dog the phone and Gunner half dragged him through the kitchen.

Cade looked back over his shoulder at Dawn. "You okay?"

"Yeah, I'm good." But she didn't sound good, and she didn't look good either. He'd never seen her so pale.

"Put your gun away," Cade said softly. "Don't let them know you have it. Call me if they take you to the station or arrest you. Club's got a lawyer, Richard—"

"I can't afford . . ."

"I'll take care of it." He had a healthy bank balance from the work he did for the club, and without a family and no desire to spend it on flashy cars, or fancy digs, he was more than able to pay Richard's fees.

"We gotta go," Gunner shouted over the wail of sirens.

"I'll ride around the block and come back when the cops leave," Cade called out to Dawn. "Then I'll take you to the clubhouse. You can't stay here with a broken-in door."

Gunner grunted his disapproval. "I thought we were gonna . . . you know . . . we had plans."

"Plans change." Cade took one last look at Dawn, and then he turned and dragged Mad Dog away.

"Fucking hell." Jagger scrubbed a hand over his face and glared at Dawn, Gunner, and Cade, seated in front of his enormous oak desk like recalcitrant children. Zane, Sparky, and Dax leaned against the walls behind them along with Shaggy and T-Rex for an impromptu and unofficial board meeting.

"What the fuck were you thinking?"

Dawn forced herself to meet his gaze. With her head still spinning from how quickly the Sinners had arranged for her door to be fixed, and the bullet holes repaired after she'd put the police off the scent last night, a confrontation with Jagger was about the last thing she was up for this afternoon.

"I was thinking Jimmy . . . er . . . Mad Dog had broken into my apartment and intended to assault me and then bring me back to his clubhouse." She raised a hand to block out the light streaming through the wall of windows beside him so she could more clearly see his face. Such a beautiful office for someone with such a menacing scowl. Dark wood shelves lined the wall behind him, and a matching credenza sat to his left beneath a polished mirror. Clearly the Sinners hadn't done much to renovate this room; its historic patina was marred only by the prints of motorcycles hung on the worn, papered walls.

"Not you." Jagger waved at her dismissively. "The two idiots beside you. What part of 'don't engage the Brethren' did you two not understand?"

"He engaged us first," Gunner said. "And he was holding Cade's old lady hostage. We had a duty to rescue her."

"Don't spin me that bullshit." Jagger thumped his fist on the desk. "You shot him. If he hadn't been wearing a vest, he would have died."

"Actually, I shot him," Cade interjected. "Gun was very expertly shooting around him to provide cover for Dawn to get out."

Gunner sniffed. "You know Cade couldn't hit a target right in front of his face. I shot him."

"I stabbed him," Dawn said, feeling left out. "In the leg. That's why he was down."

"Well, according to Wolf, he told the Brethren executive board that Cade and Gunner attacked him when he visited his wife to talk about their kids." Jagger pushed his chair away from the table. "So now we got a problem. Wolf says I broke my word, and now he can't negotiate with us without looking weak, like he's not supporting his brother."

"Did you tell him about the Jacks backing Mad Dog?" Dax always liked to know his intel was being put to good use.

"Yeah, I told him. He wasn't surprised, but he's reluctant to raise the issue before the election in case it backfires, or the Black Jack puppets outnumber his supporters. He needs us to clean house, as much as we need Brethren support."

"That might be part of the reason why Mad Dog accused Cade and Gunner," Dawn said. "He's afraid you'll actively back Wolf. With the Sinner support clubs and resources behind him, Wolf will be sure to win. By accusing Cade and Gunner, Jimmy effectively cuts Wolf off from any potential Sinner support, makes the Sinners look bad, and wins himself the sympathy vote. Wolf's only hope now is if you back him openly."

Gunner scrubbed a hand through his buzz cut. "I dunno. Then it'll look like we tried to off Mad Dog so Wolf would win. Could turn everything against us."

"Or it could be just what Wolf needs." Dawn hesitated, acutely aware that she was now the center of attention. The Sinners were listening in a way the Brethren never had. All those years sitting quietly in the corner at the Brethren clubhouse hadn't been a total waste. She'd listened and learned, watched the political game and understood the players.

Worthy. And it felt damn good.

"Keep going," Jagger said. "You know them better than we do."

"If the Brethren think Wolf is cunning and powerful enough to enlist the Sinners to take out Mad Dog, they'll vote for Wolf. Yeah, they might grumble that Wolf didn't support Mad Dog, but in the end they aren't hung up on rules or creeds or honor. The only thing they respect is power. And if the Sinners come out and show their support for Wolf instead of hiding in the shadows like the Jacks, they'll see Wolf as the strongest candidate and the Sinners as the strongest club, and they'll vote for the man who can bring a patch over to the table."

"We got intel that Mad Dog might be paying off supporters," Gunner said. "If that's the case, it won't matter who they think is stronger. They'll just follow the money."

Dawn sucked in her lips, considering. "Mad Dog came to my house demanding money. He seemed almost desperate. If he needs money that badly, he must not have paid off enough supporters yet to win the election."

Jagger's eyes narrowed. "You got any ideas?" he asked. "A good way for the Sinners to show their support for Wolf?"

"The Brethren love a good party."

"Done." Jagger slapped his hand on the table. "You organize it. Tell Banks we'll need the bar on Saturday."

Dawn's gaze flicked from Jagger to Cade and back to Jagger. She'd given them information that could tip the balance in the Sinners' favor, now it was time for payback. Only a few weeks ago, she'd considered the idea and dismissed it out of hand, not just because she lacked confidence, but also because she had nothing to offer. Now she had both.

"I want something in return." She swallowed hard and firmed her voice. "I want my girls back. Now. Wolf is president. If he tells Mad Dog to keep Shelly-Ann and the police off my back, then he'll have to do it; otherwise he risks being kicked out for disobeying his president and he'll lose his chance at running for election. He's put me at risk by making Mad Dog untouchable, and you've seen how Mad Dog took advantage. I've had enough. No more talking about it. No more negotiating. I'm a Sinner old lady and they are Sinner girls and I want them to come home."

"You've got to be fucking kidding," Zane spat out. "We're not getting involved in a fucking marital dispute."

Dawn dropped her hands to her hips and stiffened her spine. "And I didn't want to get involved in a biker war, but that's what this is. The Brethren are a pawn in the war between the Sinners and the Jacks. Yes, you can take the information I gave you, ignore my request, and help Wolf win the election so he'll patch his club over to the Sinners, but it's not the right thing to do, and it's not how our world works. I'm calling in my mark and I expect you to honor it."

"I vote in favor," Cade said. "Anyone opposed?"

Not even Zane lifted a hand.

Jagger nodded. "I'll talk to Wolf."

She thought her heart would burst.

★ EIGHTEEN ★

I will never let down my guard.

SINNER'S TRIBE CREED

Her girls were home.

Dawn sat on the floor of the bedroom that had been unused for the last year, hugging her knees to her chest, still unable to believe her angels were home. But there they were. Maia and Tia. Asleep in their twin princess beds, tucked under duvets bearing the images of handsome princes, horse-drawn carriages, and happily-ever-afters.

One call was all it had taken. Everyone was on board with her plan. Jagger called her after the deal was done, and a few minutes later she was in the Sinner SUV, and driving straight to Shelly-Ann's house.

They'd celebrated with ice cream and pizza and now the girls were asleep and Dawn couldn't bring herself to leave their room, terrified it wouldn't last. What if it wasn't real? What if Wolf changed his mind and Shelly-Ann came to take her girls away? Without a way to overturn the court decision, it was a pyrrhic victory at best. She'd used up her mark with the Sinners, and no doubt enraged

Jimmy, and as easily as the favor had been granted, it could be taken away.

Unless she took Doug up on his offer.

The buzz of her phone startled her. She pushed away her thoughts of leaving Conundrum and checked her text messages.

How's my old lady?
Best day of my life
And your girls?
Asleep
Are you sleeping?
Yes. I'm fast asleep
Wake up, babe. I'm here

Dawn heard the rattle of a key in the lock and the thud of a dead bolt. The front door creaked open and footsteps echoed through the house. When she looked up, Cade stood in the doorway, arms folded, blocking the light from the hallway.

"Where did you get the key?"

"Had it made when we replaced the door."

She lifted an eyebrow. "You didn't think to ask?"

"You're my old lady. I need easy access." He kept his voice low as he walked toward her, his handsome face partially obscured by the shadows. "What are you doing on the floor?"

"I've waited so long to have them back, spent so many nights imagining they were here, after I put them to bed, I couldn't leave. I want to watch them in case it isn't real or in case it doesn't last and they're suddenly taken away." She pressed a fist to her mouth. "I'm so confused, Cade. One moment I'm bursting with joy, and the next I'm terrified I'll lose them again. I don't think I could bear it."

A pained expression crossed Cade's face and he sat on the floor beside her, his leather creaking as he put an arm around her shoulders and pulled her against his chest.

"What are you doing?"

"Keeping you company."

"Cade . . ." She tried to push away, but he held her tight. "You don't have to do this. If you want to stay, you can take my bed."

"There aren't many precious moments in life, babe." He stroked his fingers over her bare arm. "Best to appreciate them when they happen, and even better if you're not alone. We'll watch them together. Keep them safe."

She swallowed past the lump in her throat. "You want to sit on a cold, hard floor all night watching two little girls sleep?"

"Maia and Tia," he said. "Not just two little girls. Your girls. And I know you're worried. That's why I'm here for as long as you need me."

Dawn tried to wrap her mind around the fact a big, badass biker was sitting on the floor with her, in a room full of princess toys. Not only that, he seemed prepared to stay. "That's very sweet."

Cade chuckled. "For a sinner."

"You have a good heart for a sinner. Strong, brave, loyal. And you're not so bad in bed."

Dawn leaned up and nuzzled his neck. Cade groaned.

"Don't start something that can't be finished in here with your kids. I'm supposed to get a reward for good behavior. Not a punishment."

"I'll just sit here and dream up a suitable reward."

But when he tucked her under his arm and settled her back against his chest, Dawn knew he understood. Now she needed her girls. Later was for him.

* * *

Cade startled awake when Dawn placed a hand on his shoulder. Last thing he remembered, he'd carried her to bed, fast asleep, then come back to watch over the girls.

"What are you still doing here?" She kept her voice to a low hush so she didn't wake the children.

"Thought I'd keep watch after you fell asleep." He pushed himself to his feet and Dawn reached up and stroked a hand along his jaw, rough with a five o'clock shadow.

"That's probably the nicest thing anyone has ever done for me."

"That mean it's time for my reward?" He slid a hand over her hip and along the edge of those damn sexy shorts she wore to bed. He loved her in those shorts. Probably more than he loved her in lingerie.

"You did this for sex?"

Cade leaned down and kissed her. "I did it for you."

Dawn clasped his hand and led him out of the room and down the hallway.

Cade lasted thirty seconds watching her lush ass peeking from the bottom of the shorts, and then lust destroyed the last of his patience. *Can't wait.* In one quick motion, he scooped her up, and threw her over his shoulder.

"Hey, put me down." She wriggled against him and his groin tightened. *Christ.* He'd listened to the brothers with old ladies complain about their women dressing down once they had kids, but now he understood. If he had to watch her walking around in those shorts every day, he'd be sporting a permanent erection not appropriate for family viewing.

"You got a perfect ass." Cade squeezed her cheek. "I can hardly wait to get both hands on it."

Once in her bedroom, he dropped her on the bed and immediately turned to check out her room. Feminine but not frilly. Modern but not austere. She'd clearly worked hard to fix it up, and if he hadn't known to look for signs of the break-in, he wouldn't have been able to tell the room had been totally destroyed.

He liked the ornate wrought-iron headboard, and the pristine white duvet, not so much the purple silk cushions scattered on the bed since they served no useful purpose and would inevitably wind up on the floor. The clean white lines of her night table and dresser appealed to his taste for simpler things, and of course he checked out the framed pictures of her kids and friends. No pictures of Benson, he was pleased to note, or of Mad Dog. And no pictures of her parents.

"What's with the cuckoo clock?" He pointed to the gingerbread-house-style clock on the wall, so at odds with the rest of the decor.

She blushed. "My grandparents on my mother's side were from Bavaria. When I ran away from my uncle, I left behind all my mementos, but I saw this clock in a pawnshop and it was almost identical to the one my parents had in our kitchen. I was surprised Jimmy didn't destroy it."

"If it makes any noise when I'm inside you, I might have to rip it off the wall."

"Don't worry. I turned it off. It was set to wake me for work."

"I'll find you a new job." He leaned against her dresser. "One where you can sleep in so I can fuck you all night long. Tell me where and what, and I'll make it happen."

"The restaurant." The idea formed in her mind even as the words dropped from her lips. "I want to manage it since you now own it after making Stan sign the deed over to the Sinners. We had a solid customer base and great staff, and now they've all lost their jobs. I've been working there longer than anyone, and I took business management courses when I started my degree. I think I could make a go of it."

He liked it. His woman working for a Sinner business. Anything that would keep her in Conundrum, he would do. "I gotta run it past the board. I think they'll go for it, but on one condition."

Her forehead creased in a frown and Cade laughed and kissed the creases away. Damn she was cute when she was riled.

"What condition?"

"You gotta finish your degree and then help me with the Sinner finances. You can work with the legit businesses and I'll handle everything else. We've got too much work for one person to handle, and we can't trust any outsiders."

"I would consider that, but I have a condition, too." She tugged the tank top over her head and he immediately put aside any thoughts about jobs or conditions. Damn she had nice tits. And beautiful curves. Soft, creamy skin . . .

"Cade. Up here." His mind cleared enough to warn him she'd been talking and he'd been . . . distracted.

"I'll need help with the restaurant and tuition until I get things going, but I don't want you to give me the money. I want a loan so I can buy the restaurant from you and pay back the tuition. The restaurant always turned a good profit, so I don't think it will take that long."

His heart swelled with pride. His woman. Working for his club. Was there ever a greater aphrodisiac?

Dawn slid her shorts over her hips, inch by inch, slowly revealing what he was burning to see.

Yes, there is. He lunged. She backed away.

"You didn't say anything about my conditions."

Cade gritted his teeth. The only condition he cared about right now was the condition of his cock, which was hard and throbbing and in need of release. He lunged again and Dawn shook her head.

"This is my show." Dawn held the shorts just above her mound, running her thumbs along the edge. His mouth watered and he couldn't drag his eyes away. He'd heard talk of women who had men by the balls, but he'd never thought it could happen to him.

"What does that mean?" He liked women who knew what they wanted in the bedroom, but he needed to be in charge. He'd had no control growing up as a child, watching his mother suffer and being unable to stop the abuse. Now that he had the control he so desperately craved, he couldn't give it away.

She lowered her shorts another inch. "I was going to seduce you, strip off your clothes, tie you up, take you in my mouth, and make you beg for release."

"Here's the problem with that plan." He licked his lips when she let the shorts drop just enough for him to see her golden curls, glistening in the soft light of her bedroom lamp. "First, the minute I see you I am seduced, so no effort required there. Second, you don't strip off *my* clothes unless you're naked, else I'll be ripping things off you. Third, no one ties me up and lives to tell the tale. And fourth, I never lose control."

"Never?"

"Never."

"What if I did this?" She cupped and squeezed her breasts, then rolled her nipples between her thumb and forefinger until they peaked.

"Someone's courting trouble." He crossed the floor, scooped her up, and tossed her on the bed. Dawn squealed and twisted away. But before she could get off the bed, Cade pinned her down and straddled her hips.

She looked up at him, cheeks flushed, chest heaving. "I like this kind of trouble."

He bent down and a drew a rosy nipple into his mouth,

sucking and licking until she arched on the bed beneath him.

"Fuck, you're beautiful. I wanna fuck you till you scream my name."

She lifted her hips, grinding against the bulge in his jeans. "How about if I moan your name real quiet so I don't wake the kids?"

He drew her other nipple between his teeth. "Moaning is good. Screaming is better, but I can adapt. First, though, I'm gonna tie you up, and make you so damn hot and so damn wet and so desperate for my cock, you won't know whether you're moaning or screaming, and the only thing you'll be thinking about is how bad you want me and how hard I'm gonna make you come. He climbed off the bed and rifled through her dresser drawers. Dawn sat up and frowned.

"Can I help you with something?"

"Ropes, scarves . . . these will do." He pulled a bundle of nylons from her drawer and gave her a wicked grin. "Do you trust me, babe?"

Did she trust him?

Dawn stared at the nylons in his hand, and her mouth watered in anticipation. He hadn't been kidding when he said he wanted to tie her up, and she was curiously unafraid. Jimmy had been rough, but conservative, in his sexual tastes, and since he was the only man she'd ever been with before Cade, she'd spent a long time fantasizing about something more. And Cade was all about something more.

"Kinky bastard," she murmured when he returned to the bed, resuming his position in a straddle across her hips.

"I take that as your consent to go ahead with my plan."

He tied one of the nylons around her wrist and then drew her arm up over her head, pausing as he slid it between the bars of her headboard. "Yes?"

Her heart thudded against her ribs. "Maybe I just want it missionary style."

"Says the woman who was down on her knees with her beautiful lips around my cock not so long ago."

Dawn smiled. "That was a good night."

"This one will be better." He dropped a kiss to her lips. "Do you trust me, babe?" he asked again.

"Yes." She answered without thinking, but almost immediately she felt the truth of the word. Knowing the lengths he would go to protect her, and tonight, when he'd watched over her girls . . . yes, she trusted him, in a way she'd trusted no one else.

He tied the nylon to the headboard then slid a finger between the fabric and her wrist, ensuring it wasn't too tight.

"Those are very expensive nylons. You'd better not get runs in them." She wiggled beneath him, brushing her taut nipples over the soft cotton of his T-shirt. "I'll need them for when I run the restaurant I'm going to buy from you with the skills I'll learn at college."

"Behave." He pinched her nipple hard and Dawn let out a moan.

"Christ." He tied a second nylon to her other wrist and then through the headboard slats. "Maybe I'll have to gag you, too, or I'm not gonna last."

"You don't want to do that, or you won't get the benefit of my mouth."

Cade laid a finger against her lips. "The kinda sass that comes outta that mouth makes me fucking hard, babe. So careful or I'll go ahead with that plan."

She tilted her head and drew his finger between her lips, sucking until her cheeks hollowed. Then she swirled her tongue over the tip and around the length. He tasted of leather and chrome, with a hint of outlaw danger.

Cade stilled, his eyes riveted to her mouth, his chest heaving beneath his cut. She could feel the weight of his cock beneath his jeans, pressed against her stomach. God, she wanted him bad.

Gently, he drew his finger away and brushed the hair back from her face, his hand lingering on her temple. "I'm fucking addicted to you. I can't get enough, and the more I have, the more I fucking want, till I'm thinking about you every goddamn minute of the day."

"That was sweet, except for the cuss words."

He lifted an admonishing eyebrow, and then tested her bonds. "You think you're really in a position to give me attitude?"

"If you take off your jeans, I will be." She licked her lips. He tore off his clothing.

Naked, his cock proudly erect, he knelt over her, giving her a long moment to appreciate the taut planes and angles of his body. Damn, he was perfect. From his lean, narrow waist to his broad shoulders, and from his firm pecs to the rippling six-pack, partially hidden by the soft downy trail leading to his shaft, thick and heavy, the head pink with the promise of pleasure.

"Are you wet for me?"

"I get wet just thinking about you," she whispered.

"Always knew she was a dirty girl." His words vibrated over her skin as he worked his way up her body, kissing every inch of skin. "My dirty girl."

"Your old lady."

Desire sparked in his eyes, fierce and hot. "Mine."

And then he reached her breasts and she couldn't speak for the need pounding through her veins. He took his time, his hands stroking and squeezing as he sucked and licked her nipples. Dawn writhed on the bed, pulling against the bonds until they chafed her wrists.

"If you hurt yourself, I'll throw you over my knee and spank you," he murmured against her breast.

"This just gets better and better. Or maybe it's worse and worse. I can't tell anymore. The only thing I know is that I need to come so bad it hurts."

"Hmmm." Cade stroked his jaw. "Hurting is bad."

"Very bad."

He cupped her sex with his warm hand then pushed a thick finger inside her wetness. "Does it hurt here?"

Dawn's body arched at the exquisite intrusion and she ground against his finger. "I don't think your itty-bitty finger can reach where it hurts. Maybe you should use something bigger."

A cheeky smile played over his lips, and he added a second finger, pressing against her sensitive inner walls. "Like this?"

"Not bad." She yanked impatiently against the restraints, digging her heels into the bed, trying to get more of what he was holding tantalizingly just out of reach. "But maybe you have something even bigger and more . . . satisfying."

"Maybe I do." He added a third finger, stretching her, filling her, making her eyes water with the sheer pleasure of his touch. "But you don't get that until you come for me." He thrust in deep, and then pumped hard. Dawn's hips jerked, matching his rhythm, and the headboard banged against the wall.

"Shhhh, babe." He grabbed the headboard with his free hand. "You wake the girls and I guarantee you a night of frustration."

"It's already a night of frustration." She moaned and rocked against his hand. "Make me come."

He lifted an admonishing eyebrow. "Is that a *request*?"

"It's a goddamn fucking order from your old lady," she bit out. "Make me come. Now."

"Pleasure." He slid down and settled himself on the bed between her parted legs, his breath warm against her sex. "I like this view."

"Cade . . ."

He stroked her curls. "Such a pretty pussy."

Dawn wanted to scream, but she couldn't. Not with the girls in the next room. So she growled softly instead. "Stop teasing."

Cade looked up and grinned. "I got a bossy old lady."

"You have a wet old lady. Soon to be a pissed-off old lady who will be closing the heavenly gates if you don't get down to business."

"Business? Not pleasure?" He leaned down and drew her clit into his mouth as he thrust his fingers back inside her. The sudden intense sensation of his warm, wet mouth, the velvet caress of his tongue, and the gentle suction of his lips on her clit finally took her over the edge. She climaxed hard and fast, burying her face in her shoulder to muffle her scream as a fierce burst of pleasure sizzled through her veins then faded into a gentle throb.

"Nothing I like better than watching you come." Cade feathered kisses over her mound, then slid his fingers out and wiped her moisture along her inner thigh. Deliciously dirty. Painfully erotic. But that was Cade.

"Need more?"

Dawn nodded. She was so wet, so wanting. The climax had barely taken off the edge. "I need you inside me."

He reached up and undid her restraints then flipped her over. "Wanna fuck you tied up, but I'm thinking the headboard is gonna be a problem. I want you so bad, I'm gonna take you hard, and I'm gonna take you raw, and

I'm gonna be rough 'cause I know you can handle it." He positioned her on her knees facing the headboard and knelt behind her, his chest tight against her back as he lifted her hands and wrapped her fingers around the iron rail. "There we go, beautiful girl. Don't move."

She looked behind her, drinking in his lean muscles, and received a sharp slap of reprimand. "Eyes forward."

Far from hurting, the sting on her ass only added to her frustration. She needed him to relieve the ache in her core, and she needed it now. With a quick pleading glance over her shoulder, she spread her legs by way of invitation.

"That's what I like to see. My girl open and ready for me. Needing my touch." His fingertip grazed over her folds, dipped inside testing her wetness, then brushed lightly over her clit, drawing a gasp from her lips.

"So soft." He leaned over her, his chest pressed against her back, as his fingers wandered over her body, stroking her breasts and thighs, feathering over her sex. Dawn's clit throbbed for more attention, and she clutched the headboard until her knuckles whitened. He felt so good, his body hot and hard against her, his hands confident as he touched and teased.

"Cade . . . please."

He palmed the swell of her hips and spread her thighs apart with his knees. "Since you asked so nicely this time . . ."

She felt the head of his cock probing her entrance and pushed back against him, too impatient to wait. Cade nuzzled her jaw, his breath warm on her cheek. "Not yet, babe. I want it to last."

Dawn groaned and released the headboard, dropping her arms to the pillow in mock defeat. Her cheek pressed against the cool cotton and Cade smoothed a hand over her back, from her nape to her ass, a soothing yet possessive gesture that made her bones turn liquid.

"I like you like this." His seductive whisper only served to inflame her desire. "You aren't a submissive woman and yet you have the strength to give yourself to me." He reached over the bed and pulled a condom from his jeans. He sheathed himself, then moved against her until his thighs were tight against her own.

"Gonna start slow," he said. "I want you to think of nothing but how I feel inside you, filling your pussy with my cock." He held her firm, one hand on her lower back and one on her hip as he stroked into her body, inch by inch, forcing everything from her mind but the helpless anticipation of the moment he was completely seated deep within her.

She had never enjoyed this position with Jimmy, always fearful of what was happening when she couldn't see. He was never gentle with her, never cared about her pleasure. This was a position for cold, rough, sometimes brutal sex, where any sense of intimacy was lost. But Cade was totally focused on her, angling himself to hit her sweet spot, driving her crazy with the slow gentle friction of his thick cock inside her sex, covering her body with his own. She felt nothing but devastating pleasure, and a sense of connection she had never experienced before.

"You like my cock, babe?" He slid one hand over her hip to toy with her clit, and she squirmed beneath him.

"I love your cock. Give me more." She pushed backward, taking him deeper, ripping a groan from his throat.

"Squeeze me."

Driven by a relentless hunger and a desperate need for release, she tightened her inner muscles and rocked against him.

"Just like that." He pulled out and thrust again, harder this time, while his hand continued to roam her body. He knew just how to touch her to keep her on edge, stoking her fire until she thought she would combust.

Unable to submit to his slow, controlled rhythm, she jerked back, trying to drive him deeper, but Cade held her firm, letting her know with every powerful stroke that he was in control.

"Take me." He leaned over her, engulfing her body with his own, threading his fingers through hers on the mattress, a curiously intimate gesture that made her melt inside.

And then he gave her what he had promised. With a last brush of his lips across her nape, he slid his hands down her body, grabbed her hips, and gave it to her raw and rough and hard. A soft cry tore from her lips at the intense, erotic pleasure. She wanted this—needed it—every stroke of his cock erased memories of Jimmy, made her feel powerful, wanton, and so close to climax she shuddered in anticipation.

"Now. More." She gasped the words and he twisted her hair through his hand, yanked up her hips, and drilled down into her center. Everything faded away. Fear. Shame. Pride. And the last of her inhibitions. She spread herself wider, opening herself completely to him, and he reached around and lightly pinched her clit.

"Let it go. For me."

A low, guttural groan erupted from her throat as the climax engulfed her, sensation flooding her body in a molten wave of heat that left her raw and trembling.

Cade hammered into her, using her body for his pleasure while he drew out her orgasm, sending aftershocks rippling out to her fingers and toes. His shaft thickened when he climaxed, pulsed and throbbed against her swollen tissue. Pleasure sparked through her when he groaned.

Yes, it was sex, but there intimacy, too, something she had never had with Jimmy. And although it scared her, she couldn't deny how right it felt to be here. Now. With him.

He collapsed on top of her, his chest slick with sweat against her back, his stubble prickling against her shoulder. Dawn melted beneath him, content to stay buried in his warmth.

"My beautiful girl." He nuzzled her neck. "What is it about you that makes it impossible to stay away? From the moment we met, I had to have you. Every day after you left, I thought about you. And when I saw you again, I knew I would never let you go."

Maybe it's because I feel the same way about you. But the words didn't come.

He kissed her again and withdrew to dispose of the condom. When he returned, he lay beside her on the bed, and pulled her against him, settling her head against his shoulder.

"Do I get my loan?"

Cade chuckled. "Sweetheart, after that, I'd bring you the fucking moon if I could fly."

Her body relaxed in the cradle of his arms and she sighed in contentment as his fingers stroked gently up and down her back. "I could stay like this forever."

"So could I." He pressed a soft kiss to her forehead. "Stay with me, Dawn. Even after this is all over, I want you to wear my cut."

She didn't know what to say, so she said nothing. She had managed to hold her fear at bay when this was all pretend, when she knew it wouldn't last. But now that he'd made it real, she had nowhere to hide. She cared about him, no doubt about that, but the depth of her emotion scared her. Was she really ready to do it all again? Did she trust him enough to let go and jump into the biker life for good?

★ NINETEEN ★

I will never be the aggressor. Unless someone
fucks with me. Then they will pay.

SINNER'S TRIBE CREED

"Mom. There's someone in your bed."

Dawn awakened to Maia's concerned face—her beautiful, angelic face—and Cade wrapped around her, his arm tight between her breasts, his head on her pillow, his erection pressed up against her ass. Thank God the covers were drawn around them.

"Is it Jimmy?"

"No, darling. It's . . . Cade."

Tia joined her sister staring down at them and frowned. She was always frowning, which made it easy to tell the twins apart.

"Why is he sleeping in your bed?" Maia asked.

She could feel Cade chuckling behind her, his chest warm against her back.

"Um . . . we're having a . . . sleepover."

"Can I have a sleepover with Susie?" Maia sat on the edge of the bed. "Shelly-Ann wouldn't let us have sleepovers but now that we're home, I want a sleepover, too."

Cade ground his shaft gently against her ass and she choked back a gasp. "How about we talk it over at breakfast? You have to get ready for school. Both of you go brush your teeth and you can talk to Cade when he . . . gets up."

"I'm already up." His breath on the back of her neck reminded her of their heated night together, and she shivered. "And I thought you locked the door."

"I did lock the door. You unlocked it when you went to get rid of the condom. I hope you remembered . . ."

"Mom."

"Fuck." Cade rolled away. "I think I forgot to . . ."

"Mom."

"Christ. This is more stressful than a shoot-out." He sat on the edge of the bed and scrubbed his hands over his face.

"No swearing around the girls. And no more inappropriate behavior." Dawn pushed herself up. She would have been totally screwed if it was Saturday and she had to work at the diner. With no one to look after the children, she would have had to take a few days off. And what about this afternoon when she had to work at the florist? Or tonight when she had to work at Banks Bar? She'd spent so much time dreaming about her children coming home, she hadn't thought through the practicalities. Maybe because a part of her thought it would never really happen. And another part was convinced it was all a dream.

"Mom." Maia's voice grew louder and Dawn's eyes widened.

"Pants."

"Door." Cade reached for his jeans and Dawn threw herself at the door, just before Maia arrived.

"I'll be out in a moment, darling."

"Hell . . . I mean . . . damn, this is going to take some getting used to." Cade pulled on his shirt.

Dawn grabbed some clean clothes from her drawer and slipped on her robe. Her PJs were lost somewhere in the bed. Or maybe on the floor. "I need to take a shower. Are you going to be okay with the girls for a few minutes? You've never been alone with them before . . ."

"I know everything about big girls," he said. "I figure they gotta be much the same."

After ten minutes alone with Maia and Tia, Cade revised his assessment of little girls. They were nothing like big girls. And the fact that they seemed totally immune to his charms this morning just made the situation worse. Winks and slow smiles, a slight drawl and a full-on swagger didn't even come close to winning them over like he had at the zoo and the park. In fact, the harder he tried to engage them, the more cutting Maia became. Tia hadn't said a word to him since he'd joined them in the kitchen. Maybe they didn't like him sleeping over.

"Do you have a car?" Maia sat on the counter and kicked her legs, her little heels banging against the dishwasher while Cade searched the cupboards for something to give them to eat.

"Just my bike."

"Bikes are cool," she said. "But men who don't have cars are not cool. Real men have cars. That way they can get groceries when it rains."

"Good to know."

"I saw your bike when you came to the park." She slid off the counter as Cade pulled out a box of cereal. "I liked it. Tia thought it was too shiny. Maybe you can give us a ride sometime."

"I don't know if your mom would like that." He found the bowls and filled them to the top. How much cereal did kids eat? He had no clue, but if he filled the bowls to the top they wouldn't go hungry.

"She lets us do what we want because she doesn't get to see us very much. That's Jimmy's fault. He's a bastard."

Cade found milk in the fridge and filled up the bowls. "I thought you weren't allowed to swear."

"It's not a swear if it's true and that's what everyone calls him. Even Shelly-Ann. Jimmy's a bad person. He hurts people. He hurt Mom and us. He hurt Shelly-Ann, too, because she lost his money, but then she remembered Mom had it so he left her alone."

Was that the money Mad Dog was after? Why hadn't Dawn told him about it?

"You call him Jimmy, not Dad?" He put the bowls on the table and puffed out his chest. *Success*. This wasn't so hard after all.

Maia fiddled with the strap of the bag slung across her shoulder, a small black beaded purse with a skull emblazoned on the front. "Just because we're related to him doesn't mean we have to call him Dad. He doesn't act like a dad. Dads look after you, and take you places, and spend time with you, and make sure bad things don't happen. Plus, Jimmy hates us. He tells us that every time we see him."

Lost for words, Cade stared at Maia. He didn't have the heart to tell her good dads were few and far between. His dad sure wasn't one of them.

"Sucks," he said, for lack of anything better to say, or any wisdom to impart.

"Spoon."

"What?"

"Spoon," Maia said. "Are we supposed to slurp the cereal out of the bowl?"

"Maia. Manners." Dawn appeared in the doorway wearing a filmy white blouse he could almost see through and a short, tight skirt that hugged every delicious curve of her body. Her hair was loose and partially dried, the soft golden curls hanging just above the crescents of her breasts. His groin tightened and he turned away to get himself under control.

"You got some sweats, babe? Maybe a sack?" He turned on the cold water and splashed his face. "We're a dress-down kinda club. Like hide-all-the-good-bits kinda dress down, especially when you're in public or there's brothers around."

"Why is your face red?" Maia chewed her cereal staring at him with the kind of gaze that could send a man to his knees. *Christ.* If they were his, looking as pretty as they looked now, he'd have to barricade the door when they were teenagers. He couldn't imagine how his brothers with teenage girls handled the boys who came around. He'd probably just fire off a coupla shots and keep the bastards away.

"It's . . . hot in here."

Tia lifted an eyebrow but said nothing. He had a feeling that he'd just been judged and found wanting although he didn't know how. After all, he'd managed to fix them breakfast.

"Gotta get going," he said. "Got some work to do. See you later, ladies." That got him a few smiles and giggles. At least he hadn't totally lost his touch.

Dawn followed him to the door and leaned against the wall while he pulled on his boots, her folded arms highlighting the delicious curve of her breasts.

"You working at the florist this afternoon? And then at the bar?"

"Yes." She ran her hand through her curls and her blouse opened just enough to send all his blood rushing to his cock.

Fuck. He had to get out of here or he'd be dragging her

back to the bedroom and the kids would never make it to school.

"It all happened so fast I never thought about child care," she said. "But I just called Martha, a retired neighbor who lives a couple of houses down the street. She used to watch the girls for me before Jimmy took them away. She said she could come over today."

"I'll look after them this afternoon."

Dawn hesitated. "You? Are you sure? I mean . . ."

"I got them breakfast. No one died. I can handle a coupla hours." He dug into his pocket and held up his hand. "And I got a key. I'll make sure Tank and T-Rex are outside watching the block. You can trust me, sweetheart."

Her face lit up with a smile that almost stopped his heart, and she leaned up to kiss his cheek. "They get out of school at three-thirty. They'll need a snack. No treats."

"Might have to feed them some sugar to keep them sweet, so I won't make any promises." He wrapped an arm around her waist, pulling her against him. His cock throbbed and he groaned.

"What's wrong?" Dawn's eyes lit with amusement. She knew damn well what was wrong.

"You. Too sexy. Waking up this morning with your little ass grindin' into me . . . seeing you dressed like this. Too much."

She twirled a curl around her finger. "I thought when you saw me with the kids you'd wonder what the hell you were doing with a mom of two when you have a club full of sweet butts fighting for your bed."

He heard the waver in her tone. Saw her vulnerability. And yet nothing could have been farther from the truth. He cupped her face between his hands and leaned down to kiss her. He wanted to tell her how beautiful she was to him, inside and out, and how the fact she had kids made no difference to him. He wanted to tell her how he loved her sweetly rounded curves and how he liked the idea she had created such beauty with her body. But he suspected it wouldn't come out right. He wasn't an eloquent man. So he just said, "You've got to be fucking kidding me." And then he kissed her again and walked out the door.

"This here's an axle." Cade pointed out the part on his bike to his two attentive young students, sitting side by side on the grass in the back lane behind Dawn's house. T-Rex and Tank were parked in the alley, close enough he could hear them snickering.

"You have those tattooed on your chest," Maia said. "I saw them this morning. And wings. Blue ones."

"Well, now. You shouldn't be looking at my tat. It's not for little girls to see."

"Why?"

Cade gritted his teeth. Over the last few hours he'd grown to hate that question. Maia had an uncanny ability to detect when he was trying to be evasive and called him out every time. Who knew seven-year-olds could be so smart?

"Some things are for grown-ups to see and some things are for little girls to see."

"Why did you get it if everyone can't see it? You have another one on your back, but it has cuts on it. Why did you need two?"

He scrubbed a hand over his face. Why did he need two? Every full-patch got a Sinner's Tribe tattoo, usually on his back. It represented a lifelong commitment to the club. But the second tat had been all his. The wings for freedom, blue for the sky, and the axles for his bike. No ties. No commitments. No one to answer to. Just him and the bike and the open sky.

"'Cause I wanted it just for me and for people I wanted to share it with."

"Not us?" Her mouth turned down and Tia's mouth turned down, too. One voice with two faces. Maybe one day Tia would trust him enough to talk to him. He hadn't lied when he told Dawn he thought she had a lot to say.

"Fuck. Don't look at me like that. You'll break my goddamn heart."

Maia's eyes lit up. "You swore in front of us. Let us see your tat or we'll tell Mom."

Christ. Blackmailed by a seven-year-old. And with witnesses. He'd never live it down.

"Okay. Just for a minute." He removed his cut and tugged his shirt over his head. The two girls stood to stare at his tat.

"Can we touch it?"

"No."

Maia frowned. "Why? Are you poisonous?"

"Not that I know."

She stood up on tiptoe and poked his chest. Cade froze. What the hell was he supposed to do now? He lunged forward and the girls shrieked and ran away.

"Hey, Cade. You're losing your touch," Tank yelled. "Girls are supposed to run toward you."

"Fuck off." He pulled on his shirt and cut and grabbed a polishing cloth. Dawn was due home any moment and he'd already run out of things to do. They'd watched TV, played a video game, and eaten the box of donuts he'd brought with him. But when they asked him to play princesses, he took them out to help him with his bike instead. Bike polishing had seemed a safe and useful activity. Now he wished he'd put on that princess crown.

"Can we sit on your bike?" Maia rested her little hand on his seat.

Cade shook his head. "Only a biker sits in his saddle. His old lady rides in the pillion seat."

"Is Mom your old lady?"

Unable to resist her pleading look, he lifted her onto the pillion seat while he scrambled for an answer to her question. She was so small and light he was almost afraid he would crush her with his big hands. "You'll have to ask her."

"She is," Maia settled on the seat. "We saw her leather vest. It says PROPERTY OF CADE. That means she belongs to you."

"I guess that's right." He lifted her off and held out his hands for Tia, but she shook her head and backed away.

"So if Mom belongs to you, we belong to you." Wise beyond her years, Maia continued with the awkward conversation despite Cade's less-than-forthcoming answers.

"It's not really like . . ."

"So you have to protect us." She cut him off. "You have to look after Mom and us because that's what you do when someone is yours."

Cade dropped to a crouch in front of the two little girls. "I'll protect you and your mom. If something bad happens and you need me, I'll be there."

"Even from Jimmy?"

"Even from Jimmy."

Maia cocked her head to the side. "Promise."

"You have my word," Cade said. "A biker's word is his bond. That means you can count on it."

She smiled, the same devastating smile as Dawn. "Then I won't tell Mom you swore at Tank and T-Rex."

"Thanks."

"Since we're yours, can we have our own bikes so we can ride with you?"

Cade closed his eyes and took a deep breath. He so knew what was coming.

"No. Even if you were old enough to ride, I wouldn't let you have a bike." He polished the chrome until it gleamed in the sunlight.

"Why?"

"Because they're dangerous and I promised to protect you." He braced himself to be called out on his hypocrisy but she just kept going.

"What about a leather vest? I want one that says PROPERTY OF TREVOR."

He squirted more polish on his cloth. "Who's Trevor?"

"My boyfriend. He pulls my hair in class and chases me around the playground at lunch."

Cade put down the bottle of polish, his brow creasing in a frown. "Does he live nearby?"

"No."

"I'll come by the playground tomorrow. Point him out to me and I'll make him stop."

"I don't want him to stop." Maia put a hand on her hip and gave an affected sigh. "Don't you know anything about girls?"

He thought he did. Apparently, he was wrong.

"Mommy."

Dawn waved to Maia and Tia from the back lawn. She'd been watching Cade polish his bike with her girls ever since she got off the bus and her heart warmed at how well they got on together. Even Tia, although she didn't talk, stayed by his side.

A family. Just like you always wanted. Jimmy's taunt flitted through her brain. She bet he'd never imagined she would have a family like this, albeit a temporary one.

Or was it? Their talk last night was all about a future

together. But they hadn't addressed the elephant in the room. What would happen when it was all over? Was he really thinking of becoming a one-woman man and settling down?

Tank and T-Rex were chatting at the far end of the lane, looking less than enthused that they'd pulled guard duty. Dawn crossed the grass and stepped out of the small gate separating her property from the back lane. She'd taken the evening off so she could spend time with the girls, and she could hardly wait to tell them.

She closed the gate behind her, startling when she heard the rev of an engine. A black van sped down the lane so fast it left a trail of dust behind. Cade reached out and yanked the girls to safety. Dawn froze when the van screeched to a halt. Moments later the back door opened and a body rolled out and onto the gravel.

Shocked, Dawn could only stare as the van took off down the lane, racing full tilt at Tank and T-Rex. They scrambled to safety and then took off after the van, the rev of their engines echoing through the alley.

Maia and Tia ran across the road and into her arms. As the dust cleared, Dawn took in the body, now slumped beside Cade's bike, with the letters MD spray-painted on his back. She knew that sign. MD for "Mad Dog." Her muscles went taut and she shoved the girls behind her.

"Go inside." Dawn tried to keep her voice from wavering. "Go to your bedroom and lock the door."

"But is he okay?" Maia tried to look back over her shoulder. "Should we call 911?"

"No. Cade and I will look after him. Inside. Now." She hadn't meant to shout, but the words came out in a rush of fear.

When the girls were safely in the house, she joined Cade. He slowly turned the body so the man's face was clearly visible, and Dawn gasped.

"You know him?"

"He's the private investigator from the video Jimmy produced in court to win custody."

And then the weight of what Jimmy had done hit her hard and she swayed on her feet. "I'll never get the girls back for good now," she said with dawning horror. "Not under civilian law. Not unless Bunny can find out who filmed the video, and that's a long shot without the investigator." She scrubbed her face with her hands. "God, what have I done? He's totally lost control. The risk he's taken to do this . . . And in front of the children . . ."

Cade pulled her into his arms. "We'll call Wolf. We'll make it clear that he'll have to do more than just sanction Mad Dog or he'll risk losing Sinner support for his election bid."

"He's not afraid of Wolf anymore," Dawn said, her voice rising in panic. "Don't you see? This was as much a message for Wolf as it was for me, and he clearly has men who are willing to defy Wolf as well. If he's prepared to do something like this, either he's left the club, or he knows he's going to win with the Black Jacks' backing. And if he wins, nothing will stop him. He'll come for me. And the girls . . . he doesn't want them. What if . . ."

"Dawn." Cade grasped her shoulders. "I'll protect you. You're a Sinner now. The club will look after you and the girls. You don't have to worry."

"You can't protect me." She pulled away, letting her fear spill over in words. "You weren't there when he broke into my house, or when he caught me on the street. The Sinners didn't stop him from coming into town again the night he attacked me. Tank and T-Rex couldn't stop him from throwing a body in front of my children. No one can protect me. No one ever could. I was a fool to think I could stand up to him. I'll call Doug. He'll get me into witness protection. I can't lose my girls again."

She knew she'd hurt him when his eyes hardened. "You're panicking. We'll deal with this. Together."

"There is no dealing with this." She was shaking now, her words coming thick and fast. "There's a dead body in my back lane, Cade." She gestured behind her, unable to look at the man again. "Not just dead. Murdered. Jimmy murdered him just to make a point."

"I'm not going to lose you because of him." Cade cupped her face between his palms. "Trust me, Dawn. I won't let anything happen to you. I love you. I didn't want to, but I do. I didn't think it could happen, but it did. There isn't anything I won't do for you and the girls. I'll give my life to keep you safe. Just don't run away. Give me a chance to make this right."

She stared up at his handsome face, trying to memorize every plane and angle, the scars on his cheeks and chin, the way his nose was slightly off center as if it had been broken and never properly set. His lips were perfectly shaped, full and firm. If she closed her eyes, she could imagine those lips on her body, feel his breath on her skin. She leaned forward and brushed a kiss over his cheek. His eyes darkened almost to black, and she wanted to drown in that inky sea.

"Please, Cade. Don't make me choose."

She'd made the biggest mistake of her life getting involved with the Sinners, thinking she could beat Jimmy at his own game. She'd forgotten how clever he was, how ruthless, manipulative and totally unforgiving. Jimmy played to win and he would never give up. Not until he had her back. Not until the girls were gone. Not until Cade was dead.

Never.

★ TWENTY ★

I will strive to understand myself and my machine
so that I rely on no one but me.
SINNER'S TRIBE CREED

Dawn laced her fingers together under the wooden table. She'd never been in an interrogation room before, but it was much as she'd imagined—four white walls, a one-way mirror, cold fluorescent light on the ceiling, camera in the corner, and Doug seated across from her, clearly uncomfortable, as evidenced by his constant shifting in his seat.

"Where exactly were you when you saw the body?"

"In the back alley behind my house."

He tapped on his laptop his eyes focused on the screen. "Who else was there?"

"The girls. Cade. And two Sinners."

Doug's jaw tightened almost imperceptibly when she mentioned Cade's name. "Did you know the deceased?"

"He's the private investigator from the video Jimmy showed at court to win custody of the girls. My lawyer has a copy if you need to see it."

"And the mark on his shirt?"

She'd never seen Doug so cold and detached. Professional. A little part of her died inside. He'd always been a good friend to her and he clearly felt hurt and betrayed. "MD for 'Mad Dog.'"

He stopped typing and looked up. "You think Jimmy did this?"

"I know he did. It's a message. He's angry because . . ." She cut herself off just in time.

"Because you've taken up with the Sinners." Doug slammed his laptop closed. "I can't believe it myself, Dawn. I mean, what the hell were you thinking? After what you've been through—what you're going through now—how could you do this? How could you put your children at risk? How could you go back to a world that caused you so much pain?"

"Doug . . ." Nausea gripped her belly. He was right. About all of it. She'd spent three years trying to get away from the biker world and live like a civilian. And now, not only was she fully immersed in the life, her children were, too. "I want to take you up on the witness protection offer. I want to testify against Jimmy." Bile rose from her throat as she spoke the words.

Wrong. Wrong. Wrong. She felt it in her gut, but she didn't have a choice.

Almost instantly his face softened. "Dawn . . . I don't know what to say. You've made the right choice, of course, and I'll be with you every step of the way." And then his smile faded. "But what about . . . Cade? I won't pretend I don't know you're close."

"He's a Sinner. He'll stay with his club."

"And your cut?" He gestured to her leather vest.

Dawn swallowed hard, curling her hand around the soft leather. "I'm giving it back. I have one more thing I have to do for the club—a party I organized—and then

I'm done with the Sinners. The whole biker thing was never real. It wasn't me."

"You're gonna love these twins." Gunner showed Cade a picture of two young women in a hot tub, one blond and one brunette, both with what Cade knew to be surgically enhanced breasts. Real breasts floated.

"Just what you need to get out of your black mood," Gunner continued. "So things didn't work out with your girl. You just gotta get back in the saddle."

Cade studied the picture as he sipped his beer in the clubhouse kitchen. The blonde was cute but she had nothing on Dawn. Her hair was too short, her face too thin, and her eyes hazel and not brilliant green. She had the look of a pampered princess who had never done a day of work in her life, unlike Dawn who worked three jobs. But maybe Gunner was right. He needed someone to take his mind off Dawn. He needed to go back to having casual hookups where he could have his fun without the emotional burden or intimacy of a relationship dragging him down.

"When are you going?"

"Tomorrow night. They're bringing some friends. But you're gonna have to sober up. You don't want to have to ride out there in a cage. These chicks dig our bikes."

Gunner jabbed him with his elbow but Cade couldn't even muster a smile. He hadn't heard from Dawn since the police showed up to investigate the body outside her house. And, of course, Benson was with them, and everything went downhill. Benson promised to protect her and arranged for a police detail to watch her house. Benson assured her he would find out who was responsible, and if it was Mad Dog, he would lock him up for good. Benson took her away in his police car after she'd arranged for Martha to look after the kids.

From his vantage point on the hill above Dawn's street, Cade had watched Benson put his arm around Dawn's shoulders in the police car. Was she really planning to take him up on the witness protection offer? Nothing had ever cut Cade so deep as the moment she'd called Deputy fucking Benson.

He'd texted to see how she was doing, but she hadn't returned his messages. At first, he figured she was overreacting to the body in her back lane. But then Arianne had passed on a message that she needed some time alone.

Alone from him. Not Benson.

"Yeah. I'm there. Never could resist twins." He stared at the picture and wondered if they were like Maia and Tia who had such different personalities. Maia was so damn sharp. She knew exactly what was going on. And Tia . . . he would have liked to hear her talk. Just once.

Damn Benson for giving her a way out. Damn Mad Dog for making her need it. Damn him for not doing what needed to be done. He had to get her out of his system and move on. Or was it moving back? Back into endless nights and unfulfilled mornings. Back to a search for something he had already found.

"Look what we got!" Dawn slid off Arianne's bike and held up the USB stick she had just picked up from Bunny. They had driven straight to Banks Bar to share the news and watch the video together. "Bunny interviewed the investigator before Jimmy got to him. I didn't really think he'd pull through for me, but he did."

"Gimme a minute." Banks stuck his head out from under the hood of his Jeep. "I need a new part and I gotta get a measurement."

"Your Jeep always needs parts." Arianne laughed as she parked her bike. "If not for you, I don't think Sparky would be able to keep his garage running."

"She's got no respect," Banks muttered. "You don't talk down a man's Jeep. Something happens to people when they put on that damn Sinner cut. Never happening to me. When Jagger came begging me to join the club, I told him where to go. Don't want anything to do with bikers."

"Me either." Dawn hadn't spoken to Cade since the afternoon Jimmy dumped the body in the lane, nor had she answered his text messages. She knew she'd hurt him when she called Doug, but panic set in, taking with it all her faith in Cade and the Sinners. And now she'd made a decision that meant she and her girls would be safe, together, and as far away from the Brethren as possible. She should be happy, but she couldn't shake the feeling that she was making a terrible mistake.

After Banks finished with his Jeep, they squeezed into his office and Banks downloaded the file. "Where's the popcorn?"

"You want popcorn while we watch someone being interrogated?" Dawn stared at him aghast. "That's sick."

"Buttered popcorn would be sick. Plain popcorn is a healthy snack."

They suffered through the first few minutes of the video in silence. Bunny sat across from the investigator in a dingy office. Even now, Dawn couldn't look at him without feeling sick inside. With his slightly mussed brown hair, pock-marked plain face, and rumpled short-sleeved shirt, he looked so ordinary, like anyone's dad. Which is why she had so easily fallen for his ruse.

Bunny asked a few questions. The investigator shook his head. Finally, Bunny pushed a piece of paper across the desk. The investigator paled and then everything spilled out.

"I was hired over the phone to set up some woman behind a school, and then testify in court. I've done

setups before. I don't got any issues with them, so long as I'm paid. I was given a time and place where the woman would be, and the location of a duffel bag that had half the money, a school sweatshirt, a photograph, and a small ziplock bag filled with coke."

"You sure it was coke?" Bunny said.

"Yeah. I tasted it 'cause it had a sparkly sticker on it, and I wanted to be sure it was real. You gotta use the real stuff 'cause they need it as evidence."

"Who filmed you?"

"Dunno. Usually I do that myself with a hidden camera but that wasn't the job. I put on the sweatshirt and told the woman I was selling tickets for the school picnic. She handed over the money. I handed over the coke. Usually the mark knows what's going on right away, but I think the sticker threw her off. When she figured it out, she threw the bag at me. I got the rest of the money after I testified in court that she'd approached me asking if I had anything for sale."

Dawn sighed after the video finished playing. "He's right. Because of the sticker, I thought he'd given me something for the kids—pretend fairy dust, or a sugary treat. My brain just couldn't process the danger because of the sweatshirt, and the way he looked, and because I was at the school, and who would sell drugs at a school?"

"Every drug dealer in the city," Banks said. "But your kids are young. You don't have to worry about that until they're eight or nine years old."

"Eight?" Dawn stared at him aghast.

"Got offered my first joint when I was eight. Good stuff. Got me through Mrs. Keevil's art class. I was never big on art, but when I was stoned you shoulda seen the kind of shit I painted."

"I called my lawyer before we left Bunny's place." Dawn leaned back in her chair. "He said we can offer the video as evidence but with the investigator dead it's a long shot whether the court will accept it. I looked at the video of the setup last night, and I went back to the school, but all I could figure out was that the person who took it had to be taller than me."

"Well, that narrows it down to every adult in the city," Banks said.

Dawn huffed. "I'm not that short."

"You're not that tall, either."

"I figured he must have been at the curb, and not in the shadows, which means it wasn't Jimmy because I would have recognized him."

"A mini Colonel Mustard with a pipe in the kitchen."

"Did you just tell a joke, Banks?" Dawn shared an incredulous glance with Arianne. "I think Banks just told a joke."

"Write down the date and time. I think it only happens once every five years."

Banks gave Dawn's shoulder a squeeze. "Why are you doing this? Even if you found out who it was, how would you get them to testify? Dirt bags don't answer subpoenas and they tend to disappear when they know the police are looking for them. And if you go into witness protection, they'll bury that court decision and you'll have the girls back."

"I can't let Jimmy win. When I go into witness protection, I'll lose everything I built since I came to Conundrum. Even my name. I can deal with that, although I'm going to miss you guys something fierce. I'll be back where I started, rebuilding my life all over again. But what I can't deal with is the fact that there is a document out there that says I'm an unfit mother. I'll always be afraid it will come to light and I'll lose them. I want to clear my name. I want to know no one can take my girls away. I want to fight back."

Arianne gave her a searching look. "Then why are you running away? If you run, you'll always be looking over your shoulder. You've always been a strong person. But since you hooked up with Cade, you found just how deep that strength goes, especially when you have support. Believe in yourself and the life you choose to live. That's what Sinners do. That's our creed. And that's what it means to wear the cut."

"Maybe I shouldn't be wearing it." She stroked a hand along the soft, black leather. "Ever since I put it on, I've been doing things that really aren't me."

"The cut is neither here nor there." Banks closed his laptop. "Hell, you got away from that bastard and made a life for yourself on your own and every time he threw you a curveball, you hit it out of the park. But some fights you can't win on your own. And right now, you've got a team of damn Sinners on your side. You got a coach who'll go to bat for you if you want to drive that ball straight at the pitcher."

"Write that down, too," Arianne said. "I didn't know Banks knew that many words. I also didn't know he knew anything about baseball."

"I know another word," he muttered. "Fired. I'm gonna get myself some staff that aren't old ladies and know how to treat their boss with the proper respect."

"I'm not . . ." Dawn cut herself off. *An old lady.* But she was. Although she'd been tempted to hand the cut back to Cade after she called Doug, something held her back. She wasn't ready to give up. At least, not yet.

"You wanna watch it again," Banks said. "Maybe it will trigger a memory second time around."

"No. It was pretty much what happened. Although I'd forgotten about the sticker."

A sparkly purple heart.

Dawn sucked in a sharp breath. "Oh my God. I know who took the video."

* * *

"Hey, brother." Jagger pulled up a chair across the table from Cade in the corner of Banks Bar. Cade scowled and poured himself another shot. He just wanted to be left alone to drink in peace. Just like he'd been doing for the last four days since Arianne had called to tell him Dawn was going into witness protection.

"I thought you and Gunner were heading out to a party. He said you ditched him at the last minute."

"Changed my mind." He tossed back the shot and closed his eyes as the liquor burned down his throat. He'd switched from bourbon to whiskey this afternoon, needing something with more of a kick.

Jagger covered Cade's glass when he reached for the bottle to pour another shot. "Does this mean you'll be here for the Brethren party tomorrow night?"

"Won't let my brothers down."

Cade signaled Arianne to bring Jagger a glass. Dawn still hadn't arrived for her shift and Cade wondered if she would show at all. She was running scared, and although he understood her fear, he couldn't understand why she didn't trust him to protect her. Mad Dog's scare tactic had worked too damn well.

"I shouldn't have asked her to join the club." He brushed Jagger's hand away and refilled his glass. "It just inflamed the situation. Actually, I shouldn't have stopped to talk to her that day outside the school. Then none of this would have happened."

"It was Dawn's choice to join the Sinners," Jagger said. "She knew how it might play out. And if you hadn't stopped to talk to her, we would never have found out the Brethren were looking to patch over to the Jacks. The deal would have been done and we would all be dead."

Cade lifted his glass and stared at the brilliant amber liquid. Sometimes when the light hit her just right, he saw amber flecks in Dawn's eyes, and then those beautiful lashes would sweep down over her cheeks and he'd get distracted by her lush little mouth.

"I made the wrong fucking decision when I agreed not to go after Mad Dog. And every time he stepped out of line and we didn't act, the situation just got worse."

"You did it for the club, brother. No one will forget that. And you couldn't have known how it would play out. Just like when you were ambushed and lost your men. Sometimes shit happens that we can't control. You trust yourself to make the best decision you can in the circumstances and then you deal with the consequences. But you don't let it bring you down."

"Dawn's going into witness protection because I wasn't there for her. That's not a consequence I can accept." Cade lifted the glass and lowered it again. He felt like shit: eyes bleary, stomach churning, and a headache that just wouldn't quit. Did he really want to do this to himself again? Drown his guilt in liquor and the soft arms of strangers? There was nothing down that road but pain and emptiness, and this time his brothers wouldn't be there to save him.

"You were there for her just how she needed you to be." Jagger pulled his chair closer. "You made her see the Sinner she had inside. Hell, the woman I first met here in the bar over a year ago is not the same woman who stood up in my office, instructed us on how to play our own political game, and told my executive board where to go."

But now, after Mad Dog had destroyed any chance of her clearing her name, she was thinking of running away. She'd let fear get the better of her. Just like he'd let guilt get the better of him.

"And you did the same for the club." Jagger leaned across the table, his voice insistent. "You reminded us what it means to be a Sinner, what it means to follow the creed."

"I joined the MC when I thought I had nothing left to

live for," Cade said. "I couldn't handle the guilt of living when all my men died, and not being there for my mom when she needed me. I found a home with the Sinners. Friends. A life I fucking love. But there's always been something missing. I've been looking for something, and I didn't know what it was."

Jagger glanced over at Arianne. "I know the feeling."

Cade pushed his chair away from the table. "I never really dealt with all that guilt. I never thought it through, until I met Dawn. She made me see I got a need to protect the people I care about, and when I can't, it eats at my soul."

"Your sacrifice protected the club."

"Yeah, and it put Dawn and her girls at risk."

"You can't protect everyone, brother. You can't stop people from doing what they want to do or being where they want to be. And you can't fight everyone's fight. Sometimes it's just enough that you've got your brother's back so he knows he isn't fighting alone."

He felt the truth of Jagger's words in his gut, and the burden he'd carried for so long lifted. His mother, his men . . . he'd done everything he could do to save them, but in the end, he couldn't be responsible for their choices, or for the actions of the men who had destroyed them.

But now he had another chance. He could protect the woman he loved by destroying the destroyer before he caused any harm, and maybe then he could convince her to make another choice. The right choice.

Him.

★ TWENTY-ONE ★

I will never give in, never give up, never surrender.

SINNER'S TRIBE CREED

"Where is he?" Dawn stood on tiptoe as she tried to see above the sea of heads in front of her. The makeshift boxing ring in the backyard of the clubhouse, although illuminated by floodlights, was barely visible through the crowd, and despite the late hour, the fights were still going strong. The yard smelled of sweat and stale beer, crushed grass and the sweet scent of pot.

"He's standing in the far corner." Arianne pointed through the crowd, and Dawn caught a glimpse of golden hair. "He hasn't fought yet. I think he was hoping you would show up."

"He left a message with Banks asking me to come. I guess he wants to say good-bye. I feel awful for avoiding him, but I just didn't know what to say."

"Well, I'm glad you're here. Usually these are fun fights. We invite a few support clubs and have a big party. But Cade challenged a guy from the Devil Dogs who is an amateur fighter on the MMA circuit with all sorts of wins under his belt. Cade's good, but he doesn't have a chance against a seasoned MMA fighter."

"Christ. Look at this crowd." T-Rex came up behind them, Tank at his side. "Sparky's taking bets if you want to throw in some cash." He winked at Arianne. "By the way, Jagger's still on his way back from Helena. He said to enjoy yourself."

"You texted him?"

"Thought he should know his old lady was in a dangerous place, but T-Rex and Tank had your back." T-Rex held up his arm in a classic bodybuilder pose, his biceps flexing under his T-shirt, but Arianne didn't smile.

"Like I can't look after myself," she snapped.

"Not sayin' you can't look after yourself," T-Rex said. "Just sayin' the Sinners always have your back."

A cheer rose from the crowd, signaling the start of the match. Dawn stepped to the side until she had a clear view just as Cade stepped into the ring. His fight shorts, black with a white skull on each side, reminded her of his patch, but when he turned and she saw the scarred tattoo on his back, her heart squeezed in his chest.

"Oh. My. God." Arianne's hand flew to her mouth. "What happened to his tat?"

"Jimmy."

"Goddamn bastard," T-Rex growled behind them. "That damn Brethren election can't happen too soon. Everyone's fighting to be on the team that goes after Mad Dog."

"I think you've put in enough time waiting for that election. And Cade suffered for it." She surprised herself with the sharpness of her tone, or the spark of defiance that wasn't appropriate for a soon-to-be ex-old-lady.

Arianne gestured to the ring, defusing the tension that had curled around them. "Cade's ready to fight. Nick is referee tonight, and he just gave the thumbs-up."

Cade nodded at Nick, then looked out into the crowd. She knew the moment he saw her, felt the burning intensity of his gaze as he searched her face. His unspoken question was clear. But she had no answer to give him, except in that instant, she knew with absolute certainty she wanted him more than any man she'd ever wanted before.

Nick tapped Cade on the shoulder and he turned his attention to his opponent, now standing in the center of the ring.

Taller than Cade by about two inches, broader and more muscular, the Devil Dog wore a black bandanna and sported two silver earrings in his right ear. With a chest full of tats, he looked like a pirate, save for the Devil Dog patch on his back.

The fight started before the referee left the ring.

Cade jabbed, his fist pistoning back and forth so fast, the Devil Dog stumbled back. But he wasn't fast enough. Cade followed through with a punch that dropped his opponent to the ground. Dawn almost thought the fight was over, but the man recovered quickly, jumping up and hitting Cade with a right hook that sent his head snapping to the side. Blood splattered across the grass. Dawn gasped and grabbed Arianne's arm.

"You okay with the sight of blood?" T-Rex leaned over her shoulder. "You want me to take you inside?"

"I can handle the blood." She'd cleaned up blood almost every day when she'd been with the Brethren, whether it was hers, Jimmy's, the blood of one of his brothers, or that of one of their victims. "I just don't like to see him hurt."

Cade's eyes glazed over and he snapped off a kick to avoid another punch from his opponent. Then he threw a vicious kick and a simultaneous massive right punch that dropped the Devil Dog to the ground. His opponent tried to stand and Cade thrashed him with a brutal knee.

"Oh God. Stop, Cade," Dawn whispered.

Sweat glistened on Cade's body. With his jaw slightly

swollen and blood trickling from his nose, he looked vicious and violent and so unlike the man who had been so gentle and tender in bed, and yet he'd never turned that violence on her. Not once had she ever felt threatened when she was with Cade. Instead, she'd felt cared for. Protected. Loved.

Cade followed his kick with another hard right hand, followed by another. His opponent dropped and Cade followed him down, vicious and brutal, dropping hammer fists to his head as his opponent retreated.

Dawn wanted to leave, but couldn't. Tried to look away, but didn't. This wasn't Jimmy, crazy, violent, and merciless, savoring his victim's pain. This was Cade. Fierce, strong, calculating, and always in control.

Protective by nature. Generous of heart.

He stopped when his opponent went down, although the crowd was calling for blood. Nick lifted Cade's arm for the victory salute, and moments later Cade was on his knees, helping his opponent to his feet.

Why had she doubted him? Why had she doubted herself?

After Cade left to shower and dress, Dawn mingled with the Sinners and their support clubs. Everyone was friendly, and curious about the woman who had brought the infamous Sinner playboy to his knees. By the time she made it to the edge of crowd, her face ached from smiling and she'd run out of answers to their questions about taming the untamable beast.

She sensed, rather than saw, him emerge from the clubhouse. Felt his hunger as he searched through the crowd. A thrill of fear shot down her spine at the prospect of being hunted, and she slipped away, hiding behind groups of people until she reached the far edge of the property.

He had almost caught up to her, when two Devil Dogs stopped him to talk about the fight. Dawn came out of hiding and leaned against a tree near the side of the clubhouse, watching him struggle to be polite as his gaze shifted from cool irritation to blistering heat.

He wanted her. Needed her. Just as she needed him. Instead of running away, what if she took control? What if she stayed and fought her own inner war?

With slow, deliberate movements, she unbuttoned her shirt, sliding her fingers along cool skin to the crescents of her breasts. Liquid lava spread through her body, pooling in her belly, flushing her skin with desire.

Cade's eyes widened, but he couldn't get away from his new friends. Emboldened by the fact that they had their backs to her, and no one else was around, she slid her hand into her shirt and cupped her breast, gently kneading her soft flesh as she watched sweat bead on Cade's forehead.

So much fun. She'd never really teased a man before, and watching him watch her was more arousing than she'd ever imagined. Already she was wet for him, desire flooding through her body, ratcheting up her need to a whole new level.

She closed her eyes and imagined what it would feel like to have his hands on her, his cock inside her, his body hot and hard pressed up against her. She circled her taut nipple with her finger, pretending it was his tongue and her breath hitched. With gentle tugs she pulled her skirt up, exposing her thigh to his heated gaze. Then, when she was sure no one was looking, she slid her hand between her legs and stroked along her folds.

Ah God. So good. Her head fell back against the tree with a soft thud, and one of the Devil Dogs startled and turned.

"Free beer." Cade raised his voice and pointed to the bar, diverting the Devil Dogs' attention. His companions made a hasty departure, and Cade pinned her with one scorching look.

"Don't even think about moving." His voice carried across the lawn as he stalked toward her, his muscles taut and quivering, forcing her to back away until she hit the brick retaining wall surrounding the property. Dawn's breathing quickened, her body ripe with desire and the hunger of need.

"Good fight."

Cade stopped, only inches away. "You came. You stayed."

"I am staying," she said softly. "I'm not going into the witness protection program. I left a message for Doug before I came here. I'm not going to let Jimmy take away the life I've made in Conundrum. But I can't fight him alone." It was as close as she could come to telling him she wanted him, needed him. Loved him.

Strong emotion flickered across his face, but he didn't speak.

Dawn bit her lip and let her words tumble out. "I'm sorry I hurt you, but I was scared, not just of Jimmy, but of how much I care for you and whether I can make a commitment to wear this cut."

His face softened, and he bent down and kissed her, soft and sweet. Then he pressed his body against hers, his erection hard against her stomach. "You know what it does to a man when you give him a taste of something he shouldn't see?" His voice dropped to a growl. "You know how hard I got watching you touch yourself?"

"Always about sex."

He kissed her again. "Always about you."

Dawn cupped his shaft and stroked him with the heel of her palm through his jeans. "Hmmm. It's hard to tell. Maybe if I took these off." She tugged at his belt and his hand dived between her thighs, ripping a gasp from her throat.

He was all predator. All man. Feral in his need. She had pushed him to the edge. Would he go over, or could she control her sexy beast?

"I missed you too, honey."

Cade unleashed a low growl of frustration. "No more games. Lift your skirt and turn around. I'm gonna take you against the wall, then I'm gonna bring you inside and love you for the rest of the night."

"I choose door number two." Dawn tugged down his jeans and then dropped to her knees in front of him. "Play."

Play? He didn't want to play. With the adrenaline still streaming through his veins after his fight and his cock throbbing after he watched his old lady getting herself off while he was trapped behind a wall of Devil Dogs, he wanted to bury his cock in her sweet pussy and fuck her hard. Now.

If she hadn't come to the fight, he would have gone to see her, slipped into her bed and made love to her all night. Then he would have hunted down Mad Dog and dealt with him once and for all so she wouldn't have to make a choice that would take her away from him, and endanger her forever.

You can't stop people from doing what they want to do or being where they want to be.

Despite his best intentions, she'd made her choice.

She'd chosen to stay, and she wanted to stand and fight like a Sinner. So he would have her back. And then he'd convince her to make another choice—a choice that meant she would wear his cut and always be safe.

But right now, still primed from his fight, he wanted her with an intensity that took his breath away. Hard. Fast.

Mine.

"Up." He tunneled a hand through her hair, urging her to her feet so he could claim her, sink his cock into her pussy, and give in to the incredible heat that burned between them. But it was too late. Her soft, warm hand wrapped around his cock, tugging him free, and then she licked him from balls to tip.

"I'm not going anywhere."

"Jesus Christ." His fingers tightened on in her hair, and instead of pulling her up, he drew her close. "You want to play, then we'll play. Open up those lovely lips, beautiful, and show me what else that mouth can do."

Her little pink tongue flicked out and danced over the tip of his cock, sending a jolt of lightning through his body. His woman. On her knees. Her silky blond hair a sexy tangle over her shoulders. Those lush, pink lips wrapped around his cock. Her breasts swaying gently as she moved . . .

Anyone could come around the corner. And the possibility of discovery just made the night all that much sweeter.

Too fucking much. He fisted her hair and jerked his hips, stroking into her hot, wet mouth. "Suck me, beautiful."

She wrapped her hand around the base of his cock and dragged her tongue along the underside as she pulled away. Then her hand tightened and she swirled her tongue around his length, then back again. Damn that felt good. She knew what she was doing, but he didn't want to think about how she'd learned, or his scratch list would get even longer than it was.

His cock thickened and his hips surged up, driving him deeper into her mouth. She took him easily and he dared to push a little harder. Dawn stilled for a moment, then worked her mouth in counterpoint to her hand. Fuck. He almost lost it right there. His body thrummed with need, every muscle taut to the point of breaking. But he didn't want her like this. He wanted—no, needed—her trust.

With a groan he pulled away and sat on the cool grass, his back against the brick wall. From this position he would be able to see anyone coming through the trees, and hear people coming around the corner. Still dangerous enough to keep the adrenaline pumping but secure enough to keep her safe.

"On my lap." His words came out in a husky rasp. "Back to me."

Still on her knees, Dawn tipped her head. "I want you like this."

"And I fucking wanted you like that, too. But it's my turn for a game." He gritted his teeth against the pain of his arousal. "Come."

"So demanding, but okay. I'll play." She joined him at the wall, kneeling in front of him while he sheathed himself with a condom from his pocket. When he was certain he was in control, he shoved up her skirt and lifted her onto his lap, settling her with her back to his chest.

"This game is called trust." He slid her panties down over her hips and ankles, and then he forced her knees apart, draping her legs on the outside of his, spreading her wide open.

"Cade! I can't . . . what if someone comes?"

"Close your eyes."

She stiffened and he cupped her mound with his palm. "Trust me, sweetheart. Trust me to keep you safe."

Dawn trembled against him. He could almost feel her internal struggle, and his heart pounded in his chest. He needed this. Needed her. If she trusted him, she wouldn't walk away. Even after Mad Dog was dead.

"I trust you, Cade." She softened against him and closed her eyes.

Sweeter words he had never heard.

Cade stilled, listening to the party in the background, the wind in the leaves, and the scurry of animals in the underbrush. He heard a car door slam, a gate creak, and the steady thud of bass from the speakers the prospect had set up outside. The air was warm, fragrant with the scent of rich spring earth and newly mowed grass.

"If I recall, you were touching yourself here." He slid one hand into her bra and cupped his hand over her left breast. Her heart pounded against his arm as he fondled the soft flesh, rolling her nipple until she squirmed on his lap. "This is mine to touch, sweetheart."

She moaned softly and her skin heated beneath his palm, her nipple tightening into a hard bud.

"Very nice. Now I get to play with the other one." He switched hands and teased her right breast until her breaths came fast and shallow.

"You like a little danger with your sex, don't you, babe?" He widened his legs and Dawn shuddered.

"I'm too . . . exposed."

"Yes, you are. Anyone coming around the corner will be able to see your pretty pussy, open and ready for me." He pressed his palm over her mound, resting two fingers on either side of her clit. He loved that she would do this with him; trust him, follow him where he led. And right now, with his cock rock-hard and pressed between her soft cheeks, he was leading to a quick release.

"You're so wet." He stroked her clit and moved his legs wider, spreading her even more. "I like having you open so I can play."

She sucked in a sharp breath and her fingernails dug into his thighs. So close. He pinched her nipples and Dawn whimpered. One touch and he would send her over the edge, but he wanted to be there with her, feel her pussy ripple around him. "Up, sweetheart." Hands on her hips, he lifted her and lowered her down over his cock. Her pussy clamped around him like a silken glove and he held her still and took a deep breath. The urge to thrust was almost overwhelming, but more than that, he wanted to drive her past her inhibitions, past the fear, to the point where she wanted nothing more than the pleasure he would give her.

Once he was seated deep inside her, he slid his finger over her engorged clit, breathing in the lingering scent of her perfume and the intoxicating aroma of arousal.

"More." She wriggled on his lap and his cock pulsed, demanding release. Unable to hold back anymore, he shoved up her bra and teased her breast with one hand, while he slicked his finger through her wetness and worked his way up and around her clit. When her body went taut, he slid his thumb over her swollen nub.

He barely managed to get his hand over her mouth before she let out a satisfying scream. Her back arched and her head fell back against his shoulder. But when her pussy rippled around him, he couldn't hold back. With a low groan, he scooped her up and lowered her down to the grass, barely getting her on all fours before succumbing to the urge to sink into her slick, tight heat. His balls ached, tight with the need for release. He grabbed her hips and pounded into her. Hard. Fast. Rough.

"Feels so good," she murmured breathlessly as she moved her hips against him. "I want to feel you come."

Cade yanked her against him, and came hard, every muscle in his body twitching as his cock pulsed against her inner walls. Her pussy tightened around him, drawing his orgasm out until he was totally and utterly spent.

He collapsed on top of her, twining his fingers through hers as he nuzzled the soft hair on the back of her neck.

"You did well."

She gave a muffled snort. "Not a lot of skill involved in having a mind-blowing orgasm."

"But it took a lot of courage to give me your trust after watching me fight, knowing how you feel about violence." Every moment he spent with her, he discovered even more about her he liked. He wanted to peel back all her layers and find out what made her tick. He wanted to know every detail of her life, from what she ate for breakfast to the kind of friends she'd had as a kid. And he wanted to give her the kind of life she deserved—a life free of fear and pain and hardship. A life where he could see her smile.

Stay with me always, he wanted to say.

Trust me.

But this wasn't the time. Not with Mad Dog still on the loose. So he sat back, pulled her into his arms, and held her until the party was over.

★ TWENTY-TWO ★

I will give my life for my brother as he would give his life for me.

SINNER'S TRIBE CREED

Cade didn't show for the party.

Dawn rubbed her sweaty palms over her thighs before loading up her tray. Banks had been less than willing to hand over the keys to the bar. But once Jagger's mind was set on something, there was no going back. He'd paid Banks five times the going rate and given his word he would make good any damage.

As with any biker party, the old ladies and sweet butts were expected to serve, except, of course, Arianne, who had taken up her usual station behind the bar.

With Gunner's mix of hard-rock tracks blasting through the speakers, and the Sinners working hard to charm the Brethren, the bar had a good vibe going. Only Cade's absence and Jimmy's presence kept Dawn from enjoying the evening.

She could feel Jimmy's eyes on her as she circulated the bar, and just once she'd made the mistake of meeting his cold, dark gaze. She knew that look. The hard menacing stare, the leering, supercilious expression, and the way he flipped the bottle cap into the air, catching it without a glance. He only flipped bottle caps when something bad was going to happen, usually to her.

Dawn curled her hand around the edge of her cut. Aside from the look that always filled her with dread, something was off with Jimmy tonight. Unusually confident, overly cocky, he sat like a king with his supporters huddled around him, as if he fully expected to win the upcoming election, and he was here just putting in time.

Sweat trickled down her back. If he won the election, she would have to take the girls and leave town despite the risk of the police tracking her down. He'd come for her, and nobody, police or Sinners, would be able to stop him.

No. Dawn put the brakes on the fear train and rallied herself. She was a Sinner. She wasn't alone. She had a plan to deal with the video tape of the fake drug deal and regain custody of her children. No more running away.

By contrast, Shelly-Ann was doing a lot of running away. Dawn didn't know which of the Brethren bikers had invited her ex sister-in-law, but for the first time ever she was delighted to see her. Unfortunately, Shelly-Ann clearly wasn't feeling the love, or maybe she sensed Dawn wanted to speak to her. Whatever the reason, whenever Dawn tried to corner her, she managed to slip away.

"You still worried about Cade?" Arianne opened six beers in rapid succession and placed them on Dawn's tray.

Dawn shook off her morbid thoughts. "He hasn't returned my messages, and when I asked Jagger if he knew where he was, he said it was Sinner business. I know this isn't real, but I'm wearing a cut, and Cade is . . ."

"Your old man." Arianne gave her a soft smile. "Yes, he is. And you deserve to know. I'll talk to Jagger as soon as he's done talking to Wolf."

Dawn finished serving the drinks on her tray, casting

the odd surreptitious glance at Jagger's table. For the most part, Sinners and Brethren sat with their own, but here and there Sinners and Brethren mixed, and so far no one had been shot, stabbed, or hit over the head with a bottle.

After dropping off her tray with Arianne, she headed to the restroom. Pushing open the door, she was so distracted by memories of her heated encounter with Cade by the sink, that she almost walked past Shelly-Ann drying her hands.

"Shelly-Ann. I've been wanting to speak to you all night."

"This isn't a good time. Jimmy's waiting for me. Maybe later."

Dawn stepped in front of the door and turned the lock. "How about now? We never really get a chance to talk and we might get distracted outside."

"Really, I gotta go." Shelly-Ann gestured to the door.

"Not until I say my piece." Dawn folded her arms and leaned against the door. "All this time, I've been trying to find a way to get my girls back, and you held the key."

Shelly-Ann gave her a puzzled frown. "What are you talking about?"

"You took the video of the setup. You gave the drugs to the investigator. My girls were taken away because of you. I would never have known but you're still using the same stickers on your quarters." At least she thought the bags held about twenty-five dollars worth of coke. She'd never made it close enough to the box in Shelly-Ann's living room to tell.

Relief flickered across Shelly-Ann's face so quickly Dawn wondered if she'd seen it. And then Shelly-Ann's face twisted in a sneer. "So what? Who's gonna know? You think I'm gonna testify that I helped Jimmy set you up? You saw what happened to that PI. Jimmy doesn't give a damn that I'm his sister. He'll kill me. He almost killed me when he found out his money was—"

She cut herself off with a sharp breath and leaned right up in Dawn's face. "Give it up. Stop fighting, 'cause you're not gonna win. Now get the hell out of my way."

But Dawn wasn't about to move. Not until she had the whole story. "Is that the money he's after? Why does he think I have it?"

"Because I *told* him you had it." Shelly-Ann's voice rose in pitch. "I had to do something. I didn't know that money he left with me wasn't all his, so I started dipping into it. Once I started, it was hard to stop. I never thought he'd hurt me. He never hurt me before. And there was so much. Bags and bags of the stuff. I didn't think he'd miss a few thousand here or there. But then I decided to treat my friends to a weekend in Vegas, and we had some bad luck at the tables."

"You gambled with Jimmy's money? Are you insane?" She would have felt sorry for Shelly-Ann if she hadn't fingered Dawn as the thief.

"I made a mistake, okay? And I needed to make it good so I leaned on you, and I expanded my drug distribution, got a line into some political big wigs. I figured it wouldn't take too long to make it up, but then the Sinners started putting heat on the Jacks, and Jimmy came for his money. Viper's money. He said Viper had helped him sell a few crates of guns he'd stolen from the Brethren and they'd split the proceeds."

"Oh God, Shelly-Ann. Viper's money." Now, she did feel sorry for her ex sister-in-law. Once Viper found out what had happened—and he would—he would show her no mercy.

"Jimmy went fucking crazy." Shelly-Ann dabbed at her eyes with the sleeve of her fancy jacket. "He beat me in front of the girls. He was gonna kill me. I had to tell him something. So I showed him my busted door and told him how you and the Sinners came and took it."

"How could you?" Dawn's voice echoed in the small room. "You took my children away. You put us at risk. You set Jimmy on me. He destroyed my house and almost killed me."

"How could I?" Shelly-Ann shouted. "This is the world we live in. It's not nice. It's not safe. It's not all flowers and sunshine. There are no happy families. The world breaks you when you're a kid and then you gotta deal with it the rest of your fucking life. You think Jimmy and I had it good? Our mom died of a fucking overdose and our dad drank himself to death after using us as punching bags and sex toys for a couple of years. We were bounced around from foster home to foster home because Jimmy wasn't right in the head and he'd do scary shit like kill the family pets or try to suffocate babies. We were beaten, starved, and abused. No one gave a damn. So we learned to do what it took to survive. And that's what I did when Jimmy came for the money. I survived. And if you don't know how to do the same, then you deserve whatever Jimmy's got coming for you." She grabbed Dawn by the shoulders and shoved her to the side. "Now get out my damn way."

"Don't touch me." Dawn's hand curled into a fist and she punched Shelly-Ann. Not a tentative blow, like she'd given Stan, but a real-honest-to-goodness-wind-up-and-swing-full-force punch that sent Shelly-Ann to the floor. "That's for me and my girls. And you *will* testify about the setup, because if you don't, whatever Jimmy was going to do to you will be *nothing* compared to what I will do. No one fucks with me or my girls."

Someone thudded on the door. She half expected it to be Banks, but when she heard Cade's voice, her heart warmed.

"You okay in there, babe?"

"Yeah." She stepped over Shelly-Ann lying stunned on the floor. "I got this."

"Fucking hell." Cade moved to the side as Shelly-Ann pushed her way past him in the hallway, her face swollen and red and her eye half shut. "You do that?"

"Yes, I did."

"Proud of you, sweetheart." He gave her a hug and Dawn laughed.

"You didn't even ask why."

"Didn't have to. Knowing how you feel about violence, I figure she must have deserved it."

"She did."

While Dawn told him about her altercation with Shelly-Ann, Cade discretely gestured to T-Rex and the prospect to follow Shelly-Ann. Yeah, his girl had this, but he wanted to make sure it didn't come back on her in any way.

"I thought you weren't coming," she said as he led her to the dance floor. Jagger caught his eye and frowned, but Cade didn't give a damn if he provoked Mad Dog. In fact, he hoped Mad Dog started a fight so he would have an excuse to off the bastard tonight, instead of hunting him down tomorrow.

"Got a lead on a coupla guys who were in the van with Mad Dog. I know how Banks doesn't like blood spilled on his floors, so Zane, Gun, and I took a little side trip." He tensed, worried about her reaction, but Dawn just laughed.

"I thought Mad Dog's group of supporters was looking a little thin."

"Five down. One to go." He held up his hands. "But I washed up before coming here."

"That's sweet in a fucked-up-violent-biker-gets-revenge

kinda way." She turned to face him and Cade rumbled his approval. God, she looked hot. Tight black dress showing way too much cleavage. High heels, totally inappropriate for waiting tables. Little white apron. Her beautiful hair flowing over her cut in a golden wave . . . Hell, he knew what every biker in the bar was thinking and he wanted to kill them all.

Mine.

They reached the small dance floor at the back of the bar and her gaze fixed on him as if he were her anchor in the storm. He wanted so badly to take her away—shelter her from this world—he could almost taste it. But another part of him, impressed at how she'd handled herself, wanted more.

"I'm a bad girlfriend . . ." Dawn mouthed the words to the song as she laced her hands around his neck, her body swaying to the beat.

"But you're a damn fine old lady, and I'll prove it to you when I have you alone and in my bed." Unable to stop himself, Cade slid his hand up her thigh beneath her dress, his finger tracing along the edge of her stocking.

"Later," she whispered.

Desire shot through his veins with violent intensity, and a wave of possessiveness crashed over him so hard he could barely breathe. "Banks got an office here?"

She laughed and tilted her head into his palm. "No way would he give it up. He heard what you did at Riders."

"That was a good night."

"The best."

Cade bent down to kiss her, frowning when she tensed and leaned away. He followed her gaze to Mad Dog, standing in the corner, his face a mask of rage. And although he knew it would only inflame the situation, he pulled her close and covered her mouth with his—a full-on, one-hand-in-her-hair, one-hand-on-her-ass, totally possessive kiss that was as much a statement for her as it was for Mad Dog.

Take that you fucking bastard.

"Let's get outta here, babe. I can't wait to get you home."

Jimmy followed them through the bar after the dance, gaining on them as they neared the door. Dawn tried not to look, but she couldn't help herself. She wouldn't put it past him to shoot them in the back. She couldn't understand why Cade didn't look, but he kept walking with the same even, measured steps, his arm around her, his free hand nowhere near his holster where it needed to be.

"Cade . . ."

"Shhh."

"Mad Dog."

"I know."

The door swung open when they were ten feet away and the only thing that kept her from running into the relative safety of the street was Deputy Sheriff Doug Benson and the five policemen behind him.

"Fuck," Cade muttered. "What's he doing here?"

"I don't know."

"Doug?" She took a step toward him, but he looked away. "What's going on?"

"We're looking for Jimmy 'Mad Dog' Sanchez," Doug said in a voice loud enough to be heard over the music. "I have a warrant for his arrest."

"Doug." Dawn grabbed his sleeve. "What are you doing? I said I didn't want to go ahead with this."

"Someone has to protect you since you won't protect yourself." Doug pulled his hand away.

"It's a setup," Jimmy shouted as one of the police officers snapped the handcuffs around his wrist. "The whole party was a set up to get me arrested."

The music stopped and the bar fell into silence.

"Fuck. We trusted you." Wolf glared at Jagger. "We came here in good faith and what do you do? You set us up and tipped off the cops to arrest one of our brothers." He wasn't really angry. Dawn could see it in the way his lips twitched at the corners. With Jimmy in jail, he had no challenger in the election. But he had to publicly show support for his brother, so he was doing the minimum to save face.

"Nothing to do with us." Jagger held up his hands in mock defense. "You got a brother wanted by the cops, he should know better than to show his face in town."

"Fucking bitch," Jimmy screamed at Dawn as the police dragged him to the door. "I know you did this. You set me up. You think you're so tough wearing that cut? You think they're gonna be able to hold me? Not with the friends I've got. You don't even understand what you've unleashed. I'm coming for you. I'm coming and you're gonna suffer like you never suffered before."

★ TWENTY-THREE ★

When there is nothing to lose, there is nothing to fear.

SINNER'S TRIBE CREED

Cade threw himself into the spare chair in the prospect's makeshift IT office and kicked the door shut. They had set the prospect up in an unused room at the back of the clubhouse, and Cade had authorized the purchase of what looked to be way too much computer equipment. So far nothing much had come of the investment except some fancy Sinner's Tribe screensavers and new phones for all the brothers. But then, they hadn't really given the prospect an opportunity to prove his worth. Maybe now that the situation with the Brethren was resolved . . .

He and Jagger had spent the morning on the phone with Wolf. With Mad Dog in jail and the election only one day away, Wolf had the presidency all but wrapped up, and he'd called to discuss the details of the patch-over.

A patch-over Cade still didn't want. Yeah, they could use the extra bodies, but the Sinners were still the dominant club in the state, and now that they knew how the Jacks were growing their numbers, they were in a position to take the Jacks down hard. So why did they need to put the Sinner patch on a bunch of bastards who had not only challenged Sinner dominance, but also turned a blind eye to Dawn's suffering?

"Bad day?" The prospect pounded on his keyboard, his back to Cade. He wore a red T-shirt that said AMORAL INDIVIDUALISM in white letters across the back. Cade didn't know what the hell amoral individualism was, but it sounded smart.

"You could say that."

"You look like shit."

He probably did. After the party, he'd taken Dawn home and made love to her all night long, showing her just how much he admired her courage and even more how much he liked watching her dance. But after she fell asleep, and the first rays of morning light filtered through the curtains, he lay in bed and stared at her cut, neatly folded on the dresser. Benson's actions had pushed them into an uncertain future. With Mad Dog in jail, she no longer needed the cut, and he didn't know what he would do if she tried to give it back.

"Got something for you to do." He handed the prospect a piece of paper. "Man named Lou. Lived in Seattle about ten years ago. Connected to a family named Delgado. I want to know where he lives now, and I want to know everything about him."

"Consider him found."

"Keep it quiet. Just between you and me." Although when the time came, he wouldn't have any trouble rounding up a few brothers to pay Dawn's uncle a visit. Maybe he'd bring the prospect along to toughen him up. And of course Dax, so they could have a little fun.

The prospect turned away and tapped on his keyboard. "I've been waiting for a job like this. When I first started hanging around the club, I told everyone I'm about brains not brawn. I can hurt people worse with my computer than you can with your fists. I can wipe out bank accounts, freeze credit cards, hack into secure computers and steal information. I can erase your criminal record or give you a rap sheet a mile long."

"If you could really do that, you'd have the Feds after your ass so bad . . ."

"They offered me a job." The prospect hit a button and the printer lit up. "I coulda been wearing a suit, working for the man, taking home six figures and driving a nice shiny BMW. Instead I joined an underground hacker group, learned some new skills, and put my education to good use."

"Why?"

"I got a mission. Justice and revenge. I'm gonna destroy the people who destroyed my family. But first I'm gonna make them suffer."

Cade folded his hands behind his head. "And here I was worried about you. Now you're sounding like a biker. But you gotta let that out around the club. Go pick a fight. Shoot something. You gotta make yourself stand out. The reason you don't have a name yet is 'cause you haven't done anything to make people notice you. Everyone is known for something."

"What about you?" The prospect gave him a quizzical look. "I know executive board members don't have to use a road name, but you musta had one."

"Raider. And before you tell me it's a cool name, you should know that it had nothing to do with the MC, and everything to do with a sorority that wanted some biker loving, and a night Gun and I had one too many beers."

The prospect tried and failed to hide his laughter. "That's fucking awesome. Says it all. I hope your old lady doesn't find out. Might make her worried you'll go back to doing whatever it was you did to earn that name."

"I'm done with that shit," Cade said. "No more boozing and babes for me. I'm gonna be a one-woman man." He just had to convince Dawn to keep his cut.

"So what are you still doing here when Mad Dog's outta jail? Shouldn't you be protecting your old lady?"

"What the fuck are you talking about?" Cade shot out of his chair and grabbed the prospect's shirt, yanking him forward. "We were just talking to Wolf, making plans for the patch-over this morning. He didn't say anything."

"Maybe he didn't know." Sweat beaded on the prospect's forehead. "I got a line into the sheriff's office, and a hookup to a police scanner. They released Mad Dog at noon. He got some big-shot lawyer from New York handling his case. I just found out about it, but I figured you already knew."

"Christ." He released the prospect and called Dawn. When he left early this morning she was getting ready to take the girls to the park. When she didn't answer, he sent her a text telling her to get the girls, pack some bags, and meet him at home. There was a safe house above Sparky's shop. He'd take them there until after the election.

If there was an election. Because he'd had it with all the crap. After Dawn and the girls were safe, he was going hunting.

Dawn wheeled Maia's princess suitcase into the hallway. She'd packed as quickly as she could after receiving Cade's message, but dammit, she didn't want to run again—not even to a Sinner safe house. She'd been running away since her family died. First from her uncle, and then from the streets, and now from Jimmy all over again. She wanted to stand up to him the way she had when he broke into her house. But this time, she wouldn't make any mistakes.

Her phone rang and Doug started speaking after she

said hello, his words clipped and his voice unusually abrupt.

"Jimmy's out of jail. There was nothing I could do. The lawyer he hired is a big-time criminal attorney and he had the sheriff's head spinning with all the things he said had gone wrong with the arrest. Where are you?"

"I'm at home. I know about Jimmy. But it's okay. I'm going—"

"Get out of the house, Dawn. Get out now. Get on the bus and come to the police station. I'm just outside of town. I'll meet you there in twenty minutes. I can get you into a safe house and from there we can arrange for witness protection."

"Cade is coming. He's taking me—"

"Don't make this mistake again." Doug's voice rose to a shout. "He can't save you. When Jimmy dumped the body at your house, you came to me. In your heart you knew I could protect you. Cade is a biker through and through. He's going to use you the way Jimmy did. He's playing off your fears with false promises. He doesn't care for you the way I do. I don't want to see you hurt."

Bile rose in her throat. She had done nothing to encourage Doug beyond friendship, and she couldn't understand why he didn't get the message. And Cade . . . Doug was wrong about him. She trusted him, and she trusted herself enough now to know she wasn't making the same mistake she'd made with Jimmy.

"I've made my choice. I love him. And Conundrum is my home. I'm a Sinner now, Doug. I've found myself and I've found my place. I'm not going to let Jimmy take it away."

I love him. The rightness of the words rippled softly through her body, warming her from her fingers to her toes. Why had she been such a fool? Last night, with Jimmy in jail and their deal effectively done, she had actually considered giving back her cut. Now she wished he would hurry so she could wear it for him, tell him that she loved him, and then spend a lifetime showing him just how much.

"You aren't thinking straight. I'm on my way." Doug hung up before she had a chance to say anything else, and Dawn's heart squeezed in her chest. He had been a good friend to her but he had pushed this protection thing just a little bit too far. She wondered again about his sister, and what had happened to her that had made him so determined to run roughshod over Dawn's life.

Dawn turned on the television and settled the girls on the couch as she packed up the rest of their bags. A BREAKING NEWS banner flashed on the screen, and the familiar face of Ella Masters, Conundrum's up-and-coming news reporter, appeared on the screen. Standing under an umbrella, her sleek brown bob irritatingly unaffected by the humidity, she gestured behind her to a sea of police cars and an east-end alley closed off with police tape and announced that Bernie DeMarco, otherwise known as Wolf, president of the outlaw motorcycle club the Devil's Brethren, had been found dead less than an hour ago.

Dawn's stomach heaved and she reached for her phone. Only Jimmy would have the audacity to kill Wolf, on the eve of the election. And she had no doubt who would be next. She texted Cade and Arianne but got no answer.

Damn. Where was he? She wasn't about to hop on the bus and go to the police station to meet Doug, but sitting in her house waiting for Jimmy to show up didn't make sense, either. Yes, she had her gun, but she also had two children to protect, and the last thing they needed to see was their mother shooting and killing their father.

"Girls. Grab your coats. We're going for a walk until Cade gets here."

"I want to bring blankie." Tia jumped up and raced to her bedroom. Dawn ran after her. She had just reached the bedroom when she heard a knock at the door.

"I'll get it." Maia, already dressed and standing in the hallway, turned the lock.

"No."

But it was already too late. The door swung open, and Maia fell to the side.

"Jimmy." Dawn stared at him aghast.

"That's President Jimmy, love. And I've come to take you home."

★ TWENTY-FOUR ★

I shall uphold my creed or I shall turn
in my colors.

SINNER'S TRIBE CREED

He rode like the devil was on his ass.

Streetlights, stoplights, traffic, pedestrian crossings, and school zones flew past as he raced through the streets of Conundrum.

The prospect had come running out of the clubhouse just after he started his bike, and from the look on his face Cade knew the news was gonna be bad.

Wolf is dead, he said.

Mad Dog is president, he said.

And Cade knew exactly where he was going to be.

Dawn screamed when Jimmy dragged her from the house.

"Please. Don't leave them. They're too little to be on their own."

Where were the neighbors who'd complained about shots fired at night? Where was Cade? And where was her damn purse and her gun?

"Mommy!" Maia and Tia ran after them, and Jimmy turned and pointed his gun at his two sobbing daughters.

"You want to live, you'll shut those mouths and you'll go back inside."

"Go to Martha's house after we're gone," Dawn shouted. "Then ask her to call Arianne. The number is in my phone. Please, Jimmy. Let them come with us . . ."

"Shut the fuck up." Jimmy spun around and slapped her. "I don't want those brats. They destroyed my fucking life. You draw any attention and I'll fucking shoot you and get rid of you once and for all. I'm racking up the body count today and three is my lucky number."

Dawn sucked in a sharp breath. Oh God. *Cade.* Had he killed Cade, too? Despair gripped her hard and she took a deep breath and pushed her fear away. Right now she had to survive and escape. Then she'd find her girls and get the hell out of Montana forever. There was nothing left for her here anymore.

"Why do you want me, Jimmy?" She stumbled when he shoved her toward a black SUV, parked at the side of the road. No back lanes or shadowy alleys for him anymore. No attempt to even hide the kidnapping. He was president now. Untouchable.

Two Brethren brothers she didn't recognize opened the door and Jimmy shoved her inside, before climbing in beside her.

"I don't have your money," she continued. "I never did. And you're president now. You don't have to prove anything to anyone."

"I know you don't have the money." His face twisted in anger. "Shelly-Ann caused me a whole lotta grief with her lies, and when I found out, I made sure she was damn sorry she did. As for you, I like havin' you around." He put an arm around her shoulders and pulled her against him. "Pretty face. Sexy body." He gave her nipple a cruel pinch and Dawn gasped. "Love the way you fucking scream. Nothing gets me off like your scream. Lotta girls broke when I beat them. Inside and outside. I never broke you." He squeezed her breast and Dawn had to fight back the nausea as seven years' worth of terror hit her in a rush.

She grabbed the door handle, but the driver had locked the door. She screamed and pounded at the window until Jimmy smashed her head against the glass and promised there was more of that waiting for her if she made any more noise.

After a long drive, the SUV pulled up outside the Brethren clubhouse, a converted barn in the foothills of the Tobacco Root Mountains just outside the Conundrum border. One of Jimmy's companions opened the door for him, bowing as if he were some kind of royalty. Dawn stepped out of the vehicle, and back into a nightmare.

Jimmy hadn't wasted any time. He already had a president patch pinned to his cut, and as they walked toward the clubhouse she could see workers buzzing around what used to be Wolf's house, a small bungalow near the back of the property.

Other than the construction, everything was exactly the same as when she left. The front door opened into a makeshift office foyer, complete with a potted palm, a rack of magazines and a water cooler, all designed to throw nosy cops off the scent.

Gail, the house mama and pretend receptionist, sat behind an empty desk filing her nails. She had grown her platinum-blond hair down to her waist, and her breasts threatened to explode from her low-cut fluorescent-green tank top. She waved absently when Jimmy shoved Dawn forward.

"Long time. No see."

"Gail." Dawn bit back a grimace. Gail had made it clear from day she joined the club that she wasn't interested in friendship, bonding, or female solidarity, and she definitely wasn't interested in anyone who might be a threat to her position. Gail looked out for only Gail. In that way, she was very much like Jimmy.

"Quit yapping." Jimmy pushed Dawn into the clubhouse proper. Her nose wrinkled when she inhaled the familiar stench of unwashed bodies, stale sweat, cigarette smoke and beer, as she fought back the stomach churning memories associated with the unpleasant scent.

A few Brethren members watched TV in one corner, and another cleaned guns at the worn kitchen table. Clothes hung off the free weight machine, but the pool table was busy, as usual. The bikers she knew smirked as she walked past and a few newbies gave her quizzical looks. But of course no one talked to her, because Jimmy hadn't given permission. She was nothing here until he acknowledged her.

He steered her into a small room containing a bed and dresser. Jimmy flicked on the light and closed the door, then pointed her to the bed.

Dawn's pulse kicked up a notch and she took a seat, hoping he would let her call someone to look after the girls if she was compliant. But when he leaned against the door and folded his arms, his face twisted into a cruel, victorious smile, Dawn's hands clenched on the rough polyester bedspread. There would be no mercy for her tonight.

"Lucky for you I gotta stay here until things get settled. Otherwise I would have taken you home to hear you scream." He pulled a bandanna from his pocket and dangled it in front of her. "Not that you'll get off that easy. We can always muffle the sound."

"Let me call someone to look after the girls, Jimmy, and I'll do what you want."

Jimmy snapped the bandanna between his hands. "Don't give a fucking damn about those brats. Consider it part of your punishment for trying to humiliate me at the bar."

"What are you talking about? I didn't do anything to do."

He struck her across the face with the back of his hand and she fell sideways on the bed, her cheek throbbing.

"I forgot what a goddamn slut you are. You loved being up there on the dance floor showing off to the crowd, practically fucking that Sinner in front of my brothers. You're gonna fucking dance for us, but it's me you'll be touching, me you'll be fucking, and it's me you'll be begging for mercy, which I'm not gonna give."

"I'll never dance for you, Jimmy." She pushed herself up, bracing for another blow. "Not again."

This time he just laughed. "You will dance. 'Cause if you don't I'll send someone for those girls and I'll kill them in front of you."

"You wouldn't."

"I'm president of the damn Brethren." Jimmy reached for the door handle. "Soon to be Viper's right hand man as president of his key support club. With the Jacks at my back, nothing's gonna stop me, love, and no one's coming to save you."

She threw herself at the door after the dead bolt slid into place, pounding on it and beating it with her fists. Then she screamed until her voice was raw. But of course no one came to help her. Not now.

After all, no one defied the president.

He knew he was too late when he pulled up to the curb in front of Dawn's house. First, she usually left on the light on the front porch. Second, the front door was partially open, and it seemed no one had called the police. Third, the TV was blaring hip-hop and Dawn was a jazz kind of girl.

Heart in his throat, Cade parked his bike under a streetlight and drew his gun from his cut. If the neighbors didn't notice an open door and a loud TV, they sure as heck wouldn't notice a biker with a gun, and if anyone was inside the darkened house, he hoped to hell they ran in his direction.

He approached from the side, peering in the living room window as he made his way to the back door. Using a file from his cut, he jimmied the lock and stepped into the kitchen. Hearing no sound, he crossed into the living room. The streetlights shone through the opposite window highlighting the chaos inside. Overturned chairs, furniture askew. He spotted a gym bag, half open and stuffed with clothes, near the entrance to the kitchen as well as a princess suitcase and a small stuffed toy. Dawn's purse lay open on the floor.

His hand tightened into a fist, and his chest heaved. Jimmy had his girls. The Brethren would patch-over to the Jacks. The Sinners would be destroyed. And all because he didn't do what he should have done weeks ago.

He turned to leave and then he heard a sound. Soft. Slightly muffled.

A sob.

His pulse kicked up a notch, and he made his way to the hallway leading to the bedrooms.

"Who's in there?" He flicked on the light switch, gun at the ready.

The door to Maia's and Tia's room opened a crack and then a bundle of pink flew down the hallway, hitting him so hard, he stumbled back.

"Cade." Skinny arms wrapped around his hips, holding him tight. "I told Maia you'd come. I knew you would save us. You gave us your word as a biker."

"Tia?" His voice cracked as emotion welled up in his

throat. That the one person who had the most to lose had such faith in him . . .

"Cade." Maia barreled down the hallway hitting him with such force he staggered back. "Jimmy was here. He took Mom away. He said he didn't want us." Her body shook with a sob. "He said he'd kill us if we went outside. Mom said to go to Martha's house but we were too afraid."

"But you'll save Mom." Tia tugged on his shirt. "Won't you?"

"You know I will." Or he would die trying.

After texting the prospect to bring the SUV, he helped the girls pack their bags, then called Jagger to let him know what had happened. By the time he finished the call, the prospect had arrived and Cade loaded the girls' bags, then locked up the house and led them to the vehicle.

"Where are we going?" Maia asked.

"Not sure yet. We have a safe house—"

"Why can't we stay with you?"

Why couldn't they stay with him? There were no wild parties going on tonight at the clubhouse. And he could ask Arianne to watch them until he brought Dawn home. He pulled out his phone and made the call. Arianne told him she'd ask Dax to join her. He'd just gotten back from a job down south, and since he had five kids he'd know how to have some fun.

Cade didn't know about having fun at the clubhouse, or about letting the club torturer anywhere near his girls, even if he did have five kids, but he did know he liked to see the girls smile. And the only way to do that was to bring their mom home.

"Time to get dressed, bitch. You're dancing tonight."

Dawn shot up on the bed when Jimmy burst through the door. She'd been over every inch of the room during the night, and then again over the course of the afternoon, but there were no windows, and the door was locked from the outside.

"Here." He threw a shopping bag at her. She recognized the logo from the shop where she'd bought her dance clothes when she'd been with Jimmy before.

"Put them on."

She stared at the bag. Three years ago she would have picked it up and dressed right away. But she wasn't the same person she had been three years ago. Hell, she wasn't the same person she'd been six weeks ago.

"No." The word fell from her lips before she could stop it. And even though she knew the consequences, it felt so damn good to say that word after so long, she didn't care.

"Pick up the fucking bag and put on the fucking clothes." Jimmy enunciated every word as he crossed the room toward her. He wanted her to cower and cringe and scream and beg. Like he'd said in the car, he got off on her fear and her pain. And when she thought she had nothing and was worth nothing, when she thought no one cared, and she had nowhere to run, she'd given him what he wanted. But not now. Never again.

"I'm not playing this game anymore." Her heart thundered in her chest and she backed up to the wall. "You want me to stay and play happy families so you can delude yourself into thinking that gives you legitimacy in the eyes of the senior patch, then let's go get the girls." She braced herself for the storm, but Jimmy just laughed.

"You think I want you back to be my old lady again? You think I care what the senior patch think anymore? I'm fucking president. And this isn't about getting back together. This is about punishment. Revenge. Justice. You humiliated me when you left. Only reason I didn't do anything about it was 'cause Wolf laid down the law. He didn't want any Brethren hurting civilians and drawing the attention of the cops or the ATF. It was revenge or the cut, he said. So I chose the cut, but I knew the day would come when you would be mine again. I was patient. And my patience was rewarded."

Wolf? She'd always wondered why Jimmy let her go and how she'd gotten off as easily as she had. For months she'd been unable to sleep, terrified she'd wake up with a knife against her throat. Although taking her children away had hurt her worse than any physical pain.

"That's when I knew Wolf had to go," he continued. "So I could make this club great again—the kind of club that doesn't leave a brother hanging out to dry when he's been humiliated by a fucking bitch, the kind of club my dad ran. So I went to Viper. I told him Wolf was weak and he wasn't committed to joining the Jacks. I told him I'd bring him the whole club as a support club if he helped me win the election. Viper wanted more. He wanted puppets to do his dirty work, recruiters to increase his numbers. I had no problem with that. Got me closer to the big man himself."

"You went to Viper on your own? That's treason."

"I got my supporters. Brothers who were tired of Wolf taking the teeth out of this club. And my pal Matchstick, up in Demon Spawn, he hated the Sinners. Fucking Sinners forced his club to be a support club. I recruited them for Viper and in return he helped me steal the weapons Wolf had hidden up in Whitefish, and put me in touch with a buyer. Viper told me to use what I needed to pay off Wolf's supporters first. I hid the money at Shelly-Ann's place in case any of the brothers started asking questions, and then she got her greedy paws on it. Viper almost killed me. Told me to find it. Shelly-Ann sent me after you." He reached for his belt buckle and Dawn tensed. Jimmy's belt had many uses aside from holding up his jeans, and all of them involved pain.

"Viper came through in a big way." Jimmy yanked the belt through his belt loops with a sharp crack. "Even got me outta jail. He's got connections everywhere. The Jacks got puppet members in clubs all over the state. They got cops, senators, judges, lawyers, and government officials in their pocket. Those Sinners are going down, not just in the state but nationwide."

He doubled the belt and slapped his palm. Dawn steeled herself not to flinch. Confusion flickered across his face, and then he narrowed his eyes.

"When I said no one is coming to save you, love, I meant it. No Cade, no Sinners, no deputy. You're on your own. It's you and me and a clubhouse full of Brethren just waiting for a share of what I'm gonna use and throw away. So don't pretend you're not scared, when we both know you are."

Dawn drew in a ragged breath when he closed the distance between them, the belt dangling from his hand. "Can't you see how he's used you? How he's going to use you? Wolf saw it. That's why he came to the Sinners when Viper started sniffing around. Once Viper does you a favor, he owns you forever."

"Shut the fuck up." He grabbed her hair with his free hand and pulled her forward. "We're gonna have some fun with my belt. Just like old times. Then you'll remember to keep your mouth shut. No one gives a damn what you think. You're a fucking woman. You don't know dick about club business."

Dawn fell to her knees, desperate to keep him talking so she could think her way out. There had to be a way. "Why kill Wolf? If the Jacks were backing you, and Wolf's loyalty was called into question when you were arrested at the party, you were guaranteed to win the election. You didn't need to kill him."

"You're as stupid now as you were before." Yanking

her hair, he forced her to turn to the bed. "Because of fucking Shelly-Ann, I didn't have enough money to pay off all the senior patch. And then the Sinners threw that damn party, and won over most of the brothers who had been on the fence. Even some of the brothers I'd paid off started talking about how a patch-over to the Sinners would be a good thing. I told Viper what was going on. He didn't want to take any chances. He told me what to do and I did it."

"Oh God, Jimmy."

He pushed her over the bed. "God's not gonna help you now."

Cade didn't knock before he entered Jagger's office. Instead, he slammed open the door.

Jagger looked from his desk. "Did you find her?"

His chest constricted and it took a moment before he could speak. "She's at the Brethren clubhouse. I've spent the night doing all the recon I can do. I have a plan to go in. I'll need at least twenty, maybe thirty brothers with me."

Jagger rubbed his forehead, and in that moment Cade knew something was very wrong.

"What's up?"

"Mad Dog just called. He wants to meet. Says he's interested in hearing the details of the deal I offered to Wolf."

"He's only doing that 'cause he knows I'm coming after him. It's a trap. If he made a deal with Viper and goes back on it, Viper will hunt him until he's dead." *Which is exactly what I should be doing right now.* Cade clenched his hands by his sides. Every minute he wasted was a minute Dawn might be suffering.

"I agree it doesn't feel right, but we can't just kill the president of another MC, especially if he's making overtures to the club." Jagger scrubbed his hands over his face. "Our future is at stake. The lives of all the club members are at stake. He offered to bring Dawn and the shipment of AKs Wolf promised us as a gesture of good faith if I agree to meet with him."

"Like she's a piece of property." If he'd listened to his instincts and taken care of Mad Dog in the beginning, Dawn wouldn't be in that clubhouse, and the club wouldn't be at risk. He loved the club. He loved his brothers. But he loved Dawn, too. Weeks ago, he'd made a sacrifice for his club. Now he would make a sacrifice for her. He had wasted enough of his life bearing a heavy burden of guilt over things he couldn't control. This time, there was something he could do and nothing was going to stand in his way.

He slid the cut off his shoulders and threw it on Jagger's desk.

"I'm done."

★ TWENTY-FIVE ★

I will never abandon my brother.

SINNER'S TRIBE CREED

Cade pushed himself away from the wall outside the police station and walked under the glow from the overhead streetlight, making himself visible to the cop crossing the parking lot.

"Benson."

Benson turned and frowned, then looked back over his shoulder at the police station as if assessing how close he was to safety. "Cade? You looking for me?"

Hands held high so Benson could see he wasn't armed, at least not visibly, Cade walked toward him. "It's about Dawn. I need a favor. Didn't want any brothers to see me talking to the cops. You know someplace private we can talk?"

"Jail?"

"I'm not in a joking mood."

"I wasn't joking. When we renovated the station, we built nice new comfy jail cells, so no one is using the old cellblock. The cameras are offline. It's as private as you're gonna get, and to be honest, I'm not keen on going anywhere you might stab me in the back."

"No honor in stabbing someone in the back, but fine, let's go." As long as he had his weapon, he didn't care where they talked and with the clock ticking he wasn't prepared to dick around.

Benson led him through a back door and down a dingy flight of concrete stairs. He keyed a number code into a panel beside a thick steel door. Fluorescent lights went on when the door opened and they walked along the corridor to a small, windowless room filled with monitors and a few chairs. The cellblock smelled of mold and sweat, and faintly of piss.

"Guard station." Benson waved Cade over to a metal chair. "Or maybe you're familiar with it."

"Never been incarcerated. I like to keep my nose clean."

"Sure." Benson took a seat near the door. "That's why you're in an outlaw biker gang that runs guns, shakes down small-business owners, and protects drug dealers as they transport their goods through our fine state. Oh, and I'm sure you had nothing to do with the body that was found outside Dawn's house."

Cade bristled. "We run legitimate businesses in and around Conundrum."

"To launder your money."

"To provide services to the good citizens," Cade countered. Damn. He didn't want to like Benson, but he had to admit the dude was sharp as whip. He knew the score with the Sinners. No doubt he had some plan in mind to take them down in the future.

"So what favor could you possibly need from me?" Benson folded his arms, his chair squeaking as he settled back.

"I might need you to get Dawn and her girls out of town." He leaned his forearms on his thighs and dropped his hands between his legs. "Shit is going down between the clubs. Could get ugly. I got something I have to do and if something happens to me, she'll have no one to watch out for her. If that happens, I want you to put them in the witness protection program so they can live a safe life."

He had Benson's attention now. The chair squeaked again as Benson leaned forward, mimicking Cade's position. "What do you mean by 'shit is going down'?"

"Nothing for you to worry your pretty little head about." *Fuck.* He just wanted to get Benson's agreement and get out. Biker business wasn't cop business and he didn't want to give the game away. Plus, it grated on him something fierce to have to come to Benson for help. But without Cade, Dawn had no connection to the Sinners, and the safest place for her was out of town.

Benson's mouth opened and closed and Cade prayed he didn't say something that would piss him off. He was wound too tight, a coil ready to spring. Never could he have imagined having to go to the police for help.

"You're not wearing your cut."

"Very observant," he said drily.

"So you're not a biker anymore?"

"I'm a man who's gotta protect the people he cares about whatever the cost."

"Hell." Benson stood and walked over to the wall beside the door. "You're going after Mad Dog."

Was there any reason not to tell him? Benson and Dawn were friends. She trusted him. Hell, Benson wanted her in his bed. And he'd tried to help her get out already. "He's got Dawn at his clubhouse. If I don't get to him, he's gonna kill her and destroy my club."

"The only reason he got Dawn is because of you." Benson's upper lip curled in disgust. "I called her when Mad Dog was released. I told her to get out of the house. I told her I'd meet her at the station and take her away. But would she listen? No. She said she was waiting for you. She said she loved you."

Cade's heart skipped a beat. She loved him. He'd never heard sweeter words. Too bad they had to come from Benson's damn mouth.

"Sorry, Benson."

"You're not sorry," Benson spat out. "You don't care for her the way I do. She's a victim of your world and she needs to be protected. You twisted her into something she's not. You dragged her back into the cesspool she tried so hard to escape."

Cade sat up in his chair, his skin prickling in warning at Benson's flushed face and trembling hands. Seriously, the dude was out of control. He couldn't figure out if the Benson was obsessed with Dawn or if something else was driving him.

"She's a strong woman who knows her own mind and who can look after herself. She owns her past and she's living a life she wants to live. You need to respect her choices." He stood and crossed the floor. "You're a good cop, but you're way outta line with the fucking disrespect. Stand aside. I'm gonna go get my girl and after I do, I don't want you anywhere near her."

"I'm afraid I can't let you do that." Benson pushed a button on the wall and raced into the hallway moments before a huge metal door dropped from the ceiling and slammed into place.

"What the fuck?" Cade drew his weapon and only just managed to stop himself from shooting. The bullet could very well rebound around the room and kill him.

"Benson? What the hell is going on?"

"If anyone is going to rescue her, it's going to be me." Benson's muffled voice was barely audible through the safety door. "I'll protect her and keep her safe. I'll take her away into the witness protection program and she'll live a happy life away from you and Mad Dog and every other damn biker in the state."

"You fucking bastard. Let me outta here. He'll kill her before you get to him. You know he will."

"Sorry, Cade."

"The minute I get outta here you are fucking toast. You will never breathe another breath . . ."

"You won't be getting out of there," Benson shouted. "That's a three-inch steel safety door to protect the guards in case of a riot. It can only be opened from inside the station. And if you think you can call for help, there's no phone signal down here. But I guess since you're not a Sinner anymore, there's no one for you to call."

"Benson." He roared his frustration when he heard Benson's footsteps in the hallway. "Benson!"

"Ow. Jimmy. Let go. I'll come with you."

Dawn clasped her hands to her head to soften the pull on her hair as Jimmy dragged her from the room. He'd only managed to hit her a few times with the belt before he'd been interrupted, and since she was wearing her clothes the pain had been manageable. But now, dressed in a tight red two-piece outfit, held together with Velcro strips for easy removal, she had a lot more skin at risk if she didn't obey.

By way of response, Jimmy tugged harder. "Crazy bitch like you needs a firm hand. You don't please me up there, you'll be feeling that hand tonight. Hell, you're gonna feel it anyway for all the shit you pulled on me." Jimmy led her up to a small stage against the wall with a pole in the center, and threw her to the floor. "We made some modifications since you left. Had a pole installed so we didn't have to waste our money at titty bars. Now we bring the girls here."

Dawn grabbed the pole and pulled herself to her feet. She counted forty-three bikers spread across the open space, some leaning against the corrugated metal walls, others against the wooden support pillars, and a few in metal fold-up chairs scattered around the stage.

Jimmy settled himself on a huge leather chair in front of the stage and snapped his fingers. Gail swanned over to sit on his lap, making no effort to hide her smirk from Dawn.

Well, Dawn was more than happy to step aside. She would be even happier if she could get out of the building. Aside from the front entrance there were two more exits from the clubhouse. One directly across from her and one at the back. Both guarded from the inside. Her chances weren't looking so good.

"Put on the music." Jimmy waved his .38 around like it was a Fourth of July flag. "Everyone join us. My ex is gonna dance the last fuckin' dance of her life. She's gonna show us the moves she used in the bar, but she's gonna be doing them for me and without her fucking clothes."

The bikers cheered. Dawn's stomach heaved. But Jimmy wasn't finished. He held up a hand to quiet the crowd.

"When she's finished dancing, she's yours for the taking. I'm done with her, and that bitch's disrespect to me and to our club has gotta be addressed. Everyone can have a taste of what I threw away. No limits."

This time only a few bikers cheered. The rest frowned or shifted in the seats. Were they Wolf's supporters? Given their number it looked like Wolf might have won the election if Jimmy hadn't killed him. Would they help her? She recognized some of their faces, but when she tried to make eye contact they looked away.

"Get to it, Dee-licious, or I'll start the gang bang now."

"Hey, Mad Dog . . ." An old biker, potbellied, grizzled and balding, stood and pointed at Dawn. "I got no problem with her dancin'. Used to watch her at the strip joints long time ago and she was damn good. But what you're wanting to do to her next, that ain't us. We're not into raping and trading and slaving the girls no more, especially not the mother of your kids."

She remembered Old Mick now, although he'd aged considerably since she'd last seen him. One of the quiet ones, and a good friend of Wolf.

Jimmy whispered to Gail and she giggled. Then he put his arm around her waist, aimed his. 38, and casually shot the biker in the leg. Old Mick howled and staggered back, falling heavily on the ground. Dawn's hand flew to her mouth. No one moved, and the shock on their faces suggested they were as stunned by Jimmy's arbitrary ruthlessness as she.

"Anyone else got a problem with the new regime?" Jimmy waved his gun back and forth, pointing it randomly at his brothers. "Old Mick was right. This ain't how Wolf would run the club. But I'm not Wolf. And he made pussies out of all of you. Viper and the Jacks can help us bring back the Brethren's legacy. They're gonna help us take our revenge on the Sinners and wipe them off the face of this fucking earth. Anyone got a problem with that, you know where to find the door. But I'll tell you now, I got no hesitation about shooting a coward in the back."

Old Mick groaned and clutched his leg. Another seasoned biker whipped off his bandanna and wrapped it around Mick's thigh, while a third used this shirt to put pressure on the wound. Dawn fought back wave after wave of nausea. Bloated with power, Jimmy had finally gone off the rails. Did he not realize Viper had no intention of "helping" the Brethren? He needed their numbers and Jimmy's blind anger to help defeat the Sinners, simply because no other club would stand against them. And when Viper got what he wanted, he would destroy them. Jimmy was a pawn in the game.

Jimmy grinned into the silence. "Excellent. Everyone is on board." He pointed his weapon at the two bikers helping Old Mick. "Leave him be. He can suffer through the show and think about the meaning of loyalty."

One of the bikers knelt beside Old Mick and whispered something in his ear, while the other patted him on the shoulder. Then they took some seats.

"Now let's have some entertainment."

Dawn stared at Jimmy. There was nothing left of the man who had saved her from the streets. Totally and utterly corrupted in his pursuit of power, he had become the monster she'd always known he could be.

"Dance, love," he said. "Like your life depends on it. You can finish with a scream."

Cade's anger was so deep, so fierce, he battered his knuckles bloody on the door. He'd had a bad feeling about Benson, but he'd chalked it up to pure jealousy, blinding himself to the wolf in fucking cop clothing.

He checked his phone again. No signal. No way of getting through the sheet of steel in front of him. Yet. But when he did, he would rain down a terror on the Jacks and Brethren the likes of which had never been seen in the biker world. And the fucking cop would pay in blood.

"Cade? You in there, brother?" Although muffled, he recognized the voice behind the door.

"Jagger?"

"Yeah. I'm with Zane, Gun, and Sparky. We got the prospect with us, too. He finally showed some initiative. He tracked you down with a GPS he put in all the new phones. Now he's doin' something with the door panel, hooking it up to his laptop."

"I'm hacking into their system," the prospect shouted.

"Hurry the fuck up. We got a rescue operation to perform."

The door slid up with a smooth whir and then clanged into place. Cade stepped out into the hallway and heaved a sigh of relief.

"You forgot this, brother." Jagger held up his cut.

Although his hand itched to take it, he didn't move. "I'm going after Mad Dog."

"Not without us. We're a team. Brothers. No one gets left behind and no one goes out alone."

Cade swallowed past the lump in his throat and shrugged on his cut, indulging himself for the briefest second by smoothing his hand over the cool leather. "I don't get it."

"You don't have to make a choice. Whatever path you choose, we will always have your back. Just like you had ours."

He needed to hear those words. With all that had happened he had lost sight of what was important. This was why he had joined the Sinners. Honor. Brotherhood. Loyalty. Men who would stand up for him. Men who always had his back.

His club.

His tribe.

Jagger nodded at the prospect who was detaching his computer from the panel. "If he hadn't followed you, we wouldn't have been able to pinpoint where you were so fast. The GPS lost you when you went into the building."

Cade glared at the prospect. "You followed me?"

The prospect shrugged. "Lost my old man when he went out on a job without someone at his back. Figured you might need some help."

"He left so fast, he forgot to put on his cut," Jagger said, his lips quivering at the corners.

"Rule violation." Gunner's mouth pressed into a thin line. "Not wearing his cut. He'll pay a penalty for that in blood."

"And he followed a senior patch without permission." Sparky winked and Cade fought back a smile. There was nothing the brothers enjoyed more than hazing a prospect.

"Suicide," Gunner muttered. "Fuckin' suicide."

"I'd call it plain stupid," Zane cuffed the prospect on the head. "Disrespecting the cut is an automatic kick-out. Leaving the clubhouse without permission is a night in the dungeon with Dax followed by a kick-out."

"Maybe I'll just shoot him," Gunner said as they followed Jagger out of the cellblock. "Put him out of his misery."

Jagger looked over his shoulder and glared at the prospect. "He also left his computer on. Penalty for wasting energy is death and an ass-kicking from me."

"No point kicking his ass if he's already dead." Sparky patted the prospect's shoulder. "I think he has value. and it'll be more fun to kick his ass and hear him scream. He finally showed some spine. It would be a shame to break it too soon."

The prospect choked back a gasp, and Gunner snorted. "Dead or alive, an ass is an ass to me."

Cade followed his brothers up the stairs, still trying to wrap his head around the incredible turn of events that meant (1) he was free; (2) he had his cut; (3) the Sinners were going to help him take down Mad Dog; and (4) he had been saved by a fucking prospect.

Time to give something back. "I think our prospect needs a name."

"Geek."

"Nerd."

"Gigolo."

Jagger stopped at the door and gave Cade a puzzled frown. "Gigolo?"

"Lookit him. The ladies will be falling all over themselves when he walks into a bar wearing his colors looking like some kinda frickin' biker movie star."

Everyone turned to stare at the prospect.

"You're jealous," Gunner said. "He's younger and prettier than you. You're afraid he's gonna steal your girls away."

"He's welcome to them." Cade stepped out into the cool, dark night. "Only one girl I want. But I need someone to take up the mantle, otherwise there are a lot of good titles out there that will be lost."

"How 'bout Hacker?" Sparky tapped the prospect's laptop. "He's not much use in the field, but he sure as hell knew his stuff when it came to finding you and getting into that system—"

"Don't forget the screensaver." Gunner cut him off. "Pretty damn cool to have our patch on every piece of tech in the clubhouse."

"Vote," Jagger called out from his bike. He'd parked between two police cars in a brazen show of sticking it to the cops.

Everyone lifted a hand.

"Hacker it is. Now let's go save an old lady and kick some Brethren ass. The rest of the brothers are waiting for us."

★ TWENTY-SIX ★

I will let nothing stand in the way of justice. I will never hold back in the pursuit of revenge.

SINNER'S TRIBE CREED

The first notes of White Stripes' "Icky Thump" filled the room and Dawn stared at Jimmy. After everything that had happened, she was back where she started, except this time she was twenty-six instead of sixteen, and when she danced, it wouldn't be with fear and humiliation feeding Jimmy's ego. She had a confidence she'd never felt before. She had people who cared about her. And she had a man who would do anything to keep her safe. But first she had to save herself. But she needed a gun.

Dawn kicked out one leg and twirled around the pole, checking out the room for weapons and an exit. A low hum from the street muffled the pelvic-throbbing beat of the music, and she paused midstep. What was that noise? She looked to the front door and a few bikers did the same.

Thunder? The rev of an engine? The roar of a train? The sound grew louder.

"What the hell is going on?" Jimmy pushed Gail off

his lap and pointed at the biker nearest him. "Go. Find out."

By now the sound was unmistakably that of a vehicle in full acceleration. Jimmy reached for his gun. The front door crumpled and the side of the building went with it, the sheet-metal-and-wood-frame structure collapsing under the weight of the massive black SUV barreling into the building. The clubhouse groaned under the impact. Pictures fell from walls. Beams crashed to the floor. Bikers shouted. Someone fired a gun.

Dawn ran. She didn't care who was in the vehicle or why it had come through the wall, but it was a chance of escape and she wasn't about to lose it.

The driver's-side door of the SUV swung open and Cade stepped out of the vehicle, his face a mask of fury. Using the door as a shield he sprayed bullets across the room, covering Dawn as she ran toward him. Cold, determined, calculating, he moved with confidence and purpose, scattering the Brethren in a shower of steel.

Dawn hit the vehicle running and reached for the door just as two pit bulls came racing through the hole in the wall. They went straight for Cade, knocking him to the ground. Cade lost his weapon as he fell. "Run, Dawn. Get the fuck out."

Like hell I will. She dropped to the ground and rolled under the vehicle, staying behind the wheel well as she reached for Cade's gun. She dragged it toward her by the handle, struggling with its weight. *Okay.* It was some kind of submachine gun. Not quite the same as her little .22 but she just had to pull the trigger.

Cade struggled with the dogs. One of them bit his arm and he cursed. The other clamped its jaws firmly around his leg, and Dawn slid her finger over the trigger, hoping a few rounds would scare them off.

"Heel." Jimmy's voice echoed through the clubhouse.

He snapped his fingers and the dogs released Cade. "Not so brave now, are you?" He crouched beside Cade with his weapon pointed at Cade's head while the dogs salivated beside him. Dawn couldn't see Jimmy's face but she could imagine the smirk. He always smirked before he hit her.

"Up." Jimmy barked the command and Cade heaved himself to his feet. Dawn shifted closer to the edge of the vehicle, and one of the dogs growled. *Damn.*

"You picked the wrong fucking brother and the wrong fucking club to mess with when you got involved with my old lady." Jimmy's voice slid through her like ice. "Shootin' you dead is gonna be too easy. Your death is gonna be nice and slow. I'm gonna film every minute of it and send it the Sinners so they know what's coming for them."

"I think you better be worried about what's coming for you."

Dawn drew the gun close to her chest. The dogs barked. A furry black face appeared under the vehicle and she slid back. The SUV rocked above her. Was someone inside?

"Hiding, love?" Jimmy raised his voice loud enough for her to hear. She could see his boots just in front of her. The same boots he'd used when he'd kicked her repeatedly in the stomach, trying to make her lose her babies.

"Don't think I've forgotten about you. Just in case you feel left out, you're gonna suffer, too."

Dawn leaned up on her elbows, shoved the gun between her breasts and fired. Jimmy screamed. The gun whacked her chin on recoil and her head jerked back, hitting the undercarriage with a painful thud.

Jimmy fell to the ground and into Dawn's line of sight. His weapon dropped to the side. "Jesus fucking Christ. The bitch just shot my fucking toe."

The vehicle rocked again and the rear passenger door

opened. Feet scuffed the concrete floor beside her. But she didn't have time to worry about what was going on. Jimmy was down, unarmed, injured, and for the first time vulnerable. She steadied the gun between her breasts and slid her finger over the trigger. This was it. The moment she had dreamed about for ten years. The end of Jimmy. She would finally be free.

Cade heard the SUV door open. This was it. Gunner was out. Sparky and Zane would be right behind him. It was the end of Mad Dog. And he was going to be the one to pull the trigger. He threw himself forward and grabbed Mad Dog's weapon. Then in one swift move, he rolled, aimed, and fired.

In that moment three things happened.

First, two more shots were fired, each from a different gun. Mad Dog fell backward, his hand to his chest.

Second, as Mad Dog fell, a bullet from a fourth gun hit Mad Dog from behind, a clean hit through the neck that slowed only when it pinged off the hood of the SUV.

Third, four people yelled, "I got him."

Gun at the ready, Cade surveyed the scene. Curiously none of the Brethren ran to Mad Dog's aid. Even the two dogs that had so obediently heeled at his command left him to lick the face of an old geezer lying on the floor with a gun pointed where Mad Dog's neck used to be.

"I got him." Dawn slid out from under the SUV.

"I got him," the old geezer yelled. "Right through the fucking neck."

"No fucking way." Gunner lowered his weapon. "I got him."

"No, I got him," Cade said. "Hit him in the leg."

"That's just the old injury from when I hit him in the leg." Dawn glared and then sucked in a sharp breath.

"Why are you lowering your weapons? We're still outnumbered."

"Not for long."

As the last word left Cade's lips, the Brethren dropped their weapons. He turned and smiled at the Sinners pouring through the wrecked wall on either side of the SUV.

His brothers.

His club.

And . . . *What the fuck? Benson?*

Talk about ruining the moment.

"Dawn!" Benson stared at Dawn aghast as he walked over the rubble. "What are you doing with that . . . weapon?"

"Shooting people." One hand on her hip, she held up her gun. Cade snorted a laugh. Damn, she was a sight in that tight red dress, dirty and torn, her hair tangled, scratches and bruises on her arms and legs. But with that weapon in her hand and the triumphant smile on her face she was beyond beautiful to him.

"Actually she was shooting toes, not people, but she did a good job. She's better at shooting toes than tires." He looked over at Benson and lifted an eyebrow. "We got business together, Benson. A little matter of locking me up in jail and trying to steal my girl. You got anyone you want to call before you die?"

Benson's mouth tightened. "Your girl."

"Mine."

Benson's gaze swept over Dawn, lingering, and then his shoulders slumped. "She's definitely a Sinner."

Dawn put her arm around Cade and leaned her head against his chest. "Cade's Sinner. I am sorry, Doug, but this is where I want to be."

"I wanted so badly to save you," Benson said wistfully. "My sister was taken by a biker gang when she was fourteen. We never got her back. I joined the police thinking I would make a difference and something like that would never happen on my watch. I think I lost perspective, and I might have gotten a little carried away."

"You went to fucking crazy town and back." Cade shoved his weapon in its holster. "Even coming out here alone . . . all kinds of stupid. You always gotta have someone at your back."

"I get it. I'm sorry, Dawn. I won't bother you or the Sinners again." He turned to go and Cade gestured to Tank to cut off Benson's retreat.

"You don't get off that easy. Locking up a Sinner is serious offense, but 'cause you were looking out for my girl, I'll give you a choice. I beat the shit out of you, break your fucking arms and legs, and dump you in a ditch outside of town, or you can be the Sinners' eyes and ears inside the police station. Sheriff Morton did a fine job for us, and was paid well for his trouble until he got greedy, so now there's a vacancy that needs to be filled."

Benson shrugged. "It's not really a choice, is it?"

"You always have a choice."

"He's being nice to you." Dawn's lips tugged at the corners. "He would usually smash your vehicle, too."

"And burn down his house." Cade brushed his lips over her forehead. "But I got my girl so I'm in a good mood."

"I kinda like my vehicle," Benson said. "And my arms and legs. You've got yourself a mole."

"I got the girls." Cade pulled Dawn against his side after Tank and T-Rex escorted Benson back to his police car. "They're safe at the clubhouse."

Dawn exhaled a relieved breath and leaned against SUV. "Thank you. I can't tell you how worried I was about them. But the clubhouse? Two little girls? Really?"

"Dax is with them."

"Dax? The torturer?"

"He's got his own kids. He knows how to have a good time."

"I'm sure he does." She wrapped her arms around his waist. "Probably dissecting frogs and shooting at squirrels."

Cade growled low in his throat. "Made me hot watchin' you shoot Mad Dog from under the SUV."

"Everything makes you hot. You'd probably have me naked and over the hood of the vehicle if I'd done more than shoot him in the toe." She had been bitterly disappointed after Zane checked Jimmy's wounds and pronounced Old Mick the winner of the shoot-out.

"I think you should put down that gun and we'll let the boys finish doin' what they're doin' with the Brethren and I'll show you just how hot your toe shooting made me."

Dawn glanced over at Old Mick and Jagger, deep in conversation while Doc Hegel tended to Old Mick's wound. Around them, Sinners kept watch on the disarmed Brethren, while others searched the clubhouse, and still more guarded the doors.

"I think they aren't going to be doing anything to the remaining Brethren other than taking their weapons and offering them a choice of patch-over or death," she said. "Mad Dog's supporters are already gone. The usual rats fleeing a sinking ship."

"We'll hunt them down. Guaranteed."

She tightened her arms around Cade, drinking in the warmth of his body. "That was a pretty damn awesome rescue. Very Cade. Lots of drama. No sneaking around or hiding in the shadows. Just straight plowing through the wall in an SUV like an action hero."

"I know something else I want to plow into. Hop in

and I'll take you back to the clubhouse and show you what else an action hero can do."

"You're filthy."

"And you love it."

"I love you," she said. "But the filth is a close second."

"What's this?" The skin on the back of Dawn's neck prickled when she saw the duffel bag packed on Cade's dresser. She'd checked on the girls and showered in the grimy clubhouse washroom to wash away all traces of Jimmy, easing the tension from her body. Now, freshly scrubbed and dressed in one of Cade's shirts, her anxiety returned all over again.

"You're going on the road so soon?"

"Shhhhh." He cupped her face between her hands and brushed his lips over hers. "I got a coupla things I got to do that can't wait. I'm taking T-Rex, Dax, and the prospect with me."

She tried to pull away, but he was too strong, his hands too firm, his lips too soft. "Where are you going?"

He smoothed a hand over her forehead. "Better if you don't know."

"I want to know where you're going." She shoved him back against the door. "I'll be worried, Cade. I worried when you were up in Whitefish, but at least I knew where you were. Tell me. Now."

"You trying to turn me on, babe? 'Cause I'll let you know a secret. That fire of yours, when it gets going, makes me hot like nothing else. Nothing a biker likes more than soft and sweet with a sassy inside."

"Cade . . ." She moaned when his hands slid down to her ass, pulling her hips against his hardened length.

"I want to love you, babe," he whispered in her ear. "Let me love you tonight. I promise you won't regret it."

She answered him with a kiss, her arms around his

neck, her breasts pressed against his chest. "Love me. Then tell me where you're going."

"I'll tell you where I'm going to as soon as you strip off your clothes." Cade settled himself on the bed, hands behind his head, legs spread, the quintessential alpha male.

"I've never stripped for anyone, Cade. Not after leaving Jimmy."

"You aren't stripping for anyone. You're stripping for me. And you're gonna think about how much I love your body, and how much I want you, all of you, inside and out; how I'm dying here waiting to see every beautiful inch of my beautiful girl."

Her fingers trembled as she reached for the hem of her top. Drawing in a shallow breath, she pulled it up and over her head. Why was she so nervous? They'd had sex. He'd seen her without her clothes. But she'd never felt like she was baring everything to him before, dropping the walls that protected her heart.

"Keep going."

He wanted her. Not just her body, but *her.* For the longest time she hadn't known who she was. Even after she left Jimmy, she had one goal and one goal only: to get her girls back. But Cade made her think about herself, who she was, and what she wanted. He made her see just how deep her strength ran, and how desirable she was to him. She wanted to take what he offered. To bare herself to him and not worry about what might happen after.

She dropped the shirt on the floor, shivering in her purple bra and panties as cool air brushed over her heated skin.

Cade made a low, sensual hum of approval. "Turn."

A smile tugged at her lips, and she turned for him, using the skills she'd learned when she was dancing. Smooth, elegant, slow, and seductive.

"You're killing me, babe."

Encouraged by his half-lidded gaze and obvious arousal, she slowly slipped the bra straps off her shoulders, and then she ran her finger lightly over the lace framing the crescents of her breasts.

When his eyes flared, she tucked her thumbs beneath the elastic at her hips, running them back and forth over her tummy before she slid them down her thighs.

"Stop."

Half bent over, her breasts swaying gently beneath the cups of her loosened bra, she looked up to see he had half risen from the bed.

"Don't you want me to finish?"

His low rumble reverberated through the room. "I can't wait."

"You started this. If I can do it, you can wait. I've never wanted to strip for someone before. It was never really a choice. But I'm kinda enjoying your discomfort."

Cade tensed and she could see his inner struggle in the lines of his face. His hand slid to his groin and he adjusted himself. "Discomfort is the least of what you're gonna feel when I get my hands on you."

"Promises. Promises."

"Finish."

She bent again to slide her underwear over her heels and Cade groaned. "Babe . . ."

"Would it be better if I faced away." She stood and turned, letting her hair sweep over her back, and then gave him a full rear view as she slid off her panties.

After a painful moment of silence, she looked back over her shoulder and a grin spread across her face. Cade had shoved down his clothing, freeing his cock for the firm stroke of his hand.

Mesmerized, Dawn turned back to watch him. She'd done that to him. Driven him past the point of control. Far from turning her off, she found it fiercely arousing and she wanted nothing more than to replace his hand with hers. But when she took a step toward him, he dropped his hand and waved her back.

"You're not finished."

"I think I am." She reached behind and unclipped her bra, then threw it at him, grinning when it landed on his erect cock. "I always had good aim."

His laugh warmed her inside, but when he launched himself off the bed, she startled and turned away.

"Shhhh." His T-shirt was cool against her heated skin, his half open fly rough against her ass. He shoved his clothing down and his cock, hot and thick, jerked against the small of her back.

With a moan, Dawn arched into him, rubbing her ass against his groin. Cade splayed his hand over her hips, pulling her so tight against him, his erection pressed into the cleft of her buttocks.

"Cade . . ." Her body was on fire, but when she tried to turn, he held her fast, his free hand gliding over her rib cage to her breasts, now tender and swollen with need. He rolled one nipple, then the other, working them between his thumb and forefinger until she was bucking mindlessly against him, wanting the promise of what was to come.

"My beautiful girl," he whispered, his lips warm and wet on her shoulder. "Tonight I'm gonna make you mine. All mine. Body, heart, and soul." His teeth found the sensitive spot between her neck and shoulder and he sunk his teeth into her skin with a firm, hard pressure that she knew would leave a mark.

His mark.

She writhed against him, almost delirious with pleasure and the need for release. One hand still splayed across her belly, he caged her jaw with the other, pulling her head back to his chest. Then he pushed his finger inside her mouth.

"Suck."

Her blood turned to molten lava and streamed through her veins. He was wild tonight. Dominating. Barely contained. And yet she had no fear of where he might take her. She could give her power freely to Cade, knowing in her heart he would never abuse it.

Her lips closed around his finger and she drew it into her mouth, swirling her tongue around his knuckle, drinking in the faint taste of bourbon and the essence of him.

He nudged her thighs apart and she felt the slide of his cock along her soaked folds. Back and forth, he rocked against her, always stopping just short of where she needed him to go.

Dawn closed her eyes as his fingers teased and tortured her nipples. He licked her neck, tasted her, swept his tongue along her jaw and nibbled her ear. Dawn tilted her head to give him better access and brought one arm up. She reached behind her and ran gentle fingers through his hair, soft and thick, yet another sensation to carry her past the point of no return.

"Ah God. Too much even for me." He swept her up into his arms and laid her gently on the bed. Then he shrugged off his cut, folding it neatly and placing it on the dresser. There was a reverence to his gesture that tugged at her heart, but when he pulled a second cut from his duffel bag, she melted inside.

"This is yours." His voice choked with emotion, and he placed the cut on the bed. "You left it behind. Put it on, babe. For me."

Dawn sat up and slid the cut over her shoulders. The leather was cool on her heated skin and she smoothed her hand over the soft leather. Cade's eyes darkened almost to black. He stripped off his clothes and sheathed himself, then eased her back on the bed,

"I wanna fuck you wearing my cut."

"I wouldn't want it any other way."

He stretched out on the bed and settled her over his hips, his erection, thick and strong wedged against her center.

"Take what you need from me." He clamped his hands on her hips and eased her up so the head of his cock nestled against her entrance. "I want to watch your pleasure."

Her cheeks burned but not as much as the ache in her sex. She lowered herself, slowly, inch by inch, her body stretching to accommodate his width. She was so wet, so swollen with desire, her eyes watered at the delicious sensation.

"My old lady is so fucking hot."

"Your old lady would be hotter if she got a little action down below." She gave him a little squeeze, her internal muscles tightening, and his look turned savage.

"You're playing with fire, babe. I'm holding on by a thread."

Dawn laughed and squeezed again, but his time she cupped her breasts beneath the leather vest, weighing them in her palms. She pinched her nipples, rolling each one between her thumb and forefinger until they were tight, hard buds.

"Christ. You mean to kill me before I get to loving you." He jerked beneath her. "Ride me, babe. Ride me hard. Ride until your pleasure is running down my thighs."

She rocked against him and the steel of his shaft pressed against her sensitive spot, making her gasp with pleasure. When Jimmy had put her on top, it was for his benefit only. He . . . She cut off her train of thought. Jimmy didn't belong here. And there was no point comparing her two lovers because Jimmy had never been a lover. Or a giver. Cade was both.

And Jimmy was gone.

Forever.

Dawn undulated over Cade's cock, testing her rhythm, her ability to take him deep or only partway. A muscle twitched in Cade's jaw, but other than that tiny sign of his tension, he didn't push, letting her take her time to find out what worked best, feed her insatiable hunger. Finally she discovered she could get maximum friction on her knees, rocking back and up so that every movement stroked his cock against her sensitive tissue. Cade picked up her rhythm and guided her hips, steadying her as she took her pleasure from him.

"That's it." His choked rasp of approval drove her wild. She had done this to him. Aroused him. Pushed him to the point he had to fight for control.

"Harder. I wanna watch you come all over my cock." His hand covered her pussy, fingers seeking her clit. Dawn whimpered, and he circled it, teasing, spreading her wetness up and around but never where she wanted him to go. He jerked his hips, his cock thrusting hard and fast, and she couldn't hold on any longer.

"More. Don't stop." She ground against him, rocked, and when finally he slid his finger over her clit, her orgasm crashed through her, waves of pleasure rippling outwards, carrying her away.

Cade gritted his teeth as Dawn's pussy clenched around him in wave after wave of wet heat. He'd never denied himself for so long or been so hard that he no longer knew the difference between pleasure and pain. But he wanted this night to last. He wanted to erase every last memory she had of Jimmy. With love. With him.

Dawn coming on top of him in his cut was a luscious treat: the sway of her rounded curves, the tremble of her legs, and the soft moan from her rosy lips. He slid his hands between her thighs to open her to him. Her labia glistened, pink and swollen around his cock, and he bit back a groan and tried to think about the fuel leak on his bike, the hamburger he had for dinner—anything other than the insistent throb of his cock.

He had other plans for her tonight, but when her body softened, languid on top of him, her head falling back, her beautiful golden hair falling in soft waves over her shoulders, he couldn't take any more. He'd never been so painfully aroused. He had to have her.

He rolled until he was on top, his cock still hard, throbbing inside her, and then he lifted her arms and wrapped her hands around the wooden posts of his headboard. "Hold on."

Still trembling from the aftershocks of her climax, she gasped when he caught her nipple in his teeth. He licked and sucked her nipples until she was writhing on the bed, each jerk of her body sending another pulse of desire through his cock.

"Legs over my shoulders." His breaths came in pants and sweat beaded on his forehead. He wanted to lick her all over, taste the sultry sweetness between her legs, but she was driving him insane.

Dawn braced herself on the headboard and lifted her legs, hooking them over his shoulders. The position opened her fully to him, aroused her, if her panting breaths were any indicator; his body shook with the effort of holding still.

Gritting his teeth, he pulled out of her hot, wet sheath and then slid a pillow under her hips to give her the support she would need when he took her as deep as he could go. So deep she would know only him. His cock. His passion. His love.

"Cade . . ." The pleading note in her voice pleased him. She wanted him. As much as he wanted her.

He drew back and slid into her, filling her hard and

fast, the angle giving him maximum penetration. Her moan was deep, primal, and he lost the last threads of his control. God, she was tight. And wet. And hot. So goddamn hot.

"Relax," he commanded. "Let me in. Take all of me."

He withdrew and then thrust in again, pushing deeper. This time she whimpered and he quickened his pace, hammering into her but always keeping up the pressure on her sensitive spot.

Dawn trembled, her heels digging into his back. The wounds had healed and he felt no pain. He slowed his pace, overwhelmed by how perfectly her needs met his, how beautifully she responded to his gentle commands.

"Come for me, babe." He stroked her with a slow, insistent rhythm that brought her to a powerful, rippling climax. Her deep-throated groan sent him over the edge and he pounded into her until his balls lifted and his cock stiffened. His climax came hard and fast, a frenzied burst of pleasure.

"You are mine," he whispered. "Mine to hold. Mine to protect. Mine to love." And then he slid one finger over her clit and stroked until she came again.

★ TWENTY-SEVEN ★

I will live my life with no regrets.

SINNER'S TRIBE CREED

"Mommy!"

Maia and Tia waved to Dawn from the road outside the school. They were wearing new pink-and-purple outfits, all ready for the housewarming barbecue Dawn had organized for later that afternoon.

The steady rush of an autumn breeze chilled her skin, pulling a few curls free from her ponytail. Dawn pulled her cut tight around her and pushed back the wayward strands just as Cade pulled up on his bike beside her.

"Did I make it?"

"They just got out." She looked up just as Maia and Tia clasped hands and stepped onto the road.

"Crosswalk." Cade's loud voice carried over the after-school chatter and the whistle of the wind; it carried across the street and into the ears of two little girls who knew very well that if they ran across the road, there would be hell to pay. And not just from their mom.

Dawn heard that voice at home and in the clubhouse, in restaurants and in bars. She heard it at school plays and picnics, but only once at a ballet recital because Cade didn't like to see his girls "wearing next to nothing" on stage. That voice had coaxed her deepest, darkest fantasies from her lips and made her believe, after six happy months, maybe dreams really could come true.

"Christ," Cade muttered as they made their way to the crosswalk. "Every fucking day. Why don't they remember? I'm gonna stop coming here because one of these times I'll have a goddamn heart attack. Even when I was on the road, I'd see a crosswalk and get worried all over again."

Cade had never talked about his road trip with Dax, T-Rex, and Hacker before. But he didn't have to. The morning after he returned, she found a framed photograph of her parents on his pillow when she woke up. And when she went to the kitchen and found him making pancakes with her girls, she had been too overwhelmed with emotion to ask. But she didn't have to. He had promised to protect her and now there were two people who would never hurt her again.

"Language, honey." Dawn's gentle reminder was met with a string of cusswords that would have put the boys in the playground to shame.

"I'll fucking swear all I want when they put themselves in fucking danger." He scowled as the girls crossed the road, his face softening only when they reached the sidewalk and smiled at him. "Don't know how Dax manages with five kids."

"I heard it gets easier the more you have.

Two hours later, with the barbecue in full swing, Dawn sent the girls to play with Dax's boys and grabbed a minute to chat with Arianne.

"Aren't you worried your neighbors are going to call the police about all the bikes on the street and the bikers in your yard?" Arianne sipped her vodka cooler and sat beside Dawn on the back steps.

"Apparently they're used to it. Dax lives down the street and he's had lots of biker parties, both with and without the kids. From what I hear, our little barbecue is pretty tame. And now I don't have to pretend Cade is just a bike enthusiast. Dax has never hidden who he is or what he does so he's smoothed the way for us. No one at the girls' new school seems to have an issue with him and Cade showing up for school functions wearing their cuts. It was one of the reasons we picked this house."

She didn't share with her new friends that she worked part-time for the Sinner's Tribe MC, helping Cade with the finances. But they did know she was always on the go, juggling her new restaurant and college classes with school runs and kids' activities.

"How's that new bike working out for you?" Sparky joined them on the step, a beer in his hand. He and Arianne had fixed up an old Harley Sportster for Dawn after she had officially become an old lady in the club.

"I love it, but I haven't told Cade about it yet. He's still a bit overprotective. He gets agitated if I drive the SUV too fast. I can't imagine what he's going to say about the bike."

Sparky waved a dismissive hand. "Once he sees you on that bike, he won't be thinking about anything except chasing after you. Nothing hotter than a chick on a bike."

"I thought nothing was hotter than a chick with a gun." Arianne raised an eyebrow, but Sparky just laughed. "A chick with a gun on a bike . . . now, that would be something to see."

Dawn stifled a laugh. Cade didn't need to see her on a bike to chase after her. He used any excuse to get her in bed. Dressed for job hunting? Check. Dressed for a

PTA meeting? Check. Undressed for the shower? Double check. Cleaning and unpacking their new house in her old sweats and ratty T-shirt? Check again. He thought she was sexy. Period. And there was nothing she could do that didn't make him want her all over again.

She heard a squeal of laughter and spotted Cade playing with Maia and Tia and their new dogs. He'd brought them the two pups from a shelter in Whitefish—one each—and they were already a permanent part of the family. Although both girls adored him, Tia was his closest companion, always thinking up new ways to make him smile. He had suffered through countless of her baking disasters, but he never complained. He ate whatever she made and convinced even Dawn that it was the most delicious food he'd ever tasted.

"Hope you're not giving Sparky a hard time." Banks pulled a beer from the cooler and twisted off the top. "You should see these two at the bar. They think they run the place 'cause they're old ladies. I need more staff. Normal people. Bikers are nothing but trouble."

"That's why you're always at our parties." Sparky grinned. " 'Cause you hate us."

"Just bein' polite." Banks sipped his beer. "You're good customers, and I like to keep the customers happy."

After catching up on club gossip, Dawn excused herself and went looking for Cade. She found him near the back fence with Zane, deep in conversation. Usually cold and distant, Zane greeted her with what looked suspiciously like a smile.

"Cade was just saying you have all the custody shit sorted out with your kids and they're yours free and clear."

"Yes, they're all mine and no one will ever be able to take them away." Warmth flooded her and she squeezed Cade's hand, still needing the simple assurance that she had her happily ever after. "Deputy Benson worked out a deal. Shelly-Ann testified that the video was a setup, and we were able to use the PI's confession to back it up. She also testified against a senator and some of the Brethren. In exchange Deputy Benson got her into witness protection with all charges against her dropped."

"Richard sorted out all the legal stuff," Cade said. "Family services, court case, custody order . . . and now he's looking into adoption. I'm gonna have three ladies to look after."

"I still have to pay you back for that," Dawn said. "Even though he's the club lawyer, he can't be cheap."

"You can pay me in other ways." Cade reached down and pinched her ass. "We'll start here and work our way up."

"Beast." She slapped his hand away and he pulled against his chest.

"You love my beastly side. Admit it." His mouth came down hard and fast, and Dawn wound her arms around his neck. She loved that he wasn't embarrassed by public displays of affection, although the girls teased her mercilessly every time they kissed.

"Okay. It's hot."

Cade nuzzled her neck. "How hot?

"Someone get these two a fucking hose." Zane grabbed a beer from Hacker, who had been assigned the task of ensuring no biker was without a drink, and pointed at the fence. "There are children out there. Might corrupt their young minds."

Dawn tore herself away from Cade to look. The boy peering in through the fence was no more than twelve, but tall and solidly built, his straight dark hair cut to his shoulders, and his skin a tawny gold.

"I don't recognize him."

"I'll tell him to fuck off." Zane took a step toward the fence and Dawn pulled him back.

"He's young, Zane. And he has to belong to someone. He's probably just shy and no threat. Let him be."

"Kinda looks like you." Cade clapped a hand on Zane's shoulder. "You sure you're off women? Maybe you got a coupla kids you don't know about it."

"If I had a kid, I'd know about it. And he wouldn't be running around the streets without his damn dad."

"Keep saying things like that and I might think you have a heart after all." Cade clasped Dawn's hand. "Now, if you'll excuse us, I gotta take the old lady inside."

"Cade . . ." She stopped in her tracks. "We can't just leave our own party."

"We did last time. And if I recall you weren't complaining, babe. Screaming. But not complaining."

Her body heated in an instant. "The girls . . ."

"Are in the middle of a yard full of Sinners. And I got a present for them. I want you to take a look."

Dawn pressed her lips together. "If this is just another ploy to get into my pants . . ."

He leaned over and pressed his lips to her ear. "You're not wearing pants. You're wearing a tight little fuck-me skirt that shows off your perfect ass and your beautiful legs and all I could think about the minute you put it on was ripping it off. Which I will do. But later."

"I was talking about a different kind of pants."

"I want in those, too."

She followed him into the house and up to their room. Cade had paid for the modest three-bedroom house in cash and refused her contribution, saying it was a good way to launder the club's money and he didn't want her involved. Although she loved the vaulted ceilings, sunny country kitchen, and dark hardwood floors, she didn't have the heart to tell him it might already be too small.

"Before you show me what you got the girls, I have a housewarming present for you." She turned away and leaned over the dresser. "Open it."

With a low growl, Cade reached for her skirt and undid the zipper. "I was gonna wait to sex you up, but I've suddenly changed my mind."

And then silence.

"Do you like it?" Dawn looked back over her shoulder at her very still, very quiet, very shaken old man.

"What did you do?"

"It's a Sinner's Tribe tat, exactly the same as yours, scars and all. I checked with Jagger that it would be okay and he wouldn't consider it a dishonor to the club. His reaction was kinda like yours."

Even the tattoo artist hadn't been happy to add the jagged lines to match the scars that marred Cade's tattoo. But she wanted Cade to understand that she accepted him, just the way he was. Loved him. Scars and all.

She felt the soft press of his warm lips against her back.

"You never cease to amaze me," he murmured. "Or surprise me. Or move me in ways a biker shouldn't be moved. It's the best fucking present I ever got."

"You can thank me later," she teased. "But now I want to see what you got for the girls."

Jaw still clenched with emotion, he nodded to a box on the bed. Dawn removed the lid and looked inside.

"What are these?" She lifted out two small leather vests.

"Sinner cuts. For my girls."

Dawn spun one of the vests around and stared at the miniature patches on the back. "PROPERTY OF CADE?"

He slid his arms around her waist and pulled her back against his chest, his lips brushing over the soft skin on her neck. "All three of you are mine. Mine to look after. Mine to protect. Mine to love."

"Well, if that's the case, there's one missing."

" 'Cause you're wearing it." His breath was warm and moist in her ear as his hand slid up to cup her breast. "And since we're alone, I want to see you wearing your cut and your new tat and nothing else to celebrate our new home."

She turned in his arms, her body trembling. This moment had gone so wrong with Jimmy. But this was Cade. And they had planned for this together. Wanted it. Hoped. Dreamed.

"I meant you'll need something smaller . . . baby size."

Read on for an excerpt from the next book by

SARAH CASTILLE

★ SINNER'S STEEL ★

Now available from St. Martin's Paperbacks

Zane flicked the throttle on his Harley and the bike surged forward, forcing Evie to tighten her grip around his waist.

He could do this.

The distance between Evie's house and Bill's shop couldn't be more than twenty miles. And look. He'd already made it to the highway. If she would just stop wiggling on the seat behind him . . . and if she didn't hold him quite so tight with her breasts pressed up against her back . . . and if her fingers weren't dangling over the bulge in his jeans, which was getting more pronounced the closer she pressed her body against his . . . .then he might actually make it to the shop without either crashing the bike or spilling in his pants like a teenage boy.

He couldn't remember feeling lust like this since the night he'd left Stanton. Sure he'd had women. He had an apartment separate from his room at the clubhouse so he could indulge his less than conventional tastes. The sweet butts were always warm and willing, and if he wanted to keep things discrete, the Sinners owned several strip clubs in town. But he rarely felt the need to take advantage of the opportunities the cut provided. And when he did, every woman morphed into Evie. She had been burned onto his brain, ruining him for other women forever.

And now her soft, sexy body was pressed up against him, her thighs brushing his thighs, her hips firm against his ass, and her damn fingers resting on his fly. His groin tightened and he swerved the bike.

Fuck. Concentrate. But it was so damn hard.

He wondered what Mark would think about his wife riding on the back of Zane's bike, holding on to him, legs parted, cheeks flushed from the wind. If she'd been his, there would be no way he would allow her on the back of any man's bike. Hell, he wouldn't let her near another man. Look how he reacted to her, despite the stain of her betrayal still tainting his heart.

By the time they reached the shop, he was rock hard and his body thrummed with need. Shooter pulled up beside them and Zane prayed for Evie to dismount quickly so he would have time to get himself together and calm the fuck down so she wouldn't see the evidence of his desire.

He wanted her. She'd hurt him and he wanted her. She was with another man and he wanted her. She'd slapped him and damned if seeing Evie come into her own hadn't made him want her more. And back there on the porch, when she'd brushed her breasts against his chest, the way she'd brushed up against him when they were young, telling him with her body what she couldn't say out loud, he'd almost taken her.

"Gotta talk to Shooter," he said after she slid neatly off his bike. "I'll meet you inside."

"I'll go check out the damage." She gave him a wink and then walked to the door, making his groin tighten all over again at the sight of her beautiful ass perfectly outlined in dark denim.

After the door closed behind her, he briefed Shooter

on surveillance techniques, which basically meant find somewhere to stand where you weren't visible and don't fall asleep. He sent Shooter to the picnic table across the street, then walked around his bike as he tried to get his libido in check, considering the various bike parts, how they fit together and how easily they came apart, and how hard it had been to replace his stock exhaust with a longer, harder, thicker pipe, and how he had to fight with Sparky to get an upswept ball-end megaphone muffler.

When he realized the direction his thoughts were leading, he gave up the fight, made a careful self-adjustment, and headed into the store.

Rows of motorcycles gleamed under the overhead lights. Bill had a lot of stock for a small store, mostly new models, but a few bobsters, and some custom pieces. The walls held parts and supplies, racks of leathers, helmets and boots.

He found Evie in her shop spraying primer on a gas tank perched on an A-frame stand. She had stripped down to a skin tight tank top and tied her hair back in a messy pony tail with loose strands framing her beautiful face. Damn she was hot, standing in that gritty shop, surrounded by motorcycle parts, and with a spray gun in her hand . . .

Christ. Was everything going to make him think about sex?

"Thought I'd get a head start on my work for tomorrow while I was waiting. My portfolio is over there if you need to look at it under more legitimate circumstances, or if you've brought a design, just leave it on the bench and I'll take a look."

Zane walked along the wall beside the benches filled with paint supplies, and air brush guns. He had already checked the place out, trying to find clues about her life from the personal items in her workspace: a handbook from Conundrum College, a parenting magazine, a coffee cup from a restaurant in Stanton, a motorcycle magazine, and the charcoal drawing of him, Jagger and Evie on the wall—a rendition of the picture he had given her. Even now, seeing it again, a lump welled up in his throat—not just because of the memory, but because she'd kept it, and made it larger than life.

"Find anything in the portfolio?" She came up beside him, and he couldn't stop himself from brushing one of the loose strands of hair back from her face. The sharp scent of primer took the edge off his desire, and he was finally able to untangle his tongue.

"No. But you're work is exceptional." She'd always been artistic, which was why he was so unsure of the gift he'd made for her the night of Jagger's going-away party. Although he knew her as well as one person could know another, he still worried it wasn't good enough . . . that he wasn't worthy.

"You're nothing and you come from nothing," her father had shouted as he beat Zane in the forest. "You've got nothing to offer my daughter. No future. No skills. Hell you couldn't even finish school. All you got is a trailer full of drugs, an addict for a father, and your shit for brains."

Perversely, he'd been happy for Evie, thinking at least her father cared. It was only later, when Sheriff Monroe showed up at the trailer with a gun, that he realized her father was protecting himself. Until that night, he hadn't known Zane was Doug Colton's son. And he couldn't take the risk that Zane would tell Evie or the police that he was on the take, running drugs for Zane's father across the state line, accepting bribes, and doing everything a sheriff shouldn't do.

"Thanks." She put down the spray gun. "I never made it to that fine arts program at college, and I sort of fell into custom painting when one of my friends asked if I could paint something on her husband's motorcycle as a surprise. He recommended me to his friends and it sort of spiraled from there. I never thought about it as a career until I went to a motorcycle show in Helena with a couple of my pieces and met Big Bill. He convinced me to leave Stanton and work for him."

"Ever think about setting up on your own?" He leaned against the table, all thoughts of a paint job disappearing when she pulled out her elastic and rubbed a hand through her hair.

So beautiful. He wanted to run his fingers through those red gold strands, feel that silky softness in his palm. And then he wanted to twist it in his hand and hold her head still so he could ravish her mouth, or better yet, her body. She had curves that could bring a man to his knees.

Her cheeks flushed and she looked down, as if she knew what he was thinking. "Um . . . no. I'm comfortable where I am, and this set-up gives me a good source of customers. Plus, it is sort of like my own shop. I'm a part owner with Bill." Pride shone in her eyes and Zane smiled. She had never been one to hide her emotions.

"So what do you think happened to Bill?" He clutched the table top behind him to keep from walking toward her and enacting his fantasy right here right now. What the hell could he talk about that would keep his desire at bay?

Her smile faded. "I'm not sure. Connie and I thought maybe the Jacks scared him away. He was—" She cut herself off with a grimace. "Never mind."

Zane filed that one away for later. Only way the Jacks would scare a man away from his business was if he'd done something to piss them off. Was he paying them protection money or had he got something going on the side? Damn stupid if he did, and even more stupid if he had put Evie in danger. The minute Bill showed up again,

Zane would be taking him out for a little talk about keeping Evie safe.

"You got a bike?" He was scrambling now, trying to avoid the real reason he'd brought her here, and it wasn't for paint.

"No. Can't afford it. One day though. Maybe when I make it big I'll buy myself a present. Mark has a Harley Fat Boy, which is a pretty sweet ride."

Ah. Mark. Now that killed his desire. He released the table and folded his arms. "What does he do?" Middle manager? Sportscaster? Or was he still a coach after all these years?

A pained expression crossed her face. "I wouldn't know."

"You don't know what your husband does?"

"Ex-husband. I left him a few years ago to move out here."

"You're not married?" His voice cracked and he drew in a ragged breath. She wasn't married. His Evie was . . . free. "What about his boy? Doesn't he come to see him?"

Her voice tightened. "No."

Their eyes met and the air crackled between them, as if her last word had been the spark to fan the flames that had been smoldering since that moment on the porch when all he wanted was to drown himself in her arms. "What kind of father doesn't want to see his son?" For all that Zane hated his father, and for all the abuse he had taken, when Zane needed him most, the one and only time in his life, his father had been there for him.

Evie twisted her hair around her finger and pulled her bottom lip between her teeth. "A step-father."

"He's not Mark's boy?"

A gunshot cracked the silence, and then another. Zane's heart pounded and he slid his hand into his cut, closing his fingers around his gun. "Stay here until I come back for you. Hide." He ran back into the store and spotted Shooter just outside the glass front door, firing his gun into the trees.

"Who is it?" He shouted from the cover of the doorway. "You see Axle? One of the Jacks?"

"Squirrel." Shooter yelled and fired again. "Red tail. Tricky little bugger but I got him trapped in that bush."

"Jesus fucking Christ." Zane ran over to Shooter and grabbed his wrist. "Put the weapon down." He unleashed all his tension in a volley of curses directed at Shooter, his mental state, his mother, and his dubious parentage. "This is a surveillance mission. That means you don't draw attention to yourself. You don't shoot things. Gunfire has a nasty tendency to rile up civilians and then they call the cops. You want to explain to the cops why you're shooting squirrels on private property?"

"He was on your bike, gnawing on your seat."

"Gimme that gun." Zane grabbed the weapon and fired three shots into the bush. "Take that you goddamn fucking bastard," he hollered. "You wanna eat my leather? Now you're gonna be eatin' crow."

"You missed."

Zane handed him the gun. "You got a new job now, prospect. Clean my seat, fix the leather, then bring me that fucking squirrel's hide."

"Yes, sir."

Adrenaline pounded through his veins as he returned to the store, whether from the shoot-out or finding out Evie had split with Mark he didn't know, but damned if he could get himself under control. He took a few deep breaths as he crossed through into the shop, clenching and unclenching his fists by his side.

"Evie?"

"Here." Her voice was faint. "Can I come out now?"

He followed her voice to a storage closet at the far end

of the shop and found her reaching for a tube of paint on the top shelf.

"I figured I'd tidy up while I was in here and I saw a box of paint I'd forgotten about. Could you get it down for me?" Half in the shadows of the small, musty room, she looked back over her shoulder. "I'm not quite tall enough."

Zane walked up behind her and grabbed the box. His body brushed up against her, his hips against her ass, his chest to her back. And before he could stop himself, he slid his free hand around her waist and pulled her against his chest.

"Zane!"

"You're not with Mark?" He leaned down and pressed his lips to her ear, inhaling her scent of jasmine as adrenaline streamed through his veins.

"No. But . . ."

His hand splayed over her stomach, pulling her close, and he nuzzled the hair away from her neck. "You got a man, Evie?"

"No." Her voice wavered. "But . . . I kinda . . ."

He shoved the box onto a lower shelf and reached around to catch her jaw in his hand, pulling her head back against his shoulder, exposing her neck to the heated slide of his lips. Somewhere, in the foggy recesses of his mind, he knew he was being too rough, but he was barely in control and rough was as gentle as he could be. "So no one's gonna shoot me between the eyes if I do this?" With his thumb he gently stroked the underside of her breast. Evie sucked in a sharp breath, but didn't move.

She answered in a breath whisper. "No."

His hand slid higher, tracing over her ribs until he held the full weight of her breast in his palm. "You gonna stop me from touching you, sweetheart?" He feathered kisses along the column of her neck, praying she didn't deny him because he was already so far gone he didn't know if he would be able to stop.

"Zane." She shuddered, her nipples peaking beneath her thin cotton tank top. He circled one taut nipple with his thumb and she groaned and wiggled her ass against his erection, nestled tight in the crack of her cheeks.

"Stop me, Evie. Because I can't stop myself."

She melted against him with a sigh, her body softening, and for the briefest of moments he soared, higher and higher, soaking in her light, her warmth, her essence . . .

He should have known what would happen if he flew too close to the sun.